HEART OF DARKNESS

BRUCE SPRINGSTEEN'S
NEBRASKA

First published in Great Britain in 2011 by Cherry Red Books (a division of Cherry Red Records Ltd), Power Road Studios, 114 Power Road, Chiswick, London W4 5PY

Copyright David Burke © 2011

ISBN: 978 1 901447 57 6

Design by: Becky Stewart
Cover photograph courtesy of David Michael Kennedy

Lyrics quoted are for the purposes of research and review only.

HEART OF DARKNESS

BRUCE SPRINGSTEEN'S
NEBRASKA

DAVID BURKE

CHERRY RED
BOOKS

ACKNOWLEDGEMENTS

Thanks a million to Richard Anderson at Cherry Red, Mike Appel, Jo Ashbridge at Wrasse Records, Eric Bachmann, Dan Bern, Tom Bridgewater at Loose Music, Tommaso Buzzi, Anna Canoni at the Woody Guthrie Foundation, Laura Cantrell, Robert Cantwell, Peter Case, Rosanne Cash, Andrew and Peter Cash, Rob Chute, Norm Cohen, Judy Collins, Kevin Coyne, Bob Crawford, Katherine DePaul, Aymi Derham, Steve Earle, Mark Eitzel, Glyn Emmerson, Simon Felice, Paul Fenn, Jeff Finlin, Paddy Forwood, Jeffrey Foucault, Bryan Garman, Howe Gelb, Thea Gilmore, David Gray, Gaby Green at GreenGab-PR, Kenneth Green, Sid Griffin, Nora Guthrie, John Wesley Harding, Melissa Haycraft, Claire Horton at Richard Wootton Publicity, Brian Hultgren at Maine Road Management, Bill Hurley, Tennessee Jones, Robert Earl Keen, David Michael Kennedy for his magnanimity and the most iconic Springsteen photos ever, Kevn Kinney, John Lennard at Fullfill, Julius Lester for pointing out the difference between the Sixties folk revival and the topical song movement, Samuel J. Levine, Vini Lopez, Sarah Lowe at Fifth Avenue PR, Will McCarthy, Tom McCrae, Michael McDermott, Sean McGhee, Editor of R2 magazine (formerly Rock'n'Reel), David Means, Chris Metzler at Décor Records, Matt Michaelis at Ninety Miles North Publicity, Andrew Morgan, Jim Musselman, Willie Nile, Chris Norton at IHT Records, David Pesci, Andy Prevezer at Warner Music, Chuck Prophet, Mark Radcliffe, Dolphus Ramseur, Flora Reed, Tom Russell, Jim Sampas, Jim Sclavunos, Jeremy Searle, Lesley Shone at Indiscreet PR, Southside Johnny, Brett Sparks, David Spelman, who, despite my being a noodge – or maybe because of it – came up with the goods, Mark Spence, Maryelle St Clare, Scott Steele at EMI Music, Michael Timmins, Willy Vlautin, Sean Wilentz for finding time to answer my questions while busily promoting his own excellent tome, *Bob Dylan In America*, Dar Williams and Steve Wynn

Also, to Shirley, my constant companion and greatest advocate, who, at the end of every hard-earned day, gives me many reasons to believe; Francesca, alumna of Sheffield Hallam University whom I may finally have managed to impress; and Dylan, research assistant, internet publicist and teenage rock guitar god, a superstar in waiting.

For Dylan – May you always carry the fire.

CONTENTS

Folk + Blue + Country
- highest order to be aspired
* Not genres - (Just)
Everything is pop (popular)
only like becoming a Saint
to be a blues man
or folk singer
- Dylan swaps in
(that's how rigorous
about the rules are)
Simon may/makes
are not folk -
Paul Simon - Steve is
Sea Sick - Steve is
not a ...
It's American

INTRODUCTION

Judy Collins, in an interview for this book, describes Bruce Springsteen as a folk hero. I disagree. His name may indeed be imprinted on the public consciousness as, variously, an eloquent voice of blue-collar America, a percipient diagnostician of the human condition, a stadium-filling superstar who never short changes his audience, and a compassionate liberal with a lower-case 'l'. But a folk hero is largely the stuff of myth. The veracity of the tales that enhance such a mythical reputation can only ever be challenged superficially, because that reputation derives from the long ago, before [mass media demystified] everything. There is no such entity as a 21st-Century folk hero, and anyone who tells you different has been suckered by the hype.

In Springsteen's case, the hype is largely the work of his manager Jon Landau, who has done an impressive job of convincing compliant music journalists that his protégé is a composite of Jesus Christ, Woody Guthrie, Elvis Presley and the John Wayne character in whatever John Ford film you care to think of. And those same music journalists have then done an impressive job of convincing the public that Landau's conception of Springsteen is the real deal.

Don't get me wrong, I count myself as a Springsteen loyalist. As writers in the medium of song go, he has few equals. And I don't doubt his integrity. I believe him to be a fundamentally decent man who cares about the world and the people in it. But he's also a man mindful of image and how best to project it and protect it. Landau's role in this respect should not be underestimated.

Perhaps Peter Case put it best when he said, "Fortunes were made to establish Bruce as a folk hero. It's sort of the opposite of what that word suggests."

Springsteen's tangible legacy will be his songs. And perhaps among these songs, the ten that comprise *Nebraska* will endure more than the rest. Not because of the method of the recording – although undeniably the fact that it was put out pretty much as it was produced, straight from a modest four-track recording unit, invest it with an artistic purity denied those albums meticulously assembled in hi-tech studios – but because it captures a writer at the peak of his evolution. *Nebraska* is bookended by before and after periods. In the before, as Springsteen tries to locate his own voice, every now and then he finds it, or something damn close to it, especially on parts of *Born To Run*, *Darkness On The Edge Of Town* and *The River*. But the voice that we now know as Springsteen's voice was truly born on *Nebraska*. The voice of the everyman, or more accurately, the voice of the American everyman. *Nebraska* will transcend Springsteen, will immortalise him as a writer, because of what it says about civilisation in the range of its complexity – the beauty, the ugliness, the tenderness, the cruelty, the love, the hate, the doubt, the fear – and because of what it says about the loneliness that lies at the heart of all of us.

Though I was infatuated with all things Americana from a young age, Springsteen didn't really enter my orbit until my late teens. I can't honestly say why. I'd seen him on *Rock Around The Clock*, an all-night music marathon on BBC Two television, doing 'The River' from what I later learned was the Musicians United for Safe Energy

(MUSE) concert at Madison Square Garden in 1979. It must have made an impact, the melancholy of the song, the intensity of the performance (at one point he appears to wipe a tear from his eye, though it could have been perspiration) – how could it not? But all caught up as I was in a Bob Dylan fixation (which has endured), I probably filed him away in my subconscious for another time.

That time came with *Born In The USA*. What I heard on this blockbuster was roots music given a rock'n'roll makeover – a bunch of amped-up folk songs about ordinary lives, the kind of lives that weren't really being written about in the mainstream. I was convinced that Springsteen was more than his image suggested (the baseball cap, the white T-shirt, the distressed denims and the American flag on the album cover created a redneck misapprehension among non-followers that hasn't been easy to shift), that he was a writer of considerable import, mining the seam that Woody Guthrie and Pete Seeger and Bob Dylan had before him. He was one of the good guys.

I wanted to know more. And so I went back to *Nebraska*, the album that prefaced *Born In The USA*. The sonic contrast couldn't have been more stark, and yet there was a common thread that also linked it to *The River*, *Darkness On The Edge Of Town* and *Born To Run*. Springsteen has often referred to it as a conversation with his audience. As conversations go, it's pretty heavy-duty, embracing as it does the big themes of faith and responsibility, sin and redemption. Hardly the stuff of the MTV generation. But like the best writing, whatever the idiom, such dense themes are explored through simple storytelling, the folk impulse at work.

This, essentially, was the intended thrust of *Heart Of Darkness: Bruce Springsteen's Nebraska*. I wanted to claim *Nebraska* as a great American folk album, to place it in the context of what preceded it and acknowledge its importance as a stimulus for the so-called Americana movement. In short, *Nebraska* as something of a bridge between old and new folk traditions.

This has involved a journey into the past, to the very origins of folk music itself and, specifically, American folk music; to the appropriation of the folk song both as a social document of an evolving America, and as an agent of protest during the Great Depression of the Thirties and the civil rights struggle and the Vietnam War of the Sixties.

It has involved a journey into Springsteen's own past in an attempt to identify what made him the writer he became, and a journey through his career, a necessary overview of his repertoire. *Nebraska* is, after all, but one part of a whole – an image, or rather a series of images, on an expansive canvas.

But like any journey on which the traveller pays attention, perceptions made themselves suggestible to change. I came to realise that *Nebraska* is much more than genre-confining folk music. It is blues and country and gospel and rock'n'roll and punk too. Add to that Springsteen's literary and cinematic sensibilities, as well as his awareness of how Ronald Reagan's economic polices were affecting those Americans not living the dream and you have a piece of work that resonated artistically and sociologically – and continues to do so.

DAVID BURKE, March 2011

2

I. THE DISCOVERY OF THE PEOPLE

"I like narrative storytelling as being part of a tradition, a folk tradition."
BRUCE SPRINGSTEEN

"Logically, when you talkin' about folk music and blues, you find out it's music of just plain people."
BROWNIE MCGHEE

The debate on what constitutes folk music is one dominated by two opposing factions – let's call them the purists and the progressives. Put simply (and rather simplistically), the purists want to preserve folk music as a kind of artefact, while the progressives' objective is to remake it in the evolving image of modernity.

The purists eschew the very idea of contemporary folk music. Theirs is an argument that pivots primarily on the grubby issue of commercialisation – or, to place it in a quasi-spiritual perspective, a transaction in which the soul is bartered for ambition or wealth.

The progressives, meanwhile, subscribe to an interpretation of folk music as that which reflects what goes on in the lives of folk, the little narratives that comprise the bigger story of life on earth.

Undoubtedly the purists would baulk at the suggestion that Bruce Springsteen's *Nebraska* fulfils many of the criteria for folk music. But *Nebraska* is pure folk from the compositional nature of the songs – songs populated by characters who speak in the vernacular, songs telling of hard times and of what hard times will force desperate people to do, songs in which the mundane becomes a medium for a more profound message about humanity – right down to the manner in which they are delivered using only voice, guitar, harmonica and glockenspiel, and the most basic recording technology. And *Nebraska* is uniquely an American folk album, forming part of a lineage that, in terms of its existence, is as old as the American nation itself.

So what is folk music? A cursory internet search will tell you that it is either "the traditionally and typically anonymous music that is the expression of the life of people in a community", "music transmitted by word of mouth, music of the lower classes, music with no known composer" or "any genre of music originating from the ethnic community of a specific region, often not recorded but passed down orally."
For Pete Seeger, the link between Woody Guthrie and Springsteen, it's "a way of life", though he admits hardly using the term 'folk music' "because it means different things to different people".

Judy Collins, a stalwart of the Sixties folk revival, finds it impossible to define. "In order to define it, you must be inclusive of musical history and how it has developed in the past seventy years. It's a very fluid thing. It reflects a political/personal combination of the ability to write and perform personal history. That differs from the great American songbook, although people like EY Harburg, who wrote 'Over The Rainbow', was being very political – he wanted 'Over The Rainbow' and *The Wizard Of Oz* to be a political statement. He wanted Dorothy's role in the film to be the icon-smashing young voice, in the same way that Bob Dylan was performing and singing songs that were icon-smashing.

"Folk music is a strange phenomenon, but it is combined with politics and personal expression. Personal expression trumps left, right, etcetera. Personal expression is everything. The politics of the time, left or right, is what gets talked about. Personal experience has no political grounding, left or right. Personal experience drenches the music of what we call the folk era. People take politics out of personal experience. But what politics is about is how you treat your dog, how you treat your wife, whether you want to be giving back to the culture, whether you want to be sapping it dry."

Novelist and African-American cultural commentator Cecil Brown, whose book *Stagolee Shot Billy* is a biography of the song, 'Stagolee', thinks of folk music as "black music". He explains, "It was the music of the people who were oral and did not have access to literacy and did not have access to any of the means of expression except what they could come up with themselves. It was the original music of the enslaved Africans when they came to the United States because they had no other form of expression."

Actor and occasional folksinger Theodore Bikel lauds the folk song for its myriad functions. "It tells a multitude of stories, fables, legends and jokes. It admonishes, lulls to sleep, calls to cattle, rings with hope for the prisoner, with threat for the jailer, with joy for the lovers, with bitterness for him who might have had but didn't. It heralds birth, boyhood, wedlock. It soothes the weary, the sick and the aged, and it mourns the dead."

I prefer the Louis Armstrong version of folk music: "All music is folk music. I ain't never heard a horse sing a song."

Okay, so Armstrong's remark contains an element of mischief, but only an elitist would deny its veracity. And elitism is, in a sense, what the purists espouse by insisting on authenticity in both form and framework. What they fail to acknowledge is that form and framework are transformative, not static, that they move, like all things, in concert with the movement of humanity. And besides, music – yes, even folk music – is expression, and expression isn't governed by criteria.

Although that's not how Norm Cohen, author of *Folk Music: A Regional Exploration*, sees it. "To me, what distinguishes folk music is not necessarily style or content but how it is preserved and transmitted – not via commercial media.

"So I don't label any new song a folk song until we've had a chance to see what becomes of it. 'Barbara Allen' was probably written by a professional songwriter in the 17th Century and survived in print for a long time, then disappeared from commercial media for a while but continued to be sung in rural communities and learned aurally. At that point it was a folk song. When it came to be recorded by Art

Garfunkel or Joan Baez, then it ceased being a folk song in that particular context. So it's the context and nature of transmission that is the key, rather than source, contents, style, attitude etc."

This is exactly why the purists give folk music a bad name. They thumb their academic noses at anything that falls outside the parameters delineated in a whole other time. They want to curate the music, antique it, put it behind a glass case and intellectualise it. They don't want to listen to its heartbeat, or feel its sorrow or hear its laughter. There is a particular irony in such remoteness given that one of the strengths of folk music is its social conscience. No wonder Bob Dylan went electric.

And so to the history bit. History, of course, is made as much by those who chronicle it as by those who play an active role in it. Or at least it was back in the day when the chroniclers of American folk music were the collectors, men like Francis James Child, Cecil Sharp, Howard Odum, John Lomax and his son Alan.

Folk music was one aspect of folk heritage, a phenomenon that had its roots in late 18th-Century Europe, where chin-stroking types considered the indigenous culture of peasants, farmers and craftspeople – what historian Peter Burke, described as "the discovery of the people". Chief among these chin strokers was German philosopher Johann Gottfried von Herder, who declared, "Unless our literature is founded on our *volk*, we, writers, shall write eternally for closet sages and disgusting critics, out of whose mouths and stomachs we shall get back what we have given." For him, folk culture represented a very real riposte to the artificiality that pervaded then contemporary culture.

In 1778, Herder published a set of lyrics collated and transcribed in the German border region of Riga, now the capital of Latvia, applying to them the handle *volkslieder*, or folk song. Mind you, he wasn't the first to assemble and compile traditional music. In 17th-Century England, old ballads featured in numerous collections, satisfying middle class and aristocratic curiosity of things 'country'.

More than a century before folk revivalism took hold in America, the pursuit of folk culture involved a complex series of ideological decisions, writes Benjamin Filene in his book, *Romancing the Folk: Public Memory & American Roots Music*. Not just anyone counted as 'folk'.

"Herder distinguished between the true *volk*, primarily rural peasants, and the urban rabble in the streets who 'never sing and rhyme, but scream and mutilate'. To Herder and other early collectors, true peasants were pure and artless and usually exotic," says Filene.

For Herder and the Grimm brothers, alias Jacob and Wilhelm, tellers of folk tales such as *Rumplestiltskin*, *Snow White* and *Cinderella*, unearthing folk cultures involved re-imagining, romanticising and transforming them.

Filene again: "Because of these transformations as much as in spite of them, their vision of the 'folk' had extraordinary reach, extending well beyond their borders and exerting influence long after their deaths. The work of these early philosophers and collectors showed that the idea of folk culture had power and plasticity. Scholars and intellectuals, artists and entrepreneurs, and the folk themselves, have been shaping and re-shaping the idea ever since."

The forebear of American folk music was Harvard professor Francis James Child. A Shakespeare scholar, his forte was British ballads, "a subject he pursued with the persistence of a bloodhound and the precision of a detective", and indeed his five-volume work, *The English And Scottish Popular Ballads (1882-1898)*, is widely heralded as canonical by students of the folk music idiom. For Child, America, with its relatively recent traditions, was of minimal interest, particularly as he preferred archival sources when retrieving old songs. Essentially he saw American folk music as British in origin.

Norm Cohen disagrees, positing that all immigrants to America "brought their own folk music with them and it became the basis of American folk music. As time went on, Americans created new songs and tunes based on their lives here in the New World. Gradually this became more distinct from the music of their ancestors."

The British theme was also pursued by Englishman Cecil Sharp, renowned as a founding father of the folklore revival in England during the early years of the 20th Century. Sharp journeyed to the Appalachian Mountains in 1916 and identified a cultural symbiosis with a long-gone England.

According to Filene, "Like Child, Sharp felt that the England he cherished had disappeared several hundred years ago, leaving only fragments behind. He found a way to revisit the British past he had never known. He created it in America. The key to Sharp's attraction to the Appalachian mountaineers' culture was that they fit, or could be sculpted to fit, his conception of old-time England. In his depiction of the mountaineers he encountered, he reinforced myths about the Britishness of American folk song heritage."

What Sharp was seeking to preserve – or perhaps, more accurately, to recover – was a culture that was white, Anglo-Saxon and Protestant. Race was a core component in his celebration of mountain culture. If you want confirmation of such a claim, look no further than his own conclusion that the reason "these mountain people, albeit unlettered, have acquired so many of the essentials of the culture is partly to be attributed to the large amount of leisure they enjoy, but chiefly to the fact that they have one and all entered at birth into the full enjoyment of their racial heritage".

Filene believes Sharp's emphasis on racial determination compounds the early ballad enthusiasts' insistence that the mountaineers were 100% British, adding, "…the collectors asserted that mountain culture was America's authentic folk inheritance and, at the same time, stressed that the mountaineers were British. In effect, therefore, the collectors established their heritage as the true American culture."

This notion of racial supremacy – for what else can it be called? – was challenged by the emergence of an African American sub-culture in the first flush of the 20th Century, embodied in the so-called Jazz Age and the Harlem Renaissance, both of which enforced historian Kathy J Ogren's view that "black culture, like black people, cannot be kept on the margins of American society". But sadly, that's exactly what happened as, apart from African American spirituals (which African Americans themselves rejected because of their association with slavery – their lyrical tenor implied acceptance of rather than refutation of this appalling crime, with the promise of redemption after death), the collectors paid little interest to African American music. Howard Odum, for example, "depicted them as the manifestations of a bizarre alien culture".

The British-centric advocacy of American folk music was challenged by a young Mississippian who grew up in Texas. John Lomax's family home was on the Chisholm Trail, used in the 19th Century to drive cattle from ranches in the Lone Star State to Kansas railheads, and he became captivated by the songs cowboys sang as they travelled. In 1910, as a Sheldon Fellow for the investigation of American ballads at Harvard, Lomax published *Cowboy Songs And Other Frontier Ballads*, featuring more than 100 songs from scrapbooks, newspapers and responses to a circular he himself had mailed out. Filene cites Lomax as the principal agent in changing "the face of the folk, replacing the sturdy British peasant with the mystical cowboy who lived hard, shot quick and true and died with his face to his foe".

Yet even within this elevation of the cowboy to folk (and folk song) hero, Lomax tipped his Stetson to the British folk tradition. "Out in the wild, far away place of the big, unpeopled west…yet survives the Anglo-Saxon ballad spirit that was absent in the secluded districts of England and Scotland," he mused, connecting the cowboy to the mythology of medieval England, with his "spirit and hospitality as primitive and heart as that found in the mead-halls of Beowulf."

Later, in 1933, Lomax and his then 18-year-old son Alan embarked on a trip across the American South to find and record folk musicians like Huddie 'Leadbelly' Ledbetter, promoting him to leftist audiences in New York as the personification of American folk song, and thus redefining the genre by bringing significant attention to the until then under-represented and misrepresented role of African Americans. The son continued the crusading work of the father when, between 1937 and 1942, he made hundreds of field recordings for the Archive of American Folk Song at the American Library of Congress.

Whatever the criticism levelled at the Lomaxes, particularly when it came to Alan Lomax's registration of joint copyright with his contributors, arguably they were central to the establishment of a true American folk music that acknowledged a diversity of influences. This was a vision shared by two other collectors, contemporaries of John Lomax, Carl Sandburg and Robert Winslow Gordon, who "spread the word that America had indigenous musical tradition, that American music was more than British music recycled". Sandburg, especially, "brought to attention banjo tunes, outlaw ballads, lumberjack songs and fiddle tunes, prison songs, hobo songs, Mexican border songs and bandit biographies", many strands of which can be found in the Springsteen oeuvre.

2. AMERICAN SPIRIT

"Woody Guthrie was the songwriter as advocate. He saw the song as a righteous sword and that inspired me."

BRUCE SPRINGSTEEN

"It's as close as people are going to come to Woody Guthrie and Pete Seeger."

STEVE VAN ZANDT on Springsteen

Here's a curious thing. Bruce Springsteen apparently got turned onto Woody Guthrie by, of all people, Ronald Reagan. The election of the 40th President of the United States in November 1980 horrified Springsteen; it was, he recalled, "a critical event to me and I started to address it on stage immediately". The story goes that someone had presented him with a copy of Joe Klein's *Woody Guthrie: A Life*, and that after Reagan's victory over Jimmy Carter, he immersed himself in what is properly regarded as the quintessential biography of the American folk hero.

"He was funny and entertaining," Springsteen said of Guthrie. "He knew you can't get on a soap box, you can't tell anybody anything. I remember at the time a far-left political group approached me and showed me some of their material and I said, 'The ideas are good but it isn't any fun'. You have to feel human. You can't just harangue."

American folk music earned its stripes in the Thirties when hard times hit. No more the minority pursuit of the learned, the interior monologue of native communities, it became the medium through which the struggles of all the people were articulated, banging the drum for the advancement of social justice and hollering in protest at iniquity. This was the time of the Great Depression, an unprecedented global economic slump that began in 1929 and ended 10 years later.

The whole thing was precipitated by the catastrophic collapse of prices on the New York Stock Exchange. Apart from ruining many thousands of individual investors, the decline in the value of assets (by 1932 they had dropped to about one-fifth of their 1929 value) forced banks into insolvency. Sound familiar? It should. The consequences of the slump in the United States were drastically falling manufacturing output and drastically rising unemployment, with between twelve and fifteen million out of work.

Meanwhile, in the agriculture sector, which had increased productivity through mechanisation and the cultivation of more land following the First World War, many financially overextended independent farmers lost their holdings and tenant farmers were turned out as a result of the stock market crash. As if the situation couldn't get any worse, poor soil conservation practices led to a seven-year drought, followed by the coming of the dust storms in which farms literally dried up and blew away, creating what became known as the Dust Bowl. Impelled by these factors, thousands of farmers packed up their families and journeyed across the country to California in search of a better life. Popular songs and stories, which had circulated in the oral tradition for decades, heralded the state as a veritable Eden. But the reality was starkly different, for California too was reeling from the Depression. The labour pool was disproportionate to the number of available openings, while migrants who did manage to secure a job were paid low wages; even with entire families earning, they couldn't support themselves. Camps were set up along irrigation ditches in fields, where poor sanitary conditions caused a public health problem.

Refugees within their own borders, the folk found some solace in song. Recreational activity in such impoverished circumstances was concentrated on the playing of and dancing to Anglo-Celtic ballads like 'Barbara Allen', 'The Brown Girl', 'Pretty Molly' and 'Little Mohee'.

Among the refugees was one Woodrow Wilson Guthrie from Okemah, Oklahoma, the second-born son of Charles and Nora Belle Guthrie. Charles, better known as Charley, was a cowboy, land speculator and local politician. He taught Woody Western, Indian and Scottish songs. Nora, too, was musically inclined and made an equally profound impact on the boy.

He would wait for the sound of his father's horse on the hard clay street and then run to meet him. Charley would sweep the boy into his lap. Woody was always "hopping around the house, making up snatches of rhyme and trying to sing them like his mother", Joe Klein recalls in *Woody Guthrie: A Life*.

Tragedy though blighted his childhood. His older sister, Clara, was killed in a house fire. There are two versions of how the fire started. In the version cited by Klein, Nora had kept Clara home from school to do housework and Clara, gone crazy with the anger that was a symptom of the as-yet undiagnosed Huntington's Disease, drenched her dress with coal oil, setting it alight. Indeed this was the version Clara herself told when, displaying remarkable fortitude, she granted an interview to the *Okemah Ledger* while lying on her death bed.

In a radio interview years later, Woody said, "My 14-year-old sister either set herself afire or caught afire accidentally – there were two different stories got out about it. Anyway, she was having a little difficulty with her schoolwork and she had to stay at home and do some work. She caught afire while she was doing some ironing that afternoon on the old kerosene stove. It was highly unsafe and highly uncertain in them days, and this one blew up and caught her afire and she run around the house about twice before anybody could catch her. Next day, she died."

The loss to Woody was pronounced. "She was like a surrogate mother to him," according to his daughter, Nora Lee Guthrie. "Nora (Woody's mother) was actually, without anyone knowing it at the time, showing symptoms of Huntington's Disease, probably for many years before it was diagnosed. It's very slow and incremental. So little events, little episodes, little breakdowns, maybe 10 years previous to the actual diagnosis, were happening. Clara stepped in as the older sister. She was eight years older than him. She really stepped in as a surrogate mother in the sense that she was the bright spot in his life. She was that positive, bright light, whereas his mother, Nora, was already shades of grey."

After Clara's death, Nora, prey to depression, began to descend deeper into the well until she was committed to a mental institution, where she eventually died.

In his autobiography, *Bound For Glory*, Woody remembered how the Huntington's manifested itself: "She would be all right for a while, and treat us kids as good as any mother, and all at once it would start in – something bad and awful – something would start coming over her, and it come by slow degrees. Her face would twitch and her lips would snarl and her teeth would show. Spit would run out of her mouth and she would start out in a low grumbling voice and gradually get to talking as loud as her throat could stand it; and her arms would draw up at her sides, then behind her back and swing in all kinds of curves. Her stomach would draw up into a hard ball, and she would double over into a terrible-looking hunch – and turn into another person, it looked like, standing right there before (brother) Roy and me."

He would go to sleep nights and dream "that my mama was just like anybody else's. I saw her talking, smiling and working just like other kids' mamas. But when I woke up it would still be all wrong, all twisted out of shape, helter-skelter, let go, the house not kept, the cooking skipped, the dishes not washed."

While Nora was institutionalised, Charley relocated to Pampa in Texas, finding work to repay his debts from failed real-estate deals. Woody and his siblings were left to fend for themselves. The resourceful teen came into his own, using his nascent musical ability to procure money or food.

In 1931, Woody joined his father in Texas. It was there he met and fell in love with Mary Jennings, the youngster sister of musician friend Matt Jennings. The couple married and went on to have three children together. It was with Matt, meanwhile, that Woody made his first serious attempt at doing something in music, forming the Corn Cob Trio and later the Pampa Junior Chamber of Commerce Band.

The Great Depression cut short his burgeoning career. Struggling to support his family, Woody, like the thousands of desperate others, made for Route 66, hitchhiking, jumping freight trains and even walking his way to California, picking up whatever employment he could in transit and playing his guitar, singing in saloons and painting signs in exchange for bed and board.

In Los Angeles, Woody landed a job on KFVD radio, performing both traditional and original songs. Together with his partner Maxine Crissman, alias Lefty Lou, he began to garner a following among the dislocated Okies in the migrant camps. Rather than restrict himself to the role of radio entertainer, Woody began using his programme to berate corrupt politicians, lawyers and businessmen and acclaim the compassion and humanism of Jesus Christ, outlaw hero Pretty Boy Floyd and the union organisers fighting for the rights of the workers in California's agricultural communities, becoming an advocate for truth, fairness and justice.

His peripatetic nature next took him to the east coast and New York, where Woody's authenticity saw him embraced by the city's folk music fraternity and leftist intellectuals. Author John Steinbeck, in a memorable quote, gushed: "Woody is just Woody. Thousands of people do not know he has any other name. He is just a voice and a guitar. He sings the songs of a people and I suspect that he is, in a way, that people. Harsh-voiced and nasal, his guitar hanging like a tyre iron on a rusty rim, there is nothing sweet about Woody, and there is nothing sweet about the songs he sings. But there is something more important for those who still listen. There is the will of a people to endure and fight against oppression. I think we call this the American spirit."

In New York, Woody was recorded by Alan Lomax in a series of conversations and performances for the Library of Congress in Washington DC; he also recorded his first album of self-penned compositions, *Dust Bowl Ballads*, for RCA Victor, and hundreds of discs for Moses Asch of Folkways Records. Here too, Woody befriended the likes of Leadbelly, Cisco Houston, Burl Ives, Will Geer, Sonny Terry, Brownie McGhee, Josh White and Pete Seeger, all of whom featured in a loosely-knit folk outfit that went by the name of the Almanac Singers, crusaders for various social causes.

Seeger, the son of a musicologist and concert violinist, had sat in the same class as John F Kennedy at Harvard University before dropping out and dedicating himself to folk music, what he referred to as "the music of the people". Like Woody, he served in the Second World War, at the end of which conflict he formed The Weavers with Lee Hays, Ronnie Gilbert and Fred Hellerman. They turned Woody's 'This Land Is Your Land' into an American standard and topped the charts with Leadbelly's 'Goodnight Irene'.

Unlike Woody, however, Seeger's "actual experience in relating to the American people was zero". By his own admission, he had "a rather snobbish attitude" until Woody taught him different; as an initiate into the tradition that was manifest in Woody's very gait, that came out of his every pore, Seeger was, in the words of Alan Lomax, possessed by a "pure, genuine fervour, the kind that saves souls".

His Damascene epiphany came on a cross-country trek with Woody that exposed him to privations of the people. Bryan K. Garman, in *A Race of Singers: Whitman's Working-Class Hero From Guthrie To Springsteen*, contends that hereafter Seeger changed his modus operandi. He became fascinated by Woody's radicalism, his knowledge of folk music, and his ability to interact easily with working people, Seeger mimicked Woody's working-class attributes and tried to eschew the wealth and privilege of his Harvard pedigree. There was, Garman notes, "more than a hint of affectation in Seeger's pose",

Affectation maybe, but Seeger never forgot that he didn't belong to the working class – mainly because Woody never let him forget. Garman again: "When Seeger would try to blend the American folk tradition with international folk songs so that the Almanac Singers might appeal to a more diverse audience, Guthrie insisted that only he, a self-proclaimed member of the working class, had the authority to speak on behalf of his constituents and dismissed his friend's efforts as being too commercial."

This is an apposite juncture at which to pause and consider the elemental influence of Woody and Pete on a young Bruce Springsteen. By his own admission, Springsteen grew up a rock'n'roll fan and didn't know much about either man's music or their political activism. Certainly this is borne out by his first two albums, *Greetings From Asbury Park, NJ* and *The Wild, The Innocent And The E Street Shuffle*. But by *Born To Run* there's a very discernible influence in terms of the earthier language he uses, while the narratives depict, if not the American Nightmare, then an American Dream shattered by harsh reality. Such narratives exposing the lie at the heart of the aspirational myth had already been written by Woody. Springsteen must have been aware of Woody and Pete, he must have assimilated their songs, absorbed them on some level; he must have known, even superficially, about their reputation as bulwarks of blue-collar America.

Bryan K Garman claims Woody developed into the mature Springsteen's most important cultural ancestor, acknowledging the former's politics, "emphasising that Guthrie had 'a dream for more justice, less oppression, less racism and less hatred'. By performing a song ('This Land is Your Land') written by this well-known labour activist and anti-racist, Springsteen placed himself squarely within a cultural struggle for social justice, explaining that he covered Guthrie's song 'because that is what is needed right now... I sing that song to let people know that America belongs to everybody who lives there: the blacks, Chicanos, Indians, Chinese and the whites'."

When Nora Guthrie discovered a store of more than 2,000 of her father's unfinished songs in his archives, she looked around for suitable candidates to complete them with a view to recording an album. Springsteen would have been a candidate, but "I didn't know Bruce at the time, so the idea of working with him wasn't really an option," Nora recalls.

She plumped for Billy Bragg, a British political singer-songwriter and activist who came to prominence during Margaret Thatcher's prime ministerial reign in Eighties Britain. It was Thatcher who once dismissed the very notion of the existence of society, who presided over the decimation of the country's coal mining industry and who sent a task force to fight Argentina for ownership of the disputed Falkland Islands in the South Atlantic Ocean.

"I first began thinking of the idea of working with Woody's unpublished lyrics around 1994. And I wasn't at all sure the idea was going to work," Nora admits.

"So I wanted to work a little under the radar, scouting around for who I might be able to pull this off with. If I worked with someone who was in the spotlight, too high-profile, and the project got trashed it would get so much bad press that it would make it much harder to continue with other musicians and projects. So it was better to stay humble and look for people who really shared a love of Woody's values and lyrics. That's how I found Billy. He was the perfect 'outsider', much like Woody, sharing Woody's values, politics, sense of humour, even on stage much like Woody. And he was willing to take the chance. Punk guys can be like that – they enjoy taking chances! It was an alternative idea that needed an alternative approach.

"Since then, I've got to know Bruce and love him lots. We've done some work together, and I'm sure somewhere down the line we'll do one or two of these lyrics together."

Nora hears Woody in the way Springsteen shows empathy for the people he writes about, nowhere more so than on *Nebraska*. "Both Woody and Bruce are compelled to write about people who usually don't get much press coverage. Paris Hilton gets a lot of press, so we all know about her. But no one really gets to know much about anyone else – people that aren't gorgeous, rich or on camera don't get much coverage. And therefore, we don't often get to hear what they think about, how they're doing and so on.

"So Woody and Bruce both share a real love of writing about these 'other' people, because they want us to know something about them. And they want us to know something about them because maybe we're like them in some way, or maybe we'll think of something we can do to help them out. Or maybe we can learn from them in some way, or joke with them about something, or cry with them over something. It's all about loving people, individually and collectively. That's why they both write songs.

"At the bottom of the lyric, 'This Land is Your Land', Woody wrote: 'All you can write is what you see.' That's exactly what Bruce does. He tells us what he's looking at, how he feels about it and what he thinks about it. And that's the Woody Guthrie school of songwriting, 101."

Back to Woody, then. When we left him he was an integral part of New York's counterculture decades before the sociologists coined the term. But that innate restlessness got the better of him again, a restlessness given impetus by his increasing disillusionment with the machinations of an industry intent on curbing freedom of speech.

"I got disgusted with the whole sissified and nervous rules of censorship on all my songs and ballads and drove off down the road across the southern states again," was how he rationalised his decision to decamp with wife and kids to Portland, Oregon to go on the payroll of the Bonneville Power Authority, writing songs about the construction of the Grand Coulee Dam.

It wouldn't be his last commission. Serving with the Merchant Marine and the Army during the Second World War, Woody was enlisted by the military to compose songs warning soldiers of the dangers of venereal disease.

In the late Forties, Woody's behaviour was characterised by erratic mood swings and a tendency towards violence, as the Huntington's that had destroyed his mother began affecting his body and mind. His debilitating condition was exacerbated by misdiagnoses, as he was treated for symptoms that suggested alcoholism and schizophrenia. Arrested on a vagrancy charge in New Jersey in 1954, Woody was admitted to the state's Greystone Psychiatric Hospital where an accurate identification of the degenerative nerve disorder was finally provided.

The pilgrims came in their droves to pay homage to him, many of them – Bob Dylan, Joan Baez and Phil Ochs – by this time helming the Sixties folk scene that revolved around Greenwich Village, the bohemian enclave of New York. Woody died on 3 October 1967 at Creedmoor State Hospital in the city's Queens district.

His legacy is immense, his cultural proportions "as great...as those physically more imposing men such as the athletic Paul Robeson or the lanky Pete Seeger", according to folk historian Robert Cantwell. In his essay, *Fanfare For The Little Guy*, Cantwell hails Woody as "essentially a poet and intellectual at a time when a nationalist embrace of grassroots imagery and expression, mixed up with an urban romantic conception of an heroic American people in whom one might detect the unquiet ghost of a revolutionary proletariat, had prepared a place for him, as Steinbeck observed, to *be* that People".

He elaborates, "Guthrie was a westerner, out of the old Indian territories, with Scots-Irish – read 'hillbilly' – roots, and like his hillbilly-musician brethren he had a knack for the African American way of diddling a tune, especially that down-home, make-do, hip-pocket instrument the harmonica. Once converted to New York, however, the 'clever little man', the 'bantam rooster' as his friend Jimmy Longhi called him, the 'real dustbowl refugee' and 'the great American frontier ballad writer' could never again be seen in his mundane aspect, or even as a man with any history of his own; instead he would inevitably be woven into an essentially mythic web of a socialist heroic, replete with images and ideas of a glorified working people, of labour union triumphalism, wobbly millennialism and, especially out of this last, the still unsung frontier epic we seem to glimpse in Woody's songs."

When you navigate your way through Cantwell's dense prose, what he's getting at can be summarised thus: Woody was more than flesh and blood, he was the personification of a socially inclusive ideal, in which the little guy (and gal), as stakeholders in society, had access to the same rights, the same rewards as the big enchiladas. The tragedy of such an ideology, Cantwell concludes, is its elusiveness, especially in a world gone wrong, a world in which the power resides not with elected political representatives of the people, but with corporate wealth.

"Woody Guthrie embodies, not an eventual triumph over injustice and inequality, but the awful depth and tenacity of them in the human scheme; even as we thrill to his moral idealism and luminosity of his vision we feel, as a kind of instinct, with the example and the person of Guthrie before us, the impossibility of any realisation of them, or at the very least, the spectre of that impossibility, in a world that seems daily more inhospitable to his social and political vision."

For Nora Guthrie, ascribing a legacy to Woody is problematic, a task for which she's "not really qualified to answer". But she has no doubt that "he's given a lot of people courage, hope and even some ideas. He's not the originator of any of these, but he was a wonderful communicator. He got you engaged. And he could make you feel strong, even when others told you that you weren't. He could make you laugh at injustice, and therefore take away its power. Once that was broken down, you felt like you really could do something about it.

"His songs don't have to keep his name alive – rather, they're meant to keep ideas alive. So, I think he's remembered for being an American philosopher, working the streets, back alleys, harbours, fields, train stops and bars, who taught consistently by writing songs and singing them to whoever would listen, to whoever was looking."

Seeger, meanwhile, continues to be, as Springsteen described him, "a walking, talking, singing reminder of America's history". Speaking at the folk grandee's 90th birthday celebration in New York's Madison Square Garden, Springsteen said, "He'd be a living archive of America's music and conscience, a testament of the power of song and culture to nudge history along, to push American events towards more humane and justified ends. He would have the audacity and the courage to sing in the voice of the people."

High praise indeed. And there's more. "At 90, he remains a stealth dagger through the heart of the country's illusions about itself. Pete Seeger still sings all the verses all the time, and he reminds us of our immense failures, as well as shining a light towards our better angels in the horizon, where the country we've imagined and hold dear, we hope, awaits us."

Springsteen could just as easily have been extolling the attributes of Woody Guthrie. For both he and Seeger sang all the verses all the time, both reminded us of our immense failures and both shone a light towards those better angels. And they did it through the medium of American folk music, taking it from the scholars and giving it back to the people. The folk song became their song, whatever that song was about.

 As Guthrie himself asserted, "A folk song is what's wrong and how to fix it, or it could be who's hungry and where their mouth is, or who's out of work and where the job is, or who's broke and where the money is, or who's carrying a gun and where the peace is."

As the winds of radical change swept through America in the Sixties, a new generation of American folk music exponents took their cue from the Lomaxes and from Woody and Pete, reaching deep into the rich soil of the American past in a bid to help build an American future befitting a nation whose constitution declares itself to be the land of the free.

3. CRY FREEDOM

"Nobody could have spoken better for our generation than he did."

JOAN BAEZ on Bob Dylan

"Dylan, he was a revolutionary. The way that Elvis freed your body, Bob freed your mind and showed us that just because the music was innately physical did not mean that it was anti-intellect."

BRUCE SPRINGSTEEN

The folk renaissance that had its geographical hub in the bars and coffeehouses of New York's Greenwich Village during the first years of the Sixties is indivisible from the struggle for civil rights that, along with the Cuban missile crisis, the assassination of John F Kennedy and the Vietnam War, defined the era. This renaissance was concerned with reviving the songs of America's past and placing them in the present. Many of these same songs came to be adapted by a new generation of songwriters, among them Bob Dylan, Phil Ochs and Dave Van Ronk, to fit the social issues of the day, and thus was the topical song movement subsumed by the Sixties folk revival.

The revival actually began at the tail end of the Fifties when the Kingston Trio reached the zenith of the American popular music charts with their thrusting take on 'Tom Dooley' – an Appalachian murder ballad, no less – the narrative satisfying the US consumer's fetish for homicidal entertainment. Folk singers had actually been gathering in Washington Square after the end of the Second World War since, as anecdotal history has it, a certain George Margolin turned up with his guitar on Sunday afternoons to play union ballads and familiar folk songs. By the early Fifties, it had become a focal point for folk enthusiasts.

Judy Collins arrived there at the outset of the Sixties. A native of Seattle, she was brought up in Los Angeles and Denver. It was in the Colorado capital where Collins, a classically trained pianist, gravitated to the folk movement.

"I was drawn to it by the personal stories. Vivid stories – horror stories sometimes. Stories about people's lives, what they are doing, what they are thinking about, how their lives are related in terms of their love lives, their political beliefs, how they raise their kids. The thing that struck me about it was that I could find a way to use my voice to talk about the world in a way that literature always talked about the world.

"I grew up playing the piano, playing Mozart, playing Rachmaninov, playing Debussy, and listening to my father read us Dostoevsky and *War And Peace*. I needed to combine the music with the stories. I think many of us who have prospered in this folk/popular music of the last fifty years, have moved into it because of the need to express ourselves in song as we had seen our contemporaries

17

in previous centuries express themselves in broadsides, union songs, in music that would filter into the political movement of the time. We're all about politics and personal intertwined."

By the time she hit New York, Collins was a working singer. For her, Greenwich Village offered the prospect of employment rather than the opportunity to join the vanguard of social change of which the folk movement was a component.

"I was looking for a job when I came to New York, and what I did was to sing folk music. I had arrived in the city without a record contract, but before I was there ten minutes I had one. I already was part of the movement, so I didn't have to look for that. I was doing it – I was the movement, like all the rest of the kids with the guitars. In the village I found many like-minded souls.

"Many people came to New York to be heard and to hear. There was a flock of kids of a similar age, most of them in their twenties, who would drink together, have coffee together, go and hear each other in the clubs. We went to listen, we went to learn – we were a massive collection of very creative people. There was a creative brewing vat of so much personal and politically sensitive material.

"It was extremely exciting. Did we know we were part of a great movement of change? Well, we were furious about the war. To be furious about the war is to be connected. Nowadays there's no draft – you have to volunteer to go and get your head blown off. But back then we had the draft. We were all involved in this up to our eyeballs. We were mad because we were waking up to a lot of things in the Sixties. One of the things we were waking up to was the fact that we'd been lied to by our leaders. Bruce fits right into that pattern, because Bruce knows he's being lied to. He was able to, I think, filter that experience of how to talk about those things through listening to some of that music and being a part of it. He was a kid back then, but he certainly was aware of this musical cacophony that was going on.

"A lot of the folk singers with whom I was coming up in the Sixties were reaching into the folk music revival recordings of songs which came from the Child ballads. Songs that had life stories – that's where we connect with what Springsteen's doing on *Nebraska*. He's reflecting some of the activity, in terms of the writing, that was going on among my contemporaries, particularly in the mid Sixties. There was a great pool of material in the Sixties to draw from, much of it part of the folk music revival, much of it part of the singer-songwriter tradition. I think Bruce is reaching into that with a straw, sucking it up. You manage, in the process, to do what many of us have done, which is to begin to reflect upon human experience and on your own experience within the context of writing something accessible, which he certainly has done."

The folk movement really gained momentum with the advent of Joan Baez and Bob Dylan, one reverentially reviving ballads from the British tradition, the other rough and ready for some revolution. Baez may have been the more politically engaged of the two – she walked it like she talked it – but without Dylan's songs, the rallying cry to make a difference would have been a whisper rather than a scream. Baez herself has no qualms about acknowledging this.

"The civil rights movement was in full bloom and he filled our arsenal with songs. But he (Dylan) was never a marcher. Years later, people would come up to me at a march and ask if Dylan was showing up. Well, he never showed up. That isn't what he did. He gave us the music for the marches but he didn't go on them. But whether he likes it or not – and it seems he doesn't really care – he goes down in the history books as a leader of dissent and social change, and his name will forever be associated with the radical movements of the Sixties."

Judy Collins, a contemporary of both Dylan and Baez, disagrees with the latter part of Baez's assessment of Dylan's Sixties legacy. "I would say it differently. He was a literate writer who was in touch with the politics of the time. He was very much a writer who coined the phrase, who used the metaphor, who ratcheted us into a sense of our own destiny because he was such a fabulous writer. His songs were so effective because they were so unlike anything we'd heard before. They were revolutionary.

"He was a humanist writer. The politics beat the drum alongside what he was doing, but he was a brilliant humanistic writer who was able to forge language into unusual segments in which we could see ourselves. We could see ourselves as individuals. We could also see ourselves as part of a great, great movement of spirit of politics. He was unique.

"You could say he was totally apolitical, and I think he would always say that. It was the writing, it was the nuance, the ability to see beyond the politics and to see into the soul. That's why he's important."

Dylan came out of Hibbing, Minnesota in the Midwest. After graduating from high school he set off "to follow Little Richard" but found himself trailing in the footsteps of Woody Guthrie instead.

"Dylan swallowed Woody's early autobiography, *Bound For Glory*, as if it was the Bible,' Robert Shelton wrote in *No Direction Home: The Life And Music Of Bob Dylan*.

In the same book, Harvey Abrams, a friend of Dylan's in Minneapolis during the latter's brief spell as a student at the University of Minneapolis, told of how the young singer morphed into a Woody doppelganger (just like Pete Seeger had all those years before). He started doing everything the way Woody did. He sang like him, and even modified his speech to sound more Oklahoman.

"That incredibly harsh gravel sound in his voice became more and more a part of him," said Abrams. "It really became much more than identification. People who didn't know Bob very well were repelled or angered by the change in him, because they thought he was phoney or he was making a dollar. Sometimes, we just thought that the Guthrie character and the Dylan character were very much the same, anyway. We believed Bob was born with this nature, only it had been covered up for 18 years by living in Hibbing in a fairly bourgeois set-up. We really felt that Bob's real self was coming out from underneath."

In December 1960, Dylan learned that Woody, then only 48, was a patient at Greystone. He rang the hospital to speak with him, but was informed that Woody couldn't get the phone; he could, however, have visitors. Dylan made it to Greystone the following month, after which he befriended the Guthrie family, then Bob and

Sidsel Gleason, a couple who brought Woody back to their house every Sunday for musical get togethers. Soon Dylan was a regular at these hootenannies, attended by Pete Seeger and Woody acolyte Ramblin' Jack Elliott. According to Joe Klein, "a real rapport seemed to develop between Woody and Dylan", the older man supposedly boasting to friends, "That boy's got a voice. Maybe he won't make it with his writing, but he can sing it."

For his part, Dylan was awed by his idol, enthusing in a letter to Minneapolis pal David Whitaker: "I know Woody... I know him and met him and saw him and sang to him. He's the greatest godliest one in the world."

He was sufficiently inspired to write 'Song To Woody', its melody cribbed from Woody's own '1913 Massacre' and, even when his star was in the ascendant, Dylan never forgot the debt he owed to his mentor. Take this quote from the sleevenotes to his second album, *The Freewheelin' Bob Dylan*: "The most important thing I know I learned from Woody Guthrie is I'm my own person. I've got basic common rights – whether I'm here in this country or any other place. I'll never finish saying everything I feel, but I'll be doing my part to make some sense out of the way we're living, and not living, now."

Sean Wilentz, historian-in-residence on Dylan's official website and author of the excellent *Bob Dylan In America*, says, "Dylan virtually channelled Woody Guthrie early on. The melody for 'Song To Woody' was taken from a Guthrie song. But even on the first album, other influences, including the rediscovered blues artists, were plainly in evidence. By the second album, he's already branching out on his own. And still Guthrie would remain an influence. Dylan never repudiates anything, and often comes back to things he'd appreciated earlier, albeit in new ways. For example, his performance of 'Do-Re-Mi' in 2009, or his appearance at the Guthrie memorial concert in 1968 – Guthrie songs, but in an entirely new way."

For Bryan K Garman, Woody became a heroic spiritual grandfather of the new left that appropriated the Sixties folk movement. He says, "The most successful of his cultural offspring, Bob Dylan, embodied both the possibilities and the limitations of his hero's vision.

"Dylan opened possibilities to see the world in new ways, to raise fundamental questions about justice, to engage meaningful social issues. His own artistry seemed to collide with and perhaps subsume his activism, and he never managed to address gender inequality. Consider his relationship with Joan Baez."

Just like Woody, Dylan sang it like he saw it. And just like Woody, he saw a lot that aggrieved him. If Woody's guitar killed fascists, Dylan's guitar scattergunned anyone who got in the way of the times that were a-changin'. If Woody sang about the people and for the people, Dylan sang about the people that people of his colour and class didn't know, people like the subject of 'The Lonesome Death Of Hattie Carroll', who "emptied the ashtrays on a whole other level". The label-loving media tagged him a protest singer – and, though Dylan despised the term, that's exactly how he came across on *The Freewheelin' Bob Dylan* and *The Times They Are A-Changin'*. A recurring theme of his protesting was the inequitable treatment of African Americans

– or, more accurately, the subjugation of a people through what we now refer to as institutional racism. The lawmakers didn't necessarily wear pointy hats or burn crosses, but they did ensure that might was synonymous with white. Dylan, like many of his generation (and arguably motivated by then girlfriend Suze Rotolo, a committed left-winger who worked at the Congress of Racial Equality), was appalled by it, as 'The Death Of Emmett Till', 'Oxford Town', 'Only A Pawn In Their Game' and 'The Lonesome Death Of Hattie Carroll' testify.

Judy Collins again: "Folk music was terribly important in advancing the cause of civil rights. The Newport Folk Festival was one of the few places in the country where blacks and whites could mingle. You could go to Newport and feel that you were an integrated community up there. That was not true in most of the rest of the country. Many of us went to Mississippi to work for voter registration in the black community. The integration movement was very much part of the folk music movement. The whole texture of the Sixties was coloured, pardon the expression, by the civil rights movement and vice versa."

But Sean Wilentz warns against overstating the part played by the folk movement in the campaign for civil rights. "There were some obvious connections," he says, "but it shouldn't be forgotten that the (civil rights) movement, especially the Student Non-Violent Coordinating Committee, had its own singers, the Freedom Singers. And in the south, music was a big part of organising efforts and rallies early on, quite apart from the folk revival which was a northern thing.

"The folk revival certainly came out of the left, and was deeply supportive of the civil rights movement. But 'We Shall Overcome' was the movement's anthem, not 'Blowin' In The Wind'. The folk revival did most to galvanise and widen support for the movement among young northerners."

Julius Lester, a contributor to *Broadside* magazine (a mimeographed publication, founded in 1962 by Agnes 'Sis' Cunningham and husband Gordon Friesen, which caught the folk zeitgeist) is careful to make a distinction between the folk revival and what he refers to as the topical song movement.

"The folk revival had nothing to do with the civil rights movement. When I think of the folk revival, I think of the New Los City Ramblers, Doc Watson and others who sang traditional music, whose focus was to revive some wonderful music and musicians who deserved to be better known.

"The topical song movement's focus was the use of music as an agent of social change. It used traditional songs and changed the words to fit a social issue. The civil rights movement was the catalyst for the birth of topical songs in the Sixties. The civil rights movement used many songs from black traditional religious music – spirituals – changing a few words, adding new verses. The music of the civil rights movement was rooted in the southern black community. There were some original songs that came out of the civil rights movement, but most songs in the topical song movement were composed by the singers who sang them.

"One crucial distinction between the topical song movement and the music of the civil rights movement was that most of the singers of the former were white and

the singers of the latter were black. There were a few blacks who straddled both –
myself, Jackie Washington and Len Chandler, for example. Richie Havens was
exclusively a part of the topical song movement, though he sang about the civil rights
movement. The main thrust of the topical song movement was protesting the war
in Vietnam."

There was no civil rights movement in a literal sense; rather it was a concept
predicated on equal rights for African Americans which different groups endeavoured
to realise over centuries. Between the Forties and the Sixties the movement was
generated by the Congress of Racial Equailty (CORE), the Southern Christian
Leadership Conference (SCLC), the National Association for the Advancement of
Coloured People (NAACP) and the Student Nonviolent Coordinating Committee
(SNCC). At the heart of this unofficial coalition was Dr Martin Luther King Junior.

Dylan and Dr King crossed paths on the steps of the nation's capital,
Washington, on 28 August 1963, the apotheosis of the Sixties folk movement and the
moment when it became indelibly associated with the campaign for civil rights. The
previous month at the Newport Folk Festival, Dylan, flanked by Baez, Seeger,
Theodore Bikel, Peter, Paul & Mary and the Freedom Singers, had closed proceedings
with his own 'Blowin' In The Wind' and the Baptist hymn 'We Shall Overcome', the
anthem of the movement. The same personnel gathered before Washington's Lincoln
Memorial with some 300,000 people from all over America, and, Greil Marcus
recounts in *Invisible Republic: Bob Dylan's Basement Tapes*, "called upon the sitting
administration, the Congress, the courts, their own governors, their own legislators,
their mayors, councilmen, school boards, sheriffs, police chiefs, and the people at
large to honour themselves by honouring their national charter, to reaffirm the credo
of equal justice under the law".

They listened, rapt, as Dr King proclaimed in Biblical imagery the utopian vision
he held in his heart, the same utopian vision shared by the folk movement, the dream
"that one day every valley shall be exalted, and every hill and mountain shall be made
low, and the rough places will be made plain, and the crooked places will be made
straight, and the glory of the Lord will be revealed and all flesh shall see it together".

But with Kennedy's death in November, the escalation of American involvement
in the Vietnamese conflict (from which thousands of young men, black and white,
returned home in body bags), and the murders of Bobby Kennedy, former black separatist
Malcolm X and Dr King himself, the idealism that illuminated the initial years of the
Sixties, an idealism encapsulated in folk's rebirth and its cry of freedom, was supplanted
by an incendiary radicalism in the latter years of the decade. The Black Panther Party,
formed in 1966 by Huey P Newton, Bobby Seale and David Hilliard, called for "a
redress of the longstanding grievances of the black masses in America, still alienated
from society and oppressed despite the abolition of slavery at the end of the Civil
War". In its manifesto, the party made ten key demands, chief among which was "the
power to determine the destiny of our black and oppressed communities". The Black
Panthers were about militancy rather than the diplomacy espoused by Dr King. Their
credo was: "The revolution has come, it's time to pick up the gun."

This shift towards militancy was captured in an artistic cameo at the 1969 Woodstock Music and Arts Fair when Jimi Hendrix's rendering of 'The Star Spangled Banner' echoed the howling storm of dissent within the African American community. The rousing melodic progression of the US national anthem was rent asunder, splintered into so much sonic shrapnel; it was both a rejection of American values that only applied if you were white and a symbolic act of liberation on the part of African Americans in a time of flux.

"The folk revival didn't suddenly end so much as it petered out," says Sean Wilentz. "Dylan's move to singing with his band was very important here. After Newport '65, everybody in Greenwich Village, including Dave Van Ronk, was looking to play with one form or another of electric band. And then you had bands like the Lovin' Spoonful, with Dylan's pal John Sebastian, creating a new synthesis of folk music and rock'n'roll. There were still folk singers and singer-songwriters, but the boom was over by 1965.

"As for the hope for the music as a tool for change, that continued right into the Seventies, but was transferred to rock'n'roll of certain kinds, the chief example being John Lennon's political music."

For Judy Collins, the folk movement is infinite. "It will never be ended. All you have to do is to go festivals and hear young singers writing about their personal and their political and their overarching desire to change the world. It's never going to be gone. And although the revival started seventy years ago, around the time I was born, the revival meant that there was something else going on before it happened. There have always been folk music elements within the culture. There have been broadsides, folk songs, Child ballads – these things have always been happening in the culture and they always will be.

"Springsteen is part of the ongoing flow. He's a folk hero in many ways like Woody was. He expresses a lot of the outrage and a lot of the beauty that people in the world, and he does it on a popular level. But that means that he's just expressing himself in a way that identifies with half the country, or perhaps more than half."

Yet by the end of the Sixties, there were some among those who had once believed, who had once had faith in race co-operation as the road to the promised land (a co-operation embodied in the folk movement), who disavowed such a theory.

"What did they know of these songs we would sing in church and in the field?" Julius Lester looked back with some rancour in his 1969 critique, *Search For The New Land*. "Blacks have always served as a path which whites have used to try and get out of the concentration camps of their souls."

Lester's view, while valid, was exaggerated, according to Wilentz. "The racial component was there, sure, but the Popular Front from which the folk revival sprang was about a lot more than race. It was about getting in touch with the folk traditions of the people writ large, which involved all sorts of folk music. Politically, the movement was strongly for racial integration, putting black performers up front – people like Leadbelly, Sonny Terry and Brownie McGhee, Josh White. But musically as well as politically, it had other preoccupations as well, such as forging a leftist politics that would emerge from the music of the masses, as the revivalists saw it."

Growing up in the mainly white New Jersey hamlet of Freehold didn't exempt Bruce Springsteen from the racial tensions that crackled and burned in America throughout the Sixties. As 'My Hometown', the closing track on his 1984 album, *Born In The USA*, recounts, "In '65 tension was running high/At my high school/There was a lot of fights between the black and white/There was nothing you could do/Two cars at a light on a Saturday night/In the backseat there was a gun/Words were passed, in a shotgun blast/Troubled times had come/To my hometown".

While the song deals with social issues in a personal way (including the closing down of a local mill), the problem with it, says Harvard University lecturer Jim Cullen in *Born In The USA: Bruce Springsteen And The American Tradition*, is its airlessness.

"No one is actually creating or fomenting the racial tension; it's just there," he argues. "So are the 'words'. And the 'shotgun blast'. A dismaying passivity characterises the singer (and, arguably, Springsteen himself). Perhaps even more than overt hostility, *this* was the attitude that Martin Luther King gave his life to combat: the idea that racism was natural, even inevitable."

Now whether Springsteen got the date wrong, or was exercising an artistic decision in choosing 1965, a so-called race riot did occur in Freehold on 19 May 1969. Race relations had reached a nadir as the area's economy slumped. The local government sought to address the issue through an Inter-Racial Human Relations Committee in 1968, but the powder keg blew the following year.

The *Asbury Park Press* reported: "The police log book for Monday night's racial disturbance shows the first incident involving bands of black youths, started some four hours before a window-smashing spree and a teenage shooting.

"Police broke up a band of black teenagers near the bus terminal at 6:13pm. At 8:27pm, another group was dispersed without incident at the same location. The first window was smashed at 8:27pm at a South Street poolroom by a group of black youths.

"Fifteen minutes later, a crowd of blacks again gathered at the bus station near the Borough Hall and was again dispersed. An out-of-town woman telephoned police at 8:48pm and said her son was driving into town and 'there would be trouble'.

"At 9:22pm, reports came in of two separate groups of blacks in the predominantly Negro south-east section of the borough. One caller reported the group loitering on the overpass on Centre Street and another reported a band of blacks with sticks and clubs rounding the corner of Centre Street and First Avenue.

"By 9:56pm, a large group of blacks was seen in the downtown parking lot off Court Street. At 10pm, a caller reported a crowd at Centre and First Streets pelting passing cars with bricks and bottles.

"Fifteen minutes later, one motorist had the side of his car dented and a baseball bat passed through the front window of a woman's car. Neither was injured.

"At 10:27pm, a large group of cars filled with white teenagers drove through the bus terminal area shouting catcalls to nearby black youths. The drivers then parked the cars on side streets around 10:30pm and walked through the centre of town. Around the same time a car stopped on South Street, an unidentified man got out, hit a parked car with a baseball bat and drove off.

"The log book shows reports of various store windows broken in the business section at 10:35pm, and a shooting at South Street on Route 33. Police said a carload of white youths pulled alongside a car of black youths, and a shotgun was fired into the back seat of the car of black teenagers. The victims, Dean Lewis, 16, of 8 Monmouth Avenue, who suffered buckshot wounds in the left side of his face and right eye, and Leroy Kinsey Jr, 19, Factory Street, who was hit in the neck, were taken to Jersey Shore Medical Centre, Neptune.

"Police Chief Henry T Lefkowich called for reinforcements at around that time, and police from Marlboro Township, Freehold Township and the County Sheriff's Office responded.

"At 11pm, Mayor John I Dawes ordered a curfew until 6:00am Tuesday and declared a state of emergency. State police were then called in from Princeton to assist in maintaining order. Quiet was restored shortly after midnight."

Springsteen referred to the episode again when he played a concert at the US Bank Arena, Cincinnati in 2002. The deaths of two young African Americans in police custody had sparked a boycott of the downtown area.

"As a young man, I saw it up close in my hometown," Springsteen told his audience. "While there have been many improvements since then, the core fact of racism continues to this day at all levels of society."

4. GROWIN' UP

"Springsteen is not just from Freehold, but is of and in it."

Freehold, New Jersey historian KEVIN COYNE

"Well, I got out of here hard and fast in Freehold
Everybody wanted to kick my ass back then in Freehold
Well, if you were different or black or brown
It was a pretty redneck town back in Freehold."

BRUCE SPRINGSTEEN, 'Freehold'

How much does where you're from shape what you become? It's an intriguing question. We are, after all, formed in the place we first call home; we grow up into a composite of local influences and experiences from house and neighbourhood. And then, if we're big enough and brave enough, we take ourselves off someplace else. But what do we take with us? To what extent does that gestation period prior to attaining independence affect our attitudes, our philosophy, our ideological outlook, later on? Admittedly, in this mass-media age, those local influences and experiences have been augmented by others beamed in from beyond the parameters of our immediate environment through the miracle (or curse) of technology. The local is now global, you can go anywhere without leaving where you are.

For Bruce Springsteen, home was Freehold, radio and television his links to the outside world. Freehold is a township in Monmouth County, New Jersey, situated about halfway between the Atlantic Ocean in the east and the Delaware River in the west. It borders New York State in the north and Cape May in the south.

Lenni Lenape Indians were the first inhabitants, before Scottish settlers began arriving in 1683, followed by the English and the Dutch. Freehold (adapted from the English noun meaning tenure of property held in fee simple) was one of three townships established when Monmouth County was subdivided in 1693 (Shrewsbury and Middletown were the others). It left its imprint on the American Revolution as the site of the Battle of Monmouth on 28 June 1778. General George Washington's Continental Army attacked British forces that were on the march to Sandy Hook from Philadelphia. A guide to New Jersey, published by the Works Progress Administration in 1939, cited Freehold as embodying "America's growth from farm to factory", the transition from agriculture to manufacturing.

Springsteens have lived in Freehold since the 18th Century. The earliest, John Springsteen, was born on 3 June 1759 in Middlesex County, New Jersey, to the north of Monmouth County. Bruce Springsteen, part-Italian, Irish and Dutch, came along on 23 September 1949. He was raised, along with little sister Virginia (known as Ginny), by parents Douglas and Adele at 87 Randolph Street next door to St Rose of Lima Roman Catholic Church. Many of his relatives lived nearby.

"There was my cousin's house, my aunt's house, my great-grandmother's house, my aunt's house on my mother's side with my other grandmother in it. We were all on one street, with the church in the middle."

The family moved out of Randolph Street shortly after Springsteen's fifth birthday, and settled into a duplex at 39-1/2 Institute Street three blocks east. In 1962, they relocated again, this time renting half a duplex at 68 South Street, four blocks from Institute Street.

According to Kevin Coyne, Freehold historian and author of *Marching Home: To War And Back With The Men Of One American Town*, a portrait of six Second World War veterans from the town, Springsteen's childhood coincided with an era of relative prosperity in Freehold.

"But then in the Sixties, everything started to change," he explained. "The rug mill, the biggest factory, closed down, and the downtown started to fade. Developers began buying the surrounding farmland and putting up houses for people who were abandoning New York and the cities of northern New Jersey, and Freehold became absorbed by the larger metropolitan sprawl. It was always, to an unusual degree for a town its size, ethnically and racially mixed. It had, and still has, an urban diversity mixed with a village intimacy. It was, and remains, a town of very modest means."

For Coyne, Springsteen is a man of Freehold – an everyman whose qualities were bred there. "He has deep roots in this one place. He hasn't lost touch with the family and friends who surrounded him as he grew up. He found the raw material of his songs here. He took the stories he lived and heard there and shaped them into the larger stories that touched a chord with so many other people in so many other places.

"I think he tends to see the world as Freehold writ larger – a place where people are, or should be, loyal to their families, their communities, where they try to look out for each other and extend a helping hand when needed, where they're connected deeply to the lives of others. He and his work were shaped by this town – you can hear it in every song. And he still lives nearby and returns regularly for sustenance."

Eric Alterman, in *It Ain't No Sin To Be Glad You're Alive: The Promise Of Bruce Springsteen*, equates Springsteen's childhood with a bad Charles Dickens novel soundtracked by the Who's *Quadrophenia*. The Dickens allusion smacks of hyperbole; Springsteen's mother was devoted to him, and he enjoyed a good rapport with siblings Ginny and Pamela (born in 1962). What Alterman had in mind while over-stretching himself for an appropriate analogy was undoubtedly Springsteen's fractious relationship with father Douglas – a relationship that involved "little but discipline and rebellion".

Douglas was a disappointed man, a bitter man who never could find a place for himself in the Freehold economy. He held down various jobs for brief periods, including mill worker, jail guard and cab and bus driver, but nothing at which he stuck. The conflict between father and son was only heightened by Springsteen's musical ambitions, the seeds of which were sown by seeing Elvis Presley's performance on *The Ed Sullivan Show* in 1957.

"When I first heard Elvis' voice, I knew that I wasn't going to work for anybody and nobody was going to be my boss. Hearing him for the first time was like busting out of jail," said Springsteen.

Years later, on an MTV tribute to the king of rock'n'roll, he professed, "Elvis is my religion. But for him I'd be selling encyclopaedias right now."

Springsteen bought his first guitar ("one of the most beautiful sights I'd ever seen in my life") from the Western Auto pawnshop at the age of thirteen for just $18. Frank Bruno, his cousin, taught him some basic chords. When he was sixteen, Adele, a legal secretary on the minimum wage, took out a $60 loan to get him a Japanese-made Kent electric guitar and an amplifier for Christmas.

"It was a very defining moment," Springsteen remembered, "standing in front of the music store with someone who's going to do everything she can to give you what you needed that day, and having the faith that you were going to make sense of it."

Douglas didn't share Adele's faith in their boy's chosen path. "When I was growing up, there were two things that were unpopular in my house: one was me, the other was my guitar," Springsteen used to joke to audiences. Whenever he practiced, Douglas would turn on the gas jets on the stove and direct them into the heating ducts leading to Springsteen's bedroom in an attempt to drive him out. It was a meanness that often had the required effect.

On those nights when Springsteen came in late, Douglas would sit alone in the kitchen, darkness all around but for the burning ember of his cigarette, waiting to berate the boy.

"Pretty soon we'd end up screaming at each other and my mother would come running up from the front room, trying to pull him off me, trying to keep us from fighting each other. And I'd always end up running out the back door screaming, telling him that it was my life and I could do what I wanted to do."

Springsteen's upbringing was hardly *The Waltons*, nor was it the stuff of Victorian London's slums. Rather it was one with which, I would suggest, most of us could identify – emotionally impotent, occupationally unfulfilled patriarch wreaks his revenge on completely innocent progeny, while stoic matriarch binds the whole together. This is what used to pass for the average blue-collar baptism, the essential difference being that Springsteen put it in his songs and the songs connected him to an audience because that audience knew what he was singing about.

"What would I conceivably have written without (Douglas)?" Springsteen quipped during his induction speech to the Rock'n'Roll Hall of Fame. "If everything had gone great between us, we would have had disaster. I would have written just happy songs. He never said much about my music, except that his favourite songs were the ones about him. And that was enough. Anyway, I put on his work clothes and I went to work. It was the way that I honoured him. My parents' experience forged my own. They shaped my politics, and they alerted me to what's at stake when you're Born In The USA."

His mother, Springsteen said in the same speech, gave him "a sense of work as something that was joyous and that filled you with pride and self-regard, and that committed you to your world."

Shortly after Douglas' death in 1998, Bruce admitted, "There ain't a note I play on stage can't be traced back to my mother and father." Add to that the nuns who taught him at St Rose of Lima. Springsteen had "the big hate" when it came to school. Hardly surprising when you hear that in the third grade Sister something-or-other stuffed him into a garbage can because "she told me that's where I belonged".

Then there was the incident in eighth grade when, after playing the wise guy, he was sent down to the first-grade class to sit at a desk made for a child a fraction of his size. It didn't end there. When Springsteen smiled at the nun who had forced him into the tiny seat, she turned to another pupil for a demonstration of what happened to people who smiled in the classroom.

"This kid, this six-year-old who has no doubt been taught to do this, he comes over to me – him standing up and me sitting in this little desk – and he slams me in the face."

The following year, Springsteen left for Freehold Regional, a public high school derided by the majority who saw it as the least appealing educational option and where he became invisible, refusing to take part in any activities or even apply himself much academically.

"I didn't even make it to class clown. I had nowhere near that amount of notoriety. I didn't have, like, the flair to be the complete jerk. It was like I didn't exist. It was the wall, then me."

It's not exaggerating it to suggest that Springsteen's life was saved by rock'n'roll, hackneyed though that sounds. "I tried to play football and baseball and all those things. I checked out all the alleys and just didn't fit. Music gave me something. I was running through a maze. It was never just a hobby. It was a reason to live. The first day I can remember looking in a mirror and being able to stand what I was seeing was the day I had a guitar in my hand."

Rock'n'roll gave him community, "filled with brothers and sisters who I didn't know, but who I knew were out there. We had this enormous thing in common, this 'thing' that initially felt like a secret, a home where my spirit could wander. It was the liberating thing…my connection to the rest of the human race. It reached down into all those homes where there was no music or books or any kind of creative sense, and it infiltrated the whole thing. It was like the voice of America, the real America coming into your home."

While Springsteen knew that rock'n'roll was fun, he also believed that it could be a conduit for serious ideas, "and that the people who listened to it…were looking for something."

His first band was the Rogues, who ended up throwing him out because his guitar was too cheap. Then George Theiss, a guitarist who was dating his sister, Ginny, recruited him for the Castiles, a Beatles and Motown-influenced outfit managed by Freehold factory worker Gordon 'Tex' Vineyard. They played about two dozen shows in Freehold, including five monthly appearances at the Hullabaloo Club. The Castiles were among the first of the New Jersey Shore bands to release a single ('That's What You Get', backed with 'Baby I'), and to secure a regular residency outside the area at

New York's Café Wha? They broke up in August 1968 and Springsteen went on to form Earth, a short-lived power trio in the mould of Cream.

But his first group of any real repute was Steel Mill, featuring Steve Van Zandt on guitar, Danny Federici on keyboards and Vini 'Mad Dog' Lopez on drums, the fulcrum of the E Street Band mark one.

"I first met Bruce in a band battle at the Keyport-Matawan Rollerdome, I think it was 1966," Lopez recalls. "I was in a band called Sonny and the Starfires. He was in the Castiles. They were set up right next to us. There were twenty-five bands in this thing. We finished in second place, they finished out of the top three. They were good, and we thought they would win it. We were shocked about the outcome."

What caught Lopez's attention about Springsteen back then was "a certain charisma he had that drew you into what he was doing – and he was a great guitar player".

Many of the bands on the New Jersey Shore scene congregated at the Upstage, a legendary Asbury Park club which hosted late-night jams. "Everybody went there because it was open later than the regular clubs and because between one and five in the morning you could play pretty much whatever you wanted, and if you were good enough, you could choose the guys you wanted to play with," Springsteen wrote in the liner notes for Southside Johnny and the Asbury Jukes' debut album, *I Don't Want To Go Home*.

Southside Johnny, alias John Lyon, lived half a mile from the Upstage. He used to walk there every night to sit in on sessions, and it was here he first encountered Springsteen. "I didn't drive until I was forty years old – I was too interested in drugs and alcohol. I realised I could do one or the other, and I couldn't drive and do the other things.

"The Upstage was open until five o'clock in the morning. All the musicians went there and played. One day I walked up to the upstairs, which is where the rock bands played, and there was this long-haired guy with a gold Les Paul, singing a song about how the nuns taught him about the blues. They were mean to him when he was in Catholic school, then one day one of the sisters brought in a BB King record and Bruce's eyes just got real wild. It was a talking blues about this experience he had. I thought, 'Who the hell is that?' He was definitely the competition at that point."

If the Upstage was the mecca, there were plenty of other clubs where musicians could hone their skills – clubs like The Fast Lane, Mrs Jay's, the Student Prince and the High Tide Café. Later on, in the mid Seventies, there was the Stone Pony, the place where Springsteen and the E Street Band would hang out while off the road.

Southside Johnny again: "There were all the honky-tonk towns along the Jersey Shore. They had clubs where you could go in and get a fake ID and listen to bands, and eventually end up playing at seventeen in these bars basically.

"As long as you knew twenty Chuck Berry songs and five Bo Diddley songs, three this and four that, you could get in and play. We started doing our own stuff, but any time the customers got a little antsy, you'd just go right into 'Tutti Frutti' or whatever, and they were happy. It was a chance for us to learn how to play, but also to be part of this excitement. We were not really old enough to be in those places.

Then they started opening the youth clubs where you could get in as a teenager. It was heaven on earth for us. People actually looked as us! They paid attention to us because we were playing in bands.

"We could pretend to be the Rolling Stones or Chuck Berry for three minutes on stage. There were enough places to play. It was very blue-collar, knockdown, no art rock or anything like that. We were all big admirers of Bob Dylan and that kind of stuff, but it was really more about going up and pounding it out. I think it was accepted. It gave us a chance to learn. It also gave us a chance to go out and experiment and thrash around, just like the punk people did later when they got fed up with the twenty-minute guitar solos and the art rock. Fuck that – it's rock'n'roll.

"Then you could take it where you wanted to take it. Bruce took it where he wanted to take it, Little Steven incorporated a lot of R&B into his sound, and I was always a blues guy. We started to put those elements into the bands, so there was a mongrelisation of straightahead rock'n'roll, garage rock, blues, rhythm and blues, Stax and all of that. It was a chance to find out what really pleased you and find your own path into music.

"Bruce's success was pivotal for all of us in the sense that he made it okay for record company executives from New York to get in their limos and travel an hour and fifteen minutes into Asbury Park to look for other bands. Of course, we were one of the bands there, so we were the beneficiaries of his success."

It was when fronting Steel Mill that Springsteen emerged as a writer, penning 'The Wind And The Rain', 'Going Back To Georgia' and 'Resurrection', staples of their live sets in venues along the New Jersey Shore where they developed a large following. They headed west in 1969 and nearly bagged a recording contract but, with too little money on offer, returned home. Springsteen soon dissolved Steel Mill and began taking the bus to Greenwich Village in nearby New York to play solo for food money (not unlike a certain Woody Guthrie in another lifetime).

Dr Zoom and the Sonic Boom, more a travelling circus than a band (including twirlers and Monopoly players), arrested the attention of the Shore regulars for a while before becoming the Bruce Springsteen Band, a cumbersome 10-piece unit complete with backing singers and a horn section. Too financially demanding to maintain, it went the way of the Castiles, Steel Mill and Dr Zoom and the Sonic Boom. For Springsteen, "the kicks started to wear off". That was when Mike Appel came along to take care of business.

Mike Appel has what the Irish call the gift of the gab – in other words, he talks a good game, a definite attribute in the world of music management. That he is himself three quarters Irish probably explains it. His website, which describes him as a writer, musician, singer, arranger and producer, is a shrine to his enduring ability for self-promotion. His first break, he writes, came courtesy of a duo by the name of Hugo & Luigi (who produced Sam Cooke and wrote Elvis Presley's 'Can't Help Falling In Love With You').

"The first project I did for Hugo & Luigi was the Balloon Farm, who had a *Billboard* Top 40 hit called 'Question Of Temperature'. I sang, played guitar, wrote and arranged it. I had also written several hits for David Cassidy and The Partridge Family. 'Doesn't Somebody Want To Be Wanted' went to Number 1 and sold over a million copies."

See what I mean?

Appel's legal wrangles with Springsteen are well documented, not least in Marc Eliot's book *Down Thunder Road: The Making Of Bruce Springsteen*. The two had a falling-out during the recording of *Born To Run* and Appel was eventually displaced by Jon Landau.

Despite the acrimonious circumstances of their split, Springsteen harbours no residual resentment of Appel. He told *Mojo* magazine in 2010, "I have deep feelings towards Mike to this day. However ruinous the rough sides of your relationship, not only was he my manager but we were very good friends. He was highly enjoyable company: very funny, very cynical, always very sustaining. And time passed on and he's still very similar, but we knew that happened once. It's nice to sit down with the guy that happened once with for an hour or two in the afternoon and say, 'Hey! How's it going?' We do that every once in a while."

Without Appel, Springsteen would have made it in some fashion. But it's unlikely he would have made it through the doors of Columbia A&R legend John Hammond's offices for an audition without Appel's braggadocio. Hammond was the man with the golden ear instrumental in launching or furthering the careers of Billie Holiday, Count Basie, Aretha Franklin, Bob Dylan, Leonard Cohen and Stevie Ray Vaughan.

"My first impression of Bruce as a songwriter was that he had too few songs to expect an album deal," Appel tells me. "However, I never sat next to anybody that sang with his intensity. When I told him that if he wanted to get an album deal he'd need more than two songs, he said he'd be back. True to his word, he came back for a second meeting three months later in the same offices and he knocked all of us over who were in the office that day, armed with his new songs."

Appel set up the meet at Columbia with Hammond, by the end of which Springsteen was signed to the label for a $25,000 advance and $40,000 recording budget. "Hammond was thrilled with the songs, so much so that he said to us right then and there, 'Consider yourself of Columbia Records. I have that power. Just wait here, I'm going to get Clive (Davis, Columbia president) and have him sit in with all of us'. Clive was out of town at the time, but when he heard Bruce he loved him also."

Springsteen's rather more amusing version of the audition was related to *Rolling Stone*. "A couple of weeks ago I had just finished reading Dylan's biography and now I find myself sitting in Hammond's office with my beat-up guitar, and like the whole thing I've been reading about is about to happen to me. But what Mike was doing was even weirder.

"He is a funny guy. He's like a real hyper, and he gets into the whole thing like playing the role. So I'm sitting in the corner with my old beat-up guitar, when all of a sudden Mike jumps up and starts hyping John Hammond. I couldn't believe it. I had to start laughing. John Hammond told me later that he was ready to hate me. But he asked me to do a song, so I did 'It's Hard To Be A Saint In The City'."

If Appel was, in Springsteen's parlance, "a real hyper", Springsteen himself was single-minded from the get-go.

"Bruce is, always was and always will be that way," agreed Appel. "He is coming from somewhere. You can't push him into anything. He has very definite ideas about what he wants to do and how to do it. I did not steer him in any direction. He had his own innate direction and we just tried to make the most of that direction."

This was borne out by Springsteen himself who, in *Songs*, iterated, "Though I'd never known anyone who had made a professional record, I knew two things. One, I wanted to sign to a record company as a solo artist – the music I'd been writing on my own was more individual than the material I'd been working up with my bands. The independence of being a solo performer was important to me. And two, I was going to need a good group of songs if I ever did get the chance to record."

He got that chance, cutting *Greetings From Asbury Park, NJ* in three weeks and presenting it to Columbia. Clive Davis promptly handed it back because there was nothing that could be played on the radio. Springsteen went home and wrote 'Blinded By The Light' and 'Spirit In The Night'. With Clarence Clemons on saxophone, these last two songs were laid down and the record completed.

The "new Dylan" comparisons elicited by *Greetings...* caused Springsteen to consciously steer away from ever writing in this vein again, even if "the lyrics and spirit (of the album) came from a very unselfconscious place".

The Dylan comparisons, according to Appel, were based on common stylistic traits in each man's lyrical approach, as well as mere coincidence. "Like Dylan, Bruce had a sense of humour and could string a few intelligible sentences together in a song. However, being that Bruce was discovered by Hammond – and, of course, Dylan was discovered by Hammond too – and Bruce and Bob were both on Columbia as well, the comparisons were harder to dispel."

For Appel, Springsteen has never bettered the material on *Greetings...*, *The Wild, The Innocent And The E Street Shuffle* and *Born To Run*. "They were more self-indulgent from a commercial songwriting perspective, and highly romantic and graphic. Songs like 'Thunder Road', 'Jungleland', 'Born To Run' and 'Meeting Across The River' are once-in-a-lifetime songs, arrangements, performances and productions. Yes, he may have made other great recordings since, but not greater ones in the way those early ones were great."

There is much to love about *Greetings...*, its whimsical wordplay and vividly impressionistic depiction of a bohemian Jersey Shore populated by characters with cool names like Mary Queen of Arkansas, Crazy Janey, Wild Billy, Broadway Mary, Hazy Davy and Killer Joe (although the insistence on everyone having a moniker can become tiresome). It is, nonetheless, the sound of someone who hasn't yet found his groove. The same whimsical wordplay comes over as verbiage at times, too clever (and consequently clunky) for its own good.

Journalist Adam Sweeting, writing about the album in 1985, got it right when he said, "There have been retrospective attempts to trace key themes running through the songs…and so to make of it the first step in the development of Springsteen's canon of recorded work. These have not been convincing because the rush of imagery on the album, diffused through songs which veer wildly between several musical styles, conveys too many confusing images. There's so much information being delivered, it's virtually impossible to sift it into coherent form."

Evidently the great American record-buying public weren't turned on by Springsteen's debut. It only sold around 20,000 copies and failed to bother the *Billboard* Top 200. Still, *Crawdaddy* and *Rolling Stone* liked it. The former hadn't heard a record like it in ages, "where there are words to play with, to riff off yourself, to pull out of the air and slap down with a gleam on the shiny counter of your conversation. There are individual lines worth entire records."

In *Rolling Stone* the venerable Lester Bangs declared that Springsteen "sort of catarrh-mumbles his ditties in a disgruntled mushmouth like Robbie Robertson on Quaaludes with Dylan barfing down the back of his neck". Bangs went on to describe him as "a bold new talent with more than a mouthful to say, and one look at the pic on the back will tell you he's got the glam to go places in this Gollywoodlawn world to boot".

But of course Springsteen wouldn't go anywhere until *Born To Run*. In the meantime, there was that difficult second album. *The Wild, The Innocent And The E Street Shuffle* was recorded just a few months after *Greetings…*, the line-up bolstered by David Sancious on keyboards and Clarence Clemons, a former American footballer (he played with the Cleveland Browns until a leg injury ended that particular career) who once held down a spot among James Brown's Famous Flames, on saxophone throughout.

Lyrically, it's slightly more contained than its predecessor – but only slightly. We're still in the same geographical territory, the Jersey Shore, and the cast this time includes Madame Marie, Catlong, Missy Bimbo, Little Tiny Tim, Spanish Johnny and Diamond Jackie. You can hear more of Springsteen's musical influences here than on *Greetings…*, yet the verve generated by his prospering live reputation wasn't quite there. The point was picked up by John Rockwell in *The New York Times*, who felt the songs "really function as rough models for the fully formed versions one hears live". For Ken Emerson, in *Rolling Stone*, Springsteen was maturing as a writer. "The best of the new songs," he wrote, "dart and swoop from tempo to tempo and from genre to genre, from hell-bent-for-leather rock to luscious schmaltz to what is almost recitative."

Springsteen knew what he was doing. He identified *Greetings…* as principally an acoustic album with a rhythm section, which was all very well first time out. But with *The Wild, The Innocent And The E Street Shuffle*, he was determined to put his bar-band background in the foreground. That was as specific as the planning got. There was no master plan at that stage. Springsteen was enjoying the ride and keeping things in perspective.

"With a record contract and a touring band, I was better off than most of my friends. They were either jobless or locked down in the nine-to-five. I felt lucky to be doing what I loved most."

Less lucky was 'Mad Dog' Lopez. "I was in a band that was going places. We split a lot of hot dogs in those days. Doing the albums was a dream come true. That is all we did – MUSIC. Then I got fired."

The reason for Lopez's expulsion is no clearer now than it was then. All these years later, he's still keeping quiet. One account alluded to his poor timekeeping behind the kit; another, somewhat murkier version mentioned an accusation of theft levelled by Lopez at someone close to the band, which concluded with 'Mad Dog' and a third party trading punches. Whatever the circumstances, there is no lingering resentment towards Springsteen.

"At first I was bitter. But as time went on, my feelings changed. I came to a peace with it. I was in another band – Cold Blast and Steel – instantly, so I had other things to think about. We are all still friends and I will always be part of the E Street Band."

5. TROUBLE IN THE HEARTLAND

"For me, the primary questions I'd be writing about for the rest of my work life first took form in the songs on Born To Run.*"*

BRUCE SPRINGSTEEN

"I was never a visionary like Dylan. I wasn't a revolutionary, but I had the idea of a long arc: where you could take the job that I did and create this long, emotional arc that found its own kind of richness."

BRUCE SPRINGSTEEN

Pivotal moments don't come much more pivotal than *Born To Run*. Bruce Springsteen's third album was the one that broke him big and remains, for many his magnum opus. Miles of words have been committed to print in homage to what was an audacious attempt by Springsteen to replicate the layered density of Phil Spector's 'Wall of Sound' (an audacious attempt that he pulled off memorably), without my adding to them here. But I can't resist it, so here goes.

Born To Run not only sounds great, it reads great. Lyrically, this is a leaner Springsteen, the exuberant imagery that made both *Greetings...* and *The Wild, The Innocent And The E Street Shuffle* occasionally clumsy, has been toned down. This is a writer serious about improving his craft. The songs, particularly 'Thunder Road', display astute editorial judgement; they are narratively arresting in their synthesis of romantic poetry, dirty realist fiction and cinematic imagery.

George Pelecanos, the American crime fiction author, has cited 'Meeting Across The River', the penultimate track, as a watershed for him. "As artful in its economy as a Raymond Carver short story. There are many books and movies that made me want to become a fiction writer, but very few songs. This is one that did."

Thematically, although the argot of *Born To Run* is contemporary, the songs embody the American folk tradition's preoccupation with the lives of the common people, those men and women who "get up every morning at the sound of the bell", who "sweat it out on the streets of a runaway American dream". But where Woody Guthrie would have infused them with a sense of hope, and early Dylan would have protested on their behalf, Springsteen lays it out as he sees it, and what he sees is mostly drudgery and despondency punctuated by the respite of music and the kinship of gangs. It's a soulless reality from which its characters want to flee.

There is a recognition here that everything is not as it should be, that for a whole swathe of society, choice is limited to the slender possibility of things being better someplace else. That someplace else is not just found on the map – it can be inside yourself, it can be inside another, it can be in the sounds coming out of the radio or in the bands that pump it out on stage, or, in the most extreme cases, it can be in the black economy, in those shady deals done under cover of night.

The music at times is almost symphonic in its scope, especially the title track and 'Jungleland', whose emotionally draining sax solo was arguably Clarence Clemons' finest moment as an E Streeter. And the words mark Springsteen out as more than a smart arse with access to a rhyming dictionary. On 'Thunder Road' and 'Backstreets' he displays the instinct of a dramatist with the heart of a poet – every image in the former is vividly conceived.

That Springsteen could sustain such artistic focus while the suits at Columbia were making noises about dropping him from the label unless he began shifting more units – a lot more units – was impressive. "If I fuck up now, it's over," he confided to one journalist before descending into the hell of recording an album that "ate up everyone's life".

Springsteen and the E Street Band cocooned themselves in New York's 914 Sound studio for months, grafting twelve hours a day, painstakingly building each song. Most famously, Clarence Clemons spent sixteen hours perfecting the elegiac saxophone solo on 'Jungleland'. The whole experience was pounding Springsteen into the ground. When he wasn't in the studio, he was holed up in a seedy Times Square hotel crawling with prostitutes, pimps and junkies. He became obsessed with the mirror in his room.

"The mirror was crooked. That sucker was as crooked as crooked could be; it just hung crooked. Couldn't get it to hang right. It just blew my mind after a certain amount of time. It was the album that mirror became – it was crooked, it just wouldn't hang right."

Springsteen was ready to abort the project, even told Columbia he would refuse to release it. Then along came Jon Landau.

Historically, rock managers are tough bastards. Think Allen Klein, Albert Grossman, Peter Grant and Colonel Tom Parker who, despite the jolly uncle appearance, lined his own very deep pockets with loot off the back of Elvis' naivety. But then I suppose they have to be tough to get the best for their charges; they function, after all, in a medium infested with oily characters for whom idealism is only useful as a commodity. In horseracing parlance, they have the mathematical genius of a bookie, the cunning of a trainer and a neck like a jockey's bollocks. They are charming and obnoxious, just as they are diplomatic and autocratic, complicated and simple, and they are probably among the most paranoid, neurotic creatures you will ever have the misfortune to encounter.

Now to avoid any kind of lawsuit, I'm not going to say which of the above applies to Jon Landau. Instead, I'm going to tell you a little yarn, something that came to pass while writing this book. It provided a salutary glimpse at the kind of empire Landau oversees, and indeed perhaps the kind of empire Bruce Springsteen has conceived. The latter, of course, is conjecture, for if it isn't, then 'The Boss' really is the boss and part of, rather than in opposition to, the establishment. This would be a travesty given that I and others regard him as being among that special band of brothers who channel the spirit of Woody Guthrie. The brief anecdote that follows is not designed to impugn Springsteen's reputation as a blue-collar bard, but to reveal a little of Landau's management style.

Any book of this nature involves piles of correspondence (mostly these days through the auspices of email) regarding approaches to publicists and the like. The rules governing such correspondence dictate that the writer couches their request – either for information or interview time, usually the latter – in obsequious language and prepare themselves to be flexible with their ethics.

Toby Scott was one of the engineers on *Nebraska*. That makes him a pretty important guy. Springsteen may have the production credit on the sleeve, but it was Scott who, with his colleagues, helped to finesse the rough edges on the cassette tape Springsteen had been carrying around in his back pocket. He was among the team who enabled what was essentially a domestic recording to become fit for public release. Like I said, a pretty important guy.

Scott was easy to track down on the internet. I contacted his manager Joe D'Ambrosio, outlined a synopsis of the book, told him what I was after. His reply was positive and gave me a chuckle into the bargain. The sort of wry chuckle reserved for religious disciples of a fundamentalist bent. My email address, you see, suggests a cheerless disposition, though in more profane terms. It always elicits a laugh. But not from Scott, it seems.

"You're in business. Toby will do it," D'Ambrosio informed me.

There was, however, a proviso.

"He doesn't like your email moniker. Is there a way to have him correspond with you via a different email address?"

Fair enough, I thought. I can rustle up another email address, an alternative he won't find offensive. And so I did. Same routine in the email to Scott.

"I will talk about the *Nebraska* record," he replied in a tone that bore the dramatic whiff of conspiracy, as though agreeing to impart secret knowledge. It was all a bit 'Deep Throat'.

"I will have to get permission from Bruce's manager, Jon Landau, and he will require final approval of any text or draft before publication. This will not be an issue if we stick to the subject and do not get into the intimate details of Bruce's life."

Permission? Final approval of any text or draft? From Nixon's America we were now in the old Eastern Bloc. What punitive measures was Landau going to impose on Scott if he went ahead and talked to me without consent?

This is where my principles were subjected to contortion. Sure, I can wait for Mr Landau's blessing – and as for a transcript of our chat, no problem. That was on a Friday. By Monday, Scott still hadn't heard back from Landau but set a provisional day and time for the interview and furnished me with his phone number.

Then, the day before the interview was due to take place, this: "David, I have received word that I cannot do the interview with you regarding the *Nebraska* album. Any further contact or discussion on this should be through Jon Landau Management."

And that was it. Communication ended. I fired off an email to Scott expressing my disappointment, as well as my genuine bewilderment. I fired another off to a representative at Jon Landau Management expressing considerably more. Their response? "It is customary that our office be contacted about a book being written about Bruce Springsteen and/or his music. However, since we were never notified and know nothing about it, we are forwarding your email to our attorneys."

I pointed out that Springsteen's New York-based publicist Marilyn Lafferty of Shorefire Productions had been informed months ago of my intention to write this book. On that occasion, she graciously passed on my request for an interview with Springsteen to Jon Landau Management. Inevitably it was refused, but she nonetheless wished me good luck with the project. I also composed a letter to Jon Landau himself and had it sent to him through a third party. So the claim that his management company "were never notified and knew nothing about it" was complete bollocks. And they knew it, as their next email indicated.

"David, we're contacting our attorneys simply to inform them you are writing a book. If you would like to start over and inform us of the book, who your publisher is, what the focus of the book is and what your specific requests are, we would be happy to take a look at it."

Take a look at it they did, apparently. The outcome? Well, two months later, I was tersely informed, "Bruce is not available to do an interview with you." I could have bet my liver on that one.

Now I understood why all those emails to members of the E Street Band went unanswered; why Springsteen's UK press people were giving me the electronic equivalent of the deaf ear. What did any of them hope to achieve (or what were they seeking to avoid) by not talking to me? My objective was explicitly conveyed: I wanted to laud *Nebraska* in print, celebrate a great album. There was no hidden agenda. I knew my chances of securing an interview with Springsteen were about as likely as being granted an audience with the Almighty, but talking to some of his collaborators would have been the next best thing.

What is this really about? Is it about Jon Landau letting the rest of us know he is the power behind the throne? Is it about absolute control of the Springsteen image in the public domain – a dictatorship by any other name? Or is it about ensuring that nobody but the inner circle feeds off the sacred cow? Is Jon Landau a Svengali or sentinel?

Here's a more disturbing question: is Springsteen that determined to preserve the favourable persona he has cultivated among we, the folk, that he is willing to relinquish the responsibility for doing so to Landau, regardless of the tactics he employs? Whatever your perspective, it's hard to imagine Woody or Dylan being that bothered.

For Springsteen, the clincher when it came to Landau was he that he could trust him. In 2002, he said, "There were a lot of things I hated doing, business things, which I had proven terrible at before I met Jon. I wasn't even terrible at it. I just couldn't have cared less. I just wanted to be able to do what I wanted to do. Particularly when I was younger, I was really alienated by that part of it and I felt that any involvement in it was somehow not being true to my original ideas.

"So when Jon came along, that whole thing was taken care of. I had a long period of time when I was pretty estranged from it, probably until well into my thirties, and he kept the boat afloat. He was a writer himself, and he managed because I needed a manager.

"We had a lot of discussions over the years about these issues, where people were right and where people went wrong, and it's always based around, 'How do we do the best job this time out with the record?' It was so simple. He would say, 'Well, you can do this and play a hall this size and it can still be great.' He was constantly pushing the boundaries out for me a little bit, which I needed to do because I was fearful, I was self-protective, and not unwisely so because you need to be. You need to protect your work, your music and the identity that you've worked hard to present."

Now the need to protect your work and your music, that bit I understand; the need to protect an identity, that's where the confusion sets in. An identity should reveal itself; an identity is a composite of the individual characteristics that make a person or thing recognisable. And if it's not, then it's a construct – it's not real.

There's an excellent article by Stephen Metcalf on the *Slate* magazine website in which he attributes "all the po-faced mythic resonance that now accompanies Bruce's every move" to Landau. Metcalf puts forward the argument that pre-Landau, Springsteen was an "endearing wharf rat", but that by the time Landau had worked a number on him, Springsteen "had been refined away".

Landau, he claims, "insinuated himself into Bruce's artistic life and consciousness", while simultaneously staying on the *Rolling Stone* masthead, "until he became Springsteen's producer, manager, and full-service Svengali. Unlike the down-on-their-luck Springsteens of Freehold, NJ, Landau hailed from the well-appointed suburbs of Boston and had earned an honours degree in history from Brandeis. He filled his new protégé's head with an American Studies syllabus heavy on John Ford, Steinbeck and Flannery O'Connor. At the same time that he intellectualised Bruce, he anti-intellectualised him… Bruce's musical vocabulary accordingly shrank."

More than three decades later, Springsteen, according to Metcalf, has ceased to be a musician and become a belief system. "And, like any belief system worth its salt, he brooks no in-between. You're either in or you're out."

It's a bit of a heartbreaker to learn that someone who purports to be one of us, who writes so eloquently of our hopes, dreams, doubts and fears, may not be all that he seems; may, in fact, be an actor playing a role. And, like a consummate actor, one who does his job so well that perhaps the line between flesh and fantasy has become blurred.

But the bald fact of the piece is that, without Jon Landau's intervention, *Born To Run* probably would not have turned out as it did. Landau had famously written in *Rolling Stone* that he had seen the future of rock'n'roll, and the future was Bruce Springsteen. Just the kind of pronouncement to seduce any self-respecting rock'n'roll ego, whether by default or design. The two men became friends. And so it was that, over Mike Appel's vehement objection, Springsteen invited Landau to join the *Born To Run* production team early in 1975. It wasn't as though Landau had no previous form, having manned the controls on albums by MC5 and Livingston Taylor.

The recording had stalled prior to Landau's involvement. Keyboardist David Sancious and drummer Ernest Carter lost faith and moved on to form a jazz-fusion outfit. Auditions were held for replacements, Springsteen finally deciding on Roy Bittan and Max Weinberg.

Landau's first act was to move the operation from 914 Sound in Blauvelt on the outskirts of New York, to the higher-tech Record Plant in Manhattan. He then hired Jimmy Iovine, fresh from working with Phil Spector on John Lennon's *Rock'n'Roll*, as engineer.

Another breakthrough came when Steve Van Zandt, a New Jersey compadré of Springsteen's, wandered into the studio as the band were grinding their way through a turgid 'Tenth Avenue Freeze-Out'. "I didn't know enough to be diplomatic or respectful," said Van Zandt. "I'm sitting on the floor listening, and the horns were just wrong. I said, 'Fuckin' awful. How about I go in and fix it?' So I sang the riffs to them, and that's the arrangement on the record."

'Miami' Steve became Springsteen's interpreter in the studio, translating the sounds in his head to the band. "Bruce did have a very distinct vision in his mind, but it was difficult. For those of us who lived in the live rock'n'roll world, the Record Plant sounded dead and dull and flat. And Bruce was relentlessly pursuing this live sound from the past. In our frame of reference, the whole live sound was weird and dull. So we bashed and bashed and bashed away at it to make it sound live."

Things gathered pace in the first half of 1975, and the album was officially completed in mid July. Columbia liked what they heard and allocated a $250,000 budget for promotion, with publicity and marketing departments given pep talks months in advance of *Born To Run*'s release.

And then the biggest coup of all – Springsteen appeared on the cover of both *Time* and *Newsweek* simultaneously on 27 October, the first non-politician to achieve such a feat. From virtual obscurity to national figure in months. *Time* called him "rock's new sensation" and his music "primal, directly in touch with all the impulses of wild humour and glancing melancholy, street tragedy and punk anarchy that have made rock the distinctive voice of a generation". *Newsweek* was more ambivalent: "Bruce Springsteen has been so heavily praised in the press and so tirelessly promoted by his record company, that the publicity about his publicity is now a dominant issue in his career. And some people are asking whether Bruce Springsteen will be the biggest superstar or the biggest hype of the Seventies."

The only thing that mattered to Columbia was recouping their investment, which they did big time. Yet despite *Born To Run*'s success, Springsteen found himself strapped for cash. Time to take a closer look at the contracts he'd signed with Appel. What the large print had given, in Springsteen's case, the small print had most certainly taken away. Appel, it turned out, had awarded himself an inflated management commission, and controlled the publishing rights to Springsteen's songs. The lawyers were duly summoned and legal battle commenced.

Appel told Springsteen he wouldn't let Landau produce his fourth album. Springsteen sued Appel for fraud and breach of trust. Appel took it further, filing a suit asking the court to prevent Springsteen and Landau from recording together. The court complied.

The dispute rumbled on into 1977, with a settlement concluded in May of that year. Precise details of the settlement remain sketchy to this day, although the upshot of it was that Appel won some money, as well as a portion of the profits from Springsteen's first three albums and a production deal with CBS, while Springsteen regained control of his catalogue.

"You stare at the legal papers served upon you and you feel completely at a loss; the energy just drains out of your body and you don't quite know what to do or make of it," Appel remembers the spat thirty three years on.

"When you put all your eggs in one barrel and that barrel gets split and all the goods run out, you realise that you've got nothing and you've got to start from scratch again. You are, in a very real sense, destitute. You have no more income from something that you put years into. Your celebrity shrivels right up because the press and everybody at the label must necessarily desert you. Have you ever heard of the press or record label beating an artist over the head in favour of the manager? I was the manager and, by definition, the manager is the bad guy. There are certain stereotypes you can't get away from.

"On top of everything, you look at the legal papers and you know it's all nonsense to boot. Lawyers trying to pretend that Mike Appel is a scoundrel, his contracts are unconscionable and, of course, he must have stolen money from Bruce. It's extremely frustrating to say the least. It was all a gas, but it was all over, baby blue."

With the futile benefit of hindsight, Appel would never have become Springsteen's manager. "It kept me away from him so that our personal relationship suffered. I was always a songwriter/producer, not a manager. Bruce hated all the managers he'd met, and that's why he insisted that I manage him. I managed him as a convenience because we couldn't even afford a real outside manager."

While Appel, in the kind of self-denial typical of the classic lovable rogue, would rather reinvent history, the more plausible truth is that he saw Springsteen as an opportunity for him to advance his financial cause, however passionately he believed in his artistry. And he was found out. The resultant legal feud prevented Springsteen from capitalising on *Born To Run* with the immediacy he would have liked.

The recording ban imposed on him while the lawyers bickered and the hard lessons learned from the saga forced him deeper into the kind of dark creative terrain he had begun to explore on *Born To Run*. "In a funny way," Springsteen said in 2010, "the lawsuit was not such a bad thing. Everything stopped and we had to build it up again in a different place."

During the enforced absence from the studio that was a legacy of the legal proceedings, Springsteen returned to New Jersey. It was a homecoming that provided the template for the songs on *Darkness On The Edge Of Town*. He felt a sense of accountability to the people with whom he grew up, many of whom were struggling to survive in an America that, despite having ditched the unctuous Richard Nixon, was stung by the realisation that things weren't a whole lot better under the new White

House incumbent, Jimmy Carter. Meanwhile, Springsteen himself was engaged in a different kind of struggle – a moral struggle, if you like – to reconcile his relative wealth with the poverty, financial and spiritual, of his New Jersey homies. These factors coalesced to generate a reservoir of material that "veered away from great bar band music or great singles music and veered towards music that I felt would speak of people's life experiences". The proposed title of the album (Landau's suggestion) was *American Madness*.

Another inspirational dynamic on *Darkness On The Edge Of Town* was cinema, Springsteen having become a recent (and fervent) convert to the medium, especially the work of John Ford, the four-time Academy Award-winning director whose forte was the Western in which fundamentally decent men are beset by external forces. It was Ford's adaptation of John Steinbeck's depression-era novel *The Grapes Of Wrath* that made an enduring impression on Springsteen who, incredibly, used to baulk at such black and white pictures whenever they were screened on television.

"I always remember turning it off and turning on something that was in colour. Then I realised it was a stupid thing to do, because one night Jon and I watched it and it opened up a whole particular world to me. It was very interesting, just a way to watch movies – just a way to observe things, period."

Ford's re-telling of the story of the migrant Joad family was Springsteen's 'in' to Steinbeck, an author who, like Woody Guthrie in his songs, animated the ordinary American, raising him from the realm of stereotype and caricature and giving him individual identity and dignity. He made him real – too real for some. In 1939, *The Grapes Of Wrath* was banned from public schools and libraries by the Kern County Board of Supervisors, a school board in Mississippi also removed it from school reading lists on the grounds of profanity. In Steinbeck's hometown of Salinas, California, there were ritual burnings of the book on two separate occasions.

Yet Steinbeck refused to be cowed by the reactionaries. Throughout a career in which he produced sixteen novels, six works of non-fiction and five short-story collections, he remained true to what he believed was the role of the writer, synopsised in his acceptance speech following the award of the Nobel Prize for Literature in 1962.

"The writer is charged with exposing our many grievous faults and failures for the purpose of involvement... Furthermore, the writer is delegated to declare and celebrate man's proven capacity for greatness of heart and spirit, for gallantry in defeat and for courage, compassion and love."

Wasn't this was Woody Guthrie was about? And Pete Seeger? And the Sixties folk movement spearheaded by their poster boy, Bob Dylan? And aren't there echoes of Steinbeck's mission statement in Springsteen's best writing?

If *Darkness On The Edge Of Town* resonated with the spirit of Ford and Steinbeck – a spirit that would become more manifest later on – it positively pulsated with the stylistic traits of film noir. "I always liked the flash and outlaws of B pictures – Robert Mitchum in *Thunder Road* and Arthur Ripley's *Gun Crazy*," said Springsteen.

He sought out Forties and Fifties film noir such as Jacques Tourneur's *Out Of The Past*, drawn by a feeling of men and women "struggling against a world closing in". Even the album title, by Springsteen's own admission, owed much to American noir.

With its roots in German expressionist cinematography, film noir was the term applied to Hollywood crime dramas in which, to offer a crude explanation, cynicism and sexual motivation prevailed in a world that is inherently corrupt and where fate conspired to doom its denizens. *Born To Run* was about, well, running and never looking back, about taking chances, last chances even; the characters on *Darkness On The Edge Of Town* – maybe the same characters on its predecessor, those who either couldn't get away or were determined to stay – were in it for the long haul, as Springsteen "steered away from any hint of escapism" and set them "down in the middle of a community under siege".

The tension in the lives of these characters is palpable in the music. It's a tension generated by a latent menace, a suggestion of violence in the switchblade guitars of 'Badlands' and 'Adam Raised A Cain', rumblings of a slave revolt in 'Factory'. There's anarchy in the air, Springsteen acknowledging the influence of Britain's punk explosion. Where *Born To Run* offers the chance to get out of town, *Darkness...* wants to burn the town down.

"The record was of its time," Springsteen told *The Guardian* more than twenty years later. "We had the late-Seventies recession, punk music had just come out, times were tough for a lot of the people I knew."

If Springsteen took counsel from anyone but Landau, *Darkness On The Edge Of Town* would have been a completely different album. Van Zandt, who has always fallen under the spell of the three-minute record, wanted his friend to go with his pop impulse rather than the tone poem *Darkness...* became. Springsteen had amassed a mini-library of spiral notebooks containing lyrics to songs that totalled several multiples of ten. Springsteen himself reckons it was around forty, a couple of band members put it at seventy. Either way, there was a wealth of material to play around with, much of it animatedly opposite to the intense selection finally plumped for.

You can hear it on 2010 release *The Promise*, a collection of so-called outtakes from the *Darkness...* sessions, released as a stand-alone double album and as part of a deluxe box set (*The Promise: The Darkness On The Edge Of Town Story*) helmed by director Thom Zimny's documentary, *The Making Of Darkness*, and two live gigs from 1978 and 2009.

Among the tracks that didn't make it onto *Darkness...* but make it onto *The Promise* are 'Because The Night' and 'Fire', recorded by Patti Smith and the Pointer Sisters respectively. Those that didn't make it onto either included *Born In The USA*'s 'Darlington County', and *The River*'s 'Ramrod', 'Sherry Darling', 'Independence Day' and 'Drive All Night'. The man was prolific back then and, as *The Promise* testifies, there was quality in abundance to be found among the quantity. Big tearjerking ballads like 'Someday (We'll Be Together)', 'One Way Street' and 'The Brokenhearted' (close your eyes and imagine Roy Orbison singing this one), finger-snappers like 'Gotta Get That Feeling' and the hilarious 'Ain't Good Enough for You', and alternative versions of 'Candy's Room' (renamed 'Candy's Boy' here), 'Factory' ('Come On (Let's Go Tonight)') and 'Racing In The Street'. Only Bob Dylan's *Bootleg Series* has unearthed such a bounty of buried treasures.

Bud Scoppa, writing in *Uncut*, called it "big, bold, vibrantly coloured and laced with sweeping chorus hooks and towering middle eights. In a word: spectacular." Quoting Springsteen from the Zimny documentary, when he said *The Promise* would have been a perfect fit between *Born To Run* and *Darkness*..., Scoppa added, "Seeing the light of day at long last, thirty two years hence, this music seems to have arrived from some parallel universe, enriching the history of a supreme artist at his very peak, during a vital era in rock history."

Keith Cameron in *Mojo* was more measured in his appraisal. *The Promise*, he soberly stated, "depicts a crossroads moment in Springsteen's development as a songwriter".

Dave Marsh, a friend of Jon Landau's and Springsteen's chief lobbyist in print (he has written four books, including a brace of hagiographies), completely missed the point of *Darkness On The Edge Of Town* in his *Rolling Stone* review. Where *Crawdaddy*'s Peter Knobler, like those of us listening hard, found "enough raw emotion to make you shake", and one interviewer expressed surprise that "there weren't any razor blades attached to the LP", Marsh heard optimism. "It poses once more the question that rock'n'roll's epiphanic moments always raise: do you believe in magic? And once again the answer is yes. Absolutely."

Cultural commentator Joyce Millman, in an appreciation of the album some twenty years later, called it just about right when she described *Darkness*... as "urban folk music that quotes rock'n'roll in the way that Jimmie Rodgers and Hank Williams quoted black and Appalachian spirituals".

Springsteen was about to get folkier and darker yet next time out.

6. THE HUMAN THING

"When my sister first heard it, she came backstage, gave me a hug and said, 'That's my life'."

BRUCE SPRINGSTEEN on 'The River'

"Springsteen's genius was that he always made listeners feel as if he was singing about their lives."

Novelist GEORGE PELECANOS

Strip it right down to its bare bones, denude it of the E Street Band and the multi-track production, jettison the stock rockers (perfect stadium fodder but out of kilter with much of the album) and *The River* could have been *Nebraska*. Bruce Springsteen has talked about how this bloated double set – it should have been a single – was when The E Street Band really came into its own in the studio. Could he be so dismissive of their collective contribution to *Born To Run*, which, despite the onerous sessions (maybe even because of them), was the sound of an outfit leaving nothing inside?

They struck the perfect balance between garage band and the professional nous needed to make good records, he expounded. Springsteen wanted "the snare drum to explode", he wanted less disconnection between the instruments. And after *Darkness On The Edge Of Town* he wanted to give himself greater elasticity with the songs' emotional range. The E Street Band's shows had always been "filled with fun", and this was a facet of their collective personality that he didn't want to neglect on *The River*.

As a prodigious live performer going back to his Jersey Shore days, Springsteen knew how to work a crowd, whether in the close-up environment of a club or, as was the case with his swelling status, the bigger venues in which Johnny and Mary sometimes found themselves stranded in the outer limits of Row Z. But the recorded document, with few honourable exceptions (Van Morrison's *It's Too Late To Stop Now*, The Who's *Live At Leeds* and Thin Lizzy's *Live And Dangerous* immediately come to mind), doesn't always replicate the concert experience.

And besides, the fun element of the shows that Springsteen sought to reflect on *The River* gave it an unbalanced, almost schizoid feel. Imagine settling into your cinema seat to watch a double bill featuring *Yankee Doodle Dandy* and *The Grapes Of Wrath*. Somebody should have divested Springsteen of his fuzzy vision for *The River* – so, do you want to make a rock'n'roll record or an amped-up folk record? Because you can't do both.

Musicians United for Safe Energy, or MUSE, was an activist group formed in 1979 by the liberal faction of the decadent music industry. Helmed by doe-eyed singer-songwriter Jackson Browne, it included Graham Nash, a refugee from the Hollies who had found harmonic heaven with David Crosby, Stephen Stills and occasionally Neil Young, and Bonnie Raitt, flame-haired folkie, later flame-haired blueswoman. They were against the use of nuclear energy, their activism stoked by an accident at the Three Mile Island nuclear generating station in Dauphin County, Pennsylvania, earlier the same year when radioactive gases and iodine were inadvertently released following a partial core meltdown.

MUSE organised a series of five 'No Nukes' concerts at New York's Madison Square Garden in September, some six months after the accident. On 23 September, almost 200,000 people attended a large rally staged by the organisation on the north end of the Battery Park City landfill.

Bruce Springsteen was among the Madison Square Garden cast list, alongside the aforementioned Browne, Nash (with Crosby and Stills), Raitt, James Taylor, Carly Simon, Chaka Khan, the Doobie Brothers, Jesse Colin Young, Gil Scott-Heron, Tom Petty and Poco. He blew them all away with a scorching 90-minute set, two songs of which ('Thunder Road' and the newly-premiered 'The River') were captured for posterity in the *No Nukes* movie. Springsteen wasn't bandwagoning on the nuclear issue – it was something about which he had genuine fears, going so far as to write a song, 'Roulette', after the Three Mile Island episode in which he pleads: "I need some answers, I need to know."

It's arguable to suggest that this period marked Springsteen's awakening as a political songwriter, although it's equally arguable to suggest that politics – the politics of the everyday – has always run through his songs like an underground stream. As Billy Bragg says, "He tells good stories about ordinary people – they're not overblown, but they're still deeply emotive. He finds the simple way of telling the tale, without a huge over-arching political narrative."

But what 'Roulette', 'No Nukes' and *The River* album revealed was a man, an artist, looking outward, beyond the confines of his immediate physical environment – Freehold, the Jersey Shore, New York – beyond even amorphous spiritual conflicts, into the eyes of a world that was unpredictable, uncaring and downright cruel. He has never been a badge-wearer, a marcher, a heart on his sleeve kind of guy like Woody (and, to a lesser extent, Dylan) was; but here, he began the process of coming out to rally behind the cause of humanity. Springsteen's ideology is the people's ideology – an ideology in which the principal aspirations are not dissimilar to those espoused by the French Revolution, namely liberty, equality and fraternity, appended by justice and security.

If the MUSE concerts were his tentative introduction to overt campaigning, by August 1981, as Bryan K Garman notes in *A Race Of Singers: Whitman's Working-Class Hero From Guthrie To Springsteen*, he was more outspoken still about his commitments.

"After reading Ron Kovic's *Born On The Fourth Of July*, a disturbing narrative about the Vietnam War and the social, psychological and financial problems its largely working class veterans faced, Springsteen decided to do something to help veterans such as Kovic get back on their feet. To that end, he staged a benefit concert in Los Angeles for the Vietnam Veterans Association, an organisation that provides services for veterans and lobbies for related issues. The concert, he recalled, marked the 'first time' he felt as though his music had served a 'useful' purpose, and throughout the Eighties and Nineties he would continue to assess the unsettling legacy the war had bequeathed to veterans and their families."

What Garman terms Springsteen's "half-hearted political engagement" developed with his increasing interest in classic country and traditional folk music, "useful forms for exploring working class issues". While folk music, as illustrated earlier, has a symbiotic relationship with the quest for social justice and its associated convictions, country music's so-called political concerns are less obvious. Yet the genre at its best conveys just as much information about the lot of ordinary rural Americans as any sociological report could do.

Those who parody the drinking and cheating culture that pervades country songs either don't fully grasp their subtlety or are wholly cognisant of the reduction of the protagonists' life choices to the lowest common denominators. The ability to distil such experiences was what made Hank Williams every bit as effective a political songwriter as Woody Guthrie or the young Bob Dylan – perhaps even more so because of his use of straightforward narratives to express complex truths. This is an ability Springsteen himself has perfected.

Williams' ghost passes through *The River*'s title track, an echo of the country Shakespeare's 'Long Gone Lonesome Blues'. But where the latter is a comical lament about a broken-hearted, luckless man who can't even drown himself because the river has run dry, laughs are in short supply on Springsteen's 'The River'. The narrator is a native of the valley (indeed he comes from "down in the valley", a doff of the cap to gospel, itself part of the American folk music tapestry), raised up with no more ambition than to replicate the life of his father.

He gets his high school sweetheart (Mary, a favoured girl's name in Springsteen songs, a Catholic reflex) pregnant and is thrust into a world of responsibility and harsh reality, a world in which love's sweet grace is an indulgence, in which cherished dreams become disturbing spectres and where unemployment has been ramped up "on account of the economy".

It's that simple: the economy's screwed, that's why I haven't got a job; I don't care about the machinations of the markets, how 'A' impacts on 'B' and all that other fiscal fandango – the bottom line is, I'm not working and my life, as a consequence, is bloody grim. The river, in this context, is a place of sanctuary, yet also a place of torment, and by the end, a place best forgotten about, emblematic of the indifference to a crumbling marriage ("I just act like I don't remember, Mary acts like she don't care").

It's a masterful piece of writing and a microcosm of the album's themes, "a perspicacious paring of a man's concerns down to a fundamental triumvirate of work, women and what the heck it's all about anyway", as Andrew Mueller summed up in *Uncut* magazine thirty years after its original release.

'The River' rounds off the first disc of a two-disc set which could easily have been whittled down to 'The Ties That Bind', 'Sherry Darling', 'Two Hearts', 'Crush On You', 'You Can Look (But You Better Not Touch)', 'Out In The Street' and 'I

Wanna Marry You' belong on another album. They appear too flippant alongside 'The River', 'Jackson Cage', 'Independence Day' and even 'Hungry Heart', which, despite its radio-friendly melody, is one sorry tale of a man who's quit his wife and kids in pursuit of something he hasn't found yet.

Relationships were playing on Springsteen's mind. "It took me five albums to even write about it," he told *Rolling Stone*. "People want to get involved, not because of the social pressure, not because of the romantic movies that they grew up on. It's something more basic than that, it's very physical and it presents itself. It's just the way men and women are. Everybody seems to hunger for that relationship, and you never seem happy without it."

But the relationships he sings about on *The River* are in the foreground for a reason; they are the form for the bigger context, what Mueller refers to as "what the heck's it all about anyway". That's why the likes of 'Two Hearts' and 'Crush On You' are incongruous. And if their inclusion was designed to function as some sort of light in the darkness, it doesn't work. There's something almost obscene about the trite refrain, "Two hearts are better than one, Two hearts, girl, get the job done", preceding the understated rite-of-passage drama of 'Independence Day' – like gatecrashing a monasterial retreat in a clown's outfit honking a horn.

Jimmy Guterman, in *Runaway American Dream: Listening to Bruce Springsteen*, identifies *The River* as the album on which "all the voices arguing in Springsteen's head could go public at last". He adds: "There's plenty of grit and evil here – I count several accidental deaths and at least one narrator-performed murder – but there are also a handful of some of the happiest and most liberating performances of his career."

'Independence Day' is another of those hold your breath moments in the Springsteen canon where you're loth to exhale lest you intrude on an intensely moving scene between a father and son. This is Springsteen finally laying to rest the antagonism that marred his relationship with Douglas – there's no other way of reading it. The son here speaks to the father in a gentle, respectful tone. It's as though the traditional roles have been reversed as the son assumes the wise old head –

"Nothing we can say is gonna change anything now".

The "darkness" in both house and town that has caused the blood conflict is a recognition of greater, more oppressive forces that incrementally ruin the little man and a recognition, too, that in such a milieu father and son have mutated into one ("I guess that we were just too much of the same kind"). But the son is adamant that he will not be broken like the father; perhaps the (Catholic) subtext is that he will not repeat the sins of the father, that he will be somebody better.

There is overwhelming sadness in the final verse – the empty rooms in Frankie's, the deserted highway, the evocation of barren lives. Even for those who walk away, who strive for independence, who want something more, it's a lonely journey but one they are compelled to make, because to stay is to stagnate and die.

The guy on 'Hungry Heart' has made the same journey, abdicating his marital and parental duties in the course of doing so. His journey, like all the other journeys, is directionless; he'll only know the destination when he gets there. But what he does know is that it's a place he can rest, a place he can call home, a place where he won't be alone. The song is a perfectly condensed summary of the seeker's quest, right down to the doubt that undermines it.

Meanwhile, the guy on 'Jackson Cage' has stayed put with his "little girl". They are both caged in an existence they are helpless to change, faceless people fading away to invisibility. Again, the hum-drummery of life at the bottom of the totem pole, anonymous people crushed by the politics conducted up above their heads.

Now that I've effectively reprogrammed the first disc – 'The River', 'Independence Day', 'Hungry Heart' and 'Jackson Cage' – it's time for disc two. Out would go the hoary rockers 'Cadillac Ranch', 'I'm A Rocker' and 'Ramrod', along with the turgid 'Fade Away', leaving only 'Point Blank', 'Stolen Car', 'The Price You Pay', 'Drive All Night' and 'Wreck On The Highway'. The last three especially prefaced what was to come on *Nebraska*.

On 'Point Blank' (yet another film title pilfered by Springsteen), we're back among the desperate and the broken. The "little darlin'" to whom the song is addressed is caught in the crosshairs of a world indifferent to her plight. She used to wait on Romeos, now she waits on welfare payments; the narrator swore he'd never let her go, now he sees her on the avenue, in the shadows – prostitute or drug dealer? Either one, she's just "another stranger waitin' to get blown away".

'Stolen Car' is spooky as hell. "It's a very haunting song," said New York singer-songwriter Jesse Malin. "Just listening to that in the middle of the night gives me the creeps. It's super eerie."

Adam Sweeting reckoned it's what Springsteen left out that makes the piece "resonate with such chilling emptiness." The character's terror "elevates it to a kind of mystical film noir, written by Kafka and shot by Polanski".

For Springsteen himself, 'Stolen Car' was something of a template, "the predecessor for a good deal of the music I'd be writing in the future…inner-directed, psychological".

The principal here could be a prototype for the guy on Nebraska's 'State Trooper'. He's cast adrift, from his marriage, from life itself, unable to connect, to find anchor, tempting fate, wanting to disappear.

On 'The Price You Pay' you either learn to live with yourself and what you've got, or you give yourself over to whatever the corollary of reaching out "for the open skies" will be. There are no guarantees, but then there are no limits either.

The final two songs on *The River* – 'Drive All Night' and 'Wreck On The Highway' – seem to represent a conclusion of sorts to the should I stay or should I go dilemmas that permeate the rest of the album. They seem to say that the love of another, the companionship, the solidarity they provide, is the yearning at the core of each of us. And that however rough the storms, whatever the toll they exert on the spirit, together they can be overcome. A cop-out maybe, a conveniently idealistic denouement, but far be it for me to dampen down the flickering embers of hope.

'Drive All Night' is an explicit declaration of love and an acceptance of its healing properties. The coda finds Springsteen at his most soulful, his most sensual, offering himself up to his lover, completely. If *The River* was to have ended there, that wouldn't have been such a bad thing.

But Springsteen wanted to go out on a prayer – for how else could you describe 'Wreck On The Highway'? It is, Springsteen has said, "about confronting one's own death and stepping into the adult world where time is finite". On a rain-soaked highway the principal character witnesses a fatal accident. He makes his way home, and, lying awake next to his lover the same night, realises "that you have a limited number of opportunities to love someone, to do your work, to be a part of something, to parent your children, to do something good".

Again, the title was appropriated from another source, this time from one of the many kings of country music, Roy Acuff. He in turn had appropriated the lyrics and the tune of Dorsey Dixon's 'I Didn't Hear Nobody Pray' and renamed it. The Dixon/Acuff song, while pretty graphic in its description of a crash scene: "There was whiskey and blood all together/Mixed with glass where they lay" (Springsteen sang: "There was blood and glass all over"), was essentially a clarion call to the House of God for souls foundering in their faith.

Springsteen acknowledged Acuff's influence, as well as that of other country doyens, in an interview with *Musician* magazine: "I go back further all the time. Back into Hank Williams, back into Jimmie Rodgers. Because the human thing that's in those records is just beautiful and awesome. I put on that Hank Williams and Jimmie Rodgers stuff and wow! What inspiration! It's got that beauty and the purity.

"The same with a lot of the great Fifties records, and that early rockabilly… Those records are filled with mystery; they're shrouded with mystery. Like these wild men came out of somewhere, and man, they were so alive."

It's the "human thing" that courses through at least half of *The River*. It's what brings us into the characters' lives and makes us care what happens to them. That and the fact we see ourselves, our own lives, reflected back at us. This, more than anything, is what defines Bruce Springsteen as a folksinger and songwriter; he has that faculty for taking our stories and crafting from them something vivid that enables a perception of our internal selves and of the world in which we matter.

7. THE REAL BADLANDS

"Like a lot of great American writers – John Steinbeck, Mark Twain etc – I think he sees the same injustices that many great American writers also saw, and he wanted to lend his voice to that group."

MIKE APPEL on Bruce Springsteen

"Much of Nebraska *explores the subtle and ordinary ways that working-class lives are devalued."*

BRYAN K GARMAN

There was a second-hand bookshop in the town where I grew up, a veritable trove of literary riches discarded by unwitting owners or (far less credibly) donated by altruistic readers who wanted to enlighten others. It was here, in 'The Book Nook', that I unearthed copies of Bob Dylan's *Tarantula* and *Writings & Drawings* (in excellent nick), Jack Kerouac's *The Subterraneans* and *Visions Of Cody*, Kathy Acker's *Blood And Guts In High Scho*ol and Stephen King's *The Stand*. Yes, you read that correctly – Stephen King's *The Stand* mentioned in the same sentence as Dylan, Kerouac and Acker.

You're no doubt expecting a barbed aside, a snort of derision directed at an author whose prolific pulp-horror output generates the kind of sales figures that has so-called proper authors crawling around the cramped confines of their dusty garrets in apoplectic envy. But I'm not about to throw my lot in with the elitist mob who masquerade as custodians of what constitutes literature. In fact, quite the opposite. For Stephen King, as well as being a consummate storyteller, is as undisputed a master of the horror genre as Charles Dickens was of Victorian realism. And, like Dickens, he has turned more people on to books than the self-aggrandising esotericism of critical darlings such as Martin Amis or Salman Rushdie.

Of course, he doesn't always get it right – impossible when you're churning out fiction on such a prodigious scale. And King's work doesn't always bear up under the scrutiny of second reading, as I realised when nostalgia sent me back to *The Stand* a couple of years ago. Yet when I first devoured it over several autumn nights in the mid Eighties, the post-apocalyptic world engendered by King seemed to resound in a terrifying way with the recently purchased cassette copy of *Nebraska* that was always playing in the background. It wasn't in the detail of the viral outbreak known as 'Captain Tripps' that wiped out 99.4% of the population; nor was it in King's evocation of the breakdown and destruction of society and the subsequent battle between the forces of good and evil among the remaining survivors. Rather it was in how the two very separate creative conceptions vibrated with the solitary heartbeat of individual journeys; and it was in how a sense of fatalism stalked each of those journeys. These were the real badlands, this was the real darkness on the edge of town.

King and Springsteen may have been engaged in artifice – imagined characters, imagined narratives – but it was artifice rooted in what Springsteen (when talking about country music) had referred to as "the human thing", the vicissitudes of life writ large.

The Stand is a road novel just as *Nebraska* is a road album. But where King adheres to the mass market's appetite for reassurance in the form of a definitive denouement (the end of the road brings the traveller to salvation or condemns them to damnation), in *Nebraska* the outcomes are not so straightforward.

The ambiguity in Springsteen's writing makes perfect sense when you consider the influences he was absorbing at the time of *Nebraska*'s composition. Flannery O'Connor, for one. A Catholic from Savannah, Georgia, O'Connor produced two novels and 32 short stories during her short life (she died at the age of thirty nine of complications from lupus). Her style bore some of the hallmarks of southern gothic, a sub-genre of gothic specific to the American South that relies on supernatural, ironic or unusual events to guide the plot and to explore social issues and reveal the cultural character of the region. Yet it is plausible to posit that O'Connor's fiction owed just as much to her faith in its frequent investigation of morality.

Whatever the source of her inspiration, what can certainly be said is that O'Connor, in the telling of her tales, was nothing if not vague. You, the reader, are left to reach your own conclusions. This obscurity too is a facet of the songs on *Nebraska*. Wendy Lesser, in an internet article entitled 'Southern Discomfort: The origins of Flannery O'Connor's unsettling fictional world', could have had Springsteen (and *Nebraska*) in mind when she wrote: "You could read all of O'Connor's work and conclude that she hated God with an amused and bitter hatred; you could, with somewhat less support, imagine that she loved God and all his creation; but you could not emerge from a thorough reading and conclude that she was indifferent to God."

But if the make-believe world of O'Connor's literature cast a spell on the Springsteen who realised *Nebraska*, so too did a story from the real world – a story every bit as grotesque as one of O'Connor's own.

Charles Starkweather, known as Chuck or Charlie, was born on 24 November 1938 in Lincoln, Nebraska. At elementary school he was picked on because of his thick glasses and speech impediment. He deterred his tormenters with the threat of using a knife. Starkweather, whose copper-coloured hair and piercing green eyes gave him the appearance of James Dean, was a high-school dropout. His only interests were guns, guitars, hot-rods and girlfriend Caril Ann Fugate. He got a job on a garbage truck only to be fired for laziness, and was then banned from his rented room until he paid the outstanding rent.

After robbing a Lincoln service station on 1 December, 1957, Starkweather abducted employee Robert Colvert, 21, took him to a secluded location and shot him in the head.

Caril Ann Fugate was born in 1943. At the age of fourteen she fell for Starkweather, five years her senior, despite the fact that her parents had forbidden him from seeing her.

On 21 January, 1958, Fugate returned home from school to her family's rundown, one-storey house in Lincoln's poor Belmont area. Starkweather had killed her stepfather, Marion Bartlett, 57, and her mother, Velda Bartlett, 36, and clubbed her two-and-a-half-year-old baby sister, Betty Jean, to death. He hid the bodies and the couple carried on living on the property for days. On two occasions, relatives called to find out why the Bartletts hadn't been seen; Fugate sent them away, claiming everybody was sick with the flu.

Starkweather and Fugate had fled by the time detectives were brought in to investigate by Fugate's grandmother. A search turned up Marion's body wrapped in paper in the chicken house; Velda and Betty Jean were found in an outbuilding.

What the police didn't know was that Starkweather and Fugate had, only hours earlier, driven to a Highway 77 service station to buy gas, a box of .410 shotgun shells and two boxes of .225, before heading to the rural farmlands of Bennet, 16 miles southeast of Lincoln, to hole up in a farmhouse belonging to 70 year-old August Meyer, a friend of Starkweather's. En route to Bennet, their car broke down. When high school student Robert Jensen, seventeen, and his date, Carol King, 16, pulled over to help, Starkweather shot them in the head with a .22 rife and made an unsuccessful attempt to rape the girl before stuffing their bodies in an abandoned storm cellar. They then drove to Meyer's house to procure more guns and ammunition, killing the old man with a .410-gauge shotgun.

Starkweather drove back to Lincoln. He knew his way around the city's opulent south east side. After pulling into the garage of the large French provincial-style home of Capital Steel Company President C Lauer Ward, 47, he pushed Clara Ward, 46, and housekeeper Lillian Fend, 51, to the second floor, tied them to a bed, gagged and fatally stabbed them. When Lauer Ward returned from a conference that evening, accompanied by Nebraska Governor Victor Anderson, he was shot in the head and neck and knifed in the back. Starkweather and Fugate took his 1956 black Packard and made for Wyoming.

Lincoln was in the grip of terror. When Sheriff Merle Karnopp called for a posse, one hundred men volunteered, arming themselves with deer rifles, shotguns and pistols. The National Guard was called in to protect the National Bank of Commerce, district court recessed, parents kept their children indoors, even going so far as to remove them from school. In all, more than a thousand law enforcement officers and National Guardsmen were searching for Starkweather and Fugate.

They were already five hundred miles away, outside Douglas, Wyoming. Merle Collison, 37, a travelling shoe salesman from Montana, pulled his brand new Buick off Highway 87 to grab some sleep. Fugate climbed into the back seat, while Starkweather eased open the driver's door and shot Collison nine times in the head.

Joe Sprinkle, 40, a geologist, stopped his car when he spotted Collison's Buick, believing someone might need his help. He got more than he bargained for, when Starkweather put a rifle to his head. Sprinkle managed to escape just as Deputy Sheriff William Romer was approaching the scene. Fugate ran to the deputy, screaming, as Starkweather fired up Sprinkle's Packard and sped off, crashing through a roadblock at more than one hundred miles per hour until a police bullet shattered his windscreen and brought his killing spree to an end.

Starkweather and Fugate were locked up in Douglas, neither showing much remorse for what they had done. Starkweather smiled for the media, admitted to the murders and agreed to extradition. Initially he said he had kept Fugate captive, but when she turned against him Starkweather fingered her as an accomplice.

He pleaded guilty at his trial, which began on 26 March 1958. Psychiatrists attributed the murders to paranoia; Starkweather's friends asserted it was because everyone had opposed his plans to marry Fugate; his father maintained he was a slow boy growing up too fast. On 23 May, Starkweather was found guilty.

On 27 October 1958, Fugate's trial commenced. She claimed Starkweather had held her hostage and that she had feared for her life. Starkweather, brought to court from his death cell, testified that she had been a willing participant in the crimes and could have fled when he left her with loaded guns. On 21 November, the five women and seven men on the jury handed down a life sentence for Fugate. She was taken to the Nebraska Correctional Centre for Women in York.

Starkweather went to the electric chair on 5 June, 1959, the last person to be electrocuted in Lincoln. Fugate, after serving eighteen years of her sentence, was released on 20 June, 1976, settling down in Clinton County, Michigan. She never married, nor did she ever discuss the case publicly.

And here's a footnote worth mentioning, apropos of the earlier anecdote about Stephen King in this chapter. King, as a boy, kept a scrapbook on Starkweather. "It was never like, 'Yeah, go Charlie, kill some more!' It was more like, 'Charlie, if I ever see anyone like you, I'll be able to get the hell away'," he told *The Guardian*'s Tim Adams in 2000. "And I do think that the very first time I saw a picture of him, I knew I was looking at the future. His eyes were a double zero. There was just nothing there. He was like an outsider of what America might become."

Springsteen's fascination with Starkweather and Fugate was further stoked by *Badlands*, director Terrence Malick's film dramatisation of their eight-day killing spree. Martin Sheen, like a beautiful hybrid of Elvis and James Dean, the quintessence of Fifties cool in white tee-shirt and denims, plays Kit Carruthers and Sissy Spacek, a South Dakota miss encumbered by ennui, his girlfriend Holly Sargis. Malick's laconic script refuses to judge the actions of Carruthers/Starkweather and Sargis/Fugate. These are people we should abhor because of the crimes they commit, especially Carruthers/Starkweather; yet, if anything, we find ourselves won over by the amiable character as portrayed by Sheen as even his eventual captors are in the movie.

As Malick himself explained shortly after *Badlands*' theatrical release in 1975: "Kit doesn't see himself as anything sad or pitiable, but as a subject of incredible interest, to himself and to future generations. Like Holly, like a child, he can only really believe what's going on inside him. Death, other people's feelings, the consequences of his actions – they're all sort of abstract for him.

"He thinks of himself as a successor to James Dean, a rebel without a cause, when in reality he's more like an Eisenhower conservative. 'Consider the minority opinion,' he says to the rich man's tape recorder, 'but try to get along with the majority opinion once it's accepted.' He doesn't really believe any of this, but he envies the people who do, who can. He wants to be like them, like the rich man he locks in the closet, the only man he doesn't kill, the only man he sympathises with and the one least in need of sympathy. It's not infrequently the people at the bottom who most vigorously defend the very rules that put and keep them there.

"And there's something about growing up in the Midwest. There's no check on you. People imagine it's the kind of place where your behaviour is under constant observation, where you really have to toe the line. They got that idea from Sinclair Lewis (American Nobel Prize-winning novelist and playwright). But people can really get ignored there and fall into bad soil. Kit did, and he grew up like a big poisonous weed."

Malick's *Badlands* led Springsteen to Ninette Beaver's unauthorised biography of Fugate, *Caril*, and a somewhat amusing phone call to the author herself. Beaver, then an assignment editor for KMTV news in Omaha, told *Rolling Stone*: "His name sort of rang a bell. First I asked him what he did. And he said, 'I'm a musician'. I just said, 'Honest to God, I know I should know who you are, but I'm just drawing a blank'. And he was just a doll about it – really cute." They spoke for around thirty minutes, mainly about Fugate, and Springsteen came away with the guts of the *Nebraska* title track.

If the musical sensibility that shaped *The River*'s more reflective material was down to Springsteen's discovery of country music, *Nebraska* owed a considerable debt to archival American folk music. As Dave Marsh rightly points out in *Glory Days: Bruce Springsteen In The Eighties*, Nebraska had "the quality of stillness associated with the great Library of Congress folk recordings of the Thirties and Forties, by performers actually described by critic Paul Nelson as 'traditional (and non-professional) singers and musicians you've probably never heard of: poor folks, mostly from the rural south, just sitting at home in front of that inexpensive tape or disc machine and telling their stories, sometimes artfully and sometimes artlessly, undoubtedly amazed that anyone from the urban world would place any value on what they were saying or how they were saying it...a considerable piece of Americana'."

You can also hear, on *Nebraska*, the revenants of Harry Smith's multi-volume *Anthology Of American Folk Music*, a collection that became indispensable to the callow youth, Bob Dylan, in the fertile days of the Sixties folk movement.

The bohemian Smith was an artist, filmmaker, musicologist, anthropologist, linguist, translator and occultist, a figurehead of the mid-20th Century American avant-garde. His anthology was issued by Moses Asch's Folkways label in 1952. It comprised 84 recordings made between 1927 (the year electronic recording enabled accurate reproduction) and 1932, the period between the realisation by major record companies of distinct regional markets and the Great Depression's stifling of folk-music sales.

According to Eric Alterman, the project was "an attempt by two left-wing bohemians to tell the story of another America, one that lived outside the mainstream of history and national politics. Both Asch and Smith were obsessed with the possibilities of political and cultural syncretism that folk music seemed to offer."

And just as Dylan drew on Smith's anthology for 'Maggie's Farm', a homage to the Bently Boys' 'Down On Penny's Farm', so did Springsteen plunder it for 'Johnny 99' on *Nebraska*. Springsteen's song is a rejoinder to 'Ninety-Nine-Year Blues' by Julius Daniels. The latter, recorded in 1927, concerns a young black man arrested while visiting a new town under "the poor boy law". The judge sentences him to ninety nine years in "Joe Brown's coal mine", an injustice which provokes in the boy a desire to "kill everybody" in town.

But for all the artistic forces that cohered to create *Nebraska*, it was also an album that responded to the social and economic climate that existed in Ronald Reagan's America, thus fulfilling the American folk music mandate established by Woody Guthrie and Pete Seeger in the Thirties. The country was, after all, experiencing its greatest economic decline since the Great Depression, with high inflation, double-digit unemployment (the combination of these two factors led to stagflation), hundreds of thousands of home repossessions, fractured families and crumbling communities.

It was a recession of two parts. The first, from January to July 1980, came on the back of an oil crisis, while the second occurred between July 1981 and November 1982.

Gross national product fell by 2.5% and almost one third of America's industrial plants lay idle. Major firms like General Electric and International Harvester laid off workers. Farmers were also hit hard, with numbers declining as production became concentrated in the hands of fewer. During the Seventies, American farmers had helped to prevent India, China and even the Soviet Union from suffering food shortages, and had borrowed heavily to buy land and increase output. Oil prices raised farm costs and a global economic slump in 1980 reduced the demand for farm products.

Banks, too, were affected by the downturn. Deregulation introduced in 1980 had phased out restrictions on their financial practices and broadened their lending powers. The newly liberated banks subsequently rushed into real estate and speculative lending, as well as other ventures, just as the economy began to break down. By the middle of 1982, there was a steady rise in banks that were failing.

Reagan's popularity rating plummeted to 35%, close to Richard Nixon and Jimmy Carter at their most unpopular. Many voters thought him insensitive to the needs of the average citizen. This perception was hardly improved when Reagan, in the midst of the crisis, quite incredibly complained that he was tired of hearing about it every time someone lost his job "in South Succotash".

"The chief idea behind Reaganomics was that the wealthy and the corporations were taxed much too heavily," says Sean Wilentz, Princeton University historian and author of *The Age Of Reagan*. "Also, that cutting taxes and tax rates on the rich would, at once, lead to spectacular investment and economic growth and narrow the federal deficit by increasing wealth that would make up for the loss in federal revenues. Finally, the benefits of all of this would trickle down to ordinary Americans. It didn't exactly work out that way, as inequality worsened."

In the long term, Reagan's presidency radically revamped the structure of America's tax system and, according to Wilentz, "remade the federal judiciary, turning it in a dramatically more conservative direction. While falling well short of the goal of some of its supporters, namely to repeal the New Deal (the series of economic reforms passed by Congress during President Franklin Delano Roosevelt's first term in response to the Great Depression, the Reagan era brought about fundamental shifts not just in institutions but in the broad view of how the country ought to be run. Those presumptions are far to the right today from what they were in 1980."

Springsteen, despite his wealth, was plugged into the suffering of ordinary Americans and the gradual demise of the American way of life under Reagan.

"The record was basically about people being isolated from their jobs, from their friends, from their families, their fathers, their mothers – just not feeling connected to anything that's going on," he said. "And when that happens, there's just a whole breakdown. When you lose that sense of community, there's some spiritual breakdown that occurs. And when that occurs, you just get shot off somewhere where nothing seems to matter."

8. FRONTIER MATERIAL

"I felt that it was my best writing. I felt that I was getting better as a writer. I was learning things. I was certainly taking a hard look at everything around me."

BRUCE SPRINGSTEEN

"There was no problem with nobody playing on Nebraska. *It was my idea to put it out like that. He played me the four-track home demos and I said to him, 'This is going to sound odd, but it should be released as it is – the fact you didn't intend to release it makes it the most intimate record you'll ever do.*

This is an absolutely legitimate piece of art'."

STEVE VAN ZANDT

It began on a rocking chair in his bedroom sometime after new year 1982. Bruce Springsteen, having completed *The River* tour with the E Street Band the previous October, was trying out a different approach, working alone on a cycle of songs, with the intention of evolving them sufficiently before going into the studio to record the next album.

"I decided that what always took me so long in the studio was the writing," he told *Rolling Stone*'s Kurt Loder. "I would get in there and I just wouldn't have the material written, or it wasn't written well enough, and so I'd record for a month, get a couple of things, go home, write some more, record for another month – it wasn't very efficient."

Springsteen asked his guitar tech, Mike Batlan, to go out and buy him a tape recorder. What Batlan came back with to Colts Neck, New Jersey, was a Tascam Portastudio 144. Tascam is the professional audio division of the Japan-based TEAC Corporation, a world leader in recording technology. The 144 model made its debut in 1979. Based on a standard compact audiocassette tape, it meant musicians could affordably record several instrumental and vocal parts on different tracks of the built-in four-track recorder and later blend the parts together while transferring them to another standard two-channel stereo tape deck to form a stereo recording. Usually, such machines are used to record demos.

Springsteen and Batlan rigged up the 144, along with a pair of Shure SM57 microphones and an old beat-up Echoplex (a tape-delay effect) for mixing.

"I got this little cassette recorder, plugged it in, turned it on, and the first song I did was 'Nebraska'," Springsteen recalled. "I just kinda sat there; you can hear the chair creaking on 'Highway Patrolman' in particular. I recorded them in a couple of days. Some songs I only did once, like 'Highway Patrolman'. The other songs I did maybe two times, three times at most."

And that is how the spooky underworld of *Nebraska* came to be. It's improbable that Springsteen could have heard those recordings as anything other than rough cuts,

61

templates for the band to develop later. The idea of following a blockbuster like *The River* with a bunch of what were effectively home-made demos would have been seen as pure folly on Springsteen's part, especially in the context of the hi-tech Eighties. But then wasn't that what his detractors said of John Hammond's decision to sign Bob Dylan to Columbia? One man's fool is another man's visionary.

The songs themselves, according to Springsteen, were connected to his childhood more than anything else he'd written. The tone of the music took him back to the time when the family lived with his grandparents. "I went back and recalled what that time felt like, particularly my grandmother's house," he wrote in *Songs*. "There was something about the walls, the lack of decoration, the almost painful plainness.

The house was heated by a single kerosene stove in the living room. One of Springsteen's earliest childhood memories was the smell of kerosene, his grandfather filling the spout in the rear of the stove. The cooking was done on a coal stove in the kitchen. As a child, Springsteen would shoot his water gun at its hot iron surface and watch the steam rise.

The centrepiece of the living room was a photo of his father's older sister, who had died at the age of five in a bicycle accident around the corner by the gas station. Her ethereal presence from this portrait "gave the room a feeling of being lost in time".

The sound Springsteen heard in his head, the sound he nailed on that Tascam 144, was deep and dark as a well, deep in the way that John Lee Hooker and Robert Johnson sounded deep; the kind of deep where you feel what the character being channelled by the singer is feeling. The sound of another country, at a remove from the all-singing, all-dancing, high-kicking, big-smiling Walt Disney version starring a retired Hollywood actor as the President, and his retired Hollywood actress wife as First Lady.

And the words…the words cobbled together lives from the shadows, lives that pumped with a heartbeat but lives that were barely living.

Bryan K Garman hears the Carter Family, bluesman Julius Daniels, references to classic country, while "Woody is all over the place. The old blues artists are travelling around in the background. Since the folk tradition began as an oral tradition, it is difficult to tell where its influence begins and ends. But in terms of recorded music, it goes back to the early race and hillbilly records of the Twenties.

"Springsteen's work is influenced by folk, blues, country, soul, gospel, rock'n'roll. His work is a conglomeration of a variety of traditions. I would resist, a la Dylan, the temptation to draw hard boundaries between folk music and other genres. Nebraska is influenced by that tradition – it is deeply linked to it. But as a work of art, it stands on its own."

First to hear the *Nebraska* demos was Springsteen's manager, Jon Landau. What he heard, in this order, was 'Bye Bye Johnny', 'Starkweather (Nebraska)', 'Atlantic City', 'Mansion On The Hill', 'Born In The USA', 'Johnny 99', 'Downbound Train', 'Losin' Kind', 'State Trooper', 'Used Cars', 'Wanda (Open All Night)', 'Child Bride', 'Pink Cadillac', 'Highway Patrolman' and 'Reason To Believe'. Nine of these songs wound up on *Nebraska* just as they were mixed at Colt's Neck. 'Downbound Train', 'Born In The USA' and "Child Bride' (which became 'Working On The Highway' after an extensive rewrite) were earmarked for *Born In The USA*.

While Landau found the material moving, "these songs were so dark they concerned me on a friendship level". Springsteen insisted he had the bones of his next album. Landau was less certain. Things were postponed as Springsteen put his shoulder to the wheel of Gary US Bonds' second album, *On The Line*, on which he wrote seven of the eleven tracks.

In May, Chuck Plotkin, part of the production team on *Darkness On The Edge Of Town* and *The River,* arrived in New York to work on Springsteen's new album. What he heard on the tape was "frontier material". The singer had found a new voice, the songwriter had "fetched something that was at the time mysterious to him".

What engineer Toby Scott, in an interview with Daniel Keller on the Tascam website in 2007, remembered about the demos were Mike Batlan's technical shortcomings in recording them. "Mike was a guitar roadie…and he didn't have much of a chance to get familiar with the gear before Bruce wanted to record. He got some levels and tried to make sure the meters didn't go into the red too much, and he may have listened briefly with the headphones, but Bruce was eager to get going so I don't think he got too much beyond the basics. In fact, on some of the first songs they recorded, you can hear a bit of distortion where Mike is still getting his levels."

At the Power Station, Springsteen and the E Street Band spent two weeks trying to mould the *Nebraska* songs into shape as a unit. They tried 'Atlantic City', the song that most seemed to lend itself to a band arrangement. It didn't happen. They tried 'Mansion On The Hill'. Same thing. They tried 'Nebraska' itself. They tried them with the full band, they tried them with some of the band – Springsteen even tried to re-record them solo. Nothing worked. Plotkin believed they were "losing more than we were picking up", that "it was being scaled incorrectly". The decision was taken to switch to songs Springsteen had written since recording the cassette. The latter wasn't being abandoned, merely set aside for now.

What happened at the next session was 'Born In The USA' which, Landau claimed, had already been dropped from consideration for *Nebraska* because it just didn't fit. So essentially, out of the failed *Nebraska* band rehearsals came the seeds of the album that would send Springsteen global. Everyone was excited – except Springsteen himself. His attention was still focused on the *Nebraska* songs.

"I was troubled by what was happening," said Plotkin. "The problem was that the demo tape was great and our treatments of the *Nebraska* stuff in the studio were adequate and they were less meaningful. They were less emotionally compelling, they were less honest; we were reducing the stuff, we were making less of it. We ran into a brick wall. We were screwing it up."

A meeting was called at which Landau, according to Plotkin, "had pretty much decided himself that he thought we could and ought to treat this thing as an album".

This is where it gets really technical. While listening again to the *Nebraska* tapes, Toby Scott learned some interesting details about how Springsteen and Batlan had recorded the songs. "It turns out they'd mixed everything through an old Gibson Echoplex – the ones with an endless tape loop for slapback – and that machine had since gone to meet its maker.

"It seems also that, during the recording process, Mike had never really figured out what that little round knob next to the transport controls was for and had left it at around the two o'clock position. So they'd ended up recording everything with the varispeed set fast. Then he thought, well, maybe it shouldn't be in that position so he turned it back to twelve o'clock for mixdown.

"Then there was the mixdown desk. Turns out they mixed down to the only other deck they had around that had a line input, an old Panasonic boom box with a history of its own. You see, Bruce had a canoe he liked to take out on this little branch of the river that flowed near his house, and the previous summer, during one of these trips, the boom box had fallen overboard and sunk in the mud. Later that day when the tide went out, he retrieved it, brought it back to the house, hosed off the mud and left it on the porch for dead. About a week later, he was sitting in the porch reading the Sunday paper and the boom box all of a sudden comes back to life.

"So now it's the following January and, forgetting all about that, this was the machine they used for their mix."

When Springsteen, who had been carrying the tape around in his back pocket for a couple of weeks, presented it as a master to Scott and the other engineers at Power Station, "you could just about hear the moans".

Scott again: "We were all trained to get the best sound possible on the best equipment, and here was our artist asking us to go against pretty much everything we knew. And I said, 'Yes Bruce, we could. I'm not sure you'll like it, but we could.'

"So I gave the cassette to an assistant and told him to copy it onto a good piece of tape. Then we went around to four or five different mastering facilities, but no-one could get it into a lacquer – there was so much phasing and other odd sonic characteristics the needle kept jumping out of the grooves.

"We went to Bob Ludwig, Steve Marcussen at Precision, Sterling Sound, CBS. Finally, we ended up at Atlantic in New York, and Dennis King tried one time and also couldn't get it onto disc. So we had him try a different technique, putting it onto disc at a much lower level, and that seemed to work. In the end we ended up having Bob Ludwig use his EQ and his mastering facility, but with Dennis' mastering parameters. And that's the master we ended up using.

"The album sounds the way it does because of all those factors – the multiple tapes, the dirty heads, the varispeed – it's all part of the overall atmosphere and part of what Bruce liked about the songs."

The so-called electric *Nebraska* – the attempts to remake the songs as Bruce Springsteen and the E Street Band songs – has never been released, nor have the recordings ever surfaced as bootlegs. It remains as elusive as the holy grail among Springsteen devotees, although my guess is that Jon Landau may be hoarding the tapes to form part of some kind of anniversary package along the lines of those issued for *Born To Run* and *Darkness On The Edge Of Town*. As recently as 2006, Landau insisted that "the right version of Nebraska came out", adding that he didn't think the band sessions constituted "particularly meaningful stuff".

Drummer Max Weinberg disagrees. He told *Rolling Stone* in 2010 that the E Street Band recorded *Nebraska* in its entirety and "it was killing. It was all very hard-edged. As great as it was, it wasn't what Bruce wanted to release. There is a full band *Nebraska* album. All of those songs are in the can somewhere."

While it is inevitable that *Nebraska* with Springsteen and the E Street Band will be considered ready for release sooner or later (what are the odds it will be 2012, thirty years after *Nebraska* was originally released?), interesting though it would be to hear, I would rather it remained in the vaults.

Even live renditions of the *Nebraska* songs (whether performed solo by Springsteen or with the band) jar a little, taken as they are out of context of the album as a whole piece of work. And besides, *Nebraska* is not only about the songs, it's about the atmosphere, an atmosphere that can't be reproduced in an over-populated studio where application and not art informs the process, nor in the communal gathering of a concert arena where man love is expressed by homo sapiens brandishing beer bottles in their raised firsts, while their little women sway uneasily on their shoulders singing the wrong words.

Electric *Nebraska* – who really cares?

With the *Nebraska* master finally secured, the next step was an album cover. Springsteen didn't want his image this time. He wanted something more evocative, something that cut *Nebraska* from the cord of his celebrity. This was folk music, and folk music was of the folk, by the folk and for the folk; it didn't countenance the cult of personality. It was faceless and yet had myriad faces.

Art director Andrea Klein introduced him to David Michael Kennedy, a fine art photographer who had a successful career in advertising, editorial, music and portrait photography, A photo session was arranged from which three pictures emerged, two of them of Springsteen. The shot that appeared on the *Nebraska* sleeve – a two-lane blacktop in the Midwest snapped through the windshield of a car – had been taken by Kennedy some time before.

Kennedy, who lives in New Mexico, works within the realm of analogue processes. His prints possess a mystical quality that, if such a thing is possible, portray the soul of his subjects, who have included Bob Dylan, Debbie Harry, Willie Nelson and Muddy Waters, as well as a whole series on Native Americans.

"I was doing a lot of stuff for CBS Records at the time," he recalls. "And I'd done a landscape – the one that they used on *Nebraska* – a long time ago, around the mid Seventies. I honestly don't remember where it was taken. It was a very old image. It was somewhere in the Midwest, so there's a very good possibility it was in Nebraska – it was certainly in that region of America. And Andrea Klein, who worked at CBS and did most of the Springsteen stuff, had seen my studio.

"I'd done a lot of stuff for her. I had it on the wall of my studio and she'd seen it there. So when the *Nebraska* album came along and Bruce wanted to do a landscape for it, she remembered that one. She called me and asked me if I could show it to Bruce. I don't think she asked me for any others. She was pretty specific, if I remember right, that that was the one. And Bruce loved it. He said, 'That's the one'.

"Then they needed to do the point of purchase stuff, advertising and all the other stuff, so Andi asked me if I'd also shoot a session with just Bruce. It's funny because I wasn't all that excited about Bruce Springsteen. I really liked his rock'n'roll, but it wasn't the kind of music that just really knocks me out. I like rock'n'roll but I'm much more attuned to music like what was on *Nebraska*. So I was sort of like, 'Yeah, whatever, another cover'. And then he sent over the tape. And when I heard the tape it just flipped me out. I fell in love with it. His acoustic music I think is incredible.

"It really talked about America, about the real people in America and their feelings and thoughts and emotions. Like That song, 'My Father's House', is just incredibly touching. It really spoke to an America that I'm very familiar with and have photographed a lot and seen a lot. A couple of years ago, my house burnt down, I got a divorce and I was really disillusioned with what was going on in America. I bought a vintage Airstream trailer and I just travelled around America for two years, on all the back roads, seeing the real America that you never hear about.

"There's a spirit here and a self-reliance that you see in the people that just impresses the hell out of me. It's not the America that we read about in the newspapers. It's not that greedy, corporate group of people. It's like a subterranean America – that's what America is. You travel around and so much of it is rural, so much of it is people that are creative in how they deal with their land, with their cows, with how to survive – creative in their lifestyle.

"I think it's much more what this country used to be about. What made me feel really good is that, when I went out and travelled for those two years, the majority of the country is still about that. The only problem is it's lost."

Springsteen, says Kennedy, had no preconception of what he wanted from their sessions together. "Once they decided to use that landscape for the cover, the rest of what we were doing I don't think was as important in terms of a look or feel. It was more for the advertising and point of purchase, and it needs to reflect a kind of country, folkie kind of look, but I don't think he had anything real specific in mind.

"I had to have a private meeting with Bruce. So he came down to the studio one day and we just had coffee and talked. And I realised part-way through it that I was sort of being interviewed. It was like after Bruce left he was going to decide what he felt about me as a person. I had a lot of pictures around the studio, so he had a good feel for my work. But I realised it was important to him that he wanted to know who I was and what I thought and how I felt before he decided, I want this guy to do the pictures. He needed to connect with me on a human level first. I guess I passed the interview!"

When Kennedy is given a commission, he approaches it "with an empty mind". He explains, "I try really hard not to pre-judge or to think, this is what I want to show. I want to try and understand, who is this person? Forget what we know – forget this is Bruce Springsteen, rock'n'roll star, the Boss, all of that nonsense. Who is this human being and how do I connect with him in such a way that I can share this experience of who he is with the people who look at the pictures? One of the ways I do that is I always make eye contact. When we started planning the shoot, I got pretty much told that Bruce didn't want any production values. He didn't want hair or make-up people, he didn't want any kind of a production, he just wanted to make portraits.

"We did them at my family's summer home in upstate New York. He just showed up in his old pick-up truck, just him. No limos, no entourage, this dude just pulled up in his pick-up truck and got out. I had my assistant and my daughter and my girlfriend there. My girlfriend usually did the make-up, but she didn't do it that day – she just wanted to come for a trip. It was really just a few people getting together in the country and fooling around. That's how it felt. It was very much, hey, this is the kitchen, let's play over by that window, have some coffee and let's just make a few pictures. Very loose. There are a couple of shots that I think are pretty magical, a couple that capture who he is, his spirit."

A couple of shots that are pretty magical? Kennedy is being far too modest. Those black and white images of Springsteen, perched on a kitchen chair, sat at a kitchen table, standing against the railing of a verandah, are among the most iconic ever taken of him – just like Kennedy's close-up of Bob Dylan.

"Dylan, for me, was an idol. The opportunity to photograph Bob Dylan doesn't come along too much. And I was really intimidated by that shoot. That's a whole other story – if you do a book on Dylan, I have a good story about that.

"But once we got past the surface stuff with Springsteen, it was really the same. With Dylan, it was just me and Dylan – I didn't even bring an assistant when I shot Dylan. It was very much two people fooling around, having fun and making pictures. That's kind of how I've tried to approach my whole career. I used to tell people when we started shooting, 'If we have fun today and we make horrible pictures, that's fine, because we can always come back and make more pictures. But if we don't have fun today and we make great pictures, that's really not okay because you can never get back that time that wasn't fun.'

"If you're fooling around having fun, you always make good pictures. That good time and good feelings show through in successful photographs. Unfortunately, a lot of the time you get people who are into the production values, they think they need hair and make-up and caterers – they're very much into that aspect of the industry. But Springsteen was totally not into that at all.

"That shoot remains one of the definite highpoints of my career. It meant a great deal to work with him. At the time rock'n'roll was not, as I said, a music that I got really jazzed about. His music wasn't so special to me. But looking back now, I realise how amazingly special his music is, the things he writes about. I'd work with him any time.

"And he's such an accessible guy. After *Nebraska* I pretty much lost touch with him. We worked on the project and went our separate ways. We don't live in the same world. I don't think I had any contact with him. Ten years or so after that, a friend of mine called me, she was a Jersey girl. She said, 'David, Springsteen's coming to New Mexico, I want tickets, I want us to go and I want you to introduce me to him. He's coming in three days.' I'm sitting here in New Mexico. I don't even think I'd talked to anyone in CBS Records in so long – how can I do this? I got in touch with the people at his management company. This was maybe a Friday and he was playing on the Sunday. They knew who I was, I explained the situation and they said, 'Let's see what we can do'. They couldn't put it together.

"We went to the concert, and I brought the photograph of him in the kitchen. I'm pretty sure it was that one. I signed it and I wrote a note saying, 'Bruce, we're in the audience, I'm with this Jersey girl who really wants you to autograph this picture for you and she would love to meet you.' We got to the concert. It wasn't a big venue. It was an acoustic tour (*The Ghost Of Tom Joad*) and I think there were 400-500 people in the audience. I went to one of the security guys and I explained it to him. I said, 'Look man, can you please run this backstage? If nothing else, maybe he could just sign it for her.' The guy's kind of looking at me, and he believed me, I guess. He went backstage and he came out a couple of minutes later with the print. He said, 'Look man, when the concert's over, you're going to see everybody going through that door over there. Go over to this other door over here'.

"So the concert's over, we go to this other door, knock, somebody opens it and we were brought into his dressing room. He's there all by himself. We spent ten or fifteen minutes hanging out with him. He just chatted her up, he signed the thing. He was so focused. It was like, here's this person, she's so into my music and I want to give her some time. Then he said, 'Look, I've really got to do the meet and greet thing now', so we said okay, they let the people in the other door and he hung out with everybody. I just thought, what an incredible man.

"Then another friend of mine, two or three years ago, ran into him in New York. She went up to him and said, 'Excuse me, I know people bug you all the time, but I just really want to let you know I love your music, and by the way, I'm good friends with David Kennedy'. And he immediately knew exactly who I was. Think how many covers he's done, think of how many people he's met. I've met so many people in the industry and it's so hard for me to remember everybody. He just talked to her for a couple of minutes on the street. He just stopped what he was doing and shared some of his time with her. This is who this guy is. That's so refreshing."

There was much deliberation about the title of the album. About half of the song titles were considered before it was narrowed down to three choices – *Open All Night*, *January 3, 1982* (the date on which the majority of the Colt's Neck demos were recorded) and *Nebraska*. Springsteen plumped for *Nebraska*, the first one he'd recorded, the first on the track listing, the song that, according to Dave Marsh, "set the mood and told the story".

In September, *Rolling Stone* announced its impending release with a note of caution, warning its readers that "those who've heard it say its mood is personal and darkly ruminative about America as a whole".

For an album that came out of a DIY recording session featuring just voice, guitar harmonica, a bit of glockenspiel and nothing in the way of a hit single, *Nebraska* did respectable business. Industry watchers (remember, the music industry was suffering the same as every other industry in Reagan's America) predicted it wouldn't sell much more than a quarter of what *The River* sold – they suggested a ballpark figure of between 200,000 and 300,000. It went on to shift some 800,000 units in America alone, and reached Number 4 on the *Billboard* chart.

And in a concession to the new age of MTV, which streamed videos to promote singles twenty four hours a day, Springsteen agreed to a short film for 'Atlantic City', though he himself had only nominal involvement. "The only direction I gave was to say that it should be kind of gritty looking, and it should have no images that matched up to the images in the songs," he said.

Arnold Levine's black and white drive-by video, made in one day with a hand-held camera, was voted Number 37 in *Rolling Stone*'s 100 Top Music Videos of All Time. Levine described the concept thus: "It was showing the disparity between the boardwalk and a block away from the boardwalk, after all those broken promises about how they were going to rebuild Atlantic City."

Critical opinion of *Nebraska* was overwhelmingly positive. The Eighties was such a synthetic decade in music, with British electro-pop the dominant soundtrack, that for something this raw, this uncompromising, to infiltrate the mainstream must have felt like revolution.

Robert Hilburn of the *Los Angeles Times* wrote: "In the album's best moments, Springsteen combines a captivating sense of cinematic detail with an endearing sense of America that we haven't approached in pop music since the early works of John Prine and the Band."

Paul Nelson, in *Musician*, acknowledged it wasn't easy listening. To his ears it "sounded so demoralised and demoralising, so murderously monotonous, so deprived of spark and hope". Springsteen, he added, had made an album "as bleak and unyielding as next month's rent". But for all that, Nelson heralded *Nebraska* as a descendant of works by Woody Guthrie, Bob Dylan and Neil Young, as well as redolent of the Library of Congress field recordings.

Mikal Gilmore, in *Rolling Stone*, called it "a dark-toned, brooding and unsparing record…the most successful attempt at making a sizeable statement about American life that popular music has yet produced".

Greil Marcus concurred: "*Nebraska* is the most complete and probably the most convincing statement of resistance and refusal that Ronald Reagan's USA has yet elicited from any artist or any politician.

"Because Springsteen is an artist and not a politician, his resistance is couched in terms of the bleakest acceptance, his refusal presented as a refusal that does not know itself. There isn't a trace of rhetoric, not a moment of polemic; politics are buried deep in stories of individuals who make up a nation only when their stories are heard together."

Those individuals, Marcus continued, were alone, "because in a world in which men and women are mere social and economic functions, every man and woman is separated from every other".

For Robert Palmer, writing in *The New York Times*, it had been a long time "since a mainstream rock star made an album that asks such tough questions and refuses to settle for easy answers – let alone an album that suggests there are no answers".

In Britain, the reception was less rapturous. While Chris Bohn, in *NME*, applauded Springsteen for "writing and singing in the testy troubadour tradition of entertaining with a kick", *Melody Maker*'s Paolo Hewitt castigated him for being "completely unable to move away from his overblown, romanticised view of the world".

Surely the first and last time *Nebraska* has ever been labelled overblown and romanticised.

9. THE SOUND OF SEPIA

"A multi-layered work of revisionist history narrated in working-class language, Nebraska *represents the history of class in the United States and places the social problems of the Eighties in the context of change over time.*

BRYAN K GARMAN

"If people are sick and hurting and lost, I guess it falls on everybody to address those problems in some fashion. Because injustice, and the price of that injustice, falls on everyone's heads."

BRUCE SPRINGSTEEN

Jimmy Guterman, in his book, *Runaway American Dream: Listening To Bruce Springsteen*, describes *Nebraska* as eccentric. The foremost definition of eccentric is something or someone deviating from convention. Which is exactly what Springsteen did by releasing an album of what were effectively coarsely recorded demos. Another definition of the same word is that which is "situated away from the centre or the axis". The centre, or axis, in this context would be the mainstream, which is where Springsteen was safely ensconced after *The River*. The mainstream is that constituency where an artist gets the populist vote, sometimes at the expense of artistic integrity – compromise by any other name. Subjective opinion as to whether Springsteen performed such a trade-off to enhance his commercial appeal will vary. I don't believe he did; I just think *The River* was, in parts, typified by lazy songwriting.

So here we have someone whose public stock has never been higher, someone who has had his first Top Ten US single in 'Hungry Heart'. It's a perilous place to be for a man who takes seriously what he does. The air gets thinner up there, judgement is not what it would be at a lower altitude. And then the people responsible for elevating you, consumers who have exchanged their hard-earned cash (particularly hard-earned in Reagan's America) for what you're offering, want more of the same. They want songs that make you feel good. Yeah, they understand the need for the slower stuff like 'Independence Day' and 'Wreck On The Highway' – the need for some contrast – but what they really dig are the rockers, soul-stirrers like 'The Ties That Bind', 'Sherry Darling' and 'Out In The Street'. It's Bruce Springsteen and the E Street Experience they're after. That Bruce Springsteen and the E Street formula.

Only an authentic artist – an eccentric – would mess with such a favourable method. Isn't eccentricity – that wilful determination to eschew the impregnable for the risky – the sign of the authentic artist? So in that sense, Guterman is spot-on. *Nebraska* is an eccentric album, the work of an eccentric man – an authentic artist.

In fact, I'd go further. *Nebraska* is downright weird in the way that the songs on Harry Smith's *Anthology Of American Folk Music* are weird – or at least in the way those songs sound weird to us now. They probably sounded weird even on their release in

1952; if you could put colour to sound, the anthology would sound like sepia. Just like *Nebraska*. Sepia evokes not only another time, a long ago time, but also another world. A world apart from that in which we exist on the surface, never daring to tunnel our way underneath things, fearful of what we may unearth there.

Of course, there has always been weirdness, especially in the realm of the artistic. But weirdness has either always been a peripheral pursuit or an entity indulged by the masses for their amusement. When *Nebraska* came along, because of Springsteen's status, weirdness was forced into the foreground and it was no laughing matter. I would suggest that its acceptance – an acceptance borne out by the numbers of people who actually bought it and by those who, during the nearly three decades since its release, regard it as Springsteen's masterpiece and an album of immense artistic significance – preceded the acceptance of all sorts of other weird Americana that came in its wake, from the films of the Coen brothers through the novels of Daniel Woodrell and William Gay to the music of the Handsome Family.

And yet there's nothing that immediately strikes you as weird about 'Nebraska', the song that opens the album. This is folk music, plain and simple, introduced by a gently picked acoustic guitar with an accompanying harmonica line over the top. Then the vocal comes in, and that's when it hits you. The quietness of Springsteen's delivery. But no, that's not it, not exactly. It's the quietness and the detachment – maybe remoteness is more correct. He's singing from inside himself, or outside and removed from himself.

Remember, this is a guy who cut his teeth on live performance in the Seventies, a guy whose marathon shows have become the stuff of legend, a guy who can justifiably lay claim to being among the finest rock and soul frontmen around. And here he is singing as though telling a story, a story in which he is both narrator and protagonist, a story in which Bruce Springsteen has disappeared.

Bruce Springsteen has become a medium, a channeller, a vessel for this other guy, this guy telling you about a girl, a young girl he first encounters twirling a baton on he front lawn. A majorette, perhaps? He's telling you about how him and this girl, how they took a ride – and in the next line, ten innocent people have died. This detail is conveyed without drama, as a matter of fact, and is all the more shocking because of that.

Just like when the principal in 'Banks Of The Ohio' reveals that he has drowned his love and watched her dead body float down the river (although in another version, covered by Johnny Cash among others, he plunges a knife into her breast first). We are in murder ballad territory, of which there are plentiful examples in the folk genre – 'Stagger Lee' ('Stagolee', 'Stackerlee', 'Stack O Lee', 'Stack-a-Lee), 'Down In The Willow Garden' ('Rose Connelly'), 'Lord Randall', 'Little Sadie' ('Cocaine Blues') and 'Pretty Polly' are just a handful.

In the best tradition of the murder ballad, Springsteen proffers evidence of the crime, or, in this case, multiple crimes. His character tells of how he drove through Lincoln, Nebraska, and on through Wyoming, murdering anyone he came across that he had a mind to murder.

That's all we learn before the narrative turns into a valediction of sorts. But where we, the civilised, law-abiding audience, would expect to hear penitence, there is none forthcoming. This is a man who feels no compunction for what he did. Quite the opposite.

Only those knowledgeable about such things (or those familiar with the inspiration behind the song) would have been aware that Charles Starkweather was the model for 'Nebraska'. The rest could but surmise that they were entering the psyche of a sociopath.

In the fourth verse Springsteen shifts gear again to satisfy our curiosity and confirm our suspicions – this is a man facing a death sentence, going to the chair; a dead man, if not walking, then readying himself for that walk into eternal darkness, or whatever you choose to believe awaits us after death.

And then, in the penultimate verse, an absurd request. He wants his girl, his "pretty baby", right there with him when he's electrocuted. Hopeless romantic or homicidal fetishist?

And as if we're not reeling enough from the brutal candour of the narrative, the unflinching insight into the broken mind of a murderer, the final verse, rather than offering the succour of salvation in the form of reason or, at the very least, repentance wrought by fear of "that great void", all we get is a shrug of the shoulders and a supposition that the world can be a mean place.

If it's answers you want, if it's reassurance you're after that humanity lies in the heart of every one of us, no matter how inhumane some may appear, 'Nebraska' is not the song for you. For it acknowledges the presence of depravity in our midst, a presence that impels us to examine the issue of our faith in our own god, whatever our creed. For such an entity supposedly symbolises goodness and mercy, and we are supposedly created in the image of this entity.

This is Springsteen, the songwriter, going deeper than he's ever gone before. The language, the imagery may well be uncomplicated, the human condition he is seeking to investigate, less so. Nothing is as it first appears, everything cannot be rationalised. And what if all that we believe in, all that we hold dear, is a great big con?

And this is Springsteen the singer, separating from himself and becoming someone else, a transformation that, for those six verses, is wholly credible. We buy into Springsteen as psychopath just as we buy into Robert De Niro as Travis Bickle or Marlon Brando as Colonel Kurtz. This is Springsteen as method singer.

And it is the abstruse nature of what he's singing about, combined with the convincing tenor of his performance, which makes 'Nebraska' probably the scariest four and a half minutes you'll hear on record.

The argument could feasibly be constructed that 'Nebraska' is a commentary on the moral collapse of America, assuming, of course, that you subscribed to the theory that it was collapsing. Certainly the politics of Reaganomics seemed to favour the monolithic corporations while exploiting the little man's industry – or dispensing with it, whichever proved more useful in feeding the wealth of the few. Framed in this context, it wouldn't be wholly inaccurate to suggest that the American government had relinquished its moral responsibility to its citizens.

Perhaps Springsteen's character in 'Nebraska' could be read as a personification of the indifference of the legislators on Capitol Hill towards the electorate, or, on the flip side, as the latter's anarchic response to such indifference. A variation on the Bob Dylan premise that when you've got nothing, you've got nothing to lose. But I prefer to think that 'Nebraska' transcends the politics of the day, that its concerns, and Springsteen's concerns, are of an altogether more spiritual kind.

In fact, why bother with my analysis of 'Nebraska' when there's a perfectly good primary source available? Springsteen himself, in VH1's *Storytellers*, described how, on *The River*, he began to approach the compositional process differently, taking on other characters and walking in their shoes, and, by extension, inviting us to walk in their shoes also.

"It kind of frees me to choose characters in some ways different from myself, to sing in those voices and to tell those stories along with my own," he explained.

"This type of writing is often very detailed. You're creating a physical world that's not your own. I'm in the desert, I'm in Texas, I'm in Mexico. It involves a certain amount of research.

"For this song ('Nebraska') I'd been moved by the Terrence Malick film, *Badlands*, and I got interested in the story. There was a book out at the time called *Caril*, about Charlie Starkweather's partner. Just out of the blue I decided to call a newspaper in Nebraska. I called up and the woman who had reported the story was still there, thirty years later. So I got to speak to her. And she was just friendly and helpful.

"You can put together a lot of detail, but unless you pull something up out of yourself it's just going to lie flat on the page. You've got to find out what you have in common with that character, no matter who they are or what they did. So 'Nebraska' is a song written with the premise that everybody knows what it's like to be condemned, which they do, of course.

The body of the song, the first five verses, is basically reportorial. It's information you can glean from researching the story. It's spooky because I'm singing in the voice of the dead. The music is very childlike and mystical. On the record I used a glockenspiel. I think I was interested in an aural projection of the Robert Mitchum film *Night Of The Hunter*, which is kind of this horror story told from a child's perspective.

"The character in this song is very plain-spoken. He's just storytelling, what he did, what happened. But the song takes place in a place where it's quiet now, it's after the violence. It feels like it takes place after his death. There's even a joke – 'Make sure my pretty baby sits right there on my lap'. And things kind of roll along until the end, when someone or something else steps forward. And that something else, that's me and that's you and that's him. And we all kind of meet."

If 'Nebraska' could be deemed a somewhat circumspect reaction to the dominant American politics of the day, 'Atlantic City' puts a human face to the consequences of Reaganomics. It makes real the suffering that occurs when a government abandons its accountability to the people it represents. It strips away the layers of propaganda, the words finessed into phrases designed to lull the millions into a false sense of security, to persuade them that things are good – that this, lest you forget, is America, the land of the free, the home of the brave, where anybody can be somebody.

American presidents have always been quick to employ the trump card of patriotism in times of crisis, to appeal to the people's blind loyalty to the stars and stripes. But 'Atlantic City' blows a hole in the futility of such jingoism. The people on the eastern edge of the States might as well be on the edge of the world. They are falling, and their descent is slow and agonising as everyone scrambles for a foothold, does whatever it takes to hang on.

In the furious scramble, there are victims – the Chicken Man (probably a reference to a mobster by the name of Philip 'Chicken Man' Testa, whose Philadelphia house was blown up in March, 1981), the gangs rumbling on the promenade, the gambling commissioner… The first two verses, propelled by the big, dark minor chords on Springsteen's acoustic, and by the urgency of his vocal, conjure up a nightmarish tableau – the New Jersey shore as the abyss. But hold on, the chorus brings respite, the promise of reincarnation. Everything dies, sure, but everything comes back.

So forget about the now, forget about the madness and the hardship and the heartache, and let's pretend that we still believe in magic and in magical places. And Atlantic City was once a magical place, a place where the American Dream could be realised – or at least that version of the American Dream that values wealth above enlightenment.

But after the first chorus it becomes apparent that the central character in the song, the Springsteen character, is in Atlantic City not for love, nor for dreaming. He's there looking for a break; he wants some cold cash and lots of it, fast, because he has "debts no honest man can pay". The gambling mecca along the shoreline is his last-chance saloon. He's the guy with a film of sweat where a moustache should be, jelly legs walking the plank, clutching his wife's arm for support, their life savings in the handbag slung from her exposed bony shoulder.

And then you hear him, in the bridge of the song, trying to assure her, trying to assure himself; things may be bad now, but things will get better. But suddenly we're plunged into the resignation of the final verse. You get the feeling that even the money he drew from the Central Trust, his gambling loot, has been gambled away. The promise of Atlantic City, like the promise of America, is a broken one. There is nothing down for him if he plays it straight, so he's not going to play it straight any more.

If 'Nebraska' owed much to Springsteen's fascination with the Charles Starkweather killings and with Terrence Malick's *Badlands* (although, unlike Springsteen's song, Malick's narrative perspective was that of Caril Fugate character). It was a literary device used by Flannery O'Connor that informed the structure of 'Mansion On The Hill' (and, later on the album, 'Used Cars' and 'My Father's House'). O'Connor, in common with William Faulkner and indeed another southern writer, Eudora Welty, often told her stories through the eyes of a child. Springsteen's adoption of the same device meant he could relate the bare facts of the piece as witnessed by the minor, while leaving the listener to read the white space – to unravel the subtext, if you like. This is one of his particular attributes as a songwriter, that facility (acquired or instinctive?) to judge what to show and what to tell. It's what makes him a persuasive political songwriter without being polemical.

'Mansion On The Hill' is a song about the class divide (yes, even in America), the mansion emblematic of the haves, towering above the have nots toiling in the factories and the fields. It's a song about how the American Dream is not, contrary to popular myth, available to all; how the mansion on the hill – the same American Dream – is cordoned off by "gates of hardened steel".

There is a poignancy in the image of the father taking the son to look up at the mansion in the third verse. It's not so much as if the older man is endeavouring to foster aspiration in the boy, more as though he is letting him see what will never be his, what will always be out of his reach, beyond the grasp of his kind.

On *The River* tour, Springsteen would recall how he couldn't envisage his life being different from that of his father's. "It seemed that if you were born in a certain place, things didn't change much for you," he said. "I tried to think what was the thing that we all had in common, why did it, time after time, end up that way? And it was that we didn't have enough knowledge about the forces that were controlling our lives."

Of course, Springsteen's life became the polar opposite of his father's. He chose to do something he loved, laboured hard to get good at it and enjoyed the bounty of his success. Yet not even enormous wealth has dulled his class consciousness, has prevented him from continuing to write about the guy he used to be, and perhaps at heart, remains.

"Springsteen's characters on *Nebraska* are predominantly working class and speak in a working-class dialect," says Bryan K Garman. "For example, their use of the word 'sir', a word you will often find on Nebraska, often indicates a sense of their social standing. It's a multi-layered album because it represents so many music traditions and is filled with many historical references. Think too about a song like 'Youngstown' (from *The Ghost Of Tom Joad*), or even his cover of 'How Can A Poor Man Stand Such Times And Live?' That song keeps some old references to poverty and is updated with a treatment of Hurricane Katrina and references to George Bush."

The world inside the gates of Springsteen's mansion in 'Mansion On The Hill' is exotic, a world of shining lights, music playing and people laughing – a world without care.

Then, in the final verse, the boy becomes a man. Like his father before him, he is excluded from opportunity, fated to accept the preservation of wealth in the hands of the wealthy. And not only that, but the suggestion of something worse; the suggestion that he has lost his place even among his own (working) class as he watches "the cars rushin' by home from the mill".

'Mansion On The Hill', like much of *Nebraska*, could also be heard as a spiritual, the promise of an Elysian recompense in the sweet by and by, a conceptual reflex related to Springsteen's Catholicism. Many of us confirmed in that faith have loosed the chains of its dogma only to discover that we can't fully exorcise ourselves of its mystical possession.

'Johnny 99' harbours no such delusions of redemption. The sinner has sinned, and unless the mitigating circumstances of the sin can be acknowledged, he might as well pay the ultimate tariff.

Like the guy in 'Atlantic City', Ralph has "debts no honest man can pay" – the repetition of this line two songs apart, reinforces the sense that the impossible choices imposed by Reagan's America weighed heavy on Springsteen's mind. 'Atlantic City' hints at involvement in illicit activity as a means to the end of penury. This seems to denote, at the very least, a decision reached after taking a rational overview of the situation. 'Johnny 99' is what happens when the response to a similar predicament is completely irrational.

Ralph gets soused on alcohol and shoots a night clerk. The malice of the character in 'Nebraska', the calculated reasoning of the character in 'Atlantic City', is here replaced by the tragic impulse of a man whose dignity has been incrementally eroded, a man frustrated by the fix in which he finds himself, a man who cracks under pressure. This pressure is accentuated in the second verse as Ralph/Johnny brandishes his gun and threatens to do still more damage before the cops haul him away.

The appointment of Mean John Brown as judge rules out the possibility of a sympathetic hearing – such is the unforgiving nature of Reagan's staunchly right-wing Republican administration in matters of law and order. And sure enough the harshest of sentences (short of the death penalty) is handed down.

Springsteen increases the dramatic ante in the fourth verse as, in a scene that could have come straight from a Sunday afternoon black-and-white matinée, the family of Ralph/Johnny make a desperate petition for clemency. The judge consents to hearing the statement of the condemned man before he is forever taken away.

And what a harrowing statement it is; an inventory of his poverty – economic poverty, spiritual poverty, the poverty of opportunity – that subverts fundamental decency, that precipitates the evil that men think and do. This is a man who has awoken from the American Nightmare to the loss of everything he held dear – most importantly, his freedom. He'd rather be dead.

'Johnny 99' is blues of the bluest hue. The falsetto cry that launches the song is as lonesome as anything out of the deepest, darkest Delta. The bark that punctuates its fade is strange and unsettling. The way Springsteen seems to speed up the melody in places, the way he seems to pause almost imperceptibly before the second line of the last verse ("The bank was holding my mortgage…"), the frenetic harmonica break, all of it conspires to underscore the sheer awfulness of the tale, as though it were something you don't want to hear but he has to tell you, because this is how things are.

And this is how things are still. We're almost thirty years from *Nebraska*, in a whole new century, a whole new world, where erstwhile enemies are now friends and technology has accelerated change at a pace and in ways we could never have imagined back then. But we haven't come so far as to eradicate the problems that spawn the guy in 'Nebraska' or 'Johnny 99'.

This the true measure of the ten songs that comprise Springsteen's solo masterwork – their timelessness, their continued relevance. They speak to us just as the songs of Woody Guthrie and Pete Seeger and Bob Dylan speak to us long years after they were written down and recorded. They endure just as all folk songs endure, because we are the folk and we understand what they mean because we live out their meanings every day. Our heartbeat remains the same.

It's not at all surprising that Sean Penn choose 'Highway Patrolman' as the basis of the script for *The Indian Runner*, his debut as a film director. He could have picked pretty much anything on *Nebraska*, for every narrative is a potential treatment for the big screen. Just think what Martin Scorsese, in his Seventies pomp, could have done with 'Atlantic City'. Or how the Coen bothers, before they went all Hollywood and recruited George Clooney and Brad Pitt to their pool of actors, would have left their imprint on 'Reason To Believe'.

'Highway Patrolman' is not only among the finest songs on 'Nebraska', it's among Springsteen's finest songs, period. And it's one of maybe three songs on the album that has a proper chorus.

The narrator is Joe Roberts, a small-town policeman who has always tried to be honest, to do the right thing. But he has a brother, Frankie – and Frankie, well, he just "ain't no good". It sounds ominous already, as if Joe's readying us for a confession of sorts.

And that confession comes in the second verse. Joe has sometimes compromised his position for Frankie, turned a blind eye to his misdemeanours, because blood's blood and there's nothing more important than that.

The chorus ghosts in with a fond memory of the two brothers laughing and drinking, dancing with a girl named Maria, a girl who would, we later learn, become Joe's wife. This memory of what Frankie once was, of what perhaps he could be again, is what compels Joe to catch him whenever he strays. And besides, your loyalty is to your family, and if you have no family loyalty, then you're nothing. That's Joe's whole dilemma right there – family loyalty pitted against loyalty to the law he's paid to uphold.

Springsteen provides some back story in the next verse. Frankie joined the army in 1965 as American involvement in Vietnam was escalating, while Joe settled down with Maria and worked the family farm. Three years later, Frankie came home and Joe, unable to sustain a living on the land, became a cop.

Then we're back to the chorus before the real action of the song unfolds in the fourth verse, the episode that has Joe all tangled up in angst. Trouble in a roadhouse, a kid bleeding (to death?), a girl crying, Frankie's responsible. Joe sets out after him, driving like a madman, spots Frankie's car at a crossroads and gives chase to the Canadian border. But rather than apprehend him, as he would have done had it been anyone else, Joe pulls over and watches as Frankie's light disappears.

Springsteen, as he does throughout *Nebraska*, allows you to reach your own conclusion, however obvious it may appear that Joe has bailed Frankie out yet again. Of course, the disappearing light could be the archetypal death metaphor. It could be Joe finally liberating himself from responsibility for his kin. Or it could be that Joe has realised he can't maintain the law and stay good, anomalous though that seems.

'Highway Patrolman' is a model of narrative articulation in its rendering of the imminent aloneness of belief in what we hold to be right, even when we know it to be wrong. Put another way, we sometimes do things that are wrong for the right reasons.

Five songs in and this was relentlessly wretched stuff. And they used to say Leonard Cohen was lugubrious! Most albums are composed of light and shade; five songs in, *Nebraska* was composed of dark and darker. And it was about to get darker yet.

'State Trooper' is the sound of suicide. It's unbearably desolate, Springsteen's unhinged voice eerily echoing over an insistent bluesy riff as he climbs into the skin of a character hell bent on running right off the end of the road to nowhere. You wouldn't want to be in this guy's shoes. Not here, not now. We've all of us been in his head at some time or other.

He's riding on the New Jersey Turnpike, Springsteen relocating to familiar territory after travelling through Nebraska, Wyoming and Michigan. The night's wet, the rivers are black underneath a sky illuminated only by the fire from the refinery. There are no stars upon which to make a wish, there is no moon to make you swoon. We're in the land of heavy industry, the American counterpart to the dark Satanic mills in William Blake's 'Jerusalem'. It's a picture that might have been in Cormac McCarthy's mind when he was imagining himself into a world gone wrong for *The Road*.

This driver hasn't got a licence; he is, like the guy in 'Nebraska', the guy in 'Atlantic City', like 'Johnny 99', like Frank in 'Highway Patrolman' a lawbreaker. But he has a clear conscience, he has absolved himself of whatever crime or crimes he has committed. He is his own God, his own judge. He entreats the state trooper not to stop him – why? Is he beyond the parameters of whatever punishment the law can mete out? Is he unable to trust himself not to administer his own punishment for whatever he perceives the law – or society as a whole – has done to him? You begin to fear for the state trooper. This guy could be another Charles Starkweather.

This fear is exacerbated in the next verse. "Maybe you got a kid, maybe you got a pretty wife" comes over as menacing, as though he resents the fact that others possess what he doesn't himself possess – apart from that which has been "botherin' me my whole life". This could be anything, but it's not anything good. Charles Bukowski wrote a poem about the hole in the heart that would never be filled, a certain lack of something, an emotional deficiency that meant true bliss would always be denied him. This could be what's troubling the protagonist in 'State Trooper'. Or it could be that his particular deficiency is more psychological, a form of mental illness. Whatever the nature of his torment, we've got a ringside seat, watching him as his head – filled with disparate voices on the radio stations he flicks through – comes apart. And then he's gone, or nearly gone, issuing one last plea for someone, anyone, to listen to him, to save him. You get the feeling it's too late, Springsteen's bloodcurdling wail seeming to confirm as much.

The first brace of songs on side two (in the vinyl days before CDs or downloading) are as light as it gets on *Nebraska*. 'Used Cars' is another variation on the theme of class, an amusing if heartrending anecdote about always having to settle for second best, for other people's cast-offs, of never quite having enough to afford the shiny new things. We all remember the kid in hand-me-downs, the kid dependent on the state for school meals and school books, the kid despatched with similar kids on a one-week holiday every summer to some kip of a seaside resort down the country. Some of us *were* that kid.

As in 'Mansion On The Hill', Springsteen allows us to see the whole sorry tale through a child's eyes. It's the family's big day out, a trip to the used-car lot to buy "a brand-new used car". The mother, alone in the backseat in the first verse, fingering her wedding band in the second, seems to embody the disappointment of their lives, the fact that they just about make ends meet. And if you're in any doubt about their place on the economic ladder, the line about the salesman staring at the old man's hands affirms it. For these are the hands of a manual worker, a worker who doesn't earn enough to qualify for the credit offered in purchasing a vehicle straight off the production line.

The child narrator takes it all in, he knows what's going on here. There's righteous indignation as he swears never again to ride in a used car when his lottery numbers come up. The realisation of wealth is presented as a matter of chance rather than something that can be achieved by design.

The neighbours emerge from every nook and cranny (I picture a trailer park) to gaze upon the family's second-hand acquisition, a scene that makes the boy squirm with embarrassment and seethe with anger. This is not what he wants for himself, this is not the way it's meant to be, sweating the same job day after day, interned on the same "dirty streets" he's always known. But again, other than through good fortune, there's nothing as tangible as a plan to escape the emptiness.

'Open All Night' uses some of the same imagery as 'State Trooper', but with none of the latter's sense of foreboding. The car, so often the mode of transport to the promised land in Springsteen's songs, so often a feminine object about which Springsteen's characters rhapsodise, once more assumes the principal role. She's ferrying the guy to his girl, Wanda (are there *really* girls called Wanda?), whom he met behind the counter of a fast-food joint at a service station.

Just as in 'State Trooper', he's journeying into night, "in the wee wee hours" when his "mind gets hazy", out there all on his lonesome, the last man on earth, the only man on the moon ("This New Jersey in the mornin' like a lunar landscape"), the turnpike giving him the creeps but the radio keeping him safe, keeping him sane. There's mischief in this guy where there's misery in the 'State Trooper' guy. He's going to see his baby, even if it means a "one two power-shift" spiriting him away from the motorcycle policeman on his tail, and no matter how long it takes.

There's exuberance in the final verse, a kind of amphetamine rush that comes with being up all night or from the natural high of impending reunion with your lover. This guy's wired now, poking fun at the lost souls seeking salvation on the gospel stations. He's beseeching his own god, the god of rock'n'roll, to "deliver me from nowhere". But it sounds to me as if he's already been delivered, like he's already found his somewhere.

Nebraska is loaded with religious allusions. Religious themes are implicit throughout. But it only on 'My Father's House' and 'Reason To Believe', when the God question becomes manifest. Make no mistake, these are gospel songs, though gospel songs with a difference. While traditionally such songs are written and performed in praise of a deity (whose existence is never up for debate), Springsteen's are filled with dubiety. Is there really a God in heaven, as we are taught as Christians? And how on earth, literally, do people sustain their faith in the face of adversity?

'My Father's House' begins with the narrator recalling a dream in which he was a child again, making his way home through a fairytale landscape before nightfall. Like the best fairytales, there is something forbidding about the landscape, something sinister – something wicked this way coming. The "ghostly voices" from the fields evoke the spirits of the dead, spirits lost in Catholic purgatory, maybe. The boy runs from these voices – sins of the man's past, sins of America's past, sins of slavery? Could the fields referred to be the cotton fields in which African slaves worked until they were half dead from work?

It's not impossible, given Springsteen's interest in American history and how it records the barbarism visited upon African Americans, that this was more than a subliminal thought. Though simple in terms of their composition and arrangement, the lyrics on *Nebraska* do open themselves to different strata of explication. Whatever the nature of these "ghostly voices", they instil abject terror in the boy who, with Satan himself in pursuit, finally reaches the sanctuary of his father's house. He has eluded the fiery flames of hell, fled through purgatory and reached his heavenly reward – at least in the dream.

The man emerges from his slumber and thinks about "the hard things that pulled us apart", of how vice ripped him from the heart of virtue, of how it took him away from God's church, the church to which he now vows to return and repent. But when he gets there, a woman speaks to him through "a chained door". He is like those "ghostly voices", cast out, a lost soul like so many of the lost souls on *Nebraska*. Or is it his faith that has been lost? For, according to the woman, nobody with his father's name lives at his father's house any more. There is no God and heaven is merely made-up. Yet the man can't fully shake the sense that this isn't true. He wants it not to be true, because otherwise he can't atone for his transgressions but has to carry them with him for all eternity.

Another less complicated reading of 'My Father's House' could be that as children we are systematically indoctrinated into to a certain belief (whatever the denominational origin of that belief) and consequently we accept it unconditionally.

As adults, we are more inclined towards deconstructing that belief.

So if 'My Father's House' is about lost faith, 'Reason To Believe' is about holding onto that faith come what may. The narrator here appears bemused by people's capacity for keeping on believing despite the shit that life throws at them. It's a curious song with no little humour in it, though you have to listen hard. The man by the highway poking the dead dog with a stick, as if he expects it to revive itself, is quirky enough for a Coen brothers' movie.

There's nothing funny about Mary Lou's vigil "at the end of that dirt road" for Johnny, her no-good lover who upped and left her. It's just plain pathetic. The girl needs to move on.

In the third verse, one life begins as another ends. Newborn Kyle William's (original) sin is washed away in the water. It's not clear whether the old man "in a whitewash shotgun shack" has been absolved of his sins before passing away. But if he hasn't, prayers are offered up for him in his grave, which I suppose is a form of absolution.

It could be that Springsteen had Bob Dylan's 'The Groom's Still Waiting At The Altar' in mind when he wrote the final verse – because that's exactly where the groom is still waiting at the end of it all, "wonderin' where can his baby be". He's been jilted, poor fellow, and not only that, the congregation have left him to hurt alone. This image, more than that presented in the chorus about how folk, at the end of every day, find reason to believe, is possibly the overriding image on *Nebraska*. It compresses the album's many themes into a single dominant theme: namely, that faith, like suffering, is a solitary thing.

Another theme – although it's probably more accurately described as a thread – that runs through *Nebraska* is criminality, or, as New York Professor of Law Samuel J Levine puts it, "the decisions, actions and perspectives of criminals".

According to Levine, Springsteen defies simplistic judgements and categorisations, confronting us "with an uncompromising examination of and, consequently, a more truthful and realistic reflection upon the complexities of crime, criminals and our justice system". Levine places the criminals on Nebraska into three different groups: the enigmatic criminal, the sympathetic criminal and the criminal as brother.

The enigmatic criminal is represented in the Starkweather-prototype who narrates 'Nebraska'. Here, says Levine, Springsteen offers "the disheartening but valuable lesson that exploration of the criminal mindset may not yield any insight into the mysteries of senseless criminal acts, their causes or their motivations".

Levine finds three examples of the sympathetic criminal, in 'Atlantic City', 'Johnny 99' and 'State Trooper'. In the former two, Springsteen maps the trajectory of the principals "from dejection to desperation and ultimately to the fateful submission to the pressures to cross the line and commit a crime".

Levine continues, "In contrast to the enigmatic protagonist of the title track, whose crimes linger unexplained and whose cavalier attitude shocks and dismays, the speaker in 'Atlantic City' tells us precisely how and why he has arrived at his decision to break the law, and we appreciate the suffering and struggles he has unsuccessfully tried to overcome. Although we may not condone or excuse his conduct, we understand the forces that have driven him to seek solace and success in the world of criminal activity."

'Johnny 99', meanwhile, compels us to examine more thoughtfully the criminal's predicament "and appreciate more fully the emotional and logical appeal of his argument". This is what Ralph/Johnny himself wants; he's not seeking acquittal, he just wants a measure of sympathy for his suffering and some regard for his plight.

"Thus, consistent with prevailing principles of criminal law, Springsteen does not put forth the more radical contention that the criminal's misfortune should preclude guilt; rather, through its emphatic narrative, the song makes a powerful case for the proposition that a broader understanding of the sympathetic criminal's condition warrants more careful attention in a determination of a just and fair sentence."

For Levine, 'State Trooper' (which he hears more as an urgent plea for help than a song) presents the most sympathetic criminal on the album. The narrator's troubled situation calls on us "to accept the seeming inevitability of his criminal conduct. The driver's lonely desperation stems neither from external pressures nor from financial hardship, but instead from a deeper existential angst borne out of a lifetime of suffering, apparently beyond remedy or repair.

"Springsteen's portrait evokes in us a reaction strikingly different from our response to the remorseless Starkweather. Rather than feeling puzzled or repulsed by the driver's lack of contrition, we begin not only to understand his justifications but perhaps to concur with his disquieting conclusion that he need not maintain a guilty conscience for the crimes he has committed."

If the guy in 'State Trooper' is the most sympathetic criminal, Frankie in 'Highway Patrolman' receives the most sympathetic treatment, says Levine. "As we listen to the powerful narration of the song, told through the perspective of Joe Roberts, we understand and appreciate his attitudes and actions. Indeed, putting ourselves in his place, we cannot help but begin to feel compassion for Frankie as well. After all, as the narrator repeatedly reminds us, once we picture Frankie as our own brother, we owe him our sympathy and our support, the question of whether he deserves it now proving immaterial.

"Thus, through a story of two brothers, closely connected but playing opposing roles in the legal system, Springsteen leaves us to ponder the difficult questions that stand at the boundaries of law and loyalty, questions that force us to confront the complexity of striking the appropriate balance between justice and mercy."

10. TRIAL AND ERROR

"If he's looking for a song to sound a certain way, it's going to be that way or the highway."

MIKE APPEL

"Born In The USA, I believe in the American way."

Early draft of 'Born In The USA'

Trawl the internet for Bruce Springsteen bootlegs, narrowing your search down to the keyword 'Nebraska', and you'll eventually navigate your way to an interesting two-CD compilation entitled *How Nebraska Was Born*. The general consensus among bootleggers is that these demos were laid down in the period after *The River* and before *Nebraska*. It's claimed that eleven of the songs span the two-month period from March to May 1981 and a further sixteen from June to December of the same year. The remainder supposedly came from Colt's Neck on 3 January 1982 – the session that spawned *Nebraska*. Establishing the concrete facts is problematic without Springsteen's testimony or without access to whatever recording logs (if any) were completed at the time. But it's a fair assumption that the bootleggers are correct in their speculation.

Certainly many of the songs – or bits of songs in some cases – are consistent with the themes that preoccupied Springsteen at that point in his growth as a writer. He is moving deeper into an America whose fringes he skirted on previous albums. An America of the dispossessed. He's like a man who has taken possession of a new knowledge about the way things really are in his country, and he wants to share this new knowledge with the rest of us. He wants to put it over in the only way he knows how.

At times during *How Nebraska Was Born*, whenever Springsteen scuffs a chord change or vacillates on a lyric the listener can feel like a snoop, eavesdropping on a man's inchoate fumblings. You know you shouldn't, but you can't deny this is enthralling stuff. It's largely the sound of Springsteen sketching. The creative process in the embryonic stages of gestation. Songs with which all of us are now familiar, sometimes appear in other guises. Like 'Atlantic City'. Here it begins as 'Fist Full Of Dollars', a simple major-chord strum. Two versions open the bootleg, neither particularly portending the condemned fate of the narrator in the version that made it onto *Nebraska*. Indeed Springsteen could be reprising one of his earlier dreamers as he sings of the turnpike turning to gold. He draws his money from the Central Trust not as a final, desperate throw of the dice but almost as the means with which to subsidise an adventure, as he hops with his guitar on a Greyhound bus "on a one-way ticket to the promised land".

Springsteen seems to lose his way on the song, as though what he's saying isn't quite what he intended to say. There's a hurried line about a week's pay that "in a minute just turns to dust" before what can be heard as an omniscient narrator delivers a rather banal pair of closing couplets: "Some gonna stand and some gonna fall/And some ain't gonna get to play the game at all/Well, they give you the worst and they take the best/For a fist full of dollars and a little bit less." Then Springsteen ups the ante, hollering and hammering his guitar briefly, before plodding back into the groove. By this stage the fact that the guy has hocked his guitar matters not a jot.

The second version of the same song, still listed as 'Fist Full Of Dollars', has developed slightly from its predecessor, notably in the occasional Dylanesque lilt to Springsteen's voice and more chord changes. But with the inept recording muffling the lyrics, it merely suggests potential as a standard country-rocker. It's a long way from 'Atlantic City', that's for sure.

There follows a run of nine songs best described as doodles. Only 'Johnny Bye Bye', part-Elvis elegy, part existentialist exercise ("Many men have fallen, their dreams denied/They walk down the street with death in their eyes") breaks the two-minute mark. 'Riding Horse' is cute ("I've got a girl so tall and fair/I need a step ladder to run my fingers through her hair"), while 'Party Lights' chugs along like a Buddy Holly throwback. 'Robert Ford And Jesse James' is a subject Springsteen would return to on *The Seeger Sessions* (covering the song 'Jesse James'), but on *How Nebraska Was Born* his attempts to compose an original stumble through a single melancholy verse and a chorus without a lyric. Meanwhile, 'Daniel In The Lion's Den' is 54 seconds of a chorus without a verse.

'Open All Night' is nothing like the version that made *Nebraska*. Springsteen did keep some of the images – the spooky turnpike at night "when you're all alone", the refinery towers, the counter girl – but changed the melody completely. In fact, the melody here is recognisable as 'Used Cars' in a quicker tempo.

Springsteen's increasing Vietnam fixation gets an airing on, appropriately enough, 'Vietnam', a precursor to 'Born In The USA'. According to Geoffrey Himes in his book *Born In The USA*, Springsteen "transformed his 'Vietnam' song into 'Born In The USA'" in December 1981, recycling the music from the former into 'Love Is A Dangerous Thing'.

A returning vet finds himself in the ubiquitous Main Street after finishing a tour of duty, confronted by "strange faces watching a stranger passin' by". Springsteen segues into the first chorus, "Vietnam, Vietnam, I don't man/Back in Vietnam". So far, so ordinary. In the second verse he tries to get his old job back at the factory only to be told there's "nothin' for you here". On the second chorus another voice is telling the vet, "You died in Vietnam". So it appears we're dealing with a ghost.

Undeterred, he troops down First and Grand to see his ex-girlfriend who, he finds out, "ran off with a singer in a rock'n'roll band". It's a clunky stab at humour in a song that draws attention to the invisibility of men who come home from an unpopular war. Not that war is ever popular, except among those with a vested interest in the outcome. Himes' claim that Springsteen "transformed his 'Vietnam' song into 'Born In The USA'" is correct, though perhaps he should have qualified that by indicating how much of a transformation 'Vietnam' underwent to become 'Born In The USA'. It was quite substantial. Only the line, "Went for my job back at the factory/The only thing I heard from the man at the desk/Is, 'Son, understand if it was up to me'" survived, and even then in a revised form, while musically the two couldn't be more different. 'Vietnam' has the rock'n'soul exuberance of Springsteen circa *The Wild, The Innocent And The E Street Shuffle*.

Two versions of 'Johnny 99' are faithful to the country-blues riff of *Nebraska*, although Springsteen hasn't yet finally settled on the lyrics. The first version – in which there is no fist fight in the courtroom – includes an instrumental break (with Springsteen humming over the top) after the judge sentences the hapless Ralph/Johnny to ninety eight years in prison. Then he tells him, "You're gonna to be down in some hole and you're never gonna get back out." Ralph/Johnny offers in his defence the extenuating background that led to the shooting of the night clerk, before declaring, "Let the executioner do his job on Johnny 99."

But Springsteen isn't satisfied. There's something missing. He tries an alternative ending, prefacing the verse about having "debts no honest man can pay" with some evidence from Ralph/Johnny about his crime: "$200, it was all I was asking for/Judge, just $200 dollars I'd have been on my way out the door/He reached 'neath the counter, I saw something shiny in his hand/He spewed blood like a fountain, I dropped my gun and I ran."

It is superfluous (and gory) detail, a Hollywood technique of infusing the drama of the piece with action. Springsteen's decision to omit it in the final edit was a shrewd one.

The second version does include the fist fight but, instead of having to drag Johnny's girl away, the bailiffs "drag Johnny's dad away". The judge then informs the distraught father, "I'm sorry, man, but the law must be satisfied/At your son's murderin' hands, an honest man died." The idea of a bewigged adjudicator of the law, particularly one notorious for the severity of his sentences (if you consider the occupant of the bench here later became "Mean John Brown"), uttering the sobriquet "man" certainly gave me a chuckle.

Johnny's testimony embellishes the "debts no honest man can pay" line with, "Judge, I worked the assembly line since I was eighteen/A banker held my mortgage and they were coming down hard on me". In his parting words, he thanks the judge for "making me a dead man".

Based on these working drafts of 'Johnny 99', it's what Springsteen keeps back rather than what he reveals in the *Nebraska* cut that exemplifies his authorial instinct.

'The Answer' would eventually become 'The Losin' Kind', but its story of a guy and a girl who beat up a bartender at a roadside bar and empty his cash register could just as easily be 'Nebraska', it could be 'State Trooper', it could even be 'Johnny 99'. Some of the song found its way into 'Highway 29' on *The Ghost Of Tom Joad*.

'Love Is A Dangerous Thing' is a dark psychobilly riff on the perils of sexual attraction, in which Eve and Delilah are cited as examples of temptresses who left their hapless men (Adam and Samson) "twisting in the wind".

A rough one minute, fourteen second version of 'Downbound Train' is notable only for Springsteen's train-whistle impersonation on harmonica. The even shorter 'Red River Rock' features the 'Johnny 99' chord pattern with Springsteen whistling a different melody.

The first of two versions of 'Used Cars' is adorned by some sweet harmonica. Springsteen's vocal performance has more colour. But there's no sense of the song's sadness until the final verse, the car horn echoing down Michigan Avenue like a muted trumpet.

The second version eschews the harmonica, the pace is slower and Springsteen plumps for greater restraint in the delivery. Suddenly the narrative is not so throwaway, not comical at all but tangled up in the tragedy of the mundane, profoundly personified in the lines: "6am, I get woke up to the same old sound/My old man lying on his back on the cold, cold ground/Throwing them jumper cables out of the trunk/Standing alone on Michigan Avenue waiting for a jump".

And then we come to the first of five versions of 'Born In The USA'. This is 'Vietnam' with a whole other lyric: "I was born in the shadow of the Glendale Refinery/With the air so dirty, you can hardly breathe/The dirt gets so deep, it covers your skin/You can scrub all day and scrub all night but it's never coming out again/Born In The USA". The protagonist here just turned eighteen, got in "a roadhouse jam" and was presented with the stark choice of the jailhouse or military service.

The second version drops the 'Vietnam' riff for something closer to that which appears on *Born In The USA*, though it sways rather than pounds, the vocal is cool rather than incensed. Version three refers to Nixon being on the lam after dropping bombs on the yellow man, before a scathing indictment of WASP-ish America, "I don't care what shit they say/They wouldn't have done no white man that way."

On the fifth version Springsteen is in military threads and painted face, a footsoldier in the South East Asian conflict, where "Boy, beyond that line of trees, there's a river without a name/There, deep in the dark forest, something's waiting in the jungle rain/Go crawling up there on your knees son, go crawling quiet as you can/I want to see my baby again."

Again, the existence of these tapes is a brilliant barometer of Springsteen's discernment, illustrating that while he is willing to pursue his narrative instincts, he is never afraid to take away what he doesn't need. The 'Born In The USA' lyric on the album of the same name is perfectly nuanced. Springsteen's narratives are created from his imagination, but it is his skill as a writer that serves those narratives.

After fifty nine seconds of soul testifying on 'Club Soul City', Springsteen returns to 'Fist Full of Dollars', which now bears the title 'Atlantic City'. The lyric has been fleshed out, the melody radically altered, though he's still having difficulty with the chorus.

'Fade To Black' uses the metaphor of cinema to describe love gone bad. Indeed several of the lines read like screenwriting directions: "Small bungalow, a late afternoon… A camera pans, an empty room/The picture dissolves, slowly pulls back."

On the second disc, 'Child Bride' is a slow lament rather than a rockabilly stomp. It would have been a perfect fit for *Nebraska* either way, but especially in this incarnation. The guy here has none of the swagger of his alter ego on 'Working On The Highway'. He's not swinging with the warden on the road gang – he's alone in his prison cell with nothing for company except his story, tortuously replayed, and the forlorn hope of one day going to a roadside bar to "Pick a stranger and spin around the dance floor/To a Mexican guitar."

The version of 'Highway Patrolman', also known as 'Deputy', is the closest thing on *How Nebraska Was Born* to anything that features on *Nebraska*. A second version of 'Downbound Train' has the same intensity as 'Johnny 99', a frenzied stranger accosting you on the street, bug eyed and desperately petitioning you to understand his plight.

'The Losin' Kind' is 'The Answer' with a bulkier back story. Like 'Highway Patrolman', the character introduces himself in the opening line – "My name is Frank Davis." After the violence and the robbery and the car wreck, Davis is told by the state trooper, "Son, you're lucky to be alive", to which he fatalistically replies, "Sir, I'll think that one over if you don't mind/Life ain't much good to you when you're the losin' kind." It's a mystery why this song has remained unreleased.

The second disc also includes yet another version of 'Born In The USA' – this time harder edged than the earlier versions – and a brace of undeveloped versions of 'Nebraska'. The guitar is too busy on the first, while the second brings in the harmonica and pitches the Charles Starkweather narrative firmly in the third-person perspective: "He saw her standing on her front lawn", "Him and her went for a ride, sir."

After a couple of brief stabs at Roy Orbison's 'Dream Baby' and the old spiritual 'Precious Memories', Springsteen revs up his vocal and beats out an insistent guitar rhythm on 'Pink Cadillac', less a paean to a car than to the female sexual organ.

Closing out *How Nebraska Was Born* is 'James Lincoln Deere', another Springsteen victim of Reaganomics. Deere loses his job when the Indiana factory where he works goes bust, and so he turns to raiding grocery stores with his brother-in-law until he winds up behind bars after shooting a kid at a Stop & Shop.

How Nebraska Was Born is a valuable, if not vital, archival resource in helping to piece together a picture of where Springsteen's writing head was at during the period between *The River* and *Nebraska*. He's working hard at refining a narrative style first established on *Born To Run*. He's working hard at un-becoming Bruce Springsteen and instead transmuting into the characters he begets. Sometimes – as you can hear – he's working too hard. But at those times he has the capacity to step back, listen with a neutral ear and acknowledge when something hasn't worked. This is the real gold on *How Nebraska Was Born* – the sound of a writer engaged in the game of trial and error.

Springsteen pictured by David Michael Kennedy at the photographer's upstate New York home
as part of the sessions for the *Nebraska* cover shoot

The iconic cover shot of Nebraska, a two-lane blacktop in America's Midwest
(Copyright David Michael Kennedy)

Another of David Michael Kennedy's stills of Bruce from the *Nebraska* cover shoot

Pete Seeger, "a shining light towards our better angels", according to Springsteen

Photographer David Michael Kennedy,
whose iconic landscape shot features on the cover of *Nebraska*

Woody Guthrie, "the songwriter as advocate", a touchstone for Springsteen

(Courtesy of The Woody Guthrie Archives, used by permission)

Springsteen joins the assembled cast of The Nebraska Project on stage in New York

(Copyright Glyn Emmerson)

Springsteen meets his public in Turin, 2009

11. WORKING MAN AMERICANA

"He gave us a very real depiction of our country, and it made me think of the world in a whole different way."

JIM SAMPAS

"He is an essential figure. He has done more for American music than anybody could think of, not including my dad."

ROSANNE CASH

The tribute album has become a genre all its own over the past couple of decades. The proliferation of music magazines during this period, many of them offering free CDs with each issue (and many of these CDs featuring contemporary acts covering material by less contemporary but still hip acts), has proved a boon in this respect. The best of them – I'm thinking of the Leonard Cohen homage, *I'm Your Fan*, or *The Bridge*, an encomium to Neil Young – stand alone. The worst of them, which tend to form the majority, usually end up on charity shop shelves or in plastic recycling bins. You're unlikely, though, to find anything produced by Jim Sampas in your local Oxfam.

Sampas has raised the bar for tribute albums in recent years with the likes of *This Bird Has Flown* (commemorating the 40th anniversary of the Beatles' *Rubber Soul*), *Subterranean Homesick Blues* (Bob Dylan's *Bringing It All Back Home* revised by a bunch of indie artists) *Paint It Black* (an alt-country take on The Rolling Stones) and *Kerouac – Kicks Joy Darkness* (a celebration of Beat guru Jack Kerouac, Sampas' late uncle). He also oversaw the 2000 Sub Pop release, *Badlands – A Tribute To Bruce Springsteen's Nebraska*, on which Chrissie Hynde, Hank Williams III, Los Lobos, Ben Harper and others interpret the whole of Springsteen's original album, while Johnny Cash, Raul Malo (of the Mavericks) and Damien Jurado and Rose Thomas contribute bonus versions of 'I'm On Fire', 'Downbound Train' and 'Wages Of Sin' respectively.

Not that masterminding tribute albums is the only thing Sampas does. In 2008, he produced the documentary *One Fast Move Or I'm Gone: Kerouac's Big Sur*, which recalled Kerouac's flight from post-*On The Road* fame and notoriety to the isolated retreat of a cabin at Big Sur, California, owned by publisher Lawrence Ferlinghetti (*Big Sur*, the book that came out of Kerouac's time there, is one of the most self-excoriating texts in American literature, as the Beat guru battles alcohol and madness, eventually leading to a complete mental breakdown).

He was also music supervisor on the thriller *Long Distance* and the documentary *Condo Painting*. Oh, and he has this wild idea of maybe doing a movie about *Nebraska*, in which "a rock star with a bitter past (legal hassles with manager etc) escapes to this small house in Jersey and writes these songs. He channels the characters within the songs, whereby they actually visit him one by one in this desolate house and tell their

91

awkward, sad, remorseful, joyous, bittersweet stories." Sounds like a blueprint that could work.

Sampas has always been a Springsteen fan, one of those kids among the group assembled at the local record store entrance, waiting for the shutters to be raised, on the day a new album was launched. "I was probably one of the first people in Lowell, Massachusetts to buy *Nebraska*," he recalls.

"I went home and went through the ritual of listening to it. I was pretty flabbergasted, really shocked. At first, I remember being not really crazy about it. It was a complete departure. It was almost like being a little bit pissed, a little bit angry. You don't know what to make of it at first. It was kind of like, 'What the hell is this thing?' It was something that was somewhat foreign to me. As much as I was heavily into music and listening to everything imaginable, it just wasn't in my music vocabulary. I hadn't really listened to old Folkways recordings and I didn't have a reference point.

"But as I listened to it more it really stated to grow on me and I started to understand what it was. I stuck with it. I tried to understand it. It opened up a whole new world for me – I think it did for a lot of people. It became incredibly influential. I was a singer-songwriter back in the day, and that record was really the one that inspired me to write songs. So the shift in my opinion was pretty dramatic."

'Nebraska', the song itself, blew Sampas away (no pun intended) with its "unforgiving nature", the refusal of its central character to repent for his crimes.

"The whole album has almost a documentary feel to it. It's so real. The way he can depict the characters in a real and honest manner is pretty cool. That song struck me the most and helped me to understand what this record was. Having not really known the story about how it was recorded, it didn't really matter. In hindsight, it became my whole methodology in terms of recording *Badlands*. But back then it didn't matter to me. When you're listening to that record, you're not thinking about how it was recorded. You're just in it. The way it was recorded, looking back and thinking about it as producer, it works so incredibly well in helping you to understand the characters and the songs themselves.

"Here was a time of massive recession in America. The characters within these stories are so colourful, so beautifully depicted, that you get a sense of America, a sense of the struggle and what's going on in people's lives."

Sampas had just finished working on *Condo Painting*, director John McNaughton's documentary on American visual artist George Condo, when the idea to revisit *Nebraska* came to him. "I thought about getting everybody to record on a four-track – that would be a hook to draw in people in a way that wasn't like a normal tribute album. It's more challenging and back to basics as opposed to these 24-track and 48-track recordings everybody was doing. This was a record that had influenced so many people.

"I really thought that the folks who were involved had to have similar sensibilities and styles to Springsteen. I'm really for the idea of trying to have an album where there's consistency. The idea of having the thing not be all over the map as far as genres go. I think that's a recipe for somebody wanting to get off the couch and hit the skip button. I wanted a common thread, musically.

"The whole idea of getting the artists to record in such a minimal fashion, but not necessarily following the original arrangements – I wasn't interested in that. I wanted them to record it minimally and just hear them in a very stark way, with no big effects. I wasn't so concerned about how the thing sounded from a sonic perspective, in that I didn't want everything to be crisp and crystal clear. Almost all of the artists recorded in their homes, similar to what Springsteen was doing on the original record.

Some folks recorded with four tracks, and others went so far as to record on a four-track cassette player, as Springsteen did. Ani DiFranco was one of them, along with Son Volt and Ben Harper. That helped to give it a spooky sound."

First to commit to *Badlands* were the aforementioned Ani DiFranco and Deana Carter, at which stage Sampas had secured a verbal agreement with indie Mammoth Records to issue the album. But then industry politics derailed the proposed deal.

"We were just about to get the papers going for the contracts, when Mammoth signed some hip-hop act they had been told by Disney not to sign, as I understand it. That was the tip of the iceberg from what I heard. Anyway, the bottom line is that Disney pulled their backing from Mammoth. Within just a few days staff were fired and I got the call from the president of the company telling me the project was off. I was shocked and dismayed. Sean Rogers, who really spearheaded the project and was instrumental in getting the project going with Mammoth, had left and gone to Sub Pop. He asked me why I didn't just bring the project over here, so I did."

With a record company secured, Sampas set about completing the line-up. He eventually had too many people for the number of songs at his disposal, much to the disappointment of both Johnny Cash and British singer-songwriter David Gray, for whom *Nebraska* is "a benchmark".

Gray enthuses, "The first four songs are just unbelievable. It's game over, isn't it? It's storytelling of the highest calibre. It's the naked, haunted sound and the simplicity of it – the fact that there's nothing between you and the song, that's what blew me away. He's so understated. There's no bombast, there's no shtick to Springsteen on this record at all. That was what always kept me at arm's length from him and his music.

"I don't think of him as some sort of corny performer now that I'm older and I know his stuff and I can appreciate everything that he does. But at the time I hadn't really tuned in at all to his wavelength. But this record was, and still is, my favourite Springsteen record. It's a record I return to with the same amount of pleasure every time. Something wonderful happens. If you really believe in your craft – and Springsteen clearly does, he takes it very seriously. A song has got to stand on its own first of all, before you put the band behind it and the producer gets involved. You should be able to play it and knock people down with it. He was very much making a statement from the soul with this record. It was an unusual move really, bearing in mind the success it came off the back of."

Cash, who had covered 'Johnny 99' and 'Highway Patrolman' on his 1983 album *Johnny 99*, wanted to do 'Highway Patrolman'. Sampas had already promised the song to Dar Williams.

"His manager couldn't understand that I wouldn't give him a track and he got a bit funny about it…this was Johnny Cash and if he wants that song, by God, he's going to get it. When I spoke to his manager, he was surprised that I had waited so long. He was a little bit frustrated. It was kind of dumb on my part. He should have been one of the first people I thought of," Sampas admits.

He decided to supplement *Badlands* with three additional songs which, according to his research, were recorded by Springsteen during the *Nebraska* sessions (while my research confirmed that 'Downbound Train' was recorded at Colt's Neck, I was unable to determine if this was also the case with 'I'm On Fire' and 'Wages Of Sin'). He gave one of these, 'I'm On Fire', to Cash.

Gray, meanwhile, didn't make the final cut. "I couldn't fit him in," says Sampas. "The record company wouldn't let me do it because it would have delayed the release of the record. That's one regret I have. I think he would have been perfect for it. It's an album that's really influenced him. I didn't get in touch with his management, they got in touch with me, so that shows you how much he wanted to do it."

When Gray speaks of *Nebraska* even now, almost three decades after he borrowed an art teacher's copy, you realise how much it still means to him.

"There's something very personal about it. Springsteen ploughs a certain furrow – he goes to the same terrain again and again and again. Sometimes I'm like, can you go somewhere else? But on this record, never, not for a second. It's the grainy sepia tones of the whole thing – it's just gripping, it's the right medium for the message. It's perfect. The whoops and everything, the atmosphere he gives it…

"He shows his versatility. Not a moment of flashy musicianship on the whole thing, and we all know how capable he is. He is an amazing player. There's no lacquering, no ornamentation, just the barest touches – little bells and a glockenspiel here, little bit of mandolin scratching away, just enough to give a foil to the idea of the song. Sometimes you need something to just take the pressure off the lyric, take it somewhere else. He knew that was enough. There's something that just rings on this record and just continues to ring for me.

"There's not a single song that lets me down on the record. There's an amazing variety in the way that he presents them, from the one where he's chugging on the guitar in a kind of rock'n'roll way and whooping ('State Trooper').

"It sets a standard. It's always there to remind you that less can be more. It's like when I listen to the early Dylan stuff, or Nick Drake, it's spellbinding – you don't need anything else, as long as what you've got is the real thing. That's the difficult thing, to grab that sort of ineffable substance that sometimes comes within your reach. He just bottled it on this record on every single track. I feel it's some sort of personal statement, that's what I read into it, the depth of the emotion. Everything seems to be permeated with…I wouldn't call it nostalgia, but there's a sharp, tangible sense of looking back. He uses that emotion a lot, but there's something more acute about it on this record for me."

It remains an instructive album for Gray as a songwriter, as well as one whose likeness he aspires to create one day. "There are things that it definitely taught me. Songs begin with a rhythm, even if you're a lyric writer – there's rhythm in the words or some music in language and maybe you want to add a guitar to it, or maybe you start with the guitar and then you find the rhythm of the melody and the words on top of it. But when Springsteen's playing 'Highway Patrolman', it's the most beautifully constructed, simple arrangement, chordings all very straightforward, and you're with the swing of it and the drama of the song's building. It's brilliant detail. He takes you through a decade in a couple of sentences, but you don't feel like you're being rushed towards anything. In fact, the actual pace of the story is slow in that there's not that much detail about what's actually going on, just these flashes from his life – a series of Polaroids get pinned up on the board and he beautifully tacks them all together.

"You're into the hypnosis of the song, so you're getting used to the way the lines pay off at the end. You're getting used to the rhyming scheme. And then he interrupts it with the most wonderfully deft thing. He stops playing the guitar and there's that long line about pulling over to the side of the highway and watching the tail-lights disappear. He breaks the rhythm of it and it's just the most wonderful thing because, as he stops the music, you watch the tail-lights disappear with him. It's a brilliant trick.

"He's so good at what I call dropping the shoulder. It's like someone running towards you in football; you think they're going one way and then they go the other. He's so brilliant at that sleight of hand, or whatever you want to call it. You think you can see the punchline coming but he stops and arrests you with just a moment of silence. Even on a record when there's nothing going on, he still reduces again for his moment of drama. That little moment is the key moment on that record for me.

"The whole thing is like a giant wheel with the stars turning around, and that's the sort of Pole Star, that little moment in the middle. That's something that has never left me, ever since I noticed that. And I've heard him do it again in other songs, in other ways. He's a very clever musician. He's never afraid to use the simplest means possible. That's a testament to his strength.

"There's a part of me burning to do that. It's almost where I'm ending up. I can almost see myself standing just on my own for a little while."

When Springsteen himself heard about the *Badlands* project, he expressed his support through his attorney and offered to help Sampas however he could. It was an offer the producer declined.

"When you're doing these projects, you kind of wonder if you should go the folks and ask them and get their blessing. Certainly you want to do that for contractual reasons. It's always a fine line. I don't know how much you want the artist to be involved in the process because then all of a sudden it's like an authorised biography. It's like the kiss of death. I actually never asked for Bruce's help because the project was just resonating with people so much."

Badlands is, for the most part, reverential, as if the artists are fearful of trampling over hallowed ground. Or perhaps they're inhibited by Sampas' insistence that they adhere to the four-track recording format of Springsteen's original. There is slightly more adventure musically than vocally, with nobody daring to replicate or even emulate Springsteen's ethereal delivery. Crooked Fingers' 'Mansion On The Hill' sounds as if it's been infiltrated by that pious pilgrim in the woolly hat, U2's The Edge.

"I did the exact opposite of what *Nebraska* was production-wise, and made the sounds wider and more processed, with timed delay on the piano in particular," says Crooked Fingers frontman Eric Bachmann.

"I also sampled a fiddle from Hank Williams' 'Mansion On The Hill' and placed it at the end of the song to tie it to its roots as best I could. I'm not a purist though, so I didn't do that to satisfy any musical morality I have. It just sounded cool to me at the time and still does. But if I'm interpreting someone else's song, I don't have a specific approach that I use every time. If anything, I try and not repeat any approach. That's pretty hard to do though."

Bachmann was travelling through either Utah or Montana – "some big sky place" – with his then band, the Archers of Loaf, in 1993, when the merchandise man put *Nebraska* on the tape deck. "I didn't think too much of it. I had heard bits of it before as a kid, but I never paid it too much mind because I liked rock and the E Street Band and drums and the whole thing. It wasn't really a dramatic moment or anything, but we just sat quietly and listened the whole way through. Then every day for the rest of that tour we listened to it again and again. It just kind of quietly crept its way into my favourites list, like it always existed or something and there was no real need to state the obvious about how great it was."

For Bachmann, 'Highway Patrolman', and especially the scene where the brothers, Joe and Frank, take turns dancing with Maria, is "a strikingly efficient piece of writing because that stanza encompasses a universal family dynamic so well: closeness and conflict. It's hyperbole because one's a cop and one's a criminal, but all siblings deal with that on some level and he describes it so well in only a moment."

Bachmann has a friend who believes *Nebraska* is the audio equivalent of Sherwood Anderson's short-story cycle, *Winesburg, Ohio*, which is structured around the life of one George Willard from childhood to his independence and eventual abandonment of Winesburg as a young man.

"*Nebraska* and *Winesburg* are both easy to relate to because the characters are just like dudes you went to high school with," says Bachmann. "Or worse, just like you. It doesn't matter that the stories take place in different decades. It's extremely character-driven and the characters are all emotionally devastated by the fact that they didn't become what they thought they should have become. And as a result they felt forced to make decisions based on hostility, resentment and desperation, like the American Dream is a lie."

Los Lobos turn 'Johnny 99' into swinging Tex-Mex you can almost hear Ben Harper's rocking chair on a pastoral, down-home version of 'My Father's House', while Son Volt infuse 'Open All Night' with a club-footed waltz kind of vibe.

Given that she picked it because "it seemed the least like anything I'd ever written", Dar Williams does 'Highway Patrolman' pretty much as Dar Williams –

which is not a criticism. "I paid attention to the lyrics and thought about who I would be in that in narrator's shoes," she says.

"But the amazing thing is that as I sang it I found more and more meanings to lyrics like, 'I got a brother named Frankie, and Frankie ain't no good'. The story of the song got more complicated with every take."

She hears "a landscape of struggle and loneliness" in *Nebraska*. "Every country can be depicted this way, but I think it's thanks to people like Bruce Springsteen and John Prine that we see a uniquely American way of accepting or living with it."

Ani DiFranco's 'Used Cars' is about the strangest thing on the album – strangely beautiful, that is. Stranger still, but for the wrong reasons, is Hank Williams III's 'Atlantic City', a country hoedown replete with yodelling that forgets, at least until the song's climax, that this is tragedy, not comedy. And he's supposed to be a chip off his granddaddy's block.

"Hank III was trying to do something different, take it in a different direction," explains Sampas. "I actually had to edit it. It was much longer. The raucous kind of thing he does with it, it's playful. But the thing about these tribute albums, people either love them or hate them."

A straw poll of Springsteen loyalists reveals that, when it comes to 'Atlantic City', majority opinion resides in the latter camp.

Eighteen years after *Nebraska*, Jim Sampas' *Badlands* was already an indicator of the influential reach and contemporary resonance of Springsteen's modestly recorded 1982 album.

"It's funny, because when you think of Bruce Springsteen anytime beyond *Nebraska*, you don't necessarily think of him as a musician's musician," says Sampas. "That's not an insult necessarily. But he's not the type of artist, in my experience, who a lot of musicians gravitate to. Everyday people from all walks of life get into him, of course, but *Nebraska* was very much different. That record influenced everybody.

"I think that musicians started to take him very seriously post-*Nebraska*. I think that it was really instrumental in helping to usher in the whole alt-country genre of music that we know today. Certainly there was a lot of stuff going on before. But this working man Americana, the detail and the depth of the work, and the pain inside it, the conflicts – all these things – it feels like they weren't being spoken of at that moment. And I think, not only the way that he recorded it but what he was conveying, was incredibly influential... probably the most influential album of the Eighties."

As a songwriter, Springsteen "got really efficient" on *Nebraska*, according to Eric Bachmann. "He was verbose, especially on the early stuff, and even though he got more lyrically dexterous as he got on from *Greetings...* to *The Wild, The Innocent And The E Street Shuffle* to *Born To Run*, it's really noticeable on *Nebraska*. There is absolutely no fat and all of the stories and denizens occupying them are really compelling and relatable. What's so distinctive about him is that the songs are severely character-driven. I'm surprised that there aren't more films like *The Indian Runner* based on Springsteen characters or storylines.

"I can't think of many pop musician/songwriters who start songs saying, 'My name is Joe Roberts and I work for the state.' It's almost like with the way he wrote songs he was intending for himself to be hanging out in a bar like John Prine or Townes Van Zandt, but accidentally found himself shaking his ass in front of 22,000 people. If he pulled that off on purpose, that's pretty damn impressive."

Dar Williams doesn't believe Springsteen necessarily got better as a songwriter on *Nebraska*, rather that he began exploring characters with more of a back story. "But he was always using great, loaded words in describing people on the edge," she adds.

"I think on *Nebraska* he accomplished with words and production what Martin Scorsese did with camera and direction. His voice is consistently clear and beautiful, but the narration sounds grainy, blurry, or coming from an unexpected angle – like the line, 'I pulled over the side of the highway and watched his tail-lights disappear'. It's very cinematic and it also fills out the picture of the narrator's physical and emotional terrain. Poetically, that's either a lot of permission or a lot of responsibility to pass on to future songwriters."

Eric Bachmann admits that the *Nebraska* influence on his own songwriting has been so overt at times, he's had to dispense with several songs, while others have made it into the public domain. I can think of exactly three songs that I wrote and released and probably shouldn't have because they were too influenced by Springsteen. That said, I would consider him to be less influential to me in terms of songwriting than a few other songwriters. He's just so ubiquitous that you can't avoid him, especially if your father's family is from New Jersey like mine is.

"What I find influential about him is more about the inspirational aspects of what he's doing, not a particular songwriting quality. Like music is a religious experience that can save you, or at least distract you long enough to keep you from putting a bullet in your head for another day."

Two other kinds of *Nebraska* tribute took place in 2006 and 2008, both under the banner of *The Nebraska Project*. The first was a free concert at the World Financial Centre in New York as part of that city's Guitar Festival (a three-week examination of "virtually every aspect of the guitar's musical personality") and featured a rotating cast of musicians interpreting songs from the album. The second was a drama inspired by Springsteen's narratives staged by the Chicago-based Bruised Orange Theatre Group.

Nebraska was the first Springsteen album that Guitar Festival director David Spelman, a late convert, owned. "I'm embarrassed to admit that this was almost twenty years after its release. In the late Nineties, I was living in New York City and decided to buy a summer home on the Jersey shore. A friend kidded me that I might be breaking a state ordinance in that I didn't have any Springsteen recordings at my new place. I set out to right the wrong before the local authorities caught wind of the infraction.

"I remembered reading that Springsteen recorded *Nebraska* at home on a little Tascam four-track Portastudio. I'd always been fascinated by early field recordings, as well as later-day recordings made in hotel rooms, tour buses or barns. Chris

Whitley's *Dirt Floor*, Michelle Shocked's *Texas Campfire Tapes*, and parts of Jackson Browne's *Running On Empty* are some examples of this type of record that had spoken to me. I'd even owned one of those Tascam recorders in high school, though the recordings I made on it were unlistenable!

"I also remembered that many musicians and critics considered it his best work, and that it was on many best-of-the-decade lists. So I made a trip to a nearby record store and brought home *Nebraska*.

"I was in one part flummoxed by it, and in another part fascinated and really attracted to it. It was nothing like the E Street Band sound that I associated with Springsteen. It seemed to be everything his anthemic hits were not, and I was drawn into the stripped down acoustic ballads about courageous people living on the edges of society."

For Spelman, *Nebraska* carries the spirit of great American works of literature, in particular Walker Evans and James Agee's *Let Us Now Praise Famous Men*, John Steinbeck's *The Grapes Of Wrath* and Upton Sinclair's *The Jungle*. And in common with these classics, *Nebraska* is shaped by its creator's sense of artistry.

"Five or six years ago, the Metropolitan Museum of Art in New York mounted an exhibition of Vincent Van Gogh's drawings. Seeing more than a hundred pen and ink, charcoal and chalk images, alongside related paintings of his, gave me a new sense of Van Gogh's brilliance and evolution.

"Similarly, listening to *Nebraska* alongside his work with the E Street Band, has given me a much fuller sense of the range of Springsteen's artistry. *Nebraska* may be overshadowed by the fame and the familiarity of Springsteen's other work, but without it we are left with an incomplete picture of what this artist is capable of.

"Van Gogh's comment that 'drawing is at the root of everything' reminds me of how you can often get the clearest insight into an artist by hearing his or her songs performed solo, without a band. Sometimes this happens on a stage, and some of us are fortunate enough to occasionally hear artists alone in our kitchens or our living rooms or in a recording studio. It may not be the most polished or commercially successful way for an artist to present their work, but it can be the most vulnerable and often the most revealing."

Other commitments meant that many of those on Spelman's wish list for the New York concert couldn't make it. These included Steve Earle, Jeff Tweedy of Wilco, Ryan Adams and Emmylou Harris. But according to *Backstreets*, the Springsteen fanzine, the line-up was "nonetheless impressive, and some of the evening's best performances came from lesser-known artists".

Disc jockey John Platt delivered a brief summary of *Nebraska*'s provenance before Michelle Shocked opened the show with 'Nebraska'. She was followed by Jesse Harris ('Atlantic City'), The National ('Mansion On The Hill'), Chocolate Genius (alias Marc Anthony Thompson, later a member of Springsteen's Seeger Sessions Band, who did 'Johnny 99') and Martha Wainwright ('Highway Patrolman'). Jen Chapin, daughter of Harry Chapin, diverted from the *Nebraska* running order with a version of 'Born In The USA', accompanied only by husband Stephen Crump on stand-up bass, while Harry Manx performed the one other non-*Nebraska* song, 'I'm On Fire'. Dan Zanes and Vernon Reid, formerly of Del Fuegos and Living Colour, joined forces for 'State Trooper', while Laura Cantrell did 'Used Cars' (praising *Nebraska* for having the right mix of despair and "real spirited defiance"). The set was closed out by Otis Taylor ('Open All Night') American Music Club's Mark Eitzel ('My Father's House') and Drivin'n'Cryin's Kevn Kinney (backed by Lenny Kaye on 'Reason To Believe').

And then the whole roster of artists assembled on stage for the obligatory jam – with a surprise guest. Earlier in the evening, Springsteen, who was with wife Patti Scialfa, called World Financial Centre productions director Shannon Mayers on her mobile phone. "Hey, this is Bruce Springsteen. We're close by, but I think we're lost," he said. Mayers had to give him directions.

When Spelman invited Springsteen to lead the communal choir on 'Oklahoma Hills', his response was, "Which one is that?" – even though it had featured in his set on the *Devils & Dust* tour a year earlier (and would later, of course, feature on *We Shall Overcome: The Seeger Sessions*). Spelman sang him a chorus and Springsteen was off.

"I believe the Boss is in the house," Platt announced to the audience before Springsteen stepped up to the microphone and launched into the first verse. Afterwards, as he acknowledged the other performers with a bow, Platt asked him, "Did we get any of it wrong? Is there anything I said that was misrepresented, inaccurate?" To which Springsteen quipped, "A lot of the interpretations of the songs…were wrong. Most of the songs were written, as I've said about all rock'n'roll, to get women to pull their pants down."

Bruised Orange is a not-for-profit theatre company formed in 2004 by a small group of Northern Illinois University graduates. In 2008, it staged a month-long run of *The Nebraska Project* (an original script by Clint Sheffer, storied by an ensemble cast and directed by John Morrison) at Chicago's Side Project Theatre.

Another Bruised Orange director, Mark Spence, who worked on *The Nebraska Project*, explains the premise of the drama.

"It is 1984. Two naïve and angry teens take the opportunity of a flood to take a small New Jersey town hostage. In a misled gesture to prove their competency, Mike and Barry, armed with their father's guns, guard the only exit out of town with the other exit, an old bridge, washed out by a flood. With the power out, Whitney is out looking for her drunk father, only to find a recently shot homeless man, Roy. Allie, a stranger on the run after a money grab from Atlantic City, finds herself in a small town. She is taken in by a secretive local woman, Mary.

Whitney and Roy see the lights on at Mary's house and seek help with Roy's gunshot wound. Barry and Mike, realising they accidentally shot someone, have a falling-out and Mike leaves Barry to guard the road. Mary, Whitney, Allie and Roy find shelter in Mary's bomb shelter. While discussing a way to get out of the town to find help for Roy, a local Vietnam vet, Jeffries, hiding in the bomb shelter, reveals himself to help with the plan, offering both his war experience and his gun. He is caught by

Barry. In a scuffle for Barry's rifle, Jeffries accidentally shoots Barry, but not before getting shot himself.

"Meanwhile, back at the shelter, Mary finds herself with another visitor, Mike. Seeing Mike's reaction to the now almost dead Roy, she believes Mike is the one who shot Roy. In an effort to get to the truth, Mary confesses her real identity – Caril Ann Fugate, accomplice to Charlie Starkweather. Whitney finds Jeffries and Barry. Jeffries is barely holding on, and Whitney chooses to stay with him, hoping help will come around now that the storm is over and the morning comes."

The Nebraska Project, abandoning convention, was initiated and executed as a collaboration. Spence, a native of Nebraska, didn't hear the album for the first time until he moved away to college.

"When I grew up, Springsteen was really identified with his *Born In The USA* stereotypical image – one of a bombastic, jingoistic rock star. Obviously nothing could be further from the truth, but that was always my perception of Springsteen. It wasn't until college that a friend of mine introduced me to *Darkness On The Edge Of Town* and *Nebraska* that my eyes were really opened, and from then on I re-examined the whole catalogue. I immediately became obsessed.

"Springsteen's third-person character really goes to another level on that album. He has always written characters, but they had been surrounded by varying degrees of romanticism. With *Nebraska*, the romanticism was gone."

So what did Spence hear in the songs on *Nebraska* that made him think they would work in the theatrical medium?

"Probably because of how untheatrical it is. It isn't *Born To Run*. The stories of the creation of the album, the technical difficulties, Springsteen coming to terms with his world view, his personal relationships, are much more theatrical than the album. We originally looked at the album because of the sparseness of the songs, and of course the strong sense of character. But once we delved into the mythos of the album itself, the project started to solidify.

"A project like this would very much be expected to be a series of vignettes, or a literal song to scene project. Instead we discussed the themes of the album, what was happening in the country, how we perceived Springsteen interpreting it, and went from there."

The only difficulties Bruised Orange encountered stemmed from personnel issues. "We wanted the writing of the show to be very collaborative, and spent a long time talking about how we wanted to represent the album. The song narratives became a starting point. As a company we are addicted to plot and story. Since there is no real overall plot or story on the album, we had to develop one. Of the themes on the album, we were interested in exploring job as identity, community, violence and middle class helplessness. Once we made it past our bumps in the road, the script was developed rather easily – as easy as any script is."

The play was well received by those critics, although Chicago's *Time Out* magazine felt that "the rambling poetry that can be so conducive to folk music doesn't always serve the dramatic event and, despite committed work from a resourceful young cast, Sheffer's textual sauntering and inertia occasionally allow his audience to space out".

Springsteen himself never got to see this abstract interpretation of *Nebraska*. Spence again: "We were unsure of some copyright issues regarding the show. We did send a letter, not expecting any real response. At the same time, we didn't want to push hard and run into copyright infringements. I personally thought it would have been great press if our show did get shut down! But from the research I've done on Bruce, I doubted that would happen."

12. STREET PUNK GENIUS

"I was completely unprepared for what came out of the speakers.
  My first thought was, 'What the hell is this?'"

DAVID PESCI on hearing *Nebraska* for the first time

"I remember standing back, away from the speakers, and thinking,
  'What the fuck is this?'"

DAVID MEANS has a similar reaction

To echo Eric Bachmann's comment in the previous chapter, it is surprising that *The Indian Runner* remains the only Bruce Springsteen song thus far to have been translated into the language of cinema. The medium has always been an immense influence on Springsteen's work, a fact reflected in many of his song titles. Think 'Thunder Road' (which, as has already been alluded to, was named after the 1958 noir classic starring Robert Mitchum), 'All That Heaven Will Allow' (inspired by the 1955 Douglas Sirk melodrama *All That Heaven Allows*), 'Atlantic City' (Louis Malle's 1980 fusion of romance, crime and drama, *Atlantic City*, starring Burt Lancaster and Susan Sarandon) and 'Point Blank' (John Boorman's 1967 crime classic, *Point Blank*, featuring Lee Marvin) for starters.

Springsteen himself has been involved in the medium as a songwriter on Paul Schrader's *Light Of Day* (for which he wrote the title track), Jonathan Demme's *Philadelphia* (to which he contributed the Oscar-winning 'Streets Of Philadelphia') and Darren Aronofsky's *The Wrestler*.

His songs, nowhere more so than on *Nebraska*, are ideally disposed to adaptation in other forms, as you've seen already in Bruised Orange's *The Nebraska Project*, and as you will see later in this chapter through the fiction of Tennessee Jones. I would suggest that, given the cinematic scope of Springsteen's writing, the arc and authority of his narratives and the psychological depth with which he invests his characters, they incorporate the essential raw materials with which any filmmaker worth his or her salt (and of sufficient sensibility) should be able to cast into film. Yet only Sean Penn has done so.

The Indian Runner is based on 'Highway Patrolman'. Penn has located the story in Sixties Nebraska, with David Morse playing Joe, Viggo Mortensen as Frank and Valeria Golino as Maria (there are also roles for Charles Bronson, Dennis Hopper, Patricia Arquette and even Penn's mother, Eileen Ryan). As in the song (to which Penn's script, written in just a month, is faithful), Joe is the conscientious brother, doing the job of deputy sheriff to support his young family after the bank foreclosed on his farm; Frank, according to his father (Bronson), is infected with "restlessness", shorthand for having a criminal inclination.

Penn told *Interview* magazine in 1991 that 'Highway Patrolman' addressed a problem that haunted millions of households. "What do you do when one son is noble, and the other seeks out trouble? How far will that good brother go to help a sibling who is on the road to hell? And what happens when the good brother realises that in order to keep his life so sane, and so unlike his brother's, he has given up the fire of desire?"

He adds, "It touches on a lot of things that interest me but purposely leaves them unresolved. I say purposely, but what I really mean is, we don't know the answers."

Penn, as director, found it impossible to come down on the side of one sibling or the other, "the good brother or the bad". He didn't believe in such absolutes. "Nobody is a total prick. There's shades of that in all of us."

The Indian Runner, apart from being an accomplished directorial debut by someone who, as an actor, had given very little indication until then of the artist he would later become – both before and behind the camera – realises in celluloid those pictures that *Nebraska* as a whole, and 'Highway Patrolman' in particular, conjures in the minds of the listener, not to mention the emotional conflict it provokes. In other words, Penn gets the song completely; he understands that it's not at all as simple as it seems but contains many a complex truth about what it is to be human.

Tennessee Jones was raised in the mountains of East Tennessee, where three generations of his family lived cheek by jowl in a little holler and "the horizon of opportunity was very limited". His parents grew a tobacco crop to supplement their meagre incomes as a sheet metal mechanic and seamstress.

"I grew up poor, and many of my family's attitudes about education and work made no sense to me," he explains. "The idea was that school was for elite bastards and that honest people worked hard, didn't have a lot of money and would inherit heaven. My mother in particular managed to find hope, but it was tempered with a fatalism that made it impossible for her to believe she could ever impact the world, or get a better job, or even have people take her ideas seriously."

Jones eventually left, hitchhiking around America and producing his own magazines before settling in New York and becoming an editor at Soft Skull Press. It was the latter that published *Deliver Me From Nowhere*, his collection of short stories inspired by *Nebraska*.

Where Penn is true to the tenor of 'Highway Patrolman' in *The Indian Runner*, Jones mostly uses Springsteen's words as templates for his own idiosyncratic exploration of loneliness, desperation, loss of faith and "attempting to find the courage to be after hope has left". Some of the stories do give the kind of weight to Springsteen's narratives that isn't possible within the rigidly disciplined structure of song – 'Atlantic City', 'Used Cars' and 'Johnny 99', for example, are all close to the Springsteen texts, or at least the essence of them.

Meanwhile, others take you places, in terms of plot, that are as far removed from what Springsteen wrote as it is possible to get (if anything, they owe more to Flannery O'Connor). And so Frank Roberts is revealed as a homosexual rapist in 'Highway

Patrolman', while the son in 'My Father's House' was once a daughter before he was "no longer a girl and no longer a boy". It wouldn't be fair to divulge any more about this anthology that, in the words of novelist Eileen Myles, "leaves a residue you can't escape". I would instead urge you to seek it out in your local bookstore, or, failing that, online.

Jones knew he wanted to do something in a fictional sense with *Nebraska* when he heard 'Johnny 99' for the first time. "I was somewhere in the Midwest, it was dark and cold outside and I was in a stranger's car. I had the idea pretty much immediately that I'd like to write a story to that song, but I didn't actually start writing the collection 'till I was twenty three.

"After *The Rising* came out, I saw Springsteen play about ten times in one year. I was only making a few thousand dollars a year at that time, and I spent a huge portion of my money on the shows. I started thinking more and more about *Nebraska* and what an amazing piece of work it is, and how many of the songs talked about the relationship of class and faith in America, which was exactly what I wanted to be writing about."

Jones circled around the songs, trying to figure out what he really wanted to say in his stories. "I hadn't spent a lot of time in the Midwest and I wanted to get the feeling of the landscape just right, so I talked a close friend of mine into taking a month-long camping trip. I think landscape often forms who we are, down to some of our metaphysical beliefs about the world.

"We went over back roads in the most desolate places I'd ever seen – and I grew up in a very rural place in the Appalachians. Being in that landscape helped me to get a better handle on the feeling of the album and the desolation I wanted to come out in my stories.

"I worked on a few stories at a time, usually beginning with a pretty literal translation of the lyrics that I would move away from over time. Eventually the stories began to grow and have lives of their own, and sometimes I was just along for the ride.

"One thing that's important to mention – all of *Nebraska*'s songs are told by men. Nothing wrong with that, but I wanted to write a book that could examine class at the intersections of gender and sexuality as well. Writing from the perspective of different kinds of people allowed me interesting opportunities to examine power."

One "pretty literal translation" of Springsteen is in the opening story (the stories each share the titles and follow the order of the songs on the album), 'Nebraska', although Jones' narrator is, like in Terrence Malick's *Badlands*, the Caril Fugate model rather than that of Charles Starkweather.

"That was the most difficult story for me to write, because I could find no moral redeeming quality in the character based on Starkweather. It wasn't only uninteresting to try to write the story from a sociopath's point of view, it was repugnant to me.

"A friend suggested I watch *Badlands*, and Sissy Spacek's portrayal of the young girl was definitely influential to finding a voice for my own character."

And what about Frank Roberts' sadistic assault on the boy named Luke Bloom in 'Highway Patrolman'? Where did that come from? "I wanted to write about small town queers. The stakes are often much higher for us, and for no reason other than simply just being who we are. I wanted to show how some people think they can get away with doing terrible things, especially if they feel there is a moral reason for doing it. I wanted to show how much Luke Bloom's life was devalued in that town."

The stories in *Deliver Me From Nowhere*, as has already been mentioned, are as much shaped by Flannery O'Connor as by Springsteen's songs. "She's the most obvious and salient literary influence on *Nebraska* for me – the imagery in the songs, particularly the biblical references and the expressions of faith and faithlessness contained in the lyrics. There is also occasionally a kind of droll humour – the man poking a dead dog with a stick in 'Reason To Believe' – that is also reminiscent of O'Connor. The story, 'Reason To Believe', was my attempt to pay homage to O'Connor, particularly her story, 'Revelation'. I also wanted to express a particular strain of faith that exists where I'm from in Appalachia."

Jones isn't the only writer for whom *Nebraska* is something of a touchstone. It has also informed the fiction of David Pesci and David Means.

Pesci's best known work, *Amistad*, is a fictionalised account of a 19th Century slave rebellion on board a ship bound for America. In 1997, it was filmed by Steven Spielberg and an all-star cast, including Morgan Freeman, Anthony Hopkins and Matthew McConaughey.

"Everything you respect and embrace informs your work on some level," he says. "I never said to myself, 'I want to write my *Nebraska*'. At the same time, the songs from that record still pop into my head all the time. The characters are real and I'm sure I have drawn on them, or my image of them, when I have worked on books or screenplays."

Means, whose most recent short-story collection, *The Spot*, had some critics mention him in the same breath as Johns Cheever and Updike, keeps the framed *Nebraska* album cover above his desk, a constant reminder that "the important thing is to tell stories honestly. No matter how complex a story might be, the core has to be honest and real."

The album "opened a door" for Means, serving as a creative and ethical blueprint for his own writing. "The little hoots Bruce makes, the references to 'mister', the stories of lonely souls, the fact that each song unites narrative with tone, with a sense that a man singing alone into a microphone, doing it all himself, uniting story with bare-bones music, all combined somehow for me, the way good art can, to teach me something about myself that helped me find my way into how to write the stories I wanted to write but didn't know I wanted to write.

"I think part of the complexity of listening to the record is the fact that you know that Springsteen is a big star, rich, up there on the mountain top, and yet he can dig down and find a deeply authentic voice for people who are submerged. Art can do that. The art itself has to grab hold of the real. Too many people put the artist up to a litmus test of authenticity. They think that in order to embody, or to capture, stories, you have to be living with them somehow yourself. We had that in music for a long time, the big, bombastic rock stars singing about themselves as a way of proving they were real. Springsteen tore that apart by writing songs about adults, about the real world.

"My stories are akin to songs in *Nebraska* in that they're only fragments of longer narratives, given over to the listener or the reader. They start and finish and throw the weight of the story onto the listener, who has the task of carrying them forward. Listening to Nebraska over and over, after I'd written two books, helped remind me that my obligation was to make truthful tones and songs, to leave enough space, enough reverb, to capture the isolation of that part of the world."

This space to which Means refers is a key element in Springsteen's songs post-*Born To Run*. It's something, certainly from a literary perspective (and lyrics crafted well constitute literature), that's difficult to achieve; the choice of words and images becomes crucial, as does the necessity for some hard editing.

"The best writers use very few words to tell a story. Bruce Springsteen is succinct without being incomplete. He has four-minute records that are deeper than many 300-page novels," says David Pesci. But, of course, narratives only have as much depth as their characters – another reason why, according to both Pesci and Means, *Nebraska* endures.

Pesci again: "'Used Cars' really resonated with me at the time because we'd never had a new car in my family, just a string of used cars – some real clunkers too. Different-coloured body parts, needing jumps on cold mornings, ten years old and dying kind of duds. I think we even bought a station wagon from the nuns at the local convent. Think about that – a car that even nuns, who probably only used it to go to the market and church functions in other towns, didn't want.

"When I got into my teen years I really hated our cars. They looked like crap and were always breaking down. But I knew as much as I hated them, my Dad hated them more. He'd always say, 'A good used car is better than a new car'. It must have killed him a little inside every time he had to say that to me and my brothers and sisters."

Pesci admits he found *Nebraska* challenging on the first couple of listens. "I remember getting to the third song or so, hearing the first few bars and thinking, 'Wait a second, is this just a slow side, fast side thing?' I lifted the arm, flipped the record and played the first track of side two. Same thing, very stark and acoustic. I think I dropped the needle on every song after that just to see if any rockers were on there. When I realised that this was the album, I think I actually checked the album cover and any notes to make sure it was him.

"This was so different than anything that was on the radio or anywhere. I remember thinking, 'This is like an early Bob Dylan album, only much more pissed-off and dire'. I listened to it another time through and then later told a buddy of mine who liked the Clash and more hardcore punk stuff about it. I remember saying something to him along the lines of, 'It almost sounds like someone who's been through a war, but not on the side that won. Not suicidal, just pissed off and helpless'.

"He had a much better stereo than mine, so we listened to it together. At the end he said, 'This thing is punk. It's stripped down, naked, we're all screwed, slash your wrists and walk down the street punk genius'."

Having reconciled himself to the fact this was indeed the Springsteen of *Born To Run* and *Darkness On The Edge Of Town*, having availed himself of his buddy's insight and secured the latter's seal of punk credibility for *Nebraska*, Pesci eventually connected with it through the characters. "I felt like I knew some of these people well, and the ones I didn't, I could see right away. The characters are fully drawn for the most part. And they are adults.

"Also, in much of his other music, there was a theme about hope, inspiration, the urgency of wanting to break out from your current situation and the seizing of redemption through your own actions. On *Nebraska* there's desperation and resignation. Hope and inspiration for the most part have trickled away. Some characters – the guy on 'Open All Night', 'Used Cars', the people in 'Reason To Believe' – are clinging to some sense of possibility, of a chance for something better maybe. For the rest, life has become hollow, and hope is just a way to delude yourself in off moments when you're not feeling the suffocating crush of reality."

Means grew up near a paper mill and railroad yard in the industrial heartland of Michigan. His neighbour, a drunk, had a job at the mill. Hearing *Nebraska*, he felt "a deep sense that the sound was the sound of my own world somehow.

"Some nights, when my neighbour came home drunk, he'd sit on his front porch and talk to himself in a mumble and make strange hooting sounds, and those sounds were coming out of my speakers. When great art arrives it feels totally familiar, and the strangeness is that of looking in the mirror for the first time in years and stepping back and saying, 'Holy shit!'

"'Mansion On The Hill' hit me hard because I understood the metaphor: the rich up on the hill, the guiding light of hope, the American Dream incarnate in material things, the iron fence around the estate, the lines drawn between the poor and the rich, the fact that one step away the shambles of poverty were hidden.

"The wolf howls opening 'Johnny 99'. The train-like roiling forward of that song, everything plunging forward. Then, of course, 'State Trooper', that licence registration, 'I ain't got none'. The story there, the sense of guilt, of driving through landscape and hoping not to be caught – we all live like that one way or another. Then those cold, hard, sad laments of sound at the end, again alone, in his house. That was Bruce howling, and the narrator. It felt, and still feels, extremely real. You hear it around the edge of the recording equipment when there is that wonderful distortion, uncorrected, unfixed. My problem with the way Springsteen is recording now is that he cleans all that shit up; his voice is brought up front and it's no longer real."

For David Means, these songs, these stories, nail down what art on a larger scale cannot – the vastness of and complete paradox that is America. "What you hear on *Nebraska* is the tones of the country combined with stories of hope and loss combined with the ethos of America," he says.

"Anyone can hit it big, and anyone – at least in theory – can take the fall from grace. Used cars lead to new cars. But you can suddenly find yourself back in a used car. Any great work of art, from *The Great Gatsby* to the movie *Badlands*, exposes a different part of national identity. The great thing about *Nebraska* is that all you have to do is put it on and you're in there deep.

"When *Nebraska* came out, the surface story was that Reagan's America was in full swing, the grand delusion was roaring ahead, and here comes this record laying everything bare. We all know the media side, the mythic side of America; we all know about the Hollywood side of things, and part of that story is true. But as soon as you hear something like *Nebraska*, you're brought into a correct orientation with the complete picture and suddenly become aware of the real America."

This real America that Springsteen explores on *Nebraska* – an America which, contrary to the public relations campaigns conducted through a propagandist media, bankrolled by the corporations and cheered by slavish politicians, is not so much the promised land as a land like any other; a land in which opportunity is thwarted as much as it is presented, in which hope is taken away as much as it is given; a land in which reside millions of people with broken hearts and broken minds, surrounded by the debris of their broken dreams.

And it is this real America that Springsteen conferred with a kind of legitimacy through *Nebraska*, in the same way that John Steinbeck did through *The Grapes Of Wrath* or Edward Hopper did with paintings such as 'Nighthawks' or Arthur Fellig (alias Weegee) did in his photojournalism. It also provided a stimulus for musicians who were both Springsteen's contemporaries and those who came in his wake, to explore similar thematic territory.

"I think for mainstream artists, seeing someone of Bruce's stature doing this (*Nebraska*), was empowering on a certain level," says Pesci. "It really was courageous to turn that in. I can imagine the A&R guys going nuts. But soon after you had Elvis Costello's *King Of America*, and the rise of artists like Billy Bragg. Tell me they can sell that to their record companies without *Nebraska* already on the landscape?

"Also, in the late Eighties and early Nineties, when so many artists embraced going 'unplugged', I thought this was the natural progression in the music business from *Nebraska*. I've heard people in the music press say, '*Nebraska* was the start of all this.' There may be some merit in that, but I've always thought that the whole 'unplugged' approach was more a re-presentation of established stuff, old hits in a new semi-folk format. *Nebraska* wasn't a take on old songs. It was stripped down in both instrumentation and presentation, because that was the songs for that moment in time and in his career. In a way it's a perfect album."

It may well, as Pesci suggests, have been an album of its time, an album that could only have come out of an America in the grip of an economic depression, but for David Means it has a timeless quality. This is a view I share. Great art, whatever the medium, transcends its conception and birth, reverberating down through the ages, striking a familiar chord with each new generation. After all, history does have an unfortunate habit of repeating itself.

"It drew in so many things all at once and felt obvious," he says. "It's a primary document. It's like the original American Constitution – sun-faded, weird, but alive and connected with the present moment. Already I get the sense that the culture has caught up with it again and again. It informed grunge even though grunge didn't know it at the time. And in the future, it's going to inform again and again. I have young friends who have never heard of it, and when they go listen to it, they come back and say, 'What the fuck? This is amazing, this is great. Why didn't I know about this?'"

13. DARK ALLEYS

"My heroes, from Hank Williams to Frank Sinatra to Bob Dylan, were popular musicians. They had hits. There was value in trying to connect with a larger audience."

BRUCE SPRINGSTEEN

"It needed to get thrown out there and see what happened: interpreted, correctly interpreted, misinterpreted, used upside down, ass-backwards, straight-atcha... Meaning is a communal cocktail."

BRUCE SPRINGSTEEN on the song 'Born In The USA'

How many of you remember the diktat (with the accompanying skull and crossbones logo), "Home taping is killing music"? And how many of you committed or were accessories to such a crime? I'll certainly confess to my part in this audio mass murder. Most Sunday evenings I could be found with my functional Ferguson tape recorder lined up against the radio waiting to depress the 'Play' and 'Record' buttons whenever a favourite song appeared on the chart countdown.

I wasn't that aware of my criminal activity at the time, or if I was, I wasn't that bothered. I didn't have a record player, and if I had it's unlikely I would have been successful in attempting to scrounge the requisite price of a single off my parents. So killing music by home taping seemed like the only alternative to a kid who just wanted to listen to something more contemporary than Jim Reeves or any of the other Pickwick cassettes the old man picked up cheap in Woolworths. And anyway, let's face it, the sound quality of those home recordings was shit. The beginning of each song was invariably missed because of sluggish hand-brain co-ordination, while the endings were usually interrupted by a faux North American accent gibbering away in disc jockey speak.

Anyway, here's my point: home taping didn't kill music – all it did was upset a few industry suits who saw potential revenue spooled inside a C90. If anything killed music – or certainly de-personalised the listening experience, imposing storyboards on our individual imaginations – blame MTV. If it wasn't for them, we would never have been exposed to the embarrassing spectacle of an airbrushed Bruce Springsteen throwing down some moves (like a cross between Frankenstein's monster and Bubba) alongside a then unknown Courteney Cox in the cheesy video for 'Dancing In The Dark'. Hard to believe this was the same man who, two years previously, had released *Nebraska*, and now here he was, folkie doom-monger turned pop idol.

Yet *Born In The USA*, the album from which 'Dancing In The Dark' was culled, is very much of a piece with its starker predecessor. The songs may be augmented by the E Street Band, they would eventually fill the world's stadia (not to mention the 70,000-capacity natural amphitheatre of Slane Castle in Ireland) with their bulk, but in essence they were coming from the same place as the songs Springsteen cut at Colt's Neck. 'Born In The USA' itself, along with 'Downbound Train' and 'Working On The Highway' (originally titled 'Child Bride'), featured in the early stages of their development on the four-track demos.

"Half of the *Born In The USA* album was recorded at the time of *Nebraska*," he told *Rolling Stone* in 1984. "When we initially went into the studio to try to record *Nebraska* with the band, we recorded the first side of *Born In The USA*, and the rest of the time I spent trying to come up with the second side. So if you look at the material, particularly on the first side, it's actually written very much like *Nebraska* – the characters, the stories, the style of writing – except it's just in the rock band setting."

The title track – a big, brutal anthem which, despite its sorry tale of how America had discarded its Vietnam veterans, had Ronald Reagan's aides salivating at the prospect of using it on the stump – was, according to Jon Landau, "a dead song" as it appeared in its acoustic incarnation. The words and music didn't fit. But then Springsteen found the key – the turbulence, as Landau referred to it.

"In other words, an acoustic guitar wasn't gonna get you there on this song. He needed a band that could feel the way this song was supposed to feel," Landau explained later.

The sound of 'Born In The USA' was, as Springsteen recalled in *Songs*, "martial, modal and straight ahead" (it made for a rousing, fist-pumping opener in concert on the subsequent global trek). Over the years, he has reworked the song many times live, but insisted that it exists "in its most powerful presentation" on *Born In The USA*. "If I tried to undercut the music, I would have had a record that might have been more easily understood, but not as good."

The Handsome Family's Brett Sparks has said that the misinterpretation of the song "is solid proof that most Americans don't get irony" (Reagan's spindoctors among them). That might just be a polite substitute for a harsher truth. How could anyone in possession of even the most nominal amount of grey matter misread the relentless misery and righteous anger of the verses as they unflinchingly stare into the heart of America's darkness? This is no patriotic panegyric, no rock'n'roll 'God Bless America'.

This is a scathing indictment of how men who do terrible things, and to whom terrible things are done in the service of their country, find that the same country doesn't give a fuck about them once they have fulfilled their duty. Springsteen was writing about Vietnam, but the song could just as easily be applied to those marines sent to Afghanistan and Iraq by George W Bush and his oil-greedy government.

At a concert in Los Angeles on 20 August 1981, Springsteen vented his feelings on America's marginalisation of its veterans. "It's like when you're walking down a dark street at night, and out of the corner of your eye you see somebody getting hurt in a dark alley, but you keep on walking because you think it don't have nothing to do with you and you just want to get home. Vietnam turned this whole country into that dark street, and unless we can walk down those dark alleys and look into the eyes of those men and women, we're never gonna get home."

He himself had managed to avoid the draft as a youngster. "I got a 4-F. I had a brain concussion from a motorcycle accident when I was seventeen. Plus, I did the basic Sixties rag, fillin' out the forms all crazy, not takin' the tests. When I was 19, I wasn't ready to be that generous with my life. I was called for induction, and when I got on the bus to go take my physical, I thought one thing: I ain't goin'."

But some of Springsteen's friends weren't so fortunate, including Bart Hanes, a drummer with whom he'd played in the early Freehold days. "He was one of those guys that was jokin' all the time, always playin' the clown. He came over one day and said, 'Well, I enlisted. I'm goin' to Vietnam'. I remember he said he didn't know where it was. And that was it. He left and he didn't come back. And the guys that did come back were not the same."

The Springsteen hobbyhorse of class is evident again on 'Born In The USA'. You just know the central character didn't grow up in a picture house enclosed by a white picket fence on the right side of the tracks. Like the blues song goes, if it wasn't for bad luck he wouldn't have no luck at all. The story is a familiar one. Trouble with the law followed by conscription into the army and a despatch to South East Asia, fuel for the American war machine in Vietnam. He makes it back home, unlike his brother, killed by the Viet Cong.

Who got the better deal? This is no hero's return. There is no ticker tape parade, no gratitude, no national pride in his contribution to fighting the good fight against the red menace. There is embarrassment, shame even. Mostly there is nothing, nothing down for him, less than the nothing he had before. Ten years of nothing. This "long gone daddy" is cast adrift from the society he served to protect, liable to do anything. He might be the nocturnal driver in 'State Trooper', he might be Frank Roberts, he might be 'Johnny 99'.

Let me be considerably more cruel than Brett Sparks and say that you'd have to be some kind of a idiot not to understand that 'Born In The USA' was less a celebration of America than a condemnation of America, or at least the powers behind America. And those who contented themselves with humming the verses only to raise their voices in defiant unity at the chorus (despite the unadulterated fury in Springsteen's delivery) should probably go and stand in the corner. Forever.

The failure of many people to fully grasp the import of the song was still bugging Springsteen when he spoke to Robert Santelli. In order to understand the song's intent, he said, time and effort was required to assimilate the words and music. Unfortunately, as Springsteen pointed out, that's not how many people "use pop music". For these people, it is mainly "an emotional language", and so lyrical content is subservient to "what the listener is feeling".

He cited a pair of examples of how this plays out. Firstly, when Springsteen let Vietnam vet Bobby Muller hear 'Born In The USA', "a big smile crossed his face". Secondly, he recalls the trick-or-treaters who would show up at his front door every Halloween singing the song. They all possessed ample lung power when it came to the chorus. "I guess the same fate awaited Woody Guthrie's 'This Land is Your Land' around the campfire. But that didn't make me feel any better," he deadpanned.

Springsteen actually wrote 'Cover Me' for disco queen Donna Summer. Weird, huh? Well, maybe not. One of the songs that didn't' make it onto *Darkness At The Edge Of Town* (but did make it onto *The Promise*) was 'Fire', a hit single for the Pointer Sisters. So it's not like he didn't have the knack for mainstream soul-inflected pop. Which just about describes 'Cover Me'. It was certainly not disco. Springsteen decided to keep the track for himself, though he did later give Summer another track, 'Protection', which the two of them recorded with Quincy Jones as producer.

Like the majority of *Born In The USA*, 'Cover Me' hasn't aged well sonically. It's very much of the Eighties; there's too much going on, it's too synthetic and the mix is too tinny. Bob Dylan was someone else whose sound suffered in the decade that taste forgot, though admittedly many of the songs Bob was recording at the time would have struggled to raise themselves off their knees in any decade – *Empire Burlesque*, anybody? Speaking of which, there is a common denominator between 'Cover Me' and *Empire Burlesque*, and his name is Arthur Baker. The DJ turned mixer/producer was responsible for mixing both (though the term guilty might be more applicable).

It's a shame that 'Cover Me' ended up sounding as it did, because there's a brooding ballad buried somewhere in the final mix. Neither complex in theme nor lyric, it conveys disaffection with a world that keeps getting tougher, a world that doesn't care any more. The narrator wants no part of it, he wants to escape from it with "a lover who will come on in and cover me".

'Darlington County' resembles the Rolling Stones' 'Honky Tonk Woman', cranking out a story of two New York boys heading down south in pursuit of work and women. It doesn't end well, at least not for Wayne. The last we see of him he's handcuffed to a police car, the exact nature of his suspected crime unclear.

The only crime of which the protagonist in 'Working On The Highway' is guilty, is falling hard for a young girl and eloping with her. At least that's how he would have us see it. But how trustworthy is he? And just how young is this girl? Are we talking under the age of consent – a case of paedophilia? That's certainly the inference in the final verse – the girl's brothers head to Florida and bring their sister back home, while the highway worker is carted off to prison. And maybe it's me, but I find something oddly homoerotic in the image of the prisoner and the warden going "swinging on the Charlotte County road gang".

A road gang of a different kind features on 'Downbound Train'. The narrator may not be watched over by men brandishing guns while he knocks down cross ties in the rain, but he might as well be. He had it all, "had something going" until "times got hard" and he lost his job at the lumber yard. Then his girl lit out; whatever they once had, it was long gone, gone with his hope. This guy is one of Springsteen's most disconsolate characters – and that, given some of the characters who populate *Nebraska* in particular, is saying something.

You can substitute "dangerous" for "disconsolate" in 'I'm On Fire', the song that closes out the first side of *Born In The USA*. I don't hold with those who construe this as a simple profession of love. Russell Simins of the Jon Spencer Blues Explosion has lauded it as "one of the best courtship songs ever…just a really sexy song about pursuing a girl and showing her you want to take care of her." It makes me uneasy. Just as 'Working On The Highway' hints at the sexual violation of a minor, 'I'm On Fire', brief though it is, breathes heavily and threateningly with a kind of forbidden longing. There's a sense that this guy could do anything to the "little girl" here.

Steve Van Zandt disappeared from the E Street Band during the sessions for *Born In The USA*. At least that's how it seemed. There was no dramatic exit, no official announcement. Ostensibly the explanation proffered for his departure was a desire to follow his own muse, yet there were rumours of repeated clashes with Landau over the album's production as well as the direction in which he was steering Springsteen's career. He may have been gone by the time the album was completed, but he was not forgotten – his brotherly bond with Springsteen is immortalised on 'No Surrender' and 'Bobby Jean', the brace of songs that launch side two in a redemptive blast of rock'n'roll.

This is the Springsteen not of *Nebraska*, but of *Born To Run*, the one with "romantic dreams in my head". Make no mistake, these are love songs. Not the love that dare not speak its name, but the love between friends. And like all truly great love songs, they are underscored by an ache. And it's this ache, the tear that falls unbidden on the face of joy, that connects 'No Surrender' and 'Bobby Jean' to *Born In The USA*'s central leitmotif of how things change, of how things can never again be the same as they once were. And this incontrovertible fact provokes in each of the characters different emotional responses – anger, sadness, despair, disillusionment… These songs are as happy as it gets on *Born In The USA*.

And then we're plunged back into the tormented soul on 'I'm Goin' Down', almost a companion piece to 'Downbound Train'. This could be the same guy picking at the scabs of his rotting relationship in a prelude to the girl packing her bags and buying "a ticket on the Central Line".

'Glory Days' would be funny if it wasn't so tragic – the fallen sports star, the ragged and worn beauty, the pathetic nostalgia junkie, they're all here hanging onto the vestiges of the past for survival.

And so to 'Dancing In The Dark', the song that registered Springsteen on the MTV Richter Scale thanks to that video. If the promo for 'Atlantic City' was a cult classic, this one was forgettable schlock. Except it wasn't – forgettable, I mean. For those millions of us who have seen it will never forget it. Springsteen doesn't even look like Springsteen but a shiny waxwork replica whose wiring has been screwed up to make him dance really badly and smile too much. And he can't lip-sync, though that's definitely a good thing.

The irony is that while the video undoubtedly boosted sales of the single, its goofiness trivialised the lyric. As *Rolling Stone*'s Mikhal Gilmore wrote in 1990,

'Dancing In The Dark' was "perhaps the most pointed and personal song Springsteen has ever written about isolation". Yet mention it to most people and they'll immediately think of *Friends*.

According to Eric Alterman in *It's Hard To Be A Saint In The City: The Promise Of Bruce Springsteen*, 'Dancing In The Dark' came out of a butting of heads between Springsteen and Landau (which the latter called "testy by our standards"). Springsteen thought the album was done, Landau disagreed – it still needed a hit single. "He all but ordered Springsteen to go to his room and stay there until he wrote one," says Alterman.

Well, despite his retort to Landau that if he wanted another song he could go write it himself, Springsteen did as he was told/advised/asked. 'Dancing In The Dark', he said later, "went as far in the direction of pop music as I wanted to go – and probably a little farther".

The popular palate demands a tasty chorus, one the masses can wrap their chops around. 'Dancing In The Dark' duly obliged, though, as with 'Born In The USA', feelgood it wasn't.

"A lot of people thought 'Dancing In The Dark' was one of Springsteen's most uplifting songs because of the chorus, but it's really about struggling with boredom and inertia," says Jim Sclavunos of Nick Cave's Bad Seeds and Grinderman.

The more he listened, the more Sclavunos heard it as a song about "Bruce starting to feel his age. With most icons it's hard to believe anything they say, but when Bruce sings lines like 'Can't start a fire without a spark', you know they're metaphors for how he really feels about things like mortality."

For me, the mortality metaphor wasn't intentional on Springsteen's part. The application of metaphor to any work is subjective to the listener (reader or viewer). And the argument advanced, assuming it's scaffolded by sufficient evidence, validates every metaphor. I think Sclavunos is right the way he calls it the first time – 'Dancing In The Dark' is a song about "struggling with boredom and inertia". But then I also think Gilmore is right when he refers to it as a musical essay on isolationism.

And consider this: perhaps Springsteen was just pissed off with Landau and his insistence on another song, and this revealed itself in a lyric that's bristling with frustration. 'Dancing In The Dark' might just be the sound of a guy who wants to punch something – or someone.

The narrator of 'My Hometown' has that innate goodness of character so many of Springsteen's men seem to possess. He is a vivid creation. You can see him in his lumberjack shirt and faded jeans, his work boots, the chiselled features shaded by stubble, the stoic way he holds himself. He is his father's son, the father we glimpse in the first verse tousling his hair and showing him the town that belongs to him, and to which he belongs.

The second verse, patently an allusion to the race riots that occurred in Freehold in 1969 (and recounted in some detail in Chapter Three), divests us of the notion that we have entered a small-town American idyll. There have been troubled times, he is telling us, without venturing information on which side of the line he stood – what Jim Cullen (again quoted in Chapter Three) has criticised as "a dismaying passivity".

And then Springsteen fast forwards to the present and the "whitewashed windows" and "'vacant stores", the closure of the local textile mill. The town has lost its allure, it is no longer an attractive proposition in terms of investment, residence or tourism. Think somewhere like Flint, Michigan and its demise following the closure of several of General Motors' manufacturing plants in the late Eighties, a demise powerfully documented in the work of Michael Moore, especially his 1989 film *Roger & Me*.

There's an element of procrastination in the final verse. He knows he should leave, head south (it used to be west, it used to be that California was the promised land), but will he? He perches his own son on his lap, as his father did with him all those years ago, and says the same thing his father said to him then: "This is your hometown." Whether these words are an invocation to stay and fight, or a valediction, isn't clear. Again, Springsteen knows it's better to show than tell.

A sample of the reviews that greeted the release of *Born In The USA* pre-empted the affirmation it would receive from the record-buying public. In America, *Rolling Stone*'s Debby Bull proclaimed its "rowdy, indomitable spirit", adding that although the characters were "dying of longing for some sort of payoff from the American Dream, Springsteen's exuberant voice and the swell of the music clues you that they haven't given up."

In Britain, meanwhile, *Melody Maker*'s Adam Sweeting applauded the album for making "a stand in the teeth of history" and "stirring a few unfashionable emotions". Charles Shaar Murray, in *NME*, said that Springsteen displayed "the kind of moral and artistic integrity that rock music rarely shows any more. The power of *Born In The USA* is less flashy and less intoxicating, but it's far more real than the power of his early work; this is the power of an artist telling the truth."

The dozen songs that form *Born In The USA* were cherrypicked from around eighty (according to E Street drummer Max Weinberg) that had been recorded over two years. These included 'Murder Incorporated' (which later appeared on *Greatest Hits*), 'This Hard Land', 'None But The Brave', 'Wages Of Sin', 'Cynthia', 'Brothers Under The Bridges', 'Rockaway The Days', 'My Love Will Not Let You Down', 'Stand On It', 'TV Movie', 'Man At The Top' and 'Janey Don't Lose Your Heart' (all of which appeared on *Tracks*).

Cherrypicked, it appears, for maximum commercial impact, a process of decision-making certainly paid off. Estimated sales figures can vary depending on the source, but when you're talking about units in the multi-millions does the precise figure matter? More significantly, *Born In The USA* transformed Springsteen from an American superstar into a world superstar. It's a tricky position to occupy for someone who regards himself as an artist.

The brilliant Irish writer John McGahern once wrote that there comes a time when the way we read has to change drastically or stop. This is linked to our growing consciousness – essentially the consciousness of our mortality and of the commonality of human existence. McGahern suggested that we will no longer read for the story (for him, all stories were the same story anyway) but will seek out books that serve as mirrors, reflecting "something dangerously close to our own life and the society in which we live".

Springsteen's songs, especially from *Born To Run*, had become, to increasing numbers of people, the very mirrors to which McGahern referred. This was due in no small part to the fact of his own back story, a back story not a whole lot different to that of his fans, a back story that gave him credibility as a writer about blue-collar America. But the further Springsteen strayed from this back story, the more he gravitated towards the kind of fame and wealth achieved by none but the chosen (or fortunate) few, the greater the risk to that credibility.

It was a dichotomy he acknowledged as recently as 2010 when, in an interview with the *Sunday Times*, he said, "I write very well about these things. And I think about them very seriously. I take a lot of time and effort in the music that I write to try and honour the experiences of the characters I write about. That's the best a writer can do."

The newer converts gathered in by *Born In The USA* probably didn't give it much thought. You get the feeling most of them were transient devotees anyway, just passing through on their way to the next consumer boom. The faithful though became anxious as hell. He didn't belong to them any more but to a vaster constituency. And to this constituency he was not a spokesman but an idol. He didn't emerge from among them to sing what they felt – he was, like some false god, their construct.

The commercial deification of Springsteen through the success of *Born In The USA* forced him to examine his own identity on *Tunnel Of Love*, his most personal album yet. And he didn't like what he uncovered.

14. DUAL IDENTITY

"Once you have some success a lot of what you do becomes reactionary."

BRUCE SPRINGSTEEN

"That so many people who bought Born In The USA *passed up* Tunnel Of Love *is not surprising. It is an adult album of poetry and meditation that can be called rock'n'roll only by association."*

ERIC ALTERMAN

After conquering the globe on the *Born In The USA* tour, Bruce Springsteen bunkered down at home in Rumson, New Jersey. His fame had outgrown him – it was roaming around, living large in some kind of parallel universe, advertising, through the appropriation of the *Born In The USA* image, L&M cigarettes, Citicorp checking accounts, Casio synthesisers and Koss headphones. And you know you've made it big when the skin-flick fraternity get in on the act with *Porn In The USA*. Springsteen, you sense, was hunkering down not only to record *Tunnel Of Love* but to escape the circus – the runaway American Dream, if you like.

But before beginning work on his eighth studio album, there was the live release for which the fans – the real fans, that is – had long been clamouring. Rather than a document of the *Born In The USA* set, *Live 1975-85* was a trawl through the archives spread over five vinyl LPs or three CDs. It's a collection studded with some gems, not least the opening piano version of 'Thunder Road' (the sole 1975 representative, incidentally), Woody Guthrie's 'This Land Is Your Land' and Tom Waits' 'Jersey Girl', but is possibly too ostentatious for its own good. Disappointingly, the two cuts from *Nebraska* – the title track and 'Johnny 99' – add nothing to the original recordings.

Although it wasn't apparent at the time, *Live 1975-85* foretold the dissolution of the E Street Band. According to Springsteen years later, it encapsulated what he had to say "and did what recorded work I could with the band, for the moment". It would, however, be another three years before Springsteen officially pulled the plug on what *Mojo* magazine had heralded "perhaps the greatest backing band in the history of rock'n'roll".

Tunnel Of Love is, make no mistake about it, a Springsteen solo album with contributions from members of the E Street Band. As Jimmy Guterman puts it, "Every member of the band got a credit, but barely, as they were called in to overdub their parts after Springsteen recorded the basic tracks himself." Initially they didn't even feature in Springsteen's plans, the first sessions having been recorded with a country trio.

Someone else who got a credit on the sleeve was Springsteen's wife Julianne Phillips, a model and actress who appeared in three American TV movies (*Jealousy, Summer Fantasy* and *His Mistress*) before featuring in the video for 'Glory Days'. "To

119

Juli" is hardly the most effusive dedication ever to a loved one. Suspicions that all was not well in the marriage were confirmed by the songs themselves, despite Springsteen's protestations that they were "not literally autobiographical".

He may have been writing about the "fears of the man in the house", as he insisted to Robert Santelli almost two decades on, but you can only write about such fears with any kind of precision if you are that man. Fear is, of course, the offspring of doubt, and doubt casts its unsettling shadow over virtually every track. Contrary to the sign outside the fairground in the video for the single, 'Tunnel Of Love', this is a dark ride. As dark as *Darkness On The Edge Of Town*, as dark as *Nebraska* even, albeit a different kind of dark.

"I wanted to write a different kind of romantic song," Springsteen explained to *Rolling Stone* in 1988, "one that took in the different types of emotional experiences of any relationship where you are really engaging with that other person and not involved in a narcissistic romantic fantasy or intoxication or whatever.

"In my life previously, I hadn't allowed myself to get into a situation where I would even have cause to reflect on these things. But when this particular record came around, I wanted to make a record about what I felt, about really letting another person in your life and trying to be part of someone else's life. That's a frightening thing, something that's always filled with shadows and doubts and also wonderful things and beautiful things.

"I couldn't have written any of those songs at any other point in my career. I wouldn't have had the knowledge or the insight or the experience to do it."

So what of the knowledge, insight or experience that informs the frustration of 'Ain't Got You', a rockabilly shuffle in which the protagonist, a man of enormous wealth, the object of unconditional worship, bemoans unrequited love? Is this Springsteen addressing Phillips? Is she emotionally or sexually elusive as a spouse? Or is this Springsteen addressing a third party? Perhaps Patti Scialfa, the E Street Band's recently recruited backing vocalist who would eventually become Springsteen's second wife and the mother of his three children?

There is another possibility, though admittedly a slight one and requires a stretch of the imagination. It might just be that Springsteen is singing about the loss of self – the loss of his core identity – which has become a casualty of his celebrity. Because gone with the Freehold boy made good is the hunger. And it's the hunger, after all, that motivates the artist to dig deep, to unearth the unpalatable truths for the rest of us because we're too lily-livered or inept to do so ourselves. Whatever your take on it, scratch beneath its neatly rhyming couplets, shot through with no little comedy, 'Ain't Got You' is uncomfortable listening. There is, it would seem, a toll to be paid for reaching the mountain top.

'Tougher Than The Rest' finds Springsteen in macho posture – or does it? There's an unconvincing bravado in his patter as he tries to persuade the object of his desire that he can handle what the other guys can't. This is either aimed at Phillips or Scialfa – or maybe neither. Maybe it's Springsteen telling himself he can commit to a serious relationship, that he's got what it takes. After all, he has, as he sings, "been around a time or two", suggesting an aversion to enduring romantic liaisons. He had no such difficulty devoting himself to the music, or indeed in bonding with the all-male community (at least until Scialfa's arrival) of the E Street Band.

'All That Heaven Will Allow' blows in like a bracing breeze after the neurosis of the first two songs. The title is a play on Douglas Sirk's 1959 film, *All That Heaven Allows*, in which Jane Wyman's upper-class widow falls in love with younger nurseryman Rock Hudson, much to the disapproval of her family and criticism of her country-club peers. That's where the similarity ends. There is no conflict in Springsteen's song, there is nothing that threatens the source of the singer's unbridled happiness. This is the declaration of a man in love, a man who is loved in return. Set against the bleak landscape of the rest of the album – and it's impossible to disassociate this landscape from what was going on in his personal life, the failure of his marriage, his rumoured affair with Scialfa – it's positively exuberant.

We're deeper into that bleak landscape on 'Spare Parts'. You could say we're in the sinister world of a Grimm fairytale, or the Irish folk song 'Weile Weile Waile', in which an old hag who lives in the woods kills a baby by sticking a penknife into its heart "down by the River Saile". It begins prosaically enough, Bobby, like so many earlier Springsteen models, taking to the highway, this time fleeing the responsibility of impending fatherhood, while a pregnant Janey moves in with her mother – unwed mothers both? The chorus is a curious refrain about the spare parts and broken hearts that keep the world turning; surely those same spare parts and broken hearts cause the world to tilt precariously on its axis?

While Bobby "swore he wasn't ever goin' back", Janey, walking the floor with her baby night after endless night, is looking for a way out herself, even if the way out involves infanticide. We find her distraught, her dilemma driving her to prayer before she wades into the water with her son. It could go either way, Springsteen mounting the suspense like a man well versed in the techniques of film noir. Eventually Janey raises her son from river and carries him home. A reprieve from death – from murder – or a form of baptism, confirmation of his place on God's earth? You get to decide. What matters, when it all comes down, is the child, the life made and born into a world of spare parts and broken hearts.

I was just thinking as I listened to 'Spare Parts' again recently how feasible it would be to postulate that Springsteen was either writing about post-natal depression or writing a pro-life parable. Unlikely, I know, but then you can fix any hat onto the most shapeless head.

'Cautious Man' represents, I believe, the Springsteen ideal – the man of integrity, the man who wants to do right, but one who is haunted by something "he couldn't name" (maybe the same thing that was bothering the guy in 'State Trooper' on *Nebraska*). This is a recurring theme on *Tunnel Of Love*, that of dual identity. You can hear it more explicitly in 'Two Faces' and 'Brilliant Disguise'.

Bill Horton is perhaps Springsteen's alter ego, the one that for all those years remained wary of commitment to anything other than his art. But then he meets a girl and his guard collapses. It's not happy ever after though – how can it be when the knuckles on each hand bear the words 'love' and 'fear' (an allusion perhaps to Robert Mitchum's Harry Powell in *Night Of The Hunter*, though the knuckles of this self-appointed preacher freighted the words 'love' and 'hate')? Fear of what? Is it the fear that he won't measure up, that he won't stay the distance, that his "restless heart" will betray him? Or is it the fear that she will leave? That's the impression conveyed in the penultimate verse when Billy wakes from a dream calling out his wife's name. And then, as he looks down upon her face, lit by the moon, he realises that while the fear will be his constant companion, it is the love that prevails, at least for now.

'Walk Like A Man' might just be Springsteen's love song to father Douglas, acknowledgement that despite the acrimony of their earlier years he still wants to emulate his example. Or it might again just be Springsteen's ideal of a father whose example the protagonist wants to emulate. A father who is strong yet unafraid to cry, a very modern representation of what is a man. The Catholicism of Springsteen's upbringing enters the second verse, his mother dragging the kids along to church whenever there's a wedding, enforcing the idea of the sanctity of marriage. Yet as the boy looks on, he wonders if the bride and groom will ever again be as happy as on their wedding day – doubt rearing its mixed up head once more.

The boy has become a man in the final verse, and the journey, though often lonely, has taught him the folly of his youthful rebellion and how it blinded him from finding empathy with his father's struggle when his "best steps" were stolen away. But that was then, and now he recognises his merits as a role model, now he endeavours to follow in his footsteps.

If hope, and perhaps no little faith, closes out the first side of *Tunnel Of Love*, mistrust overshadows the title track that opens side two. Love is a fairground ride, a crapshoot, a game of chance, a tunnel like the ones we've all gone through on the ghost train. Tunnels are terrifying and thrilling, they disempower the traveller, render them unable to navigate their own course. Love, and by extension marriage, is a union governed by suspicion and worse, paranoia. Yet it shouldn't be like this. And surely if it is, it's wrong – isn't it? If the house really is haunted, if the ride really is that rough, maybe you've not met your soulmate, your mirror image, your life partner. Isn't it better to own up, to admit that you got it wrong, rather than "learn to live with what you can't rise above"?

You start to feel for Springsteen's sanity at this stage of the album. He comes over like a man beating himself up unnecessarily, a man torn between values inherited from his parents, who stuck it out though thin and thinner, and the instinctive knowledge that everything is not as it should be in his own marriage. So what or who is the problem here? Is it Springsteen himself?

If 'Two Faces' is the writer's creative subconscious, then the answer is in the affirmative. For as well as playing into the theme of dual identity, it glimpses the mind of a manic depressive – one minute "sunny and wild", the next prey to "dark clouds". As so often in his songs, Springsteen looks to the Almighty for assistance. It strikes me that anti-depressants might be a more viable alternative.

Bermudian singer-songwriter and poet Heather Nova has described 'Brilliant Disguise' as "a great song about insecurity", that unbidden element in a relationship that makes it "both scary and fun, that element of, 'Do I really know you and do you really know me or are we just two strangers in this bed?'"

She's not wrong. Insecurity, another symptom of depression, bleeds through every line. Maybe this guy has good reason to feel insecure – or it could be that his insecurity is nourished by an over-active imagination. And if you're projecting Springsteen's marriage to Phillips onto the song, there's a strong case for theorising that his insecurity is a class thing, a tic of his blue-collar background against her suburban childhood in Lake Oswego, Oregon. Of course, it could be that he's a repository for her insecurity, that every doubt he expresses in the song is, in fact, the expression of her doubts about him, especially given the opportunity to stray presented by his profession.

For Springsteen himself, as he told *Mojo* in 2006, 'Brilliant Disguise' is "about identity. And your identity is so multi-faceted and diffuse it's amazing that every part of you is in the same place at the same time! That song is asking, 'Is it me or a brilliant disguise?' And the answer is it's almost always both. You know, you've got to put out an enormous amount of your real self for it to feel real."

The insecurity seems to give way to infidelity – or at least thoughts of infidelity – on 'One Step Up'. Here, marriage is a "dirty little war", a series of battles that destroy the aspirations of the two principals, that reveal the wedding day in 'Walk Like A Man' to be nothing but a bunch of lies.

'When You're Alone' is not nearly as lightweight as it first appears. It states a bald fact – "When you're alone you're alone" – but it's a fact that not everyone accepts. And those who hold on, whether it be to memory or hope or a divine presence, will never truly be free, will never be able to move ahead, until they embrace the singularity of their existence. At which point this is beginning to read like a pseudo-psychoanalytical paper!

'Valentine's Day' ends *Tunnel Of Love* on a relative high. Yet another of Springsteen's drivers is on the highway, but this time he's not escaping from anything – this time he's going home to someone. You get the feeling that if Springsteen's singing about Springsteen – and he has always denied that *Tunnel Of Love* was "literally autobiographical" – the girl he's heading to see is not Phillips but Scialfa, though in keeping with most of what's gone before he's not wholly comfortable in this relationship either. That old devil anxiety is riding in the passenger seat, nagging at him all the way, attempting to subvert his contentment.

Springsteen took a bold step with *Tunnel Of Love*. He could have capitalised on the phenomenal success of *Born In The USA* by repeating the formula that obviously worked with the masses. But instead of being enervated by the immensity of his reputation, he retreated from it, reconnected, at least in spirit, with the guy on the rocking chair in Colt's Neck, the guy who spoke in tongues on *Nebraska*. Springsteen the writer rather than Springsteen the performer. This time, that writer was pulling from personal experience to tell a story with which we could all identify. He was holding up the mirror again. It makes for uneasy listening, and is, whatever Springsteen's protestations, his *Blood On The Tracks*.

In Britain, *Melody Maker*'s Steve Sutherland welcomed *Tunnel Of Love* as "a return to old habits, a chastened, harsh and often surprisingly humble record from a man for whom the world is his oyster." *NME*, meanwhile, hailed it as one of Springsteen's finest albums "and easily his best this decade". Neil Taylor obviously hadn't heard *Nebraska*.

Steve Pond, in *Rolling Stone*, wrote that it was "an album of songs about meeting a girl, falling in love and getting married", adding that far from being "a series of hymns to cosy domesticity, *Tunnel Of Love* is an unsettled and unsettling collection of hard looks at the perils of commitment. A decade or so ago, Springsteen acquired a reputation for romanticising his subject matter; on this album he doesn't even romanticise romance."

Some six months after *Tunnel Of Love*'s release, Springsteen and Phillips separated. Their divorce was finalised the following year. Springsteen and Scialfa made their relationship public when they moved, as a couple, to his new Hollywood estate. They wouldn't marry until 1991.

Musically, Springsteen was also ringing the changes. On 18 October 1989, he telephoned every member of the E-Street Band individually to tell them their services were no longer required. They were generously compensated, each apparently pocketing $2 million, but the money wasn't enough for some. Drummer Max Weinberg was hurt "at being left with the legacy I was fired", while saxophonist Clarence Clemons was "shocked, hurt, angry all at once".

Springsteen was unapologetic. He insisted to one interviewer, "The way I look at it is, I get paid to write a new song and I can't keep rewriting the old stuff. I played with a single set of musicians for a long time, and I thought it was time to play with other people."

15. CLOCKING IN

"There's a lot of groping around on Human Touch *and more on* Lucky Town *about finding your place and re-finding yourself, getting back in touch with your own humanity and the good things that you feel about yourself."*

BRUCE SPRINGSTEEN

*"*Human Touch *is a boring record by a rock star."*

JIMMY GUTERMAN

You can't begrudge a fella his happiness. Especially if that fella is Bruce Springsteen who, since *Born To Run*, had done more than his share of artistic suffering on behalf of blue-collars everywhere, and who, on the evidence of the self-flagellating *Tunnel Of Love*, was undergoing considerable emotional torment of his own. But the trouble with happiness is that it's only of interest to those revelling in it. The rest of us would rather stick needles in our eyes. Or listen to Frank Sinatra's *Only The Lonely*.

Happy is what Springsteen was as he relocated to Los Angeles with Patti Scialfa in 1989. They lived thirty minutes from the mountains, the oceans and the desert, and it was here they started a family. Music, for once, became secondary to home-making. And therapy.

Yep, Springsteen decided it was high time he dealt with some issues. Never a laconic interviewee, he revealed all to James Henke of *Rolling Stone* in 1992. "I crashed into myself and saw a lot of myself as I really was. And I questioned my motivations. Why am I writing what I'm writing? Why am I saying what I'm saying? Do I mean it? Am I bullshitting? Am I just trying to be the most popular guy in town? Do I need to be liked that much? I questioned everything I'd ever done, and it was good. You should do that. And then you realise there is no single motivation to anything. You're doing it for all of those reasons.

"So I went through a real intense period of self-examination. I knew that I had to sit in my room for eight hours a day with a guitar and learn how to play it, and now I had to put in that kind of time just to find my place again."

While Springsteen had plenty to say on the psychoanalyst's couch, he had absolutely nothing to say as a writer for two years after *Tunnel Of Love*. Everything he attempted "was just sort of rehashing". Domestic bliss, enormous wealth and regular sessions with a shrink were snuffing out his fire.

Human Touch was meant to be "an exercise", a means of reacquainting Springsteen with what it was he did best. It was also an initiation of sorts, marking the first time that he had collaborated with musicians other than the E Street Band, although keyboard player Roy Bittan did get a couple of co-writes (on 'Roll Of The Dice' and 'Real World') and joined the production team with Jon Landau and Chuck

Plotkin. The roll call of session men included Jeff Porcaro of Toto on drums, Sam Moore, Bobby King and Bobby Hatfield on vocals, David Sancious, a member of the original E Street Band, on organ, Ian McLagan of the Faces on piano, Mark Isham on trumpet and Michael Fisher on percussion.

The album took a year to compose and record. At the end of the process, Springsteen wanted one more song. That song was 'Living Proof'. But he didn't stop there. In the following three weeks he put together another album. *Lucky Town* became the companion piece to *Human Touch*, "both about the blessings and the unanswerable questions that come with adult life, mortality and human love". He released them simultaneously in March 1992, six months after Guns N'Roses had done the same thing with *Use Your Illusion I* and *II*.

The critics, with the exception of *Rolling Stone* (always in Springsteen's corner – perhaps it's the Landau association), were underwhelmed. David Stubbs wrote in *Melody Maker* that *Human Touch* offered us a glimpse of the real Springsteen of recent years, "sitting in his T-shirt and underpants, bored, flicking peanuts at the screen. It also points to his utter failure of imagination."

For Stuart Bailie in *NME*, listening to it was "like being harangued across the garden fence by your boring neighbour who wants to tell you about his geraniums and seed packets and the rubbish road movie he got out on video last week".

They weren't much kinder about *Lucky Town*, "the work of a man who has grown up with rock'n'roll, but has seen it replaced as the Holy Grail by marriage and fatherhood", according to Patrick Humphries in *Vox*. Everett True in *Melody Maker* compared Springsteen to "a suburban American leafing through the lexicon of Beautiful South lyrics while strumming a guitar with the amps turned to half-volume in case the neighbours hear."

Human Touch is not a bad album. It's just not very good, way below the benchmark set by its eight predecessors. You can almost hear a man clocking in for work when he might have been better advised to extend his sabbatical, enjoy some quality time with the young family. Sometimes he's trying too hard to be Bruce Springsteen, other times he's not trying hard enough. Sure, it's radio-friendly – but then so are jingles.

Lucky Town is better, but not by much. At least Springsteen gives us a laugh on 'Local Hero', where *Human Touch*'s '57 Channels (And Nothin' On)' makes us want to deny him three times before the cock crows twice. 'If I Should Fall Behind' is probably the best love song he's ever written, and 'My Beautiful Reward' pure secular gospel. 'Souls Of The Departed' is proof that even those who reside in mansions of glory aren't completely sealed off from what's happening beyond their gates, as Springsteen conflates the death of an American soldier in Basra during the Gulf War with the fatal shooting of a seven year-old boy in Los Angeles' notorious East Compton. He feared for his own son in an America that had inherited "a legacy of dread", he told James Henke later that year as LA recovered from the riots.

"That's a big part of what growing up in America is about right now: dread, fear, mistrust, blind hatred. We're being worn down to the point where who you are, what you think, what you believe, where you stand, what you feel if your soul means nothing on a given day. Instead it's, 'What do you look like? Where are you from?' That's frightening."

Yet while Springsteen's social conscience could still be pricked, it didn't inhibit his gallivanting around Hollywood. After a tour to promote *Human Touch* and *Lucky Town* (his first without the E Street Band), he could be found jamming at private parties with the likes of Woody Harrelson, Wesley Snipes, Dan Aykroyd, Magic Johnson, Stephen King, Amy Tan and Matt Groening.

It was also in Los Angeles that Springsteen first met Willie Nile, alias Robert Anthony Noonan, a New York singer-songwriter with a degree in philosophy from the University of Buffalo who cut his teeth on the Seventies Greenwich Village scene. Nile was garlanded with critical plaudits for his eponymously-titled 1981 debut and the following year's *Golden Down* before legal difficulties derailed his career for a good decade. Then came 1991's *Places I Have Never Been*, which, he learned, was essential listening chez Springsteen.

"I met Bruce in 1991. I was in LA doing interviews for an album. I was walking through the Sunset Marquis and Patti Scialfa was having some lunch. I knew her from the early Eighties, from when she used to sing with Southside Johnny. We were all friends back then. She said, 'Bruce and I love your new album. We listen to it every morning and work out to it.' She couldn't have been nicer," he recalls.

"A few months later he was playing at the Bottom Line in New York. My son was working there. So I went over and Bruce was by the stage. He saw me come in and pointed the finger across the whole room and asked me over. He has been so supportive.

"In 2009, he did five shows at Giants Stadium. I got a phone call to come and play a few songs. I was on stage with him for half an hour. In 2003, he played Shea Stadium in New York, 60,000 people. I went backstage to see him and he said, 'Get the guitar, come on up and play "Glory Days"'. Bruce is so much fun to play with. He loves to have fun on stage, he loves to rock. When you stand next to him it's like standing next to a volcano. He's generous. How many people do that, bring their friends up at a big show? It's happened a bunch of times.

"In the same year I took my daughters to see him in Buffalo. We were in the third row. I didn't get a chance to see Bruce beforehand. At one stage he came near us during the concert. I said to my daughter, 'I think he just saw me'. And a couple of minutes later I get a text message saying, 'Come back now'. I went backstage and his assistant said, 'Bruce wants you to come up.' We did that great Jackie Wilson song. 'Higher And Higher'. What a blast!

"As a writer he keeps trying to step outside the envelope. I remember reading something that Allen Ginsberg said about Springsteen in an interview. He said he was the howl from the belly of the streets. He's a real compassionate guy. You be that famous, you be that much of an icon and still have your head screwed on your shoulders – not easy to do, but he's managed to do that.

"He's written some classics. I told him once, 'You put us all on your back and you carry us up the mountain. We get to see from the top of the mountain.' I love the optimism. Even though a lot of the songs he writes are about how tough life is, at the end of the day nobody can throw a party like that. When he's up there raising the roof, there's nobody like that alive. He's incredible. As a writer he's masterful at what he does."

It's hard to argue against Nile's assertion, but by the mid Nineties Springsteen was far from masterful. Ordinary probably just about sums it up. He was treading water, kept afloat by a reputation carved out two decades earlier. Said reputation wasn't exactly enhanced by a largely forgettable *MTV Plugged*, on which a poor backing band (including hirsute, swaggering guitarist Shayne Fontayne) made you wish Springsteen would admit he'd got it wrong in dismissing the E Streeters.

By 1995, he seemed to have reached this conclusion. On the back of an Oscar nomination for 'Streets Of Philadelphia', his contribution to director Jonathan Demme's movie *Philadelphia* in which Tom Hanks plays a lawyer struck down with AIDS, Springsteen agreed to Columbia's suggestion that he put out a greatest hits package. Being Springsteen, it wasn't straightforward. He felt the compilation needed some new songs, or at least some old songs newly recorded. So he called up the E Street Band and summoned them to New York for a series of typically intensive recording sessions. One of the songs to come out of these sessions, and featured on *Greatest Hits*, was 'Blood Brothers', written the night before Springsteen reunited with his buddies in the Hit Factory.

"The song is filled with the ambivalence and deep affection of revisiting a relationship spanning twenty five-plus years," he said in *Songs*.

It's a relationship he wouldn't revive again until the new millennium.

16. STATE OF THE UNION

"I don't need to sell records that are going to make millions. I need to do work that I feel is central, vital, that sets me in the present. What I'm interested in now is finding my place in the world as it stands."

BRUCE SPRINGSTEEN

"The Ghost Of Tom Joad…represents Springsteen's most sustained exploration of race relations."

JIM CULLEN

Having made his peace with the E Street Band, Bruce Springsteen returned to California unsure of his next move. One of the songs he'd tried to record with the band in New York was 'The Ghost Of Tom Joad', but the rock version "didn't feel right" so it was shelved. Back home, Springsteen revived it. He had other songs too – 'Straight Time' and 'Highway 29' – and the ubiquitous spiral notebook stuffed with unfinished ideas. Springsteen assembled a five-piece group and together they cut what would become the title track of his next album.

Joad is, of course, the fictional character from John Steinbeck's *The Grapes Of Wrath*, the second son of a family of Okies who join the migration to California in search of work during the Great Depression of the Thirties. He personifies the political awakening of the common man and the rise of the union movement at a time of rank employer exploitation of labourers, particularly among corporate farmers. By the book's end, Joad has become a crusader for the oppressed, vowing to his mother in a stirring monologue that, wherever he goes, he will stand firm against injustice. It's little wonder, given Springsteen's affinity with the righteous characters of director John Ford's films, that he found Joad such a compelling figure. And, as already mentioned, he first came to *The Grapes Of Wrath* through Ford's big-screen re-telling of Steinbeck's novel.

And Joad also forms another link in the chain from Springsteen to Woody Guthrie. On 3 March, 1940, Woody appeared at New York's Forrest Theatre in a benefit performance for agricultural workers organised by Steinbeck. Shortly afterwards, he recorded 'Tom Joad', a 17-verse ballad that tracked the plot of both book and movie.

With 'The Ghost Of Tom Joad' recorded, Springsteen knew what he wanted to do next. It was, he told Robert Santelli, "an acoustic album where I picked up elements of the themes I had worked on in the past and set the stories in the mid Nineties." *Nebraska*, this wasn't. For starters, *The Ghost Of Tom Joad* had an outline, Springsteen had a clarity of vision. What's more, he did research to ensure that the voices he inhabited on the album were accurate in representing those people crushed under the wheels of the new world order.

The precision of the storytelling was important, he said. The correct detail could speak volumes about the character, the wrong one could shred the credibility of the story. When both words and music came together, "your voice disappears into the voices of those you've chosen to write about". Springsteen found the characters and listened to them, a method which prompted a number of questions about their behaviour, what they would and wouldn't do. He tried to locate "the rhythm of their speech and the nature of their expression".

It sounds like a folk collector's approach, though instead of collecting songs, Springsteen collected voices. Among the research he did was to immerse himself in Pulitzer Prize winners Dale Maharidge and Michael Williamson's *Journey To Nowhere: The Sage Of The New Underclass*, whose self-explanatory title provided Springsteen with the guts of 'Youngstown' and 'The New Timer' on *The Ghost Of Tom Joad*.

Living in California, "a place where issues that are alive and confronting America", a place "where you see the political machinations of how the issue of immigration is being used, and a lot of the bullshit that goes down with it", had its benefits as a source of information.

There were also chance encounters, as he told *NME*'s Gavin Martin in 1996. "I met a guy in Arizona who told me a story about his brother who rode in a teenage motorcycle gang in the San Fernando Valley, called the Vagos. I just happened to meet this guy by the side of the road in this little motel. I don't know, it just stayed with me for a very long time and when I went to write it, I kept hearing his voice."

So Springsteen set about constructing *The Ghost Of Tom Joad* as Woody Guthrie and Pete Seeger would have done back in the day, and as the champions of topical song did later on in the Sixties. He equipped himself with knowledge from primary and secondary sources and applied that knowledge to working up narratives that substantiated the lives of those who were merely digits on sociological studies.

The Ghost Of Tom Joad is demanding. Springsteen's vocal is so hushed that at times you strain to hear, while the melodies are largely low key, unremarkable. This was intentional on Springsteen's part – apparently "the simplicity and plainness, the austere rhythms" are in keeping with the identities of the characters and how they express themselves. If fidelity to these characters were such an imperative, perhaps he could have delivered some of the immigrant narratives with a Mexican lilt. Pardon my facetiousness. There is much to commend in Springsteen's determination to make it real. But worthiness doesn't always sustain the punters' attention.

For me, the songs actually only came alive in concert on the Born To Stand And Sit Down Tour, also known as The Shut The Fuck Up And Listen Tour. They are among his most accomplished stories, and storytelling is an oral tradition. There are few better exponents of this tradition than Springsteen, as anyone who has listened to his banter on stage will testify.

I saw Springsteen twice within a week on the European leg of the tour, at London's Royal Albert Hall and Brixton Academy. Kitted out as though he were going to work in the local sweatshop (on a night pass from the big house!), he brought us into the songs in a way the album doesn't. He caused us to care about the people whose lives he was singing about, just as he cared about them.

This is an important point to make, because many critics questioned Springsteen's entitlement to sing about issues from which his wealth removed him. They found it hard to stomach that a guy who lived in a $14 million Beverly Hills home was playing at being dirt poor and desperate in these songs. While it's a legitimate argument, it's one that cracks under pressure. Springsteen is a writer first and a millionaire second.

His dedication to his writing has always been vocational. He walks in the shoes of those outside his experience, at least metaphorically, to better understand – and help us to better understand – their concerns. As a writer he's curious about the human condition and recognises that the condition of all humans is not the same – that many, in fact, are in a worse condition than he is or you are or I am. Alongside the writer's curiosity is Springsteen the man's compassion. Wealth doesn't preclude the wealthy from wanting to engage in the cause for social justice.

The album's first image, almost whispered into being, is from another America, the America of Woody Guthrie, the America of the Great Depression – an America from another lifetime. Except this man, this hobo lumbering along the railroad tracks, destination unknown but far from where he began, belongs to the now. He is not a dustbowl refugee, an Okie fleeing west, but the modern incarnation of those thousands of Joads.

The country may have prospered during the previous six decades, but the march of progress leaves in its wake a trail of poverty, a trail that can be found, in Springsteen's telling, on the edge of things, in the shadows, where the exiled are hounded by the authorities and kept alive by the kindness of strangers. The soup kitchen still has a place in the most powerful country on the planet, and so too the homeless shelter. The families who sleep in their cars could be straight out of *The Grapes Of Wrath*.

The highway, so often the way to somewhere better, something better, in the land of Springsteen, is going nowhere. It's nothing but road (just like Bill Horton realised on *Tunnel Of Love*'s 'Cautious Man'), endless road, infinite suffering. And not a sign of Tom Joad anywhere – nobody to carry the fight, nobody to speak up for those who don't have a voice.

All they have indeed is faith, or what remains of their faith. The good book says the last shall be first, but such prophesy sounds hollow in the cardboard city beneath the underpass. As does the prophesy of the promised land when there's "a hole in your belly and a gun in your hand", when you're laying your head down on solid ground at night and washing in a canal.

This is not the America of MTV, Coca-Cola or Hollywood. Nor the America hailed by Woodrow Wilson as "the only idealistic nation in the world", the America in which, according to the Declaration of Independence, "all men are created equal...endowed by their Creator with certain unalienable rights", chief among them "life, liberty and the pursuit of happiness". This is an America scarred by police brutality, starving children, violence, hatred, division, unemployment, oppression… All of these things Tom Joad would have stood against, all of these wrongs he would have vowed to right. But there is no Tom Joad. And his spirit has been banished.

'The Ghost Of Tom Joad' is Springsteen's State of the Union address 1995, one you'd never hear from the mouth of a president. The song is a sort of précis, an overview of the underside of American society. It sets the scene for the stories that follow, ghost stories in which lives are haunted by poverty, whether those lives are those of Vietnam veterans, illegal migrants, iron workers, rent boys or drug mules.

Stories like 'Straight Time' in which an ex-con, eight years out of the joint, is struggling to stay on the straight and narrow, tormented by his "cold mind". Or the bank robber and his accomplice (Bonnie to his Clyde) crossing the border into Mexico after a heist, You just know how it's going to end. This is the aimless driver of *Nebraska*'s 'State Trooper' finally undone by "something in me".

'Youngstown' is a lift from Maharidge and Williamson's *Journey To Nowhere*, a eulogy for the immense blast furnace of Youngstown's Sheet & Tube company in Ohio, nicknamed Jeannette (abbreviated to Jenny in Springsteen's song), which was eventually demolished in 1997, two years after *The Ghost Of Tom Joad*. Of course, it's a eulogy for American industry and the men who worked in it, the men who made the moguls rich enough to forget their names.

'Sinaloa Cowboys' takes us into Mexico's drug heartland, a place where boys become methamphetamine cooks because they can earn half as much money in ten hours as they could toiling in the orchards for a year, despite the life-threatening conditions, the hydriodic acid that burns through your skin and leaves you spitting blood. Such is the fate that befalls Miguel's younger brother Luis.

'The Line' is yet another example of how peerless Springsteen is as a screenwriter in song. It's the kind of film you'd like John Sayles to direct. The set-up introduces us to a former marine turned border cop, another Springsteen archetype, a man who wants to do the right thing. But then he falls hard for a Mexican migrant girl and breaks the law he's paid to uphold by helping to bring her family into America. He is undone, this one mistake costing him everything. What becomes of the broken-hearted? He drifts through the migrant towns, a migrant now himself, seeking but never finding his Luisa.

The migrant experience features again in 'Balboa Park', the hustlers and the dope smugglers and the dealers and the users doing what they have to, selling what they can, ingesting what they can to survive. 'Dry Lightning' is defined by one of those Springsteen aphorisms that should be bolded and italicised and underlined on the lyric sheets – "Ain't nobody can give nobody/What they really need anyway."

'The New Timer' unites the Tom Joad generation with its descendants, the old vagrant jumping boxcars "since the Great Depression", the new kid travelling cross country in pursuit of work. It's a tale of the meanness in the world of which the Charles Starkweather character spoke about on 'Nebraska', a meanness illustrated by people "killin' just to kill", and of men who lie awake in a foreboding of evil. It's a tale of outsiders looking in but excluded from "the glow of the saviour's beautiful light".

'Across The Border' returns to the migrant theme, the narrator, in contrast to all that has gone before, buoyed by dreams of that utopia where "sweet blossoms fill the air", the pastures roll in colours gold and green and fruit can be picked from the vine.

Throughout *The Ghost Of Tom Joad*, Springsteen examines, "albeit awkwardly", according to Bryan K Garman, "the politics of race". And if his border ballads do assume a non-committal position on the subject, they seem to say that the plight of Mexican migrants is precisely because of their Mexican origins. Or as Jim Cullen writes in *Born In The USA: Bruce Springsteen And The American Tradition*, "the racism that enmeshes the non-white characters of *Tom Joad* is not personal, but systemic". While Cullen identifies this depiction of racism as "an inescapable fog that cannot be fought and only sometimes escaped," he concedes that Springsteen displays an "increasingly sophisticated understanding of the ways in which oppression depends on silence, ignorance, facelessness at least as much as it does on overt ill will."

'Galveston Bay' shows a side of America that America doesn't like to acknowledge. A reactionary America. A xenophobic America. An America "for Americans". And for all that he has turned an honest living as a shrimper since fleeing Vietnam, Le Bin Son will never be that American. Which is why, when hard times hit, his kind are fair game, legitimate targets for the frustration boiling inside Billy Sutter and his Texan compatriots. But when Le defends himself, when he kills these pure progeny of America, he is acquitted by another America – the America that upholds the right to bear arms, the right to self-defence. Billy Sutter swears revenge for his brethren, but when the opportunity arises he allows Le to live – a conscious reprieve on the part of the writer.

"I wanted a character who is driven to do the wrong thing, but does not," Springsteen said. "He instinctively refuses to add to the violence in the world around him. With great difficulty and against his own grain, he transcends his circumstances. He finds the strength and grace to save himself and the part of the world he touches."

'Galveston Bay' would have been the perfect grace note on which to conclude *The Ghost Of Tom Joad*. Bad intentions can be transformed into good actions. Compassion, humanity, call it what you will, is a choice.

But Springsteen wants to go out on a laugh and so, in the year *Forrest Gump* cleaned up at the Academy Awards, he pokes fun at the platitudinous that sugar coats so much of what is wrong with America on 'My Best Was Never Good Enough'. It's an amusing but curious parting shot.

After the dual disappointment of *Human Touch* and *Lucky Town*, certainly as far as the critics were concerned *The Ghost Of Tom Joad* restored Springsteen's reputation as a writer, and an American writer at that. One who penetrated the incessant propaganda pumped out about his country and got to the very heart of it – what made it beat, what made it rotten.

It was, according to Mikhail Gilmore in *Rolling Stone*, a timely record, being as how these were "times for lamentations, for measuring how much of the American promise has been broken or abandoned, and how much of our figure is being transfigured into a vista of ruin". Springsteen gave voice "to people who rarely have one in this culture", an act that, "as we move into the rough times and badlands that lie ahead…will count for more than ever before."

Mat Smith, in *Melody Maker*, wrote that Springsteen had illuminated "how the outside forces of chance and fate shape personal destiny in such a way that leaves you with a discernible lump in the throat."

Springsteen's only other release in the Nineties was a capacious four-CD box set of material plundered from the archives. *Tracks* comprised 66 songs, from the John Hammond demo 'Mary Queen Of Arkansas' (1972) to the sole outtake from *The Ghost Of Tom Joad*, 'Brothers Under The Bridge'. Only Springsteen can explain why this was overlooked in favour of 'My Best Was Never Good Enough', a travesty.

It's a middling collection. Those of us hoping for, or indeed expecting, something from the *Nebraska* sessions featuring the E Street Band were sorely let down. All we got was an acoustic 'Born In The USA' from Colt's Neck.

There was, however, a significant reunion before the close of the century and the beginning of a new millennium, as Springsteen rounded up the E Street Band for a world tour, 18 years since they had last gone on the road with *Born In The USA*.

The set included new versions of 'Mansion On The Hill' and 'Atlantic City' from *Nebraska* – full band versions that caused the faithful to wonder if this was how the electric sessions might have sounded. Gavin Martin, writing in *Uncut* more than a decade later, referred to 'Mansion On The Hill' as "a moveable feast, relocated from its original austere and foreboding Midwest Nebraska setting to become a Tex-Mex border ballad of awed contemplation", while 'Atlantic City' became "a festering epic of corruption, a declaration of war by a rabble-rousing army of Pogues-style brigands."

Other than a more muscular arrangement – insistent backing vocals, a slight Nils Lofgren guitar lick, a vein-bursting refrain of "Meet me tonight in Atlantic City" followed by Max Weinberg's intrusive drum roll at the finale, and the vexatiously obligatory but unnecessary communal handclap – this slow burning band version of 'Atlantic City' adds nothing to the original. It would have sounded good on *Darkness On The Edge Of Town*, say, but it sounds a whole lot better on *Nebraska*.

'Mansion On The Hill' becomes a two-handed ballad – Springsteen and wife sharing the vocal – sweetened by Danny Federici's accordion solo and Nils Lofgren's pedal steel. Again, if you'd not heard it before, or if it had appeared on any Springsteen album except *Nebraska*, you'd be smitten. The fact is, though, it's impossible to hear the *Nebraska* songs in any way other than how they were recorded.

Springsteen captured something on that four-track – some kind of spirit that was hovering in the ether at the time – that he never captured before and has never captured since. You see, *Nebraska* wasn't a made album, it was an album that just happened. What you hear on it is the act of inventiveness in its purest form – a voice, a sound, a feeling, all channelled through an indefinable essence. A Muse by any other name. Yet why does it need a name?

A new song on the reunion tour provoked hostility from a usually reliable section of Springsteen's blue-collar constituency, the New York City Police Department. That song was 'American Skin (41 Shots)'. Several weeks before the Madison Square Garden, New York dates, an African immigrant, Amadou Diallo, had been gunned down by undercover officers outside his apartment in the city. He was shot 41 times. The officers involved were acquitted of any wrongdoing.

"The sheer number of shots seemed to gauge the size of our betrayal of one another," said Springsteen.

New York Mayor Rudy Giuliani, the instigator of the macho zero tolerance policy that had supposedly reduced the level of crime on the streets, and police unions called for a boycott of Springsteen's concerts. When that didn't work, the unions formed a picket outside the Garden, which, when you think about it, was a bit of an extreme reaction to a song most of them hadn't even heard. And while it was critical of the police, it wasn't, according to Springsteen, as anti-police as many thought.

He worked hard for a balanced voice and was acutely aware that a diatribe would serve no valuable purpose – he just wanted to present "the other guy's point of view". The idea, as he explained it, was that a "price in blood" was paid for systematic racial injustice, fear and paranoia.

Two years on from this episode, Springsteen crossed paths once more with the NYPD, though this time in completely different and tragic circumstances.

17. THE LAZARUS EFFECT

"You can trace the characters on The Rising *back to* The River *or even further. They're the same people. They're just living in what America is now."*

BRUCE SPRINGSTEEN

"In the surrounding communities there were quite a few people affected. You knew this woman and her husband, someone else's son, someone else's brother."

BRUCE SPRINGSTEEN on 9/11

The world changed on 9/11. At least that's what the international media told us so it must be true, right? Wrong. What changed on 9/11 was that those who would not be enslaved by America's omnipresent brand of capitalism, by its cultural homogenisation of the planet, struck back. What changed was that indiscriminate killing on a scale unprecedented outside military engagement between nations came to America. What changed was that an American President under suspicion for stealing the election the previous December, exploited the suffering of thousands of grieving families to seize the moral high ground and wage a phoney war on a fundamentalist Islamist terrorist group that probably doesn't even exist.

For what is the 'War on Terror' but a war invented for America's strategic benefit, to facilitate a foothold in the oil rich Middle East? The American lives sacrificed to that aim (and it's arguable these include the poor souls that perished in the Twin Towers) are of little consequence to the power junkies on Capitol Hill or Wall Street, though they matter marginally more than those Iraqi and Afghan lives claimed as collateral damage. No, the world didn't change on 9/11. America's attitude to the world, particularly the Muslim world, is what changed. Along with America itself.

Everybody can remember where they were and what they were doing when news of the attacks on the World Trade Centre broke. Bruce Springsteen was at home.

"Thought it was an accident, but it was a really clear day. I tried to figure that out and went to the television just before the second plane hit. I was just, like everybody, watching the television, a lot of us together. Nobody wanted to be alone, waiting to see what was going to happen."

What did happen was mass murder, a slaughter to which each of us watching wide-eyed and incredulous on our TV screens, was witness. We couldn't believe what we were seeing, we didn't want to believe it. We wanted not to look but we couldn't turn away.

And then there was the aftermath, the agony of the relatives as they waited for news of the missing, all the while knowing, feeling it in their gut, that their loved ones were never coming back. The funerals, the interment of empty caskets, the terrible grief of the widowed, the children, the men in uniform, granite faces stained by tears for their brothers.

"Because we're so close to the city, there were a lot of people lost and there were a lot of town meetings and vigils, and we did our best to take the children out to those things," Springsteen told Robert Crampton in *The Times* ten months later.

And he did more than that. He read the obituaries and called the bereaved, offered sympathy, shared their grief and their memories. Stacey Farrelly, whose husband Joe was among the firemen who went to his death while trying to evacuate the towers, was one of them.

"At the beginning of October I was at home alone and heavily medicated," she recalled. "I picked up the phone and a voice said, 'May I speak to Stacey? This is Bruce Springsteen.' After I got off the phone with him, the world just felt a little smaller. I got through Joe's memorial and a good month and a half on that phone call."

Suzanne Berger, whose husband Jim was an insurance broker, was another Springsteen called. "He said, 'I want to respect your privacy, but I just want you to know that I was very touched and I want to know more about your husband.' He wanted to hear Jim's story, so I told him."

While Springsteen the man reached out to complete strangers in their unbearable anguish, Springsteen the writer's response to 9/11 was *The Rising*, a bunch of songs composed between September 2001 and May 2002 augmented by previously unrecorded material such as 'Nothing Man' and 'Further On (Up The Road)'. America needed consoling, and the greatest form of consolation is to give hope. Who better to deliver that hope than Springsteen and the E Street Band, reunited on a long player for the first time since 1984's *Born In The USA*?

The songs came almost of their own volition, with Springsteen "acting virtually as a receiver of messages flashing in from his own subconscious or from out of the disturbances in the collective ether," according to Adam Sweeting in *Uncut* magazine a year after 9/11. In the same piece, Springsteen told Sweeting, "I think the second or third week in September I'd written 'Into The Fire' for a telethon they had here in the States after 9/11, and I was gonna sing it on the telethon, but instead I sang a song I already had called 'My City Of Ruins'.

"Then I wrote 'You're Missing', then after that I woke up one night and I had this song, 'The Fuse', and so all of a sudden you have these elements of the story you're compelled to tell at a certain moment. That you're kind of asked to tell. Then you look at it and listen to it and it begins to say, there's just a wide variety of emotional elements to make it thoughtful and complete, and the songs kind of present themselves as such and in that fashion.

"It's not necessarily linear and it's not necessarily directly literal – in fact, hopefully it's not really literal. That was something I was trying not to do. I wanted to feel emotionally in that context but not directly literal, though on some songs I was gonna be a little more literal than on others. Those songs kind of anchored the theme of the record, so when you get to the other ones you start to look into it and check the verses and realise it's a piece of the whole thing. That was pretty much how it developed, very instinctively. It wasn't over thought-out."

Lyrically, *The Rising* is at the other end of the spectrum from Springsteen's previous album, *The Ghost Of Tom Joad*. Where the latter, like *Nebraska*, displays a novelist's eye for detail in depicting scene and characterisation, the former owes more to the populist approach of a visual artist intent on making an immediate impact. In this instance the image is vivified by the colour of sound, a sound generated by Springsteen and the E Street Band and finessed by Brendan O'Brien, a new production recruit renowned for his collaborations with Pearl Jam, Soundgarden and Rage Against The Machine. It is the sound of *The Rising* more than the words that inspires the hope referred to earlier – that curious ability music has to manipulate the emotions, to raise us up. Call it the Lazarus effect, if you will. Unlike *Nebraska* or *The Ghost Of Tom Joad*, these songs had to be made bigger by the band.

Springsteen again: "On *Nebraska*, immediately the band played those songs they overruled the lyrics. It didn't work. Those two forms didn't fit. The band comes in and generally makes noise, and the lyrics wanted silence. They make arrangement, and the lyrics wanted less arrangement. The lyrics wanted to be at the centre and there was a minimal amount of music. The music was very necessary but it wanted to be minimal, and so with *The Rising* I was trying to make an exciting record with the E Street Band which I hadn't done in a long time, so that form was kind of driving me."

In settling on a form dominated by anthemic choruses and irresistible hooks, Springsteen intuitively gave America what it needed at that particular moment. His was an outfit built "for difficult times". When people wanted a dialogue, "a conversation of events, internal and external, we developed a language that suited those moments, a language I hoped would entertain, inspire, comfort and reveal."

'Lonesome Day' sets the tone for much of what follows on *The Rising*. There are flash pictures of hell brewing, dark sun, storm, a house ablaze, a viper in the grass, revenge…but in the end a promise that this will all come to pass, that we will find the courage to navigate our way through the lonesome day.

Courage is manifest too in 'Into The Fire' – the courage of the firefighters who ascended the stairs of the Twin Towers on an impossible rescue mission, an ascension into the fire, into the sky, "somewhere higher", into heaven. The refrain is gospel, Springsteen praying for the same fortitude and faith and hope and love that these brave men carried with them to their deaths.

'Waitin' On A Sunny Day' could jar but doesn't. It's an innocuous pop song, yes, but never underestimate the invigorating properties of the innocuous pop song. Springsteen told VH1's *Storytellers* that this is the kind of song he writes to hear it sung back at him by a live audience. Yet on *The Rising* it serves a purpose too, reminding us that hard times come to everyone but that blues are temporary and that sunny day is never far away. You've just got to keep faith. Later on the album, 'Mary's Place' is similar in its design and intention.

'Nothing Man' is about a small-town hero who doesn't feel like a hero at all but is assailed by remorse for having survived whatever incident earned him his status. It's difficult not to associate the sentiments expressed in the song with the post-9/11 guilt felt by those members of the emergency services who lived while their comrades died, yet the song was actually written in 1994.

On 'Countin' On A Miracle', the protagonist is "still waiting on, insisting on life". Along with 'Let's Be Friends (Skin To Skin)' and 'Further On (Up The Road)', this is Springsteen and the E Street Band doing what they do best, "tearin' down the house".

As you listen to 'Empty Sky', you can't help but see the space where the Twin Towers used to stand. There is fleeting anger here, a suggestion of Biblical payback, "an eye for an eye". This may have been the manifesto of George W Bush's administration, but such bloodlust has no place on *The Rising*, which is about healing not hating. And part of that healing process involved the introduction of voices other than American voices, situations other than American situations.

"I wanted Eastern voices, the presence of Allah. I wanted to find a place where worlds collide and meet," said Springsteen.

The Eastern voices on 'Worlds Apart' (in which blood builds a bridge, peoples on opposite sides of tragedy are united) are those of Pakistani Qawwali singers Asif Ali Kahn and his group.

'The Fuse' is stuffed full of unsettling images of "life during wartime, scenes from home in the days immediately following the eleventh" – the lowered flag, the funeral cortege, the black dust...

'You're Missing' was apparently inspired by Springsteen's conversations with Suzanne Berger. It's a heartbreaking litany of absence, everyday reminders of a life that was once shared by another and that now hangs in some kind of purgatorial suspense.

'The Rising' itself, Springsteen told Robert Santelli, is a bookend to 'Into The Fire', a sort of secular Stations of the Cross in which the steps of duty are "irretraceable, the hard realisation of all the life and love left behind".

For Steve Wynn, founder member of Dream Syndicate, this was Springsteen's vast songwriting experience coming into its own. "There's a challenge – write an uplifting and positive song about the sad and doomed task of the firefighters in the World Trade Centre. And make it poetic. And fill it with hooks, something easy to sing with in both arenas and solitary rides on the freeway. And don't slip into cheap and obvious sentimentality or grandstanding. The kind of songwriting challenge that could be pulled off only after many decades of songwriting."

'Paradise' offers different impressions of the afterlife, including a Palestinian suicide bomber contemplating his last moments, and a Navy wife yearning for the husband lost at the Pentagon. The 'I' in the song bridges the gap between life and death in the final verse, glimpsing a loved one on the far shore, eyes "empty as paradise" – perhaps a reference to the futility of the 9/11 bombers' self-sacrifice in seeking their place in the Islamic Paradise.

'My City Of Ruins' closes *The Rising* on an exhortation – "Come on, rise up!" Like the earlier 'Nothing Man', eerily prescient of 9/11 in its self-reproach for surviving when others did not, it was written beforehand. A whole year beforehand, as a lament for Springsteen's old stomping ground, Asbury Park. Or at least it begins as a lament. But by the end it's a plea to the Lord (Springsteen's Catholic impulse kicking in again) to fill the American people with strength and faith and love – not dissimilar indeed to 'Into The Fire' – so that they may rise again from the ashes of that dreadful day in September.

The Rising resurrected Springsteen's profile too after what could arguably be called his wilderness years. Not only was it a massive seller and a wow with the critics, but it restored his reputation as the unofficial All American voice, a man who understood what the nation was feeling and who knew exactly how to salve its wounds.

"Springsteen wades into the wreckage and pain of that horrendous event and emerges bearing 15 songs that genuflect with enormous grace before the sorrows that drift in its wake," wrote Kurt Loder in *Rolling Stone*.

"The small miracle of his accomplishment is that at no point does he give vent to the anger felt by so many Americans: the hunger for revenge. The music is often fierce in its execution, but in essence it is a requiem for those who perished in that sudden inferno, and those who died trying to save them. Springsteen grandly salutes their innocence and their courage and holds out a hand to those who mourn them, who seek the comfort of an explanation for the inexplicable."

The Rising, Loder enthused, was "a singular triumph. I can't think of another album in which such an abundance of great songs might be said to seem the least of its achievements."

For Alan Light, in *The New Yorker*, *The Rising* contained "none of the political engagement we might have expected to find on a Bruce Springsteen 9/11 album. In fact, this is ultimately an album about love."

AO Scott, in his *Slate* magazine review, identified a link between the recurring nouns used by Springsteen (blood, fire, rain, sky, strength, hope, faith, love) and the repetition that psychologists say "is part of the work of grief".

He explained, "Over the course of the 15 songs on *The Rising*, the reiteration of key words and phrases – now sung in agony, now in resignation, now in hope – has a cathartic effect. In the weeks and months after 9/11, people told and retold their stories almost compulsively and plunged again and again into their terror and confusion in a paradoxical effort to move beyond the experience and to keep it close. *The Rising*...has a similar effect. It neither assuages the horror with false hope nor allows it to slip into nihilistic despair."

In Britain, *Uncut*'s Sarfraz Manzoor described it as "a brave and beautiful album of humanity, hurt and hope from the songwriter best qualified to speak to and for his country," while Sylvie Simmons in *Mojo* hailed the album's message of indomitability.

18. THE FINALITY OF DEATH

"These are all songs about people whose souls are in danger, or at risk, through where they are in the world and what the world is bringing to them."

BRUCE SPRINGSTEEN on *Devils & Dust*

"I try to find small shifts in musical tone that complement the characters I'm singing about. You're always trying to find a voice you haven't used before, to make each new character come alive. You're writing from the essential core of who you are, but if you're doing it correctly your own voice is supposed to disappear into the voice of the person you're singing about."

BRUCE SPRINGSTEEN

If the fans thought *The Rising* represented a permanent reunion of Bruce Springsteen and the E Street Band, *Devils & Dust* stripped them of that notion. With the exception of Danny Federici on keys and Patti Scialfa on backing vocals, there isn't an E Streeter to be heard. Co-producers Brendan O'Brien and Chuck Plotkin were enlisted to play bass, tambora, sitar, electric sarangi, hurdy gurdy and piano, while the rest of the personnel were session musicians (although Soozie Tyrell would later become a bona fide E Street member).

It is acoustic in form in the same way that *Tunnel Of Love* was acoustic, even if some reviewers lazily insisted the album was the final part of a trilogy that included *Nebraska* and *The Ghost Of Tom Joad*. Admittedly it is occasionally close in lyrical content to the latter (hardly surprising as many of the songs were written when Springsteen was touring *The Ghost Of Tom Joad*), but the comparison with *Nebraska* begins and ends with Springsteen's narrative modus operandi, the way in which he inhabits the characters in the songs, playing the roles of soldier, immigrant, boxer and prostitute's client.

But none of these characterisations are ever as interesting or as convincing as the ones on *Nebraska*. His commitment to them isn't as wholehearted – it's as though he's keeping something back, like he's shadowing them without wanting to become them. Remember a young Marlon Brando, in *A Streetcar Named Desire*, say, or *On The Waterfront*. Remember how you forgot he was Marlon Brando at all, how you bought into him completely as Stanley Kowalski or Terry Malloy.

Then fast forward to his autumn years when, for whatever reasons (disillusionment, apathy, the vacuity of the parts), he couldn't summon up (or couldn't be bothered to summon up) the same intensity. This is Springsteen on *Devils & Dust*. So while something like 'The Hitter' is well written, it doesn't work precisely because it's so well written. Tension has been sacrificed for technique, and it's the absence of tension that means 'The Hitter' is never anything more than a admirable but desperately dull song, a song that prompts a 'so what?' shrug of the shoulders on the part of the listener. Springsteen just doesn't make us care enough.

Six months before *Devils & Dust* was released, Springsteen was a visible presence on the campaign trail of American presidential candidate John Kerry. While we always knew his politics were more Democratic than Republican, more left than right, he had never before declared his allegiance so publicly. He effectively became a Kerry activist, touring the country's swing states as part of the *Vote For Change* bandwagon alongside REM and Conor Oberst's Bright Eyes, and addressing mass rallies, urging undecided Americans "to fight for a government that is open, rational, forward-looking and humane". In short, everything that George W Bush's administration was not. Springsteen wanted an America "where everyone can make a living wage that's going to tie them into the fabric of their nation and of their community and of their society, and give people a stake in life."

Unfortunately not enough of the electorate shared his vision. They endorsed Bush for a second term in office (though many would claim it was, in fact, his first term in office given the alleged electoral larceny that occurred first time round) and condemned Kerry to political obscurity. The experience didn't deter Springsteen, who would throw his weight behind Barack Obama four years later, with an altogether more satisfactory outcome.

Given what was happening in America under Bush – the clampdown on civil liberties, the corporate dictatorship that ran the White House, the disastrous invasions of Afghanistan and Iraq – and given his own full-on engagement with the political process and its disappointing, dispiriting conclusion, it wasn't unreasonable to expect that Springsteen would do a Woody and get topical on *Devils & Dust*. Maybe get angry at what was being done in America's name, in the so-called name of freedom.

Yet with the exception of the title track (written on *The Rising* tour shortly after America entered Iraq), he chooses to avoid that particular minefield. Instead we get more songs about "people who have something eating at them". I'd rather have heard what was eating Bruce Springsteen, probably because it was the same thing that was eating most of us – the flagrant abuse of the democratic ideology by America and its allies, chief cheerleader among which was Britain under Tony Blair, an opportunist untroubled by the blood of innocents on his hands, so intoxicated was he by the fantasy of returning imperial status to a nation washed up on the world stage.

This was surely a time for Springsteen and other conscientious artists to emerge from behind their art, to stop citing the neutrality of their art as grounds for immunity from becoming involved in the struggle against the new world order. This was a time when we needed our artists to stand up and, yes, be counted, to play their part in righting the wrongs, to rouse the sheep from their torpor with some shocking truths, because the usual suspects aside (Michael Moore, John Pilger, Robert Fisk), the media was reneging on its responsibility. But the only artists tough enough to kick against the pricks were Steve Earle, on *Jerusalem* and *The Revolution Starts Now* (in 2002 and 2004 respectively), and, in 2006, Neil Young on *Living With War*.

It's not a little disconcerting to learn that Springsteen – for reasons only he (and perhaps Mr Landau) can explain – ditched a direct reference to the Iraq occupation from the version of 'Devils & Dust' he and the E Street Band had soundchecked on *The Rising* tour, a reference that chimed with what Moore, Pilger, Fisk, Earle and Young were claiming, namely that "It's a world of earth and oil/Paid for with gunpowder and blood."

Springsteen provided a fascinating glimpse of his compositional strategy in VH1's *Storytellers* shortly after the release of *Devils & Dust*. He performed eight of his songs completely solo, either on acoustic guitar or piano, and followed the performances with a commentary on each song. The set, before a 300-strong crowd of mostly prize-winning fans at the Two River Theatre in Red Bank, New Jersey, featured selections from *Greetings...* ('Blinded By The Light'), *Born To Run* ('Thunder Road'), *Nebraska* ('Nebraska'), *Tunnel Of Love* ('Brilliant Disguise'), *The Rising* ('Waitin' On A Sunny Day' and 'The Rising') and *Devils & Dust* ('Devils & Dust' and 'Jesus Was An Only Son').

Speaking about the title track of his then latest album, he said, "You need a strong metaphor. It focuses and shapes the rest of the song. 'Devils & Dust' suggests confusion. It's a story about being placed in a situation where your choices are untenable, and the price that that inflicts on blood and on spirit.

"In the first two lines of the song, that's where the political and personal aspects collide. I'm talking about him, I'm talking about us. A lot of what you need to know about the song is contained in those first two lines and has been played out over the past few years.

"When I'm looking at you, I don't know if I'm seeing you. I don't know if I'm seeing myself. I don't know if I'm seeing my fears. I don't know if I'm seeing my highest ideals that I have promised to sacrifice my life for. I don't know if I'm seeing my death coming at me. The problem is, I have to know right now.

"I've been separated from all the things that have given my life shape and meaning until now. My family, my home, my work, the things that ground me and that I recognise as myself. "What if what you do to stay alive, destroys some part of you? What if what we do destroys our ideals? We're experiencing an erosion of our civil liberties, which is what I was thinking about when I was writing this chorus. What's been going on is very dangerous and un-American.

"The music is working against the lyrics. It's the unspoken subtext that the lyrics rest on. So you're hearing a regular guy caught in the crosshairs of history, and you're hearing his conversation with himself, and you're hearing his inner struggle. And what gives the song its power and its tension, is the tension between the lyrics – what he knows is happening to him – and his resistance, his refusal, which is given voice in the music and the performance. The music informs the lyric with so much extra information.

"Faith ain't enough. You've got to be active in some action. You've got to be in the physical world and take action. All of this is inside. These are my times, this is my house, this is my fight and these are my choices. We've been bitten by the snake, but we don't have to all succumb to its poison."

'All The Way Home' was actually recorded by Southside Johnny in 1991, and finds Springsteen and band (including Brendan O'Brien on electric sarangi and sitar, and Marty Rifkin on steel guitar) stretching out in that awkward, stiff-legged way that characterised much of *Human Touch* and *Lucky Town*. It's a fire without a spark, a musical idea as jaded as the lyrical sentiment – a half-hearted end-of-the-night overture with sexual undertones.

There's nothing so suggestive about 'Reno'. Springsteen lays it all out in his most explicitly erotic song, earning *Devils & Dust* a parental advisory sticker and giving Starbucks the willies – they withdrew from a deal to stock the album in their coffee houses. Instead of ramping up the pressure on the Bush administration with a stinging attack on its fascistic policies, Springsteen's post-Iraq invasion album offended the moral sensibility of a corporate giant with no moral scruples whatsoever about charging the equivalent of the minimum wage for a tall skinny Latte.

'Reno' could have been discomfiting for a writer – and, indeed, a man, of Springsteen's high-minded virtue. The character here is what the sex trade labels a 'John', someone who pays for sex. It's not a particularly gratifying pursuit. But then nor it is particularly exceptional. What saves Springsteen's skin is the forlornness of the episode. There's nothing horny about the way in which he details the transaction ("Two hundred dollars straight in, two-fifty up the ass"), nothing triumphantly macho about the ending. There is nothing, in fact, but emptiness, an unfulfilled longing that transcends the physical. It is, if you'll excuse the double entendre, a ballsy piece of writing.

'Long Time Comin'' is – and be warned, this is going to come over toe-curlingly corny – a lovely affirmation of life, a gently rousing rocker on which Springsteen proclaims that he's going to get "birth naked" and bury his old soul before dancing naked on its grave. This is a Springsteen archetype, a perfect coalition of words, music and feeling that warms you like the sun.

'Black Cowboys' is one of several songs on *Devils & Dust* about mothers and sons. Rainey Williams' mother declares him to be her blessing and pride, his love the sustenance that keeps her soul alive; her son always has her "smile to depend upon". But their relationship is undermined when she takes up with a man "whose business was the boulevard, whose smile was fixed in a face that was never off guard." Rainey heads for the hills of Oklahoma, where once the "black cowboys" fought the Indian tribes. He's seeking communion with his spiritual ancestors, having been rejected by his own blood. 'Black Cowboys' is another of Springsteen's gripping narratives couched in poetic language – echoes of Cormac McCarthy. But like many of the songs on *The Ghost Of Tom Joad*, musically it plods along.

The same could be said of 'Silver Palomino'. Again it's impossible to listen to this without thinking of McCarthy's border trilogy, *All The Pretty Horses*, *The Crossing* and *Cities Of The Plain*, and the intensity of the bond between boy and beast in these three novels. The mother in this story is dead (it was written in remembrance of

Fiona Chappel, a neighbour and close friend of the Springsteen's, for her sons, Tyler and Oliver), and her son wrestles with reconciling himself to her loss. He talks about his beloved horse, the Palomino of the title, and everything else but the person he wants to talk about. Until the final verse, when, riding deep into the mountains, the air he breathes brings her back to him, the sensuality of nature working its magic on memory.

The third song exploring the mother/son theme is 'Jesus Was An Only Son' which, for my money, is among the finest Springsteen has written. It makes Jesus Christ human, flesh and blood – a boy, a man, adored by his mother, desirous of what life had to offer him, fearful of death. Not unlike most of us when it all comes down. Springsteen plays simple churchy organ (as well as guitar, bass and drums), while Patti Scialfa, Soozie Tyrell and Lisa Lowell chip in with some heavenly backing vocals.

"That's a song that starts from the premise that everybody knows what it's like to be saved," he said on *Storytellers*. "On *Devils & Dust* I wrote several songs about mothers and sons. This was really one of them. I was kind of interested in the relationship between parent and child, which is why Mary figures so prominently in the song. I felt if I approached the song from the secular side, the rest of it would come through. 'Jesus Was An Only Son' – that's my main metaphor, but of course, Jesus had earthly brothers and sisters, but not on this particular day."

Springsteen plays a snatch of 'Darkness On The Edge Of Town' on the piano for a rapt VH1 congregation, to illustrate the idea of the proving ground that unifies the two songs. Jesus' proving ground was, of course, Calvary Hill. In the song, Mary walks by his side, "in the path where his blood spilled" – a path identified by Springsteen as "the path of consequence".

The second verse captures a precious moment in their Nazarene home, as Jesus reads the psalms by his mother's feet. I wanted an image of parental love and nurturing, and of life and of promise and of peace before what was to come." The third verse is a mother's prayer for her child, a petition simply to protect them, to keep them safe.

"Every parent wants to keep their children from all harm. It's such a primal thing. I was shocked when I first felt it so deep inside myself. And then I had a conversation with a friend, where I was afraid that my kids were going to grow up... I said, 'Gee, they might not have to struggle like I struggled. Maybe that's not such a good thing.' And he said, 'No, no, no, no, you're a parent, man. You give them the best because the world is going to take care of the rest.' And that's true. The world awaits us all, and there's not much that parents can do about it."

The fourth verse, in which Jesus awaits his fate in the garden of Gethsemane, reveals him not as the resigned self-sacrificial lamb depicted in the Bible but as someone who doesn't want to die, who beseeches God to spare him so that he may spread the word on earth.

"You'd have to be thinking, gee, there was that little bar in Galilee, a pretty nice little place. The weather's good down there too. I could manage the place. Mary Magdalene could tend bar. We could have some kids. And the preaching? I could do it on the weekends. I don't have to give it up. You'd have to be thinking that."

The penultimate verse is "the finality of death". Springsteen, in a moving reference to Fiona Chappel, though not by name, continued, "Regardless of what Jesus was going to meet, for Mary, she was just losing her boy. And we lose one another, and people don't get replaced. I had a friend, my wife and I had a friend, young lady lived next door to us, who passed away at a very young age. She used to come over to our house every night. There was a moment where she'd be framed in the front window, just before she knocked on the door. And I'd look up – she was this very tall and elegant lady. I still wait to see her in that window."

In the final verse, Jesus almost assumes the paternal role, kissing his mother's hands, wiping away her tears, as he moves forward into the unknown with faith to guide and nurture him.

"That's transformation. Our children have their own destiny apart from us. And I think my idea was to try and reach into the idea of Jesus as son, as somebody's boy. Because I think that whatever divinity we can lay claim to is hidden in the core of our humanity. And when we let our compassion go, we let go of whatever claim we have to a divine. So it's spooky out there sometimes."

A striking feature of *Devils & Dust* is Springsteen's voice. The falsetto that first surfaced on the acoustic tour that followed the release of *The Ghost Of Tom Joad* is revisited here, notably on 'All I'm Thinkin' About' and, to a lesser extent, on 'Maria's Bed'. It's a voice he explored further during the *Devils & Dust* concerts, alongside a distorted Tom Waits growl on *Nebraska*'s 'Reason To Believe'. Together with 'Leah', 'All I'm Thinkin' About' and 'Maria's Bed' embody whimsical respite from the dense subject matter elsewhere.

'The Hitter', already mentioned in this chapter, is a turgid trawl through the career of a weary, punch drunk ex-boxer returning home to his ma. The third mother/son song is the story of the prodigal son, though the welcome isn't as forthcoming here. This pitiful character is on the other side of a locked door, imploring his mother to open up. He wants nothing from her, nothing more than to lie down and rest. And we leave him standing outside that locked door still imploring, defeated again.

'Metamoros Banks' closes the album. This is the place along the Rio Grande at which Mexicans illegally enter America at Brownsville in Texas, the place where hundreds of impoverished people have perished in search of a better life. Springsteen shows himself to be a writer unafraid to play with form by telling the tale of one such unfortunate casualty in reverse. The first two verses follow a body past children's playgrounds "and empty switching yards", a body to which other living things, "the things of the earth", have already laid claim.

The chorus rewinds to the man who once inhabited the body, serenading his lover as she makes the crossing. And then it's his turn to dive "into the silty red river", his yearning for her kiss becoming an eternal yearning as he is swallowed up by the currents. Springsteen sings the last chorus tenderly, compassionately. It's utterly harrowing.

Where critical reaction to *The Rising* was on the whole acclamatory, *Devils & Dust* didn't win everybody over. *Mojo* magazine, however, hailed it as "music that observes and feels life in the way that any worthwhile political vision must", before mentioning Springsteen in the same breath as Woody Guthrie, Bob Dylan, Muddy Waters, John Lee Hooker, Johnny Cash and Willie Nelson as artists "born to live into middle age, old age and burn on down that road."

For Cat Goodwin in *NME*, *Devils & Dust* reaffirmed Springsteen's worth as he "swaps the political back to the personal and fact for fiction with an album of fabricated folk (lore) tales", while *Q* described it as "an inspired stopgap". Springsteen would surely baulk at the implication that anything he produces is a stopgap.

Alex Petridis in *The Guardian* was even less enamoured, though he admitted the album "rarely does what you expect it to: even the Iraq war-inspired title track is strangely subdued and ambiguous, given Springsteen's vocal opposition to the war. You're carried through its bumpier moments by the winning sound of an artist hanging the consequences and doing what he wants to," he adds, before concluding: "Not all its experiments work, but the last thing you feel like doing is blaming Bruce Springsteen for trying."

In America, *Rolling Stone*'s David Fricke reckoned *Devils & Dust* represented Springsteen's "most conventional singer-songwriter record since his 1973 debut, *Greetings From Asbury Park, NJ*." Its twelve songs were "rendered with a subdued, mostly acoustic flair that smells of wood smoke and sparkles in the right places like stars in a clear Plains sky. "

The Village Voice verdict disagreed in no uncertain terms. It was, according to their reviewer, "long and boring and preachy".

19. CARNIVAL RIDE

"It was a carnival ride, the sound of surprise and the pure joy of playing."
BRUCE SPRINGSTEEN on We Shall Overcome: The Seeger Sessions

"Bruce is carrying on the folk tradition, not just musically but in so many other ways."
JIM MUSSELMAN

Bruce Springsteen's next project gave licence to his folk alter ego to express itself more overtly than ever before. Long and boring and preachy it wasn't. Rather it was verification, if any were needed, that his heart was in the country as much as in the city, that he was as comfortable in the company of fiddles and banjos and accordions as he was standing out front of probably the greatest live rock'n'roll band of its generation.

Given the manifest influence of Woody Guthrie on Springsteen's later writing, nobody would have blinked an eye had he decided to record an album covering songs by or associated with the Oklahoma troubadour. But instead he turned to Woody's erstwhile straight man, Pete Seeger. By his own admission, Springsteen wasn't too familiar with Seeger's music or history when invited by Appleseed Recordings chief Jim Musselman to contribute a version of 'We Shall Overcome' to *Where Have All The Flowers Gone: The Songs Of Pete Seeger* in 1997.

Musselman had only just established the label with the twin aim of using it as a vehicle for socially conscious contemporary folk and roots music and to ensure that old folk songs would not be forgotten.

He explains, "I had been an activist attorney for years in Washington, working on social issues. I had conversations with Pete Seeger and Roger McGuinn of the Byrds, and we were talking about how so many folk songs were not being sung any more. A lot of these songs came over from England, Ireland and Scotland – all the immigrants brought with them was the shirt on their back and the songs. I felt these songs were in danger of being lost forever. Nobody was singing them any more."

The Appleseed roster now boasts the likes of Dick Gaughan, Buffy Sainte-Marie, Tom Paxton and Johnny Clegg, alongside Springsteen and Seeger.

Musselman's courting of Springsteen wasn't initially successful. "When I started doing *Where Have All The Flowers Gone*, I wanted to do songs of Pete Seeger with artists who were representative of Pete. I had grown up a fan of Bruce, but it was actually albums like *Nebraska* and *The Ghost Of Tom Joad* that made me ask him, because I realised that he was an artist who had guts and wasn't afraid to take chances. He wasn't afraid to go out of the box and do something totally different, the antithesis of what was expected of him. So he was on my shortlist.

"I contacted him and he said no the first time, he said no the second time. I decided to be persistent and went back a third time. The irony of it all was (that) when he said yes there was only a week left in the project and most of the songs had already been recorded. I told him to take a shot at a folk song or two. I never knew how much he was going to immerse himself in the whole project. I sent him tapes. He went out and bought some of Pete's old records. Bruce likes to understand the roots of all music, be it rock, blues, folk or anything. And he just immersed himself in Pete's music. He usually takes a long time to record, but he recorded seven songs for the project.

"It's ironic that *The Seeger Sessions* came out of this, because it was just a lot of persistence and not giving up on the dream of having Bruce on *Where Have All The Flowers Gone.* I sort of opened the door and he jumped into it. It was amazing to see how he immersed himself in the folk songs and in the folk genre. It wasn't a big leap, I didn't think, because he had always written about working class people – real people, real stories. That's what Pete had always written about and sung about too. Bruce is carrying on the tradition, not just musically but in so many other ways. I think he is one of the people carrying the torch very strongly."

Musselman could hear the folk signposts in Springsteen's work as early as *Greetings…*, signposts which opened out onto a fully-formed folk landscape on *Nebraska.* "I was just blown away by how real it was. I always appreciate stripped-down acoustic music. There was an honesty to it, but also the characters in the songs and the stories – it was just quintessential storytelling along with just a lot of guts to do an album like that.

"It was a surprise because you had the biggest rock artist in the world doing an album with him and his guitar just recorded on a tape recorder. A lot of musicians would love to do something like that, but they feel like they can't, that it's not going to sell as much, the fans aren't going to like it. I think in many ways Bruce has liberated musicians when he's done things like *The Seeger Sessions, Nebraska* and *The Ghost Of Tom Joad,* because now musicians feel more strongly about what they do in their heart, as opposed to just going through the motions. Obviously I had been a fan of *Greetings…*, the Bruce singer-songwriter. But to do what he did with *Nebraska* at the time that he did it was very shocking.

"I think it speaks of the desolation at times of America, of how big a country it is but also how there is a whole other side to America that you don't see a lot of times. It's sort of bringing attention to this – as (political satirist) Jon Stewart would say, the forgotten people, never heard and never seen. It sort of paints a real picture of America, not the picture you might see on the television set at times."

Springsteen's involvement on the Musselman-commandeered Seeger tribute album gave him an appetite for more of the same. Through Soozie Tyrell, the most recent addition to the E Street Band on violin, he assembled a dozen of the finest folk players out of New York City later the same year. These players included Charles Giordano on accordion and keyboards (a mainstay of Pat Benatar's Eighties band and, since Danny Federici's passing, a permanent member of the E Street Band), Sam Barfield on violin and Mark Clifford on banjo. Augmenting the folkie line-up were the horns of Ed Manion, Mark Pender and Richie 'La Bamba' Rosenberg, an original member of Springsteen's New Jersey ally John Lyon's Southside Johnny and the Asbury Jukes.

"I counted off the opening chords to 'Jesse James' and away we went," Springsteen writes in the liner notes for *We Shall Overcome: The Seeger Sessions*. Yet for all the fun of those first sessions in the living room of Springsteen's New Jersey farmhouse (there was no room for the brass section, who had to move out to the hallway), it was another eight years before, in 2005, the group resumed recording to finish the album.

It was released in April 2006, exactly a year after *Devils & Dust*, and was probably as much of a curve ball to casual Springsteen listeners as *Nebraska*. To the rest of us, it made perfect sense. Springsteen was not only flagging up his folk roots, but he was reviving songs written in other eras to reflect what was happening in the here and now – the title track, 'Mrs McGrath', 'How Can A Poor Man Stand Such Times And Live?' and 'Bring 'Em Home' (both on the *American Land* edition) – as well as delivering a kind of spiritual infusion at a time when American spirits in particular were depleting as increasing numbers of young men were sacrificed on the bloodthirsty streets of Baghdad, and America itself was in paranoid, lockdown mode.

A good tune has always been the perfect antidote to feeling bad. And *The Seeger Sessions* is full of good tunes – tunes performed with the rowdy fervour of an Irish hooley, a country hoedown, a happy clappy churchy celebration, a rock'n'roll party. Springsteen is in his element, less a leader than a band member. This is as much about the other musicians as it is about him. And, of course, ultimately it's about those tunes.

'Old Dan Tucker' dates back to 1843 – or at least that's when the version Springsteen chose was written by one Dan Emmett for the Virginia Minstrels. Prior to that it was a fiddle tune played at square dances. It later became renowned as a popular blackface song during the American Civil War. The models for the Dan Tucker character were said to be Reverend Daniel Tucker of Ebert County, Georgia, and Captain Daniel Tucker, a Virginian who was the second British Governor of Bermuda.

'Jesse James', a ballad immortalising the American outlaw, was written by Billy Gashade in the 1880s, not long after James' assassination by the mercenary Robert Ford (himself gunned down ten years later by Edward O'Kelly out of revenge for James' death). Many other songs have been penned about James, who has also been the subject of just as many movies, but this, alongside Woody Guthrie's 'Jesse James', remains the most enduring, having been recorded by the likes of the Kingston Trio, Burl Ives, Ry Cooder and Van Morrison.

'Mrs McGrath', whose origins can be traced back to the Napoleonic Wars, was a staple of the Irish Republican movement during the 1916 Easter Rising. It's a potent anti-war lyric which, though written in the 19th Century, finds a parallel in the recent conflicts wrought by America and its British ally in Afghanistan and Iraq. Mrs McGrath is welcoming her son home from the navy, his legs having been blown away by a cannonball. For cannonball, substitute improvised explosive devices, the scourge of occupying British forces in Afghanistan's Helmand province.

And then we're into gospel territory for the first time on the album. 'O Mary Don't You Weep' is a spiritual predating the American Civil War. The Mary of the title is Mary of Bethany who, with her sister Martha, implored Jesus Christ to raise their brother Lazarus from the dead. However, much of this version of the song is culled from the Book of Exodus in the Bible's Old Testament, with its references to Pharoah's Army being "drownded". This, like 'We Shall Overcome' itself and 'Eyes On The Prize', were adopted as anthems of the civil rights struggle in the Fifties and Sixties.

'John Henry' is among the most recorded American folk songs. It tells the unlikely but apparently true story of man versus machine during the building of America's eastern railroads in the late 19th Century. The man, John Henry, offered to race against a steam drill to determine which of them could dig a deeper hole in the mountain (folklore has it that the mountain was West Virginia's Big Bend Mountain, though a University of Georgia academic suggest it was the Coosa or Oak Mountain tunnel of the former C&W Railroad in Alabama). He did indeed beat the steam drill, only to die at the point of victory. 'John Henry' has been covered by Dock Boggs, Big Bill Broonzy, Odetta, Woody Guthrie, Arlo Guthrie, John Lee Hooker, Leadbelly, Jerry Lee Lewis, Bill Monroe, Paul Robeson and countless others.

'Erie Canal' was written by Thomas S Allen as 'Low Bridge, Everybody Down' in 1905, about the canal of the title that was constructed some 80 years earlier to link New York City in the east with Buffalo and the west.

'Jacob's Ladder' is another spiritual. It references the prophetic dream given to Jacob at Beth-El (in the Book of Genesis) as he flees his brother Esau whose inheritance he has stolen. In the dream, angels climb a ladder to heaven while God promises Jacob that his seed "shall be the dust of the earth". This was a dream that America's slaves could identify with, as it concluded with a covenant promising liberation.

'My Oklahoma Home' was written (with her brother Bill) by Agnes 'Sis' Cunningham, cohort of Woody Guthrie and Pete Seeger, member of the Almanac Singers, co-editor of *Broadside* magazine and Dust Bowl refugee. It's a humorous take on a natural disaster and became a particular favourite among audiences on *The Seeger Sessions* tour, as they got to indulge in the call and response chorus.

'Eyes On The Prize' is a hymn also known as 'Gospel Plow', 'Paul And Silas', 'Keep Your Hand On The Plow' and 'Hold On'. Composed in the early 20th Century, the version Springsteen calls on here was written by civil rights activist Alice Wine in 1956. The prize, in this context, is freedom from the chains of racial oppression. The lyric is in keeping with the non-violent manifesto of Dr Martin Luther King Junior.

'Shenandoah' is an American pioneer's homesick lament from the first years of the 19th Century. Its melody, like so many American folk songs, carries a melancholy strain that pulses with Irishness, something accentuated by the Chieftains in their 1998 recording with Van Morrison on the *Long Journey Home* album. Take my advice and check out the essential reading of it by Paul Robeson.

'Pay Me My Money Down' was originally a protest song of black stevedores exploited by unscrupulous ship captains in the ports of Georgia and South Carolina.

'We Shall Overcome' has been described by Springsteen biographer Dave Marsh as "the most important political protest song of all-time, sung around the world wherever people fight for justice and equality." A big statement, yet one it would be difficult to counter. It was certainly the mainstay of the campaign for civil rights. Pete

Seeger calls it "a portfolio song" in its accommodation of new verses, often extemporary. Before its association with civil rights, 'We Shall Overcome' was first sang politically by the Southern Tenant Farmers' Union in Arkansas and later by striking workers at a cigar warehouse in Charleston, South Carolina. The royalties from the song once went to the Student Nonviolent Coordinating Committee (SNCC). But as that organisation no longer exists, the beneficiaries are now the Highlander Centre in Tennessee, whose mission statement declares that they "work with people fighting for justice, equality and sustainability, supporting their efforts to take collective action to shape their own destiny". The monies earned from 'We Shall Overcome' are, fittingly enough, distributed in small grants for cultural expression to African-American groups working in the south.

'Froggie Went A-Courtin' is the oldest song on *The Seeger Sessions*, the earliest version having appeared in the book, *Complaynt of Scotland*, in 1549. It featured on Harry Smith's *Anthology of American Folk Music* as 'King Kong Kitchie Kitchie Ki-Me-O' (by Chubby Parker), and has been recorded by Woody Guthrie (with Sonny Terry and Cisco Houston), Tex Ritter and Bob Dylan.

And there ends the version of *The Seeger Sessions* issued in April 2006. Six months later, it was re-issued as the *American Land* version with five bonus tracks. 'Buffalo Gals' harks back to the days of the 'Erie Canal', the girls of the title being prostitutes. It was initially known as 'Lubly Fan', and has had several other incarnations, including 'Alabama Gals', 'As I Walked Down On Broadway' and 'Dance With The Dolly'.

The hymn, 'How Can I Keep From Singing', was first published by Robert Lowry, a Pennsylvania Baptist minister from the 19th Century, in the 1969 collection *Bright Jewels For The Sunday School*.

'How Can A Poor Man Stand Such Times And Live' was written and recorded by Blind Alfred Reed a month after the stock market crash that ushered in the Great Depression. Springsteen, outraged by George Bush's inept response to the devastation wreaked on New Orleans in the wake of Hurricane Katrina, updated the song during *The Seeger Sessions* tour with a scathing attack on the White House puppet.

'Bring 'Em Home' was written by Pete Seeger during the Vietnam War. As with 'How Can A Poor Man Stand Such Times And Live', Springsteen added his own spin, charging the warmongers in Washington and Downing Street with wanting "to test their grand theories/With the blood of you and me."

Finally, 'American Land' is a Springsteen original (though it might easily have been written by Shane MacGowan of the Pogues). Its inspiration was the poem *He Lies In The American Land* by a Slovakian immigrant worker, which Pete Seeger unearthed in 1947 and then set to music. The only part of the poem Springsteen retained was the opening verse.

And there you have it, the provenance of *The Seeger Sessions*. It was an album that proved, if proof were needed, that Springsteen, as a writer, owes a huge debt to American folk music – whether he himself knew it or not at the time he embarked on the journey to discover Pete Seeger. And like the folk progressive that he is (he is a purist only in the sense that he pays due respect to the source, and doesn't attempt to replicate it), Springsteen contemporised these songs, infused them with a modern sensibility, made them new and germane for the new century.

"Bruce has said that singing folk songs is like going on a ride at an amusement park," says Jim Musselman. "You get on a ride, you have fun with it and then you go to the next ride. He just added more to the songs. When I showed him 'We Shall Overcome', I said, 'Change it around if you want to. The sign of a good song is its adaptability and how you change it.' And he changed it.

"It was amazing what came out of that song. It was used for hope and healing after 9/11, and a lot of other things in the United States. He put his own signature on those songs, and he really made them fun and upbeat. And within a 19-piece band, he had a lot of room to move, to give things interesting arrangements."

So how did Pete Seeger, often (wrongly in my view) castigated for being a purist, hear *The Seeger Sessions*? Musselman again: "Pete was like, 'This key is wrong and that key is wrong'! When I put out the first *Where Have All The Flowers Gone*, Pete had written me criticisms of it. That's how Pete is. I said to Bruce and his manager, 'Don't worry, Pete likes it'. Like Pete himself says, he's a very tough teacher."

What really pissed Musselman off (and still seems to) is how *The Seeger Sessions* was received by the American folk establishment. "The folk community didn't embrace this the way that they should have. There was a lot of resistance to Springsteen doing it. I thought what Bruce was doing was amazing. He was bringing these songs to a whole new generation. Kids were coming out singing 'O Mary Don't You Weep' and 'Jacob's Ladder'. It was wonderful to see how he had re-popularised these songs. It took a hell of a lot of guts on Bruce's part. He didn't get as much support here in America as he did in Europe. In Ireland, England, Denmark they loved it. There was more resistance in America than anywhere, which was crazy because it was a celebration of American music in so many ways."

Where Musselman heard *The Seeger Sessions* as a celebration of American music, *Rolling Stone* heard it as an appropriation of "the music of our shared past to find a moral compass for a nation that's gone off the rails".

In Britain, *The Guardian*'s Mat Snow identified the use of the Miami Horns as a key factor in lifting *The Seeger Sessions* "above the common run of folk revival albums...reminding us that round the corner from the Greenwich Village coffeehouse of Seeger's heyday, you would find Charlie Mingus's parallel world of sanctified protest jazz."

20. SOUNDTRACK TO CHANGE

"I'm the President but he's The Boss."
PRESIDENT BARACK OBAMA

"A moment comes when you cash in whatever credibility a guy can have who plays and sings rock songs for a living, and you put your chips where you think they might do some good."
BRUCE SPRINGSTEEN

The 20th Century Bruce Springsteen was never prolific as a recording artist. Not for him the classic industry template of regular album releases and supplementary tours. Springsteen, other than while trying to build a reputation in those early years of the Seventies, has always listened to his own heartbeat which, in many respects, is the heartbeat of America.

That heartbeat has been louder in the new century than for some considerable time. Possibly since Richard Nixon and Watergate, since the humiliating endgame in Vietnam. There have always been dark forces, long before the term became the mantra of the conspiracy theorists. Power is seldom gained benignly. The public faces of power are seldom as powerful as they seem.

Real power is orchestrated in the shadows by shadowy people. The American electorate thought they were electing George Bush in 2000, but they were really electing an ideology – the Neoconservative ideology. An ideology that brandishes the bible in one hand and an American Express card in the other, with a gun tucked inside the belt of a well-fed waistline just in case. An ideology that wants to impose democracy – you read it right, *impose democracy* – on parts of the planet that are strategically beneficial to their cause. The objective of which, when you boil it down, is the pursuit of global domination.

My own favourite definition of Neoconservatives can be found in the *Urban Dictionary* online: "Criminally insane spenders that believe in killing brown people for the new world order. Huge Orwellian government, unfathomable amounts of spending, bomb tens of thousands of people to death to rearrange the globe. Take the worst aspects of the liberal and conservative positions and combine them into one and you would have a NeoCon."

These were the dark forces that, in the first decade of the millennium, really ruled America while George Bush did his 'good ole boy' routine front of stage. These were the dark forces that contravened international law to ensure that Iraq and its oil reserves were secured, and fuck the human cost, gullible, gung-ho American marines included. And these were the dark forces that seemed to be on Springsteen's mind as, after *The Seeger Sessions* tour, he rounded up the troops, his E Street comrades, and went to work on his third album in three years.

Is the 21st Century Springsteen prolific? Damn right he is.

It had been five years since *The Rising*. Five years since Springsteen and the E Street Band gave the American people the succour they needed after 9/11. Five years during which the American government – or at least what, in the eyes of the world, constituted the American government – had done terrible things in its country's name, in the name of what Bush and his fellow Republican stooges absurdly labelled freedom (absurd because freedom was what was increasingly being denied to American citizens).

Yet even though he had just emerged from Pete Seeger's America – an America in which the populace sang out against injustice, sang out against oppression, sang out against inequality, sang out against war – Springsteen himself wasn't about to morph into a modern day Seeger. That is not the way he writes, never has been. He is not a political writer. Nor indeed is he a political singer. *The Seeger Sessions* is as close as he's ever got and, for my money, will ever get. And remember, he was singing other people's songs.

For this reason, and at the risk of repetition (go back two chapters and you'll know what I mean), some of us found *Magic* frustrating. Yes, there were allusions to what was happening in America, what was happening in Iraq, but we wanted more.

"I didn't want a big Bush-bashing record. I've found ways to express my political concerns and personal concerns and I always found them best combined, because that's how people live," he told Joe Levy in *Rolling Stone*. What would have been so wrong about a Bush-bashing record? What would have been so wrong about singing out against a regime that was spreading fear and ignorance and death?

Yes, there are songs on which Springsteen the writer lets us glimpse Springsteen the man, when he lays bare his hurt, his disillusionment, his anger; the same hurt and disillusionment and anger anyone who's not a NeoCon junkie feels. Songs like 'Magic' itself, "about living in a time when anything that is true can be made to seem like a lie, and anything that is a lie can be made to seem true". Songs like 'Livin' In The Future', where the narrator recalls the morning after Bush's re-election in November 2004, the morning after Springsteen's candidate, John Kerry, was returned to political obscurity. His faith, he sings, has been "torn asunder", as he listens to the sound of righteousness going under.

Songs like 'Gypsy Biker', another of those Springsteen story songs, this time following a bunch of guys as they prepare for the repatriation of their dead buddy from Iraq. Songs like 'Last To Die', the title part of a question posed by Kerry in 1971 when, as a disaffected Vietnam vet coming home, he asked, "Who'll be the last to die for a mistake?"

But these songs are too few, and even their negligible number are eclipsed by Springsteen's self-confessed re-infatuation with pop music on 'You'll Be Comin' Down', 'I'll Work For Your Love' and 'Girls In Their Summer Clothes'.

Of course, the reviews were overwhelmingly flattering, Springsteen, by virtue of his longevity alone, is beyond the censure of most critics. And let's face it, music magazines these days read more like glossy publicity brochures for record companies and their charges. Objective criticism is a fine idea, but it can't possibly work in the absence of independent resources. *Magic* is an average album by Springsteen's standards.

But you wouldn't think it from Keith Cameron's fawning analysis in *Mojo*. Springsteen, he wrote, was "a man with one eye on the clock, eager to make permanent records of this creative virility". He further applauded him for continuing to disinter "the ancient rock'n'roll texts, trying to fathom new meaning, grappling with the eternal issues", among them the classic soul searcher, "I wanna know if love is real", when we all know that love, as Bob Dylan once declared, is just a four-letter word.

Uncut was no less effusive in its praise, Andrew Mueller claiming it as a hybrid between *Born To Run* and *Tunnel Of Love*, "an attempt to recover the indomitable youthful fury of the former, astutely tempered by the older, wiser, sadder resignation of the latter".

Calm down, guys, calm down.

If Springsteen was re-infatuated with pop on *Magic*, he was stark bollock naked on all fours with it on *Working On A Dream*. And who, in the first month of 2009, when America was ushering in its first ever African American President – a momentous day that diehards like Pete Seeger couldn't have imagined he would ever see – could deny that joyous pop wasn't the perfect soundtrack to change?

Barack Obama's inauguration was party time, a time to rejoice in the achievement of the prize that many good people, black and white, had strived for. The prize for which Dr Martin Luther King Junior and Malcolm X had sacrificed themselves. The prize that had sadly eluded generations of African Americans. But for that one day at least, their blood, instead of screaming in the ground, sang in the ground, the sweetest melody.

Working On A Dream caught the mood perfectly. It belongs to those halcyon weeks and months of the Obama presidency as much as it belongs to Springsteen. Despite being crushed by Kerry's defeat to Bush four years earlier, Springsteen nonetheless threw his weight fully behind the Obama campaign. 'The Rising' became the anthem of the Democrats' rallies, and blasted from the speakers at Obama's victory celebration in Chicago.

But two years on, speaking to Nick Rufford in *The Sunday Times*, Springsteen sought to temper the optimism of late 2008/early 2009, by acknowledging that there was only so much one guy could do, even if that guy was supposedly the leader of the free world.

"The climate (in America) is very, very ugly for getting things done. The moderate reforms President Obama fought to make are called Marxist, socialist. I mean, the most extreme language is put into play to describe the most modest reforms that would move the economy back towards serving a majority of its citizens. There's a tremendous distortion of information. The biggest problem we have now is almost 10% unemployment, but we also have the disparity of wealth. You can't have an American civilisation with the kind of disparity of wealth we have. It will eat away at the country's heart and soul and spirit."

He placed the blame squarely at the door of Conservative America, part of whose constituency is part of Springsteen's own constituency (don't forget, the blue-collars voted in their millions for Bush).

"You have a guy (Obama) who comes in, he gets to be president for four years. Maybe eight. But you have the financial institutions, you have the military, the corporations. They're in play constantly and, in truth, they're shaping the economy and shaping the direction the US is moving in. Those forces are huge. The money and lobbyists are pouring in to do everything they can (to preserve the status quo). It's a very tough time, a very hard time here in the States.

"Our economy has oriented itself away from the mass of US citizens and oriented itself to be at the service of the folks at the top, the plutocracy. It has to be oriented back to where it serves the health and purposes of a majority of American citizens. That's not on the books right now."

Although there is a whiff of fatalism in Springsteen's depiction of the new America (and he didn't even mention the internecine conflict instigated by Sarah Palin that has riven the Republican Party), his are fighting words as well. Sounds to me like Springsteen's pretty hacked off with what's happening to the good folk in his country who are just trying to get by. Sounds to me like Springsteen from another time. Think about it. He could be talking about Reagan's America, the very era that created *Nebraska*. How pertinent those songs are now to the hard times sweeping the States once more.

Nearly three decades on, the America of *Nebraska* remains largely unchanged despite the great changes that have occurred, none greater than Obama's election. For what is Obama but a man? A man within a machine stoked by economics and worked by political operatives. Political operatives whose functionality is guided by those dark forces. Obama's political power is illusory – his real power is as an illusionist. He makes believe he is in charge, and he makes us believe that under this charge we will all – American citizens and citizens of the globe – be delivered to the promised land.

Springsteen's songs, too, believe in the same biblical concept. You can still hear it on *Working On A Dream*. And of course the world needs its dreamers, it needs something and somewhere to which it can aspire. But it needs truth more, however unpalatable or ugly that truth may be. The kind of truth that Springsteen captured in the stories on *Nebraska*. Stories that stand up however often they are recounted, stories that remain relevant, stories that have their genesis in human beings, stories that go to the very heart of darkness in all of us.

21. HAUNTED ROAD-POETRY

"He's not afraid to try things that are not necessarily popular and 'in'. He can be a stone in a stream when he wants to be. If he believes in one of his artistic visions, he actualises it, no matter what resistance he might get from outside influences. He is the creative arbiter of his musical soul."

MIKE APPEL on Bruce Springsteen

"He's a poet with a working-class perspective and a truly American spiritual language."

BILL HURLEY

I began this book with the idea to write about *Nebraska* as a folk album – an American folk album – which, in the same way that events in history radicalise new generations of young people, played an influential role in radicalising new generations of young musicians, drawing them back to the root (or roots) of their country's music; drawing them back to blues and country and gospel and, yes, folk. Enlightening them that they could write about real people leading real lives in another America, an underground America

At the book's end, however, I am more inclined to be swayed by what *Nebraska* suggests to me when I listen to it now, almost three decades after its release. *Nebraska* is as much a punk album as it is a folk album. It is punk in attitude, it is punk by design, it is punk in the outsider status of many of the characters that populate its songs.

Nebraska is as much a blues album as it is a folk album. It is blues in the simplicity of the sound. For the blues is, as Albert Collins said, "a simple music". The blues is felt, difficult to put into words, but you know it when you've got it. And there isn't anyone on *Nebraska* who hasn't got the blues.

Nebraska is as much a country album as it is a folk album. Country music is, after all, just the blues with melodrama on top and a neater, more buttoned up but no less elementary sound.

Nebraska is as much a rock'n'roll album as it is a folk album. Rock'n'roll in its visceral nature, rock'n'roll in its rebellious streak.

Nebraska is as much a gospel album as it is a folk album. Gospel in its allusions to a (Christian) God, heaven, hell, good, evil, and in its preoccupation with and interrogation of faith.

My original working title was *Bruce Springsteen's Nebraska: The Heart Of Americana*. Americana, in this context, was meant to denote the music rather than the altogether more complicated broader application of the term. Yet Jeremy Searle, who oversees the website Americana UK, feels the use of the term in a musical sense has "lost any real meaning" in the same way that the term folk has.

161

"Any genre that can encompass current-period Wilco, the Byrds, Drive-By Truckers and Johnny Cash is so wide as to be practically pointless as a guide or reference point. It's also one of those genres where everybody knows what it means but each version is different. For me, it's music that's rooted in American traditional styles. In those I would include country, folk and bluegrass, but also things like blues and rock'n'roll. I'd exclude soul and jazz, though a case could be made for them, because for me they lack that connection to the roots that is the core of Americana."

For Searle, Springsteen meets the criteria of his definition. "As well as the more obvious Americana albums like *Nebraska*, *Tom Joad* and *The Seeger Sessions*, it could be argued that almost everything he's ever done is Americana. *Born To Run*, for example, taps into American (self-) mythology – small towns and cars (perhaps the most potent American symbols), as well as universal themes like escape and dreams. He has that ability to go deep into the well of the American experience and make connections.

"*Nebraska* is an Americana album through and through. Musically it has that sparse, stripped bare, lo-fi style that is the hallmark of American country and blues. More importantly, the songs are contemporary folk songs. Bleak, desolate, full of death and despair (which is, of course, almost a prerequisite for a folk song!), they are rooted in the dark side of the American Dream. It's also a true American album. Nobody who wasn't American could have written or recorded it, in the same way that nobody who wasn't British could have written the songs that Ray Davies or Chris Difford write."

This is true to some extent. The writing style is undoubtedly American, and the geography of the songs is culled from the American landscape. But *Nebraska*'s themes are universal. And it was this acknowledgement which persuaded me that to include 'Americana' in the title would be to impose limits on its scope and the far-reaching impact of its influence.

Bill Hurley of the American roots music website the Alternate Root hears Americana as "traditional music played on traditional instruments and written in traditional styles that incorporate varying elements from blues, folk, country, gospel, jazz and rock" – with a broad church in which *Nebraska* belongs.

"The album is very sparsely recorded on acoustic instruments, which at the time was risky for a major superstar performer. The songs themselves are written in traditional storytelling 'troubadour' style, if you will. They are common tales of everyman America, about failure, triumph, deception, struggle – the things everyday Americans have toiled with for centuries."

Both Searle and Hurley are in agreement that *Nebraska*'s influence on the new generation of Americana artists has been minimal. "That movement is rooted in country, hence the various sub-genres that all have 'country' in their titles: alt-country, renegade country, outlaw country and so on," says Searle.

"For those people, apart from Gram Parsons and Neil Young, they look back to Hank Williams, the Carter Family, Bob Wills, Johnny Cash – the pioneers of country and bluegrass – rather than Springsteen." Hurley believes other Springsteen releases have been more influential, especially *The Seeger Sessions*.

Nebraska is raw, primitive, ancient, other-worldly, spiritual, nihilistic, heartbreaking, horrifying and a whole bunch of other things that come to you like apparitions whenever you enter its province (ideally under cover of darkness). And it was made by someone who was regarded as a rock messiah. It took balls for Springsteen to defy the expectations foisted on him by dint of his success. It took balls to scramble the methodology he'd used on previous albums and go instead with gut instinct. He hung himself out there, he was prepared to run the risk of sullying his reputation and, something which probably didn't thrill his management, damaging his bankability. He had the courage of his conviction – his artistic conviction. He knew what he wanted, he knew how *Nebraska* should be presented, and he went ahead and presented it as it was conceived.

And like the great films and the great novels, it holds up well. It holds up well because it still has something to teach us about ourselves and the world we live in, and maybe even the world beyond this one. That's why we return to it, like we return to the movies of John Ford or Martin Scorsese, or the books of John Steinbeck, William Faulkner or Ernest Hemingway. And the people who come after us will, I believe, return to it for the same reasons.

But don't take my word for it. There are many others better qualified than I to pontificate on *Nebraska*'s import.

Dan Bern is an American singer-songwriter, novelist (he wrote the novel Quitting Science under the pen-name Cunliffe Merriwether) and painter. His song, 'Talkin' Woody, Bob, Bruce And Dan Blues' (on the album *Smartie Mine*), humorously pays homage to Guthrie, Dylan and Springsteen with some rib-tickling impersonations.

"I think the first time I heard *Nebraska* was right about the time it came out. I might have first heard a track on the radio, probably 'Atlantic City'. I remember that the *Midnight Special*, the once-a-week radio show on the Fine Arts station in Chicago, played the song. Which was unusual, because they usually played folk songs, old blues, not much rock'n'roll at all. But they sensed that it was a different kind of record, even though it was made by a 'rocker'.

"The language of it, and the sound of it. It was at once bleak and rich. It seemed to tap into something that was right in front of us, and yet just out of reach. Timeless and out of time, the way some of the first Dylan records did, the way Woody or Hank Williams did.

"Maybe the rootlessness. There's a lot of motion in the record, a lot of moving around, without necessarily having a destination. As long as you keep moving you'll be all right. Well, maybe not all right, but at least it's better than the alternative, which is stopping, stagnating…

"That's one of the main themes of the album – moving. Staying just ahead of something nipping at your heels, whether it's the law or some dark, unnamed forces…time, maybe. Mortality. Settling for something less than your dreams, which is probably the way it goes. But staying one step ahead, of the bill collector, of the grim reaper, of the cops, of your own dark thoughts. Maybe there will be some salvation at the end.

"My definition of folk music is pretty broad, so, yes, of course *Nebraska* is a folk album. I mean, I would include, 'Smells Like Teen Spirit' and I would include the White Stripes in my American folk music tent. But *Nebraska* is something else, it snuggles right up nicely next to Elizabeth Cotton, Leadbelly… It's really spooky, it's really simple and stripped down, and sounds home-made, which it pretty much was. And it's about simple, unglamorous things and people, who are just trying to get to next week. It's not about flying first class and finding hookers and the best caviar.

"A lot of the whole roots thing, the Uncle Tupelo-Wilco alt-country thing, maybe have stemmed from *Nebraska*. I was living in Chicago at the time, playing open mics seven nights a week, and everyone was pretty excited. You know, 'Springsteen made a folk record, now everyone is gonna listen to us.' Didn't quite work that way! But at a time, when it was still about how loud your gear could get, it was a great, unexpected way to go.

"It seems like he simultaneously went inward and outward. Like, went real deep into himself, but also used that to focus outward, to speak through characters that were not him, but related to him. But he'd done that before, on *Darkness On The Edge Of Town*, and the song 'The River'. The whole of Nebraska is really spare, there's none of that wild, free-flowing stuff like in 'Thunder Road' or 'Jungleland', or the stuff on his first couple of records. A really tightly focussed lens.

"He chooses images and characters that convey a lot of meaning. He can be big and wild and effusive, and tight and spare and controlled. He's obviously got more than one way of getting from A to B. He seems like he's tougher on himself than anyone else could ever be on him. I don't know that he writes every day from ten to four, but it seems like he's very disciplined, in his way, when he's writing. I'd love to see what a novel or a short story by him would be like. But with his guitar and his voice and his harp, he's got a lot of colours going to convey the stories.

"He's able to be so big and heroic, and so small and specific. Just a huge range in his writing. Ridiculous range. He doesn't waste words, he's tough on himself and he always writes within the scope of what he is able and wants to do vocally.

"*Nebraska*'s legacy? That's tough. I mean, we're living in it. We exist in the wake of it. It's hard to describe something that you exist within the fabric of. It's one of his very great records, as great as his big rock records, the two 'Born' records. It opened a lot of doors, probably. Obviously a lot of people love it and listen to it, and are still inspired by it."

Laura Cantrell is a country singer-songwriter and erstwhile presenter of *The Radio Thrift Shop* on New Jersey radio station WFMU. Her 2000 debut album, *Not The Tremblin' Kind*, was described by legendary British radio presenter John Peel as his "favourite record of the last ten years and possibly my life".

"I was in college when I became aware of *Nebraska*, in the late Eighties, and I had also recently heard the Hank Williams record put out by the Country Music Hall of Fame record label called *Just Me And My Guitar*. There was speculation among my friends that the tapes of Hank singing into a reel to reel recorder were floating around during the period just before Springsteen made the *Nebraska* recordings, and that there was a conscious effort on Bruce's part to tap into, if not emulate, the same type of naked emotion that is evident on the Hank recordings.

"The use of 'Mansion On The Hill' as a song title seemed to be an obvious nod to that influence on Springsteen's part, but this was the stuff of dorm room and college radio station speculation. Being of the MTV generation, my impression of Springsteen to that point involved the white T-shirt, jeans and bandana image of *Born In The USA*, and I wasn't particularly familiar with the rest of his work beyond the radio hits. So *Nebraska* was intriguing to say the least.

"There are a lot of great stories on it – 'Highway Patrolman', 'Atlantic City', 'Used Cars', they have a lot of narrative detail. They're intriguing, use a lot of words but still manage to be memorable melodically, catchy even – they stick.

"The songs have a sort of wide open quality to them that reminds me of Woody Guthrie. Even though they tell very particular stories about particular characters, as a collection there is this richness, like you've just read a novel full of great characters, or seen a post-dustbowl film about real folks in this country, people themselves, not just a 'type' of people but well intentioned, flawed, hardworking characters.

The details multiply into a sort of panorama that becomes very believable. I think *Nebraska* is an emotional, personal portrait of different American characters that is very engrossing – the struggles, the flaws, the bonds, the heavy things we carry with us, how fleeting those joyful moments that leaven the burdens. I'm not sure the message is so much American as it is just human.

"It isn't so much Springsteen's writing that seems to have evolved on *Nebraska*, but the fact that he chose to present these songs with that greater sense of quiet that lets us experience them in a different way. If we ever get to hear the E Street Band's versions of *Nebraska*, it would be interesting to note whether their sheer exuberance casts the songs in a different light. The demo versions as they were originally presented are a very potent batch of songs, strong stuff, almost to me like the effect of hearing the country blues or some other intimate form that draws you into the shadows.

"Springsteen's writing always amazes me again in its volume of words and details that seem to not overwhelm the structure of the songs. That to tell a story you might need the right amount of words and to feel free to do that in song form. I have found myself conscious of his melodies and wanting to emulate them."

Peter Case is a New York singer-songwriter who, in the mid Seventies, was part of San Francisco outfit the Nerves (their song, 'Hanging On The Telephone', was a hit for Blondie). He released his first solo album in 1986 (which I bought!), and has been the subject of a triple tribute album, *A Case For Case*.

"Somewhere in the year after it came out, a copy walked into my pad. I believe a guitarist who played with my band, named Andrew Williams, brought it over and left it for a while. I was interested in it, but never gave it an entire play. It felt to me that it lacked rhythm. I did appreciate bleakness in regards to life in America. I was sympathetic, politically, in that I resented the Reagan government etcetera.

"I didn't like the fact that he borrowed titles – 'Mansion On The Hill' and 'Reason To Believe' were songs I knew by Hank Williams and Tim Hardin. That bugged me then more than now. I found some of the techniques used in the songs to ring false – addressing people as 'Sir', for example. It was not realistic in my experience of America.

"*Nebraska* really did change the tone in the air at the time. It was a very different voice from Eighties culture. Springsteen deserves a lot of credit for that. He went the other way. He was a big star and he put out this flipped-out record. The Suicide influence was pretty far out. I took heart from that, as did a lot of others. He sort of put the Beat/Dylan/(Henry)Miller/Guthrie ball back in play, rock-culturally. And it sounds amazing – it is the opening shot in the lo-fi movement

"But the title kind of says it all – the emptiness at the heart of the land mass, a place where basically only white people live. No Native American voice, no black. People left behind the American juggernaut, human wreckage in the wake of our attempts at world dominance. I think it was prophetic in terms of where the country has gone.

"It reflects the bleakness of America. The great Kerouac line, 'America is a lonely piece of shit' in *On The Road* kind of hits it. I hitch-hiked a lot in the late Sixties and early Seventies, and that told me a lot. *Nebraska* is a very limited, focused vision by an artist trying to make a particular point.

"But I'd already read and understood this strain – Kerouac in *Visions Of Neal, Dr Sax, Visions Of Gerard*, even. Ginsberg in all of his work, Henry Miller in *Sexus, Plexus* and *Nexus*, (Herman) Melville in *The Confidence Man*, Mark Twain in *Huckleberry Finn*, (Edgar Allan) Poe in general, Kenneth Patchen's poetry, Lenny Bruce and the entire catalogue of Bob Dylan had all been read or experienced by me at that time, and they coloured my knowledge of America. *Nebraska* fits into that, but its tone is very limited in comparison to the visions of Miller and the rest.

"It's folk music without the rhythm – and without the influence of black music. That makes it very different from Woody or Dylan, and less appealing, to me at least. It was important to people who were just getting into the swing at the time, sort of like the Beatles to Motown to R&B, or the Stones to blues. Which is very important, but secondary."

The Cash Brothers are Canadian siblings Andrew and Peter Cash. Andrew began his career as a member of Toronto punk outfit L'Etranger before signing with Island Records as a solo artist. Three albums later he formed Ursula, whose demise came after their one and only release, *Happy To Be Outraged*. He has exchanged the grubby music business for the even grubbier business of politics, as a member of Canada's New Democratic Party. Peter Cash was a member of Skydiggers until he and his kin became the Cash Brothers in 1996. Their 2001 album, *How Was Tomorrow*, features the *Nebraska* homage 'Listening To Nebraska'. The band have been on extended hiatus since 2006.

Andrew Cash: "The first time I heard *Nebraska* was on a very snowy, dreary and quiet night in Toronto. I was listening to it with a friend who was going through a hard time. She said she wasn't a fan of Springsteen, but she loved this album. As soon as she put it on I understood why. There was such desolation, desperation and loneliness coming out of the speakers, that I could imagine it connecting to all the lonely people huddled in all the dimly lit and draughty rooms of the city that night.

"Like anyone who has spent time in the US I'm always struck by the American duality: they are the most welcoming, friendly, hospitable folks on the planet, and yet they are very steeped in a culture of individualism and of violence. Americans seem to be on the move constantly. There is an edge to America that is both enlivening and imbued with danger. So it is a culture deeply rooted in community, but that carries with it a shiftlessness, a restlessness. And these two qualities exist in tension side by side. Some of this tension is captured in *Nebraska*'s cover photo of a solitary driver on an open and empty highway. It is at once an image of independence and a tally of the cost.

"*Nebraska* drew many of us back to, or at least reminded us of, American folk music. After all, the punk era, which had given music a right kick in the arse, was winding down. The Clash were imploding, Elvis Costello had moved beyond the Attractions and there was a real sense that popular music was in the doldrums. Springsteen surprised everyone with this record – the first DIY album from a major recording star. It was very inspiring in the way punk rock was. It showed young musicians like us a way forward, where you didn't need expensive studios and elaborate arrangements.

"He was always a great storyteller. The first time we saw him was on *The River* Tour in Buffalo, and one of the things I still remember is a long story he told about his father cutting his hair when he was asleep. But I think on *Nebraska* he finally understood that less is more. The resulting stories are linear, spare, exacting and haunting. It takes a kind of discipline usually not associated with rock'n'rollers to pull this kind of writing off. I think, ever since, his writing has been lean and spare.

"Once on tour we had a break in New Jersey and I spent an afternoon walking through the streets of his hometown of Freehold. I felt as though I was journeying through his catalogue of songs. In other words, he follows the adage that you should write what you know. But of course writing isn't just about what you know, it is about pulling apart what you know and trying to put it back together in a way that makes sense, a way that you can understand, a way that you can be yourself in. I think this sense of belonging and restlessness in Springsteen's writing is the tension of America.

"When I first saw him during *The River* tour, my band at the time was going through its angry, intense punk-rock phase – we made a point of not smiling on stage. And here was Springsteen having the time of his life on stage. His music was joyful, ultimately positive and redemptive. His ability to bring very large, politically charged issues down to the level of how outside forces affect people in their homes, in their marriages, in their jobs and in their souls, is something which has very much influenced my own writing.

167

"It bears saying that music without a social conscience tends to have a relatively short lifespan. Now I'm not saying that music with a social conscience is always transcendent – there are a lot of bad protest tunes out there. But great songwriting touches on our humanity, matters of the heart and the historic struggle for social and economic justice that defines any age. Springsteen's songs, written against the backdrop of the hollowing-out of the American manufacturing base, never ignored the forces that were shaking the core of the American Dream. Instead he fully embraced his times and tried to understand them. Springsteen's public activism begins around this period in his career. Themes that gain mainstream radio play two years later on *Born In The USA* are worked through on *Nebraska* – America's rust belt, its lost Vietnam generation and Reaganomics' direct attack on America's New Deal principles. Springsteen took the punk rock political stance of the late Seventies, married it to his own Catholic school social justice upbringing and then fed it through the blender of America's working class, highway romanticism. All of that wouldn't be enough to make him a folk hero if also did not truly ROCK! And that he does.

"*Nebraska* was a hugely influential record, coming a good decade before the whole *Unplugged* phenomenon. It arguably spawned the alt-country genre. It wasn't quite a folk record, not a country or blues record either. There was rock'n'roll in there, but there were no thundering drums or electric guitar solos. It was filmic without being a 'concept' record. In other words, it stood out as a very rare, unique, genre-busting gem. Also, because it was recorded on a cassette four-track machine, it showed a generation of artists that you didn't need expensive recording studios and big bands to create lasting music."

Peter Cash: "I remember getting *Nebraska* for Christmas, I guess it was 1982 or 1983. I can remember leaving my parents' place that night and heading downtown to where I was living. There was no-one on the streets, and it was cold and blustery night. I sat up in my room and listened to the wind almost breaking my window, and *Nebraska*. It was a great Christmas. To be able to capture these songs by himself, with no band, I think it led to new ground on later records. *Nebraska* showed off his writing even more. After that, he must have felt like anything is possible.

"I love the detail, the way he is able to put the listener right in the song. You can picture being in the car, or the house, or city, or town, that he is singing about. And the geographical detail is amazing.

"In 1982, I was trying to teach myself the guitar and possibly become a songwriter. The fact that he recorded the album on a four-track machine was big for me as well, as I went on to record hours and hours of songs on a machine just like the one he used. At the time I don't remember a lot of records sounding like the production of *Nebraska*. As someone who was just getting into writing, it was so inspirational, because it was so stripped down yet so powerful. I remember thinking, you can put a record out that's not all band and have it be striking. On the song that I wrote as a tribute to that album (also called 'Nebraska'), I remember I started with the one line, 'Listening To Nebraska', and then walked around with just that line for months, maybe years, because I wanted the song to be as close to the feel and mood of that record as possible. I waited and waited, and the rest of the song happened."

Rosanne Cash is the eldest daughter of the venerable Johnny Cash. In the more than 30 years since jettisoning a prospective acting career, she has released a dozen albums. These include *The List*, a selection of songs culled from a list of one hundred essential country songs her father compiled for her when she joined his travelling road show after graduating high school. She has also written a short story collection, *Bodies Of Water*, a children's book, *Penelope Jane: A Fairy's Tale*, and a memoir, *Composed*.

"I remember hearing *Nebraska* the first time, and being stunned by the clarity of the songs; how the landscape of the record was like a film, or a photo-realistic painting. Every song was cinematic, and so emotionally resonant. I felt it was the perfect 'American' record. I also remember thinking that the album cover was perfect, and completely reflected the feel of the record – something in itself that is hard to achieve.

"'Highway Patrolman' leaped out at me. It is an amazing narrative. The love between brothers, which is a love so seldom discussed in popular music, was refreshing and painfully beautiful.

"The album is an American landscape of ordinary people with timeless themes – violence and crime, family connection, loss, hardship, love, belonging to a place and time, hard work, integrity. Thematically, it can feel bleak – there are no easy answers or tidy redemptions – but the truth, and the stark narratives, are in themselves the redemption.

"I think it is one of the great documents of American life. I am not connected in any way with the Midwest, or with the lives of the characters who come to life in these songs, the kind of work they do, the lives they lead, their impulses and regrets, and yet I feel a kinship, as you do to an extended family. *Nebraska* defines the maxim in art and literature that 'the more personal, the more universal'.

"I don't know that I necessarily believe in evolution as a songwriter. I have had many discussions about this with a friend who teaches a history of popular music. He maintains that there is no such thing as progress or evolution in a true artist – that there are only different phases and stages. This stage, when Springsteen wrote *Nebraska*, was very deep. He touched something in himself that was vast and resonant and universal but exquisitely specific.

"He is the definitive living 'American' songwriter, in my mind. In his song are vast landscapes, particular lives, love that is so much more complex than just romantic love, death, hard work, bitterness, travel, struggles with integrity. He has no limits, in my mind. He also can find killer backbeats, and exhilarating melodies. I can't tell you how many times I have put on 'Tenth Avenue Freeze-Out' and danced around my kitchen.

"He has influenced me just with his integrity as a songwriter – his complexity and wide range of subject matter. I think *Nebraska* helped me to see that not every song had to deal with romantic love!

"He has made us value ourselves, see ourselves more clearly, embrace our legacy and our future. He has helped us see that quiet, ordinary lives are worth documenting, worthy of respect. He has been authentically himself, which helps us all be more authentic. I cannot imagine the landscape of American music without him. It would be like having musical theatre without Rodgers and Hammerstein. Or having jazz without Miles Davis. Or having roots music without my Dad. My Dad, too, offered up those landscapes and articulated and painted America in a most poetic way – in 'Big River', 'Hey Porter', 'Get Rhythm' and so many more. Both Springsteen and my Dad are distinctly American poets as well as masters of the backbeat!

"I sent my Dad *Nebraska* as soon as I heard it, and told him that this was an important record he should hear, and I thought he would love. He subsequently recorded 'Johnny 99' and 'Highway Patrolman', and I was thrilled. I think Dad immediately responded to the album. He wanted to record the songs as soon as he heard them. I know he was deeply affected, so much so that he wanted to embody the characters. Look at the cover of his record 'Johnny 99'.

"I saw Bruce at a White House event in 1997 when my Dad received the Kennedy Centre honour. He told me how much it had meant to him that my Dad had recorded those songs. I said, 'Who do you think sent him *Nebraska*?' and we had a laugh. I thought that maybe he recorded 'Sea Of Heartbreak' (on *The List*) with me as a thank you... but maybe he just really loved the song!

"*Nebraska* is as important as the work of Woody Guthrie, Jimmie Rodgers or Pete Seeger. It is essential, and central, to the American songbook now."

Bob Crawford is bassist with the Avett Brothers. Formed by North Carolina siblings Seth and Scott Avett, the band have been described by the *San Francisco Chronicle* as having "the heavy sadness of Townes Van Zandt, the light pop concision of Buddy Holly, the tuneful jangle of The Beatles and the raw energy of the Ramones". The Americana Music Association honoured them as Best Duo/Group of the Year in 2007. Their big label breakthrough came in 2009 with the American Recordings release *I And Love And You*, produced by Rick Rubin.

"I grew up about in South Jersey, about an hour outside of Asbury Park. Bruce was always like a patron saint there, a lost, distant big brother.

"When I was a freshman in high school, I got into *Born In The USA*. I backtracked to all the albums. Me and my friends, there were about five of us, and we were just Springsteen nuts. We would sit in this common area and talk about Bruce and the band and the albums. For about six years of my life, it was the biggest thing on my horizon.

"Before I got into him, we had a paid-movie service called HBO. They would have a half hour of programmes featuring music videos. One of the first videos I ever saw was for 'Atlantic City'. We made that drive from West Atlantic City into Atlantic City a thousand times to see my grandparents. That song really means something to me.

"MTV started doing these *Unplugged* TV shows in the early Nineties. I'm thinking to myself, when this *Unplugged* wave started, this is *Nebraska*. Springsteen did this.

"Americans are a hopeful people, very idealistic. It has been and will be a beacon of hope for the world. But as grand as we can be as a people at times, we live in a world where things are very accessible, and that doesn't suit the soul. And on *Nebraska* there are a lot of tortured souls. But they're no more tortured than you and I are or could be. We're not all Charles Starkweather! But we're not too far away, most of us, on our worst days from making life-changing mistakes. We all need hope in our lives, we all need a warm touch and we all need to feel the bonds of kinship and family and community. A lot of the characters on this album are struggling for it.

"The social conscience aspect of who Springsteen has become since *Nebraska* took a major leap on the album. He came outside of himself more and began to embody someone that he was not, and made those people breathe, made those characters live and made them believable. It was a major evolution for Bruce."

Steve Earle served his songwriting apprenticeship under Townes Van Zandt and Guy Clark. He hit big in the Eighties with *Guitar Town* and *Copperhead* Road, before drug problems sidelined him to "a vacation in the ghetto" and a stint in prison, after which he found his stride again with albums like *Train A Comin'*, *Transcendental Blues*, *The Revolution Starts Now* and *Washington Square Serenade*. Earle is also a published author, having written a short-story collection, *Doghouse Roses*, and the novel *I'll Never Get Out Of This World Alive*.

"*Nebraska* is my favourite Bruce Springsteen record. I think maybe his best record is *Born In The USA*, although people tend to play that record down. But *Born In The USA* can't exist without *Nebraska*.

"The thing about *Nebraska* is it completely and totally establishes Bruce Springsteen's place as the greatest songwriter of that generation, of that moment, in rock'n'roll history. Sometimes you've got to strip away. It came along at a time where the only way he was going to be recognised as the best singer-songwriter around was to have a band and to essentially be a rock act.

"Naturally he was this level of entertainer – I think he may be the greatest entertainer rock'n'roll has ever produced, period. It will be a long time before anybody comes close to that. This record is almost the antithesis of that. He's not using any of that armour. He's basically decided, if I don't do this now I'm never going to get a chance to do it, and he puts it out and then he goes about his business, to go on to become the biggest fucking act in the world.

"When I wrote *Guitar Town*, I began putting that record together after seeing the *Born In The USA* tour. I'd been in Nashville for 13 or 14 years, I was in my early thirties, I still didn't have a record deal. And I thought, fuck it, I'm going to write an album to be an album. I wrote 'Guitar Town' to be the opening song, because I saw him open his show with 'Born In The USA' – which is also the opening song on the album – and something clicked.

"But *Nebraska*, when it came along, it stuck with me the longest. It's the record I go back to the most. I played the song, 'Nebraska', at Carnegie Hall a couple of years ago with Springsteen standing about 15 feet away, literally. Springsteen and I had never met up to that point. A lot of people were saying that we knew each other, but we didn't. I knew Garry Tallent (the E Street Band bass player) really well, but Bruce and I had never met. Then we were playing the Palace in Los Angeles, and my steel player comes back and says, 'Bruce Springsteen and John Fogerty just walked in'. And I said, 'Cool'. He said, 'Yeah, you're not going to do 'Nebraska', are you?' I said, 'Fuck, yeah I'm going to do it!' So I did it and I knew he was there.

"After the show I was sitting there soaked in the dressing room. We'd just played three hours and 15 minutes – Springsteen had raised the bar for live performance! Springsteen and Fogerty came walking in. And the very first thing Bruce Springsteen ever said to me was, 'Ballsy cover, man'."

"That record was a conscious decision to walk out there naked. And I think he was right. If he hadn't done it then, it never would have happened. We would have had a different Bruce Springsteen and a different world, at least as far as my world goes."

Mark Eitzel is singer and songwriter of American Music Club. He was once described by _The Guardian_ newspaper as being "America's greatest living lyricist".

"My room-mate Scott bought _Nebraska_ the day it came out. I remember how excited we all were that he had made this close personal record. Really beautiful.

"The history of this country has been constantly overwritten by the robber barons that own it, by the mediocre that rule it, and the big empty spaces in between. This is a quiet record by an American artist and these are true stories. It is a history seldom heard. It's the torture of the big empty spaces in between that wait for us to become them.

"For my generation it was key in that it was substance over style, and proof that he is a fucking genius."

Simon Felice is a songwriter, author and poet, formerly of the Felice Brothers (with brother Ian), latterly of The Duke & The King. His debut novel, _Black Jesus_, was published in 2011.

"Growing up in my nowhere town in the mountains of New York in the Eighties, you couldn't escape the influence of the Boss. 'Dancing In The Dark' was the first song I ever played on the jukebox when I was eleven, learning to play billiards at the local bar. But when I heard _Nebraska_ for the first time it knocked the wind out of me. It was road-poetry in its most haunted and fragile form.

"It said to me that I was born in a land where buzzards circle, where empty strip-malls are king, where we exalt our lady of the gun. It speaks to me most of loneliness, that even when we're 'taking turns dancing with Maria', or confronted by a cop or a judge or a lover, we all still remain hopelessly remote from one another.

"Springsteen let his guard down. He told the whole truth and nothing but the truth. The Boss is a poet, a visceral one, a people's poet. More than anything he taught me it's okay to be where I'm from. _Nebraska_ is like a statue of a soldier on the town green – he'll be standing weathered, equally sad and proud, long after we're gone."

Jeff Finlin is an American artist variously compared to Raymond Carver, Walt Whitman, Kurt Vonnegut, Jack Kerouac, Mark Twain, Steve Earle, John Hiatt and John Prine. *The Times* lauded "his ability to craft a deep emotion out of mere words, recall the songwriting skill of Dylan (and) the original arrangement and producer skills of Springsteen."

"The first time I heard *Nebraska* it was in my apartment in Nashville. I had been becoming disillusioned with contemporary music, other than a few T Bone Burnett records, and was listening to old stuff – Stax, and lots of blues like Lightnin' Hopkins, Howlin' Wolf and Sonny Boy (Williamson). And it seemed like it fit right in that mould. It had a timeless feel about it.

"'Open All Night', 'State Trooper' and 'Atlantic City', I think, hit me first. I was a huge Chuck Berry fan and had immersed myself in the Chess box set. I recall 'Open All Night' was like a lost Berry tune. In that reverb I could see the neon and smell the carbon monoxide dreams floating off the upper lip of America on its colossal suicidal ride to nowhere.

"I listened to Springsteen a bit before *Nebraska*, but was never one of those crazy fans. Loved *Born To Run*, but I think *Nebraska* is his best record bar none.

"He found the power of space on this record. All great things come out of the space first. If I can't feel the air or the space in a piece of music, something is always missing for me. So as a writer he simplified and got to the point of his stories a lot better. As a writer he has great storytelling ability and a sense of history and craft. He has the ability to suck you in and make you listen.

"I tend to undervalue the legacy of most music these days, where when I was young I used to put it up on a pedestal. Very few artists in the 20th Century deserve a legacy. Picasso, Dylan, maybe Charlie Chaplin or Louis Armstrong – the ones who are innovators. Muddy Waters, (Duke) Ellington (John) Coltrane, (Jimi) Hendrix. The innovators are the guys they'll be talking about 100 years from now. Springsteen or this record won't even be mentioned."

Jeffrey Foucault is an American singer-songwriter who "sings stark, literate songs that are as wide as the landscape of his native Midwest" (*The New Yorker*). His debut album, *Miles From The Lightning*, sent the critics rifling through the thesaurus in a bid to outdo each other with plaudits.

"I didn't hear *Nebraska* until I was out of college and had made my first record. I'd heard a few of the songs here and there, and eventually I borrowed a vinyl copy from the owners of the local bar where I played occasionally, when they were cleaning out their basement. I listened to it pretty hard for a few months, usually while going to sleep at night. It's been a reliable album since then, and I still marvel at some of the songs, the integrity of the collection.

"It's all of a piece and that's one reason it's such a great record. It's hard for me to remember now because at one point I learned all the songs to perform them live at a local bar for a short-lived side project, but when I think of the album the songs 'Highway Patrolman', 'State Trooper' and 'Johnny 99' all leap to mind first, and that line (in 'Used Cars') about the salesmen staring at his old man's hands.

"*Nebraska* succeeds because it resonates. Like all great art, it feels true. But I don't know whether you could give it to someone from elsewhere and have them walk away knowing much about America. To say that *Nebraska* somehow exceeds the literature of Twain, (Willa) Cather, Steinbeck, (Cormac) McCarthy, and (Jim) Harrison in any general way is probably foolishness. Great art teaches you what it means to be human, not what it means to be an American. *Nebraska* has much more to say about the former than the latter.

"Folk music means either the music that everyone knows and sings – a category that no longer exists in our culture – or a genre so broadly inclusive as to be useless as a descriptor. I think *Nebraska* fits squarely within the tradition of American popular music. So does 'Centerfold' by the J Geils Band, released the same year. I'd guess Peter Wolf and Bruce Springsteen listened to a lot of the same music coming up, and were just interested in different things then.

"I'm not sure there is an Americana movement. I'd go so far as to say that most of the people who play Americana – if we're speaking widely about musical forms derived from American blues, country blues, country, and rock'n'roll in all its various permutations – probably heard *Nebraska* at some point and thought it was good. But I don't know that I'd go much further.

"There are no pure influences. Western culture saturates to a degree that the same folks who heard *Nebraska* coming up also heard everything else along the way – *The Brady Bunch* theme song, 'Superfreak', commercial jingles, that sort of thing.

"I don't have real depth of field on Springsteen's career as a whole. I love that album and, though I have heard some others, I never cared much about them. As a writer what I find compelling is the grammar of *Nebraska*: the four-track tape, the way he screams the backing vocals from across the room, the hushed claustrophobic feeling, the reverb. It feels like a field recording of a place that never existed.

"I would describe Springsteen as a great songwriter, performer and businessman, but not a folk hero. Dillinger was a folk hero, or maybe Pretty Boy Floyd. Woody Guthrie might be a folk hero, or even Dylan, though much of the mythos of each is self-created. That kid who was stealing airplanes last year in the Northwest of the States, Colton Harris Moore, he's a folk hero. A folk hero has to leave us with more questions than he answers, and he can't be known. I find Springsteen straightforward and explicable as a writer and performer.

"I think *Nebraska* is an incredibly fine record, and particularly fulsome example of what the album as an art form can be."

Howe Gelb has collected bands in Denmark, Spain and Canada (a full gospel choir), but the critics still call his music Americana. Gelb prefers to say he's from planet earth. In 1980, he formed the post-punk outfit Giant Sandworms with close friend Rainer Ptacek. Three years later, Giant Sand emerged, and they released their debut album, *Valley Of Rain*, in 1985. Among those who have guested with them over the years are Victoria Williams, Neko Case, the late Vic Chesnutt and Isobel Campbell.

"I remember the effect of *Nebraska*. The four-track cassette quality had an immediate intimacy. The analogue delay on his voice was inspiring and made perfect sense. You have to remember how much the Eighties sucked as far as production values and the recording trends of the so-called state of the art. This record was a great relief.

"It sounded like some sanity in an insane decade. Springsteen made it more impressionable, this sound, that he brought it all back to that first sketch of a song in that first moment it writes itself.

"The whole record sings like one long song, the same song re-attacked and re-delivered, a natural evolution the way the mind changes along the way when a notion transponds in the middle of an original thought and changes the trajectory of description.

"It's a time in between autumn and winter, a place where the landscape offers no escape, a colour scheme of diluted greys and charcoal, nothing but the pulse of the impulsive heart and the heat of boiling tears ready to tipple over the eyelid dam and water the sage of rage. Of course, a lot was taken from the film *Badlands*, but that's the same thing.

"This is what every one of his songs sounds like if the clutches of production and the storming trends of the day leaves him the hell alone. Don't get me going on convenient categories, but the fact that a so-called pop artist would allow himself this kind of elbow room definitely made an impact on what is at the core of so-called Americana and how impressively the raw material stands up.

"Springsteen has elements of the best of writers in knowing when not to overthink it, and when not to underestimate its value in its relative simplicity. But the delivery has to offer proof of this, and the evidence lies in how effective he becomes the character, the voice and the offhandedness of displayed lyric.

"Every man has a gambler within him. His own legacy will be how he gambled the rest of his life on the choices he's made prior. These songs could have just as well been made to sound like any of Springsteen's before or after, but he offered them up as they were because of the gambler inside him. No safety net. Ready to endure the repercussions. That which makes a man a man.

"Here's what is usually misunderstood ever since Dylan showed that writing your own songs might be a good idea. There are two arts at work within every singer-songwriter (a notorious term, and ill-fitting at best). One is the 'fine art' of crafting a song, coming up with the 'goods', making something out of nothing. The other is the 'performing art', taking it to market and delivering it yourself by whatever displaying tactic is deemed necessary.

"Each has its own artistry. They should be seen as that. When a writer sings his own songs, it's partly because there is no time to wait for someone to come along and sing it for him, and also because he doesn't know how not to. And there, by the simple thrust of 'spitting it out', a force of nature is captured, especially if the red recording button is depressed.

"The biggest gamble of all will be in what the earth thirsts for at the time of impact, the moment of its release. You never really know, although the writing and recording in this manner is so immediate and intimate, the process of pressing and releasing it is painfully slow and public, and so there's no telling if the tracks will smoulder like the smoke from a future fire, or lay there unnoticed and trampled over like useless ash.

"I just summed up the gamble as threatening to make an ash out of yourself!

"*Nebraska* is a shot in the dark. Springsteen's cannon is well loaded, fuse sparked, taking aim, originally at his own foot, but instead, on target and said shot heard around the world."

Thea Gilmore is a British singer-songwriter who can count among her disciples a certain Bruce Springsteen. Joan Baez, who contributed to her 2008 album *Liejacker*, **personally invited Gilmore to tour America with her in 2004.**

"My way into Bruce was admittedly a tortuous one in that I heard 'Born In The USA' first all over the radio when I was at primary school. It didn't really resonate with me. At the time it didn't hint at what I now know to be Bruce's range. I heard *Nebraska* years later, circa 2000, when a good friend chastised me for not knowing it, but by that time I had heard and loved *The Ghost Of Tom Joad*.

"In some respects market clouds the issue on where it fits into the tradition of American folk music. *Nebraska* was a fearless, uncompromising album. Its subject matter, its ethos, does plant it firmly in the tradition of American folk balladry. But it was also promoted and packaged by a multi-million conglomerate to a waiting fan base, so the commercial playing field is not a level one. Basically I think it will take a century to two to find out, but I do think it merits a place amongst the best American folk music.

"I think in releasing these raw home-recorded songs, mostly stories about people around the margins and in the depths, Bruce made a generation re-evaluate American folk and roots music and start listening to important stuff that had gone before. Remember, nothing was less cool in 1982 than an acoustic guitar. So I think he facilitated a generation, making room for bands like Wilco, for early trailblazers like Green On Red and for songwriters like Steve Earle who must have felt they were as out of fashion as they could possibly be at the time.

"In most of the songs he'd recorded up to that point, you were invited to believe – probably did believe – that the 'I' and the 'me' in the songs was Bruce himself. I would be the last person to want to stumble into that trap where you take a songwriter's work to be autobiographical, but Bruce certainly wanted us to feel we were sharing his experiences, his dreams as a young man. On *Nebraska* he switched almost exclusively to the role of balladeer, storyteller – he created characters, sketched portraits of them, always leaving just enough room for you to add your own interpretation in there.

"The portraits are very detailed, and some of the lines are very long and free, but for all that there's an economy about the writing. Plenty of stuff, you feel, is being left out. And with no rock'n'roll band behind him, inviting you to drown in the sound, he left you no option but to go to the lyrics, to feel those characters. Joe Roberts in

'Highway Patrolman', 'Johnny 99' and the characters skulking in the shadows who condemn him.

"He has a natural ability to invoke empathy. And an honesty so many writers lack. Whether he writes in character, like so much of *Nebraska*, or whether he's letting you into his world, he does so with an openness and genuine heart."

Sid Griffin is a Kentucky native now living in England. He once fronted the Long Ryders (named after director Walter Hill's film *The Long Riders*), credited by many as playing a pioneering role in the emergence of the neo-Americana movement at the end of the last 20th Century. Although the band split in 1987, they got back together for a reunion tour in 2004. Griffin keeps busy these days as a member of bluegrass outfit the Coal Porters, and has written two volumes on Bob Dylan, *Million Dollar Bash* and *Shelter From The Storm*.

"When *Nebraska* came out I was a confirmed Springsteen fan already. I saw him at the Township Auditorium in Columbia, South Carolina in early 1976, a great, great gig. And I bought the second LP in 1974, so I had it and *Born To Run* by this time. I had heard that *Nebraska* was going to be home recordings, really stripped-down stuff, so I was ready for it. But the primitiveness of the project and the stark, austere sound of the record was really something to behold. I am almost surprised Columbia Records issued the album, but I guess they didn't wanna piss off one of their big artists.

"Springsteen is, to me, merely articulating the home truths of life with the *Nebraska* album. Things like the man living in the mansion on the hill may well not only be a stranger to you, he may be your enemy, even though you have never ever met him and never will. Springsteen knows driving, driving, driving a car across a vast expanse of land is only a temporary escape. It does not attack, much less conquer the root cause of the aliments the guy compelled to drive the car so obviously has. *Nebraska* has so many home truths like this.

"Another one would be that no matter how hard you try in life, fate, be it in the guise of bad luck or romance or tragic error or whatever, may play a greater role in your ultimate destiny than you ever knew, and yet you have to, have to, have to try anyway! Top that for a riddle. It was brilliant of Springsteen to be able to identify these things and put them into song with such canny ability.

"Although there is an electric guitar used at times, *Nebraska* is another chapter, another link on the chain of the grand American folk tradition. I could draw you a pretty fun, pretty silly, possibly wrong (but I doubt it) line from a Revolutionary War fiddler playing 'Turkey In The Straw' to George Washington before a battle, to songs of the American Civil War, to Woody Guthrie, to early Dylan, to *Nebraska*, and then to the young folk poets of today – and to Springsteen's Seeger session album too! Another link on the chain and an important one. And if those *Nebraska* songs stand the test of time, as I suspect they will, they will enter the folk lexicon and I will be right.

"*Nebraska* has had a medium amount of influence on the Americana movement. Obviously it is a link on the chain, yes, but it is not mentioned in interviews nearly as much as Gram Parsons' work with the Flying Burrito Brothers or Hank Williams or

Sweetheart Of The Rodeo by the Byrds or Alex Chilton and Dan Penn. I do think, however, it pointed the way for many people to have the courage to go against the artistic grain of the day. And for that alone I would applaud it heartily.

"On *Nebraska* I feel, and I might be wrong, we are hearing a man growing up. The next time we would hear it so readily is on *Tunnel Of Love*. But on *Nebraska* we literally heard a man singing very adult themes with the absence of party anthems and celebratory rave-ups. This was the sound of one man's mind thinking and brooding, of a human clock, tick, tick, ticking away and wondering where the time went. He was leaving the party boy behind, starting to downplay car songs a bit, beginning to wonder where all this guitar playing and brooding was gonna end up. He was looking himself in the mirror and taking stock, and while he did so he allowed us a peek in his musical diary. Bless him.

"Springsteen as a songwriter has a wonderful sense of self, yet he knows how to keep the audience involved. He thinks of his own feelings and how they matter but, and this is very important, not just to himself but to others he knows are listening and are along for the ride as well. You gotta admire his skill here. And he can write a catchy melody and remember the arrangement is important, even though it is just him and a guitar and a tape recorder. Remember when he wrote these songs, he began to feel more and more and more that the E Street Band could not really perform them – and in fact, should not perform them. He knows, then, what shape and feel a tune must have to maintain the greatest emotional impact.

"*Nebraska* is completely underrated, like *Sandinista* by the Clash. Sure, both are popular albums, but not in the big, big way they should be. *Nebraska* is one of those records that really grows on you the more you hear it, and the more you think about the lyrics and the story Springsteen is telling. My money is it will stand the test of time about as much, if not more, than his other records. I kid you not."

John Wesley Harding is an English singer-songwriter, the progenitor of folk noir and gangsta folk. He took his name from Bob Dylan's album *John Wesley Harding*, itself a misspelling of outlaw John Wesley Hardin's name. And talking of names, Harding's given one is Wesley Stace, under which appellation he has published the novels *Charles Jessold, Considered As A Murderer*, *By George* and *Misfortune*. He is also artist-in-residence at Fairleigh Dickinson University in the garden state of New Jersey. In 2010, as curator of the university's Words in Music Festival, he hosted an interview with Bruce Springsteen and former American Poet Laureate Robert Pinsky before a lucky audience of more than 300 students.

"To a Bob Dylan fan at the time, which I primarily was, one wished that Bob Dylan could have done something like *Nebraska*. I used to go to Bob Dylan shows and he used to play all this thudding rock music which I absolutely adored. In 1981, I saw him at Earls Court in London, and he played one song on the acoustic guitar at the end of the night, as if it was a favour. It was the bit you lived for, it was what you really wanted to hear. So when *Nebraska* came out, my initial response was, 'Fuck me, why can't Bob Dylan do this?'

"This is exactly what you want. And this is exactly what you want from Bruce Springsteen. This is exactly what you want from a musician – you just want to hear them playing the guitar and singing their songs. That's what really turned me on about music. That's why I was listening to a lot of things like John Prine and Loudon Wainwright, because I like blokes playing the acoustic guitar. So *Nebraska* was a mind blower on that level.

"What did hit me, although not as hard as it would hit me nowadays (although, on the other hand, the album wouldn't be as effective nowadays because only one person could make that album and it was only then that he could make it, and now if he did it, it would surprise nobody because roots music is more a more acceptable career move nowadays), was the message and the brutality of the recording, with its solo-ness and the way one had to focus on the lyric.

"What is so fantastic about it is the way it turns all those car metaphors upside down. 'Stolen Car', for example, on *The River* is not a happy song about driving, yet the ones on *Nebraska* make you think about that geography and space and movement that seems to be a liberating dream of all the earlier Bruce Springsteen albums, and makes it very claustrophobic and kind of end of the road seeming. There is a singularity of focus that was very shocking.

"Even the cover was very shocking, the starkness of it. It didn't look a lot like *The River* and it didn't look a lot like *Born To Run*. I think I was rather disappointed later when I found out it was just a bunch of demos, and it just ended up being used that way. One wants to believe more that it was an incredibly focused idea. But at the same time, that's what makes it interesting, because he knew to stop then. He knew he had achieved a clarity of vision and that it was exactly what it should be.

"And clearly, there's a level of stripping away the myth of everything, including himself. That is a very naked thing. As he does at the beginning of *Tunnel Of Love*, which starts off with a very *Nebraska*-esque acoustic performance ('Ain't Got You'). It would be even extra super amazing if he'd gone, 'I'm just going to make an album next with just me and an acoustic guitar, and that's that.'

"There's no doubt that it was the first time of one or two times in his career when he has put on his Woody Guthrie coat. Obviously *The Ghost Of Tom Joad* is another period of that, with a different slant. Springsteen started off with all that wordplay thing. And then he got flowery for a bit – what most people considered the classic period, 'Jungleland' and 'The Promised Land', all incredibly flowery and incredibly well observed.

"*The River* and *Darkness On The Edge Of Town* seem to represent to me a deflowering of the language, a greater focus and a less reliant use of metaphor, apart from the overriding metaphors of cars and driving and freedom and darkness, what I think of as biblical metaphors, the big metaphors. You just see that process taken to further extremes on *Nebraska*. The language is very simple, the characters are very clearly drawn, first-person narratives, and are facing moral dilemmas. So definitely, you see immediately an American tradition of short story writing. That is probably what he was reading at the time. Each song is a short story – in some cases, very short stories. There are characters facing stuff, and those things are very clearly drawn.

"I would say that it's not an album I listen to a lot these days. It's not easy listening. It's a very, very important cultural artefact, and it was an incredibly important album in Springsteen's career. He could not have known how big *Born In The USA* was going to be. He might have had a big album in him, and it might have been that things were looking that way, but nobody could predict that kind of phenomenon. The fact that the album before that was *Nebraska* is just astonishing. Like he needed to get the brutality out of his system, the visceral stuff out of his system, so he could make something that showed a willingness to accept production sounds and face what the contemporary audience might like. It's almost as if *Nebraska* cleansed the palate a bit."

Robert Earl Keen is a Texan singer-songwriter whose sound is predominantly traditional country, though his popularity isn't confined to that particular idiom – he's big among the folk, Americana and college radio fraternities. In 1974, at Willie Nelson's Fourth of July concert, his car caught fire, a story immortalised in 'The Road Goes On Forever' on Keen's 1996 album *No 2 Live Dinner*.

"When I first heard *Nebraska*, I said, 'Thank God somebody big had the guts to put out a record that was voice, acoustic guitar and good songs'. I really loved 'Atlantic City', because of the mystery involved and the hint of criminal activity, and I thought 'Used Cars' had a great perspective to it, and 'Reason To Believe' had a memorable chorus and a great story.

"I would say it was definitely American folk music. It has an everyman feel to it. You can relate to the characters personally, or you know someone, but primarily the biggest folk characteristics are the simplicity of the production.

"Based on *Nebraska*, Springsteen seems to enjoy writing in narratives. He's not afraid to go against the meter with some of his writing. To clarify, it seems important to him to get the meaning of the story out in any way possible

"He has influenced me as a writer in this way, I will tend to make sure the story is correct regardless how it flows with the music. *Nebraska* influenced many songwriters from the time it was put out until today. It also gives us all hope that we to can make a record with a guitar and a great song."

Kevn Kinney is frontman with hard-rocking Atlanta, Georgia-formed southern roots outfit Drivin'n'Cryin'. His solo side projects have included collaborations with REM's Peter Buck.

"I bought *Nebraska* the first day it came out. I was, as I am today, a huge Springsteen fan. The difference is though that back when it came out, Springsteen was a necessary lifeline of sanity. He was huge in the Midwest. You could feel the energy in the room after one of his shows. And it wasn't like New York or Los Angeles, where there are celebrities and movie stars.

"We are just regular folks who needed a revival – a revival from years of Styx and Yes and the whole Mega Fog Arena shows. He was our Jesus, and like every good

Jesus we were his disciples, frustratingly spreading the word of his working-class street genius, subway shop to subway shop. So when *Nebraska* came out, it was so intimate and Kerouacian, a sonic *Bound For Glory*, because in the early Eighties it was still just you, your speakers and the record cover.

"He still had shunned all television appearances. At the time, if you wanted to testify you had to wait and see it live. It was a bit of a validation to all the disciples that he was a man of the people, he made this record just for us, no big hits, no big sound, no hype – just him and me and a reason to believe. It was time to buy an acoustic guitar!

"I think Springsteen described it best when inducting U2 into the Rock'n'Roll Hospice of Fame. I think he described them as a sonic landscape. And that's what *Nebraska* was. It wasn't just memories of the boardwalk and Jersey and the city. You could really hear the days of his time out west, and things he probably had forgotten about but were reawakened by five years of touring. I could hear Steinbeck in his slightly southern-tinged vocals, and could picture myself, his Dean Moriarty, sitting next to him, window down, on our way to California.

"Like all good novels, it should serve as a catalyst to go out and find it on your own. It must have inspired me greatly, because it was just months later I would have a yard sale and sell everything I owned, hop in the Honda Civic, drive to Graceland for some more divine intervention, settle down in the south for the next 30 years and make my living telling people of the Bible Belt that I'm going straight to hell and get them to sing along en masse. I think anything well written can inspire you enough to change your own perceptions of boundaries. Growing up in Milwaukee, a trip to Madison on the Badger bus lines for an afternoon of used book shopping and exotic foods like the gyro, was a far out tale of American exploration. *Nebraska* just made it bigger.

"I hated folk music until I saw *Don't Look Back*. In the Seventies, it was all sweater vests and well trimmed beards. I never saw the punk in it until I discovered Dylan on that afternoon at the Oriental Theatre. And then came *Nebraska*. Wow, this is fantastic – thank you!

"It was the first new wave of Americana. I don't think anyone who wanted to be the next thing didn't listen to it. Folk music to me now means something different. I now think that of it as a term that should describe any true representation of one's own surroundings, life and upbringing. I don't think acoustic music is necessarily folk music. I think the Ramones were one of the greatest folk bands ever. I think folk music is anything that has your personal truth in it – your story. And Springsteen's stories of highway patrolmen and mansions on the hill were true to him.

"On *Nebraska* he evolved as a presenter of his story. He was willing to deconstruct his sound to the bare essentials, which I think was very brave at the time for someone who, I'm sure, had every entertainment exec whispering in his ear, 'What about *Born To Run*? You think you got another one of them in you?'"

Tom McCrae is a British singer-songwriter whose eponymously-titled debut album was nominated for the Mercury Music Prize. The follow-up, *Just Like Blood*,

received critical plaudits in America, which is hardly surprising given that McCrae sounds like he was born on the wrong side of the Atlantic.

"I was a latecomer to Springsteen as a real fan. Like many of my generation I'd misjudged him from *Born In The USA*. The stadium rock of it had left me largely unmoved. But when I started making music I revisited his earlier stuff, working back through his catalogue until I stumbled across *Nebraska*. I'd missed it when it first came out – still in my pre-teen metal phase! – but even from the first listen I was transfixed. It was the first record I remember listening to that seemed to totally create its own universe, populated with characters, stories and a consistency of tone that made it completely believable. Until that point I thought you had to live everything yourself in order to write about it with authority and integrity, yet here was a multi-platinum-selling artist singing about being a serial killer, a highway patrolman, a gambler and doing it with total conviction. It changed the way I thought about everything, not just songwriting.

"From the opening bars of the record, you know you're being immersed in a world, something that could almost be an early blues recording, or something from the Library of Congress Field Recordings. It sounded real, rough, organic – but more than that, it sounded like anyone could make it. A four-track, an Echoplex and some fucking good songs and you too could make a *Nebraska*. In a decade that gave rise to some of the worst-sounding records of all time, here was an album that seemed to give primacy to the strength of an idea, not to overpowering production. That's rare at anytime; it was almost non-existent in the early Eighties.

"'Nebraska' and 'Atlantic City' spoke to me most. I'll have stand up rows with people who say Dylan is a better lyricist. But give a monkey a rhyming dictionary and some speed, and he'll hit upon some Dylanisms pretty quickly – the best lyrics sound simple but run deep. Springsteen's a master of those, 'Nebraska' sounds like a film treatment (which is fair enough if he was paying homage to Terrence Malick's *Badlands*). It skips from scene to scene with an economy that has characterised his later writing, and is still utterly compelling despite the fact there's no real structure and no chorus. It handed me a lesson in songwriting that didn't seem to be coming from any other contemporary artist.

"The album mined a seam of American life that, if it was written about at all, it was only in government statistics. *Nebraska* is often referred to as the middle of America – typical fly-over territory – and with most pop culture in the States (let's face it, the world) being driven by the East and West coasts, it was an album that at least admitted the rest of the States existed. Those 'badlands' where the American Dream had turned sour, or worse, been stillborn. Springsteen has always been a genius at teaching America about itself. Anyone can preach to the choir. It takes a unique talent to get a room full of rednecks singing anti-war songs.

"I think *Nebraska* was the sound of someone having the confidence to fail. The 'future of rock'n'roll' was behind him, he was yet to revisit the success of *Born To Run*, and when it all comes down to it every songwriter knows it's just you, alone in a room with your songs, and that's the album he made. To not release the full band recordings of the songs shows bravery. You can bet the label and the band weren't happy.

"The best songwriting is the simplest – a twist here or there, but there's nothing you can't play from his canon after a few hours basic guitar tuition. That's the hardest trick to pull off. Elvis Costello can fit too many words to too many chords and be a genius in his own way, but if you want to be direct, like an arrow to the heart Bruce has the surest aim. Over the years, it's the sparseness of the lyrics that appeals to me. Melodies come and go – there are only so many in the ether – but he always gets the opening line right. Take 'Highway 29' from *The Ghost Of Tom Joad*: "It was a small town bank, it was a mess/I had a gun, you know the rest" What more do you need to know?

"I've always loved the American traditional folk writing, from Guthrie through Dylan via traditional songs by Pete Seeger and Burl Ives. But I've never really sought to emulate it, other than its apparent simplicity. But what *Nebraska* did for me, and subsequently on *The Ghost Of Tom Joad*, is give me permission to speak as or through someone else in a song. It's still something I'm learning to be comfortable with, but when you're young you think you're the most fascinating person in the world, as you age you realise it's other people who are so much more interesting.

"*Nebraska* will stay as a touchstone for many, not just for what it meant musically, but for what it represents. More than *Born To Run*, more than the stadium rabble-rousing, more than the hoary old rock'n'roll dream of continual escape, it's the sound of each one of us, alone in a room, coming to terms with reality, coming to terms with ageing, coming to terms with failure yet each of us still looking for beauty, still looking for love. That's what music does best."

Michael McDermott is an American folk rocker whose lyrics have been quoted in Stephen King's books *Insomnia* and *Rose Madder*. Do yourself a favour, and hunt down his 2007 album, *Noise From Words* online.

"I was standing in line in the grocery store with my Mom waiting to check out and I flipped through *People* magazine. There was an article on *Nebraska* and it sounded exactly what I was kind of getting into at the time – Dylan, Odetta, Woody Guthrie. I rode my bike to the mall the day after and bought it. I fell asleep listening to it, woke up to hear the needle on the turntable, so I didn't go right back to it when I woke. A few days later, I thought I'd try it again and it knocked me out in a completely different way. It changed my life. Twenty nine years later and it still is my favourite album

"Like all great albums, different songs serve you at different times. 'Highway Patrolman' was the first song I'd listen to over and over for its movie-like quality. It seemed to me more haunted than *Badlands*, which, unbeknownst to me, was an inspiration for this album. To me it surpassed that movie in its intimacy.

"I think it kind of redefined American folk music. Its fearlessness is what is so striking. Here was a guy on the brink of superstardom and what does he do? Puts out an album of demos about kids and killers, demystifies the American Dream by himself, guitar, harmonica and a whole lot of reverb!

"I learned about the America I was too young to understand in 1982. *Nebraska* painted a picture of the America that your father never talked about at the dinner table, but it was the America that people prayed for on their knees at night when they'd tuck their children into bed. It was the America that middle America never saw, didn't want to see.

"I really do think it was the last amazing album from Bruce. Of course, he has amazing songs and is still an amazing artist, but I think he has yet to yield such a complete, cohesive piece of brilliance like this since. He uses what he learned from the creation of this album and these characters here and there, and you can see moments of it in his more modern characters. I think this was the height of his cinematic peak. His attention to detail is pretty amazing. And his ability to put the listener in the backseat watching it all unfold as its happening. A rare gift.

"*Nebraska* is the part of Bruce you can still archaeologically trace back from my writing to this day. It is up there with *The Times They Are A-Changin'*. *Nebraska* could be traced back to 'The Ballad Of Hollis Brown'. It is a staggering piece of work. It's still current – the same cannot be said about *Born In The USA*.

"Hard to say where America is headed, but many years from now, hopefully if America is still around, when Bruce is just a name a kid remembers his grandfather talking about, when they discuss this period in American history I think *Nebraska* would be something to play history classes. It will paint them an exhilarating, frightening picture of a very dark chapter in America."

Chuck Prophet once formed the core of American rock outfit Green On Red with Dan Stuart. Since their demise in 1992, he has made quite an impression as a solo artist with albums like *Feast Of Hearts* and *No Other Love*, while occasionally moonlighting as a session guitarist for the likes of Lucinda Williams, Aimee Mann and the late Warren Zevon.

"*Nebraska* is from a time where all of a sudden rock'n'roll people had to bootstrap onto literature. And when record reviews were mentioning people like Raymond Carver. It's a song! It's a short story! It's a short story in a song! It's literature in a can! I suppose rock'n'roll wasn't good enough somehow.

"I fell in love with 'Atlantic City' and the black and white video. Who was the Chicken Man? They blew him up. And they blew up his house too! What Bruce tapped into there, that's some secret sauce. And it towers over the record for me. It was great. It was like Scorsese. It was cinematic. What Springsteen did was greater than the chords of the songs.

"I guess he was having new experiences at the time. He was able to see noir films, maybe? Beats me. Maybe he had them screened in his home theatre – for all I know he's got one. He was reading books. American history and stuff. It's all in there. It says more about Bruce, really. I still wonder if many people noticed how deeply personal that record was.

"*Nebraska* probably helped Bruce out of the New Jersey teen quest fodder, maybe put him behind the wheel of the beater he's driving in 'Stolen Car' instead of the big balls of 'Racing In The Street'. He may have been digging around, looking for a way out of the post-teenage *Born To Run*. And he dug into the heartland. I guess it's just something that he had to do. It was about personal growth for Bruce. But it's not my favourite record of his by a long shot. Even though they're all great on some level.

"You know, songwriters have problems. Everybody's got their problems with songs. Except Jonathan Richman and Loudon Wainwright, guys like that, that just take you on their journey. Bruce was a voice for all the people around him. He's always kept his eye on the ball. Where are his characters going? Where are they running to? What are they going to do when they get there? He cares deeply about that stuff. With someone like Jonathan or Loudon, where you're going – you're going to the shoe store, you're going dancing in a lesbian bar in a strip mall, heck, you're going to the proctologist! Your son likes breast-feeding, so it becomes 'Rufus Is A Tit Man'. There may be shit on the finger of the song. And no, it's not sexy, but that's what happens when you go on their journey. I hate to act smart enough to use these words, but Bruce's best stuff isn't mundane. It's not quotidian, plodding through life with a clever grin. Springsteen has created archetypes. I believe that.

"I'd say that the second wave of so-called Americana musicians have pretty much pissed on him. That's a shame, but the truth is Bruce introduced us to a kind of arcane America. Much like Dylan did for another generation with *The Basement Tapes* and *The Harry Smith Anthology*. I remember a friend giving me a Jimmy Rogers record and I dug into it. Told me this was the marinade Bruce was soaking in to get to *Nebraska*. I touched on that secret shared language of the blues. Decided it was cool. But Bruce is still tar-brushed with the image of the semi-literate Jersey Italian sleeping under the boardwalk. The very early Americana gig? We dug him. Soon enough though, there were Americana intellectuals galore who disagreed. You could see those assholes thinking: Springsteen's a greaser. I don't know where I'm going with any of this!

"It occurs to me TEAC should pay Bruce for all the four-tracks he sold. Like a colour TV, it's all there in black and white. Johnny Cash liked 'Johnny 99' enough to cover it. For anyone paying attention, Johnny changes the last line on the song from 'Shave off my hair and put me on that killin' line', to 'Shave off my head and burn Johnny 99.' The devil is in the details.

"Bruce grew as a writer on *Nebraska*. His eyesight improved. He worked out. Maybe he learned linear thinking toward lateral solutions. He grew. I mean that sincerely. But he grew into some clear pain and less of the idolatry he might have gotten used to. His eyesight improved and he got pissed on."

Mark Radcliffe is a British radio presenter, author, raconteur, wit and frontman with boisterous folk outfit the Family Mahone. He released his first solo album, *What Remains Of The Day*, in 2011.

"I guess like everyone else I was surprised when I first heard *Nebraska*, as we'd got so used to the huge E Street Band wall of sound. To hear something so minimal seemed almost like eavesdropping, and I think that's what helps to give it this haunting quality.

"It's an album that gets under your skin in a slightly creepy kind of way. I think it is a classic American album in some ways. The big *Born To Run/Born In The USA* albums portray big-city life in the States. This seems very much the darker music of the vast interior we outsiders know so little about.

"As you'd expect, the lyrics explore the lives of ordinary working people. It's hard to imagine any other artist opening songs with lines as prosaic as, 'My name is Joe Roberts – I work for the state' or 'My little sister's in the front seat with an ice cream cone.' But, of course, we are led down darker paths than we're used to from Bruce on this record. There is a general air of spookiness and menace and isolation throughout, and in many ways it is kind of a musical cousin to *In Cold Blood* by Truman Capote. There are these little towns, and little shacks and little people out there but who knows what really lies beneath the surface?

"The songs are simple to mirror the ostensibly simple lives being led, but there is a lot more trouble afoot here than the normal blue-collar concerns of the car plant and the union card that Springsteen has dealt with on so many occasions.

"Again, the stripped-down nature of the music seems to evoke a basic backwoods way of life, in contrast to the big-city blast of *Born To Run* and many others. When he sings, for example, of the 'badlands of Wyoming', we feel closer to knowing what that is like through these songs. The essence of those great 'lost' states seems to be captured here in some way.

"I suppose that is testimony to his skill as a songwriter, though you would have to say that he rarely strays from the classic pop construction of his beloved Orbisons and Spectors. None of these songs throw you off balance with an odd chord or key change. They are brutally simple. In fact, they would seem to be inhabited by the ghost of Hank Williams in many ways. We're certainly on a 'lost highway' here.

"With its clunks and bumps and guitars occasionally faltering rhythmically, it is nowhere near being perfect, and its Portastudio recording is primitive to say the least, but that all adds to the sustained atmosphere.

"I think it may well be Springsteen's most influential album on the modern crop of Americana artists, and certainly part of its legacy has been to appreciate that songs like this are often most effective at their most bare, which would appear to have been the driving thought behind Rick Rubin's work with Johnny Cash and Neil Diamond for sure. It also makes me warm to Bruce even more as, before *Nebraska*, it was hard to think of another artist operating at that level of success who would have taken a chance by doing something like this."

Tom Russell's songs have been recorded by Johnny Cash, Nanci Griffith, Guy Clark, Iris DeMent, Suzy Bogguss and, of course, himself. He is also an established painter in the folk art genre, and has published three books – And Then I Wrote (a compendium of songwriting quotes with Sylvia Tyson), *Tough Company* (a volume of letters with Charles Bukowski) and a detective novel in Scandinavia.

"I think I got *Nebraska* right after it came out. I loved the record on first listening. Haunting. It reminded me of Dylan's *The Times They Are A-Changin'*, a black and white documentary album about blue-collar blues and violence. Inward violence, outward violence. Country music began to turn into suburban dogwash in the Eighties, and folk music was dead. You could add on a steel guitar to *Nebraska* and you'd have true, blue-collar country-folk, to the bone.

"I think it's one of the strongest post-Sixties American folk records. It fits into the tradition because it's stark and acoustic, and speaks about working class people and folks up against the wall. It echoes Woody Guthrie, early Dylan, and reeks of the great outlaw ballads like 'John Hardy', 'Pretty Boy Floyd', 'Jesse James', 'Billy The Kid' and 'Sam Hall'. It speaks with a hillbilly, poverty-stricken outlaw drawl that sort of says, 'Kiss my ass, I'm drunk, poor and violent, and I can't get to the bottom of what's eating me up, so I'm gonna shoot my way out.'

"It says to me that the human condition is raw and violent right below the surface. It's an angry record. I guess it's all these down people trying to find a reason to believe. Springsteen's always struggling with the meaning of blue-collar existence.

"As a writer, he took it more inside on *Nebraska*. Sort of like Dylan on *Another Side Of Bob Dylan* and *Blood On The Tracks*. I think Springsteen was reading a lot of Flannery O'Connor, dark southern gothic fiction. It was more rural than the early records. We were not really in Jersey any more, except for 'Atlantic City'. We were somewhere in the Bible Belt, with a gun in our hand.

"He has sincerity and passion, honesty and soul as a writer. He may not be as literate and poetic as Dylan and Leonard Cohen, and he may not hit the mark all the time, but he tries harder than anyone. He gives a shit in a world that's lost its give a shit.

"All great writing will last. This record hit me in 1982 when there wasn't much to listen to. It stood out when a lot of us had given up on folk and country music. It will stand."

Jim Sclavunos, when not a member of Nick Cave & the Bad Seeds, is a member of Grinderman. And when not a member of either, is a member of the Vanity Set. Although it could be said that he's a member of all three bands at the same time but at different times. A prime mover in New York's underground scene back in the Seventies, he helped to kick start the No Wave movement with the likes of Teenage Jesus & the Jerks and 8 Eyed Spy before brief stints in Sonic Youth and the Cramps. Standing at six foot and seven inches, you don't mess around with Jim.

"*Nebraska* was my 'way in' to Bruce. I, of course, was already more than well aware of the man and his output, all the hype and drama that circulated around his earlier efforts. But none of the albums he'd recorded prior to *Nebraska* appealed to me. They were simply not my musical tastes at the time. *Nebraska*'s Spartan existentialism, on the other hand, I connected with immediately.

"For me, *Nebraska* wasn't weird. It was perfect unto itself, in the same way, for example, Big Star *Third* or *The Madcap Laughs* were idiosyncratic works one had to approach on their own unique terms. The only thing really weird for me about *Nebraska* was that up to that point I couldn't picture myself liking a Springsteen record.

Nebraska appeared to be the polar opposite of what I had come to assume his music was all about. In its aftermath I was able to see the rest of his work in a different light.

"The title track is particularly beautiful to me, probably the most touching song ever inspired by a spree killer.

"There is one theme that I hear loud and clear on the *Nebraska*: whether right or wrong, an individual's emotional imperatives supersede any societal considerations. The lyrics seem to suggest that there is a higher sense of justice and dignity one can strive for that transcends the banal or reprehensible conditions of one's life.

"The dark desperate spirit of *Nebraska* haunts Springsteen's entire body of work. *Nebraska*'s setting may be sparser, the landscape may be bleaker, but the same moral dilemmas so nakedly expressed on this album, I think, lurk in the shadows of all his albums and trouble all the characters he's created over the years. On *Nebraska*, understatement was more than just another device in the songwriter's bag of tricks, it was his entire aesthetic platform.

"Springsteen was getting compared to Dylan from early on and the folk influence has been evident in his work for some time (the Seeger album being just one of the more blatant nods). But personally, I don't think Springsteen has anything especially to do with the tradition of American folk music any more than any other pop songwriter of his generation. He adopted the folk idiom and the high lonesome sound for this particular album because it suited the alienated mood he wanted to express. But to my ears, *Nebraska* owes as much to Suicide's 'Frankie Teardrop' as it does to folk.

"Indisputably, Springsteen's imagery has always been deeply steeped in what is broadly called Americana. As far as the Americana movement goes, however, if I genuinely cared about the Americana movement (or the folk music tradition for that matter), I might be willing to stick my neck out in the debate about where *Nebraska* fits in with these genres. But I think ultimately, like any album, *Nebraska* is best judged on its own: a timeless listening experience that eclipses any genre considerations."

Jeremy Searle is a journalist who runs the website www.americana-uk.com.

"*Nebraska* wasn't one of those albums that hit me like that. I know that as a Springsteen fan I would have bought it when it came out. I remember having trouble with it. The previous two, *The River* and *Darkness On The Edge Of Town*, both touched on some similar themes, but were still rock albums, ones you could sing along and punch the air with, whereas *Nebraska* was anything but. I'd been into Townes Van Zandt for a while, and there seemed to be a relationship between his songs and those on *Nebraska*, but I didn't really make a connection between it and the new wave of American country that I was getting into.

"It says to me that for most people the American Dream is dead. It says that most people are struggling to get by, making compromises and hard decisions. Although 'Reason To Believe' offers a crumb of hope, and there's the odd nod to the positive here and there, in the end it's a series of portraits from the dark end of the street, where people are 'hanging on in quiet desperation', as Roger Waters has it.

"In one sense it's a logical progression from *Darkness On The Edge Of Town* and *The River* – similar themes, similar songs. I think that the key difference is that he learned to cut back to the absolute bare bones, keeping only what was essential to the song, in contrast to the torrent of words that poured out of *Greetings…*, for example.

"On the first three albums he had the ability to encapsulate the American Dream and its cultural touchstones, cars and girls, in Paddy McAloon's famous (but inaccurate) dismissive song. Post-*Darkness On The Edge Of Town*, he has the ability to articulate the truth and the everyday experience of the American working man. He can also offer the listener faith and hope. He's perhaps the last rock'n'roller, the last one who truly believed in the redemptive power of the music. And that comes through strongly in his songs.

"*Nebraska* is not an easy listen or a casual one, nor one of the enormously popular ones that Springsteen will be remembered for by the masses and mass media. It also hasn't attracted a lot of covers, again probably because of the darkness of the material and because of the difficulty of improving on Springsteen's own takes. All these things are what tend to contribute to establishing an album's reputation down the years. So I think that *Nebraska* is destined to be remembered chiefly by the cognoscenti as one of the great Springsteen albums, perhaps one that foreshadowed the direction much of his music would take in the future. Personally I'd go further and say that it's one of the great American albums, regardless of genre."

Brett Sparks is one half of the Handsome Family, the other half being wife Rennie. How to describe the Handsomes? Well, Rennie makes up stories whose plots and language are rooted in the traditions of gothic literature and murder ballads, while Brett conveys them through mainly folk and country templates. Their songs are magnificently morbid.

"I was in college. I had heard *The River* and responded very strongly to it, especially the more acoustic numbers. I heard *Nebraska* on a cassette tape someone gave me. I listened to it for the first time in my car. It blew me away. It sounded surprising and stark perhaps, but not weird. It seemed contiguous with his more introspective work on *The River*. And some of his earlier work, particularly on *Darkness On the Edge of Town*, like 'Racing In The Street'. And I had already heard early Dylan, so it's not like it was without precedent. There was a long tradition for this style of songwriting and production (its sparseness, whatever you want to call it). But I must say there was a certain 'otherness' that permeated the record. An indefinable feeling of isolation, loneliness, desperation. Hard to define tangibly. And that title, *Nebraska* – very mysterious."

Musically and lyrically, the whole album was revelatory. The arrangements, although minimal, are very well-thought out and evocative. When the bells come in on the last verse of the song, 'Nebraska, it still gives me shivers. Like a doorbell, they open up the record and say, 'Come in, this is going to be a long journey'. Is there a darker, more obscene way for the Boss to open a record than the song 'Nebraska'?

"It's about family, love, God ('Mansion On The Hill', 'My Father's House'), desperation, the inevitable trajectory of existence ('Nebraska') – or the 'meanness' in this world.

"I think it is a logical extension of themes explored on his earlier albums. If you look, you'll find them. 'Atlantic City' deals with very similar theme to 'Tenth Avenue Freeze-Out'. 'Open All Night' is very reminiscent of 'Racing In The Street'. 'The River' is thematically analogous to 'Reason To Believe'.

"It's more a marvellous footnote in the history of rock'n'roll than a folk album. I think it transcends that label. Although it does embrace folk concerns and has a folk tone (whatever that means), *Nebraska* made Springsteen no more a practitioner of folk music than Lennon did with 'Working Class Hero'. I guess it depends on how you define 'folk'. I don't think Bruce was out to create an addendum to *The Harry Smith Anthology*. That said, it does remind me of the cinematic quality of Woody Guthrie's 'Tom Joad' song cycle. It certainly has folk elements.

"If it were a big influence on the Americana movement, the music coming out of that movement would be much better, more intelligent, more reflective. But let's face it, most Americana is a sad caricature of itself. Banal, yee-haw, bullshit clichés, bad regurgitations of early country and rockabilly.

"Springsteen influenced me enormously. The first time I heard him in high school, it was *Born to Run*, and it was like a bell rang in my head. My girlfriend's father bought the record and hated it. So he gave it to her. She hated it, so she gave it to me. I had no reference point for this music. This was before I had heard Dylan, Lou Reed, or any decent country or folk. I listened to classical music mostly. And Led Zeppelin and Van Halen. Bruce's music sounded real, guttural and true. I had a muscle car (1972 Chevrolet Camaro) and drove around the strip in Odessa, Texas listening to that record over and over again.

"He stripped the song down to its bare essentials on that record. He eliminated the role of the producer. Above all, he nailed the storytelling. He got back in touch with the essence, in an almost desperate way.

"With all due respect to Judy Collins, her pronouncement (that Springsteen is a folk hero) sounds a bit like hyperbole to me. I'm sure he is a folk hero to many. Personally, I don't know exactly what I believe about Bruce's persona. I have thought about this a lot over the years. I've struggled with it. At times I think this folk/workingman's hero thing is just an ingenious role on his part. And I think he plays this role brilliantly. At the end of the day I think this line of inquiry is essentially irrelevant. In the folk world, arguments about authenticity always come up sadly lacking. The bottom line for me, the only important thing, is that *Nebraska* is a monumental work of art. It transcends any proclamation like folk hero we foist upon its creator. In the end, the art is the only thing that truly matters.

"The legacy of *Nebraska* is that simpler is better. It made a generation of guys with acoustic guitars realise they could do it all by themselves. It made me go out and buy a four-track recorder.

"It's the best record Springsteen ever made. Perhaps the best record of its kind. It's hard to believe one man could do it."

Michael Timmins is guitarist and songwriter-in-chief with the Cowboy Junkies, the Canadian outfit with the impossibly cool name. Fronted by Timmins' sister Margo, and including another sibling, Peter, on drums, they recorded their second album, *The Trinity Session*, on a single microphone in Toronto's Church of the Holy Trinity. Bruce Springsteen would have approved.

"I was living in London, working at the Record and Tape Exchange, playing in my band Germinal, which was an improvisational noise-band: a band inspired by my complete disillusion with the rock scene. I was listening to Cecil Taylor, Anthony Braxton, Ornette Coleman, Ascension, anything that didn't have vocals and a verse/chorus/verse structure. Despite the fact that a few years earlier, *Darkness on The Edge Of Town* had an enormous emotional impact on my life, Springsteen had become irrelevant to my world. Someone put the album on in the store and that drifting harmonica, delicate acoustic guitar and those dark, murmured vocals made us all stop and listen. It brought me back to folk music.

"It's one of those albums that I never tire of and that's because I don't think there is any chaff on it. No one song is that much better than another. But if I was forced to choose, I guess it would be 'Nebraska', the detail and pacing of that song is astounding.

"I think the primary theme is alienation. All of the characters have detached themselves (or have been detached) from their families, societies, beliefs. They find themselves on an enormous, empty, moral-less landscape, with no sense of direction, no sense of right or wrong.

"There is an ingrained romantic attachment to the outlaw in America, but these songs don't emphasis the romance. They tell stories of people hamstrung by their fear and their loss of hope. Amazingly enough, almost thirty years later, it has become all too apparent that it is fear and loss of hope that is running the agenda in the USA today.

"It absolutely fits into the tradition of American folk music. It stands with the best of Woody Guthrie, Bob Dylan, Leadbelly and all those other people that nobody listens to any more. Some of the songs on *Nebraska* would not be out of place next to some of the genre's most celebrated standards.

"I would say it has been a huge influence on the Americana movement. Personally speaking, *Nebraska* is one of the two albums (the other was Muddy Waters' *Folk Singer*) that we used as a template when we were developing our sound for Cowboy Junkies (which explains why on our first album we covered 'State Trooper'). We weren't thinking in terms of the style of songs on the album, but more the overall vibe, the other-worldly ambience.

"From a writing point of view it seems like there was a natural progression from *Darkness On The Edge Of Town* to *The River* to *Nebraska*. A song like 'Racing In The Street' could easily fit on *Nebraska*. It was his approach to those songs that changed the most. He took a huge leap of faith and decided to trust what he had written to carry the weight of emotion. He did away with all those musical exclamation points (the E Street Band) and just let his words carry the load.

191

"Like any great writer, his most important attribute is honesty. He is able to create characters and situations that generally don't fall back on cliché: the relationships, the emotions and the situations that they face mirror the lives and emotions of most of his listeners. When listening to Springsteen at his best. you hear your life laid out in song and there is a sense of comfort in the realisation that you are not alone.

"It is said that the Velvet Underground didn't sell many albums in their short existence, but everyone that heard a VU album started a band. *Nebraska* may not have had the visceral energy of *Born to Run* or grown into the cultural phenomenon that was *Born In The USA*, but every strummer that heard it was inspired to write a 'folk' song."

Willy Vlautin is frontman and songwriter-in-chief with Richmond Fontaine, a band that, like so many to come out of America, get more recognition in Europe and Australia than they do in their own country. Vlautin is also a novelist, his three books, *This Motel Life, Northline* and *Lean On Pete,* having elicited favourable comparisons with John Steinbeck, Raymond Carver and Charles Bukowski, and leading one critic to label him "the Dylan of the dislocated". High and not altogether exaggerated praise.

"I've been listening to Springsteen's music since I was kid, since *Greetings From Asbury Park, NJ*. My brother had that record, and when he left home I stole it from him. Afterwards, I remember I was thirteen or fourteen, I went into a record store and asked this old hippy clerk if he knew which Bruce Springsteen record to buy, that I only had *Greetings...* This is three or four years before *Born In The USA*, and the clerk put his hands on my shoulders and said, 'You don't know how lucky you are.'

"The thing about Springsteen that first killed was his sense of place. I'd never been anywhere and he transported me to the East Coast, to New Jersey, to Asbury Park, to refinery towers and boardwalks, to Atlantic City, to the Midwest. All these places I had never been to.

"There's a great sadness to many of his songs, and even as a kid I felt at home in those. He came across to me as a romantic with a big edge on him. It's like he lived in an SE Hinton novel, and as a kid those were my favourites.

"As a writer, I've always tried to have a sense of place like he has. His songs seem so honest and clear. Not like an art project, but songs to help you get by. I've always tried to do that. He has this dark romanticism. He's overconfident and deathly insecure at the same time. He's got that edge, the swagger. I admire that more than I can say, but it's not me. I get swagger once in a while and usually it's right before I pass out.

"My favourite songs of his are his darker, more brooding ballads. He's very cinematic. You can live inside them. There's a world going on in his albums, and to me each song lets you live in that world for three or four minutes. When he's good there's this quality of innocence, a hopeful romantic wrapped in a reality that's rough, that's a never-ending working-class life, a life with little stability or hope or home.

"I remember the day I bought *Nebraska*. It was the cover that got me. What a cover. When I got it home I liked it but I didn't understand a lot of it. Just out the gate 'Atlantic City' killed me, and then I learned how to play 'Used Cars' on guitar and that song has always meant a lot to me. The edge of that song reminds of my life as a kid. As I got older different songs would hit me. 'State Trooper' started making a lot of sense! Ha, ha, ha! And 'Reason To Believe' seemed to say how I felt most of the time but was unable to articulate. It's a record I go to every year or so, and for a week or two I disappear into the world of it.

"When I started playing in a band and writing stories, I'd always look at *Nebraska* to give me confidence. Here's a really raw committed non-commercial record released by a famous rock star. He had crews of people working for him and families depending on his songs, and he had the guts to put out *Nebraska*. If he could do that, then the least I could do was try to do something I thought had merit and not worry about anything else or anyone. That's hard enough to do in your own basement.

"It's a record with no bad songs. Some mean more than others on a certain listen, and sometimes all ten songs devastate me, and sometimes I put the record in and I'm like, 'Jesus I don't want to be around Charlie Starkweather.' And then I'll put it away. But for me it's like *Swordfishtrombones* (Tom Waits). I always go back to it. There's a loneliness stamped on that record that's always made sense to me, that I've never outgrown.

"It's about alienation and desperation and its relationship to violence. There's a sense that there is no meaning in life, that the working class life has failed and in its place are anger, alienation and frustration. It's a young man edge. Some of the frustration is justified, but some of it you can see is used as an excuse. Some people are violent, some people are dark, and a bad situation just makes it easier for them to let that side out."

Steve Wynn, founder member of Dream Syndicate, has been hailed "one of rock's true heroes of the underground" *(The Philadelphia Weekly)*, **"a veritable PhD of timeless rock songcraft"** *(The Chicago Tribune)* **and "a force to be reckoned with and cherished"** *(The Sunday Times)*. **He's also a bit of a Springsteen fan.**

"I don't see *Nebraska*'s importance in terms of it being a folk record. Bruce was making great folk music right there on his first record. You don't get much better folk songs than 'For You', 'Lost In The Flood' and 'Does This Bus Stop At 82nd Street?' And I don't see the record's importance in terms of telling the great American tales. He had already done that more convincingly from the very specific New Jersey perspective of his early records, as well as on *Darkness On The Edge Of Town*'s better songs.

"No, for me, the importance of *Nebraska* was the spontaneity, immediacy, lo-fi sound, and, most of all, that he had recorded all by himself at home. This was something that had almost never been done before, especially by a platinum-selling artist. This was what blew my mind about *Nebraska*. He made this at home! Alone! In his kitchen! On a fucking four-track cassette machine!

"Needless to say, I bought one of those Fostex X-15s within a few years. Bruce Springsteen, in a way, invented and pioneered the idea that you could make a record by yourself at home. Everyone could be their own Jackie Lomax! Now in 2010, it's common and easy to make records at home. It's a great equaliser and also a contributor to the overwhelming buzz and noise that's out there.

"There's good and bad in everything. But when I hear *Nebraska*, I hear a superstar bored with the machine and daring to reinvent it in a brand new way."

SOURCE NOTES

Any project of this kind, particularly one without the involvement of its principal subject, is the product of authorial opinion, original interviews and, of course, considerable research. In the case of the latter, the following books were invaluable:

A Race Of Singers: Whitman's Working-Class Hero From Guthrie to Springsteen, Bryan K Garman
Bob Dylan In America, Sean Wilentz
Born In The USA: Bruce Springsteen and the American Tradition, Jim Cullen
Born In The USA, Geoffrey Himes
Bound for Glory, Woody Guthrie
Bruce Springsteen: The Rolling Stone Files
Folk Music: A Regional Exploration, Norm Cohen
Glory Days: A Biography Of Bruce Springsteen, Dave Marsh
Invisible Republic: Bob Dylan's Basement Tapes, Greil Marcus
It Ain't No Sin to Be Glad You're Alive: The Promise Of Bruce Springsteen, Eric Alterman
No Direction Home: The Life And Music Of Bob Dylan, Robert Shelton
Racing in the Street: The Bruce Springsteen Reader, ed. by June Skinner Sawyers
Rainbow quest: The Folk Music Revival and American Society 1940-1970, Ronald D. Cohen
Romancing the Folk: Public Memory and American Roots Music, Benjamin Filene
Runaway American Dream: Listening To Bruce Springsteen, Jimmy Guterman
Woody Guthrie: A Life, Joe Klein
Songs, Bruce Springsteen
Deliver Me From Nowhere, Tennessee Jones' short story collection based on *Nebraska,* was also referenced, as was John McGahern's prose anthology, *Love Of The World.*

Among other publications that provided a wealth of detail were *Mojo* – January 2006, *Q Collectors' Edition: Dylan, Uncut Legends # 1: Bob Dylan, Uncut Legends # 4: Bruce Springsteen, Uncut – The Ultimate Music Guide: Bruce Springsteen, Springsteen: Visions of America,* Adam Sweeting, *Uncut* – September 2002, April 2003 and November 2005, *Interview* – September 1991, *The Sunday Times* – November 2010 and *The Guardian* – September 2010.

Visual sources included BBC Four Television's *Folk America* series and the DVDs, *Woody Guthrie – This Machine Kills Fascists* and *VH1 Storytellers: Bruce Springsteen.* As well as Springsteen's entire discography, the one other aural source used was the bootleg CD, *How Nebraska Was Born.*

Academic sources included Robert Cantwell's treatise on Woody Guthrie, *Fanfare For The Little Guy, Greetings From Freehold: How Bruce Springsteen's Hometown Shaped His Life And Work* by David Wilson and Samuel J. Levine's *Portraits Of Criminals On Bruce Springsteen's Nebraska: The Enigmatic Criminal, The Sympathetic Criminal And The Criminal As Brother.*

The internet enabled me to pull together various strands of information. While the many sites visited are too numerous to cite individually, those that proved particularly useful were www.freeholdnj.homestead.com for material on Springsteen's home town, www.karisable.com and www.lincoln.libraries.org for accounts of the Charles Starkweather/Caril Fugate killings, www.tascam.com for Daniel Keller's interview with Toby Scott, www.slate.com for Stephen Metcalf's article, '*Faux Americana: Why I Still Love Bruce Springsteen*', www.bookforum.com for Wendy Lesser's article '*Southern Discomfort: The Origins Of Flannery O'Connor's Unsettling Fictional World*', www.eskimo.com for the 1975 interview with *Badlands* director Terrence Malick, www.brucespringsteen.net for '*Dave Marsh's Notes For Bruce Springsteen's We Shall Overcome: The Seeger Sessions*', and www.urbandictionary.com for its hilariously accurate definition of Neoconservatism.

Finally, the full roll call of interviewees was Mike Appel, Eric Bachmann, Dan Bern, Laura Cantrell, Rosanne Cash, The Cash Brothers, Peter Case, Norm Cohen, Judy Collins, Kevin Coyne, Bob Crawford, Steve Earle, Mark Eitzel, Simon Felice, Jeff Finlin, Jeffrey Foucault, Bryan Garman, Howe Gelb, Thea Gilmore, David Gray, Sid Griffin, Nora Guthrie, John Wesley Harding, Bill Hurley, Tennessee Jones, Robert Earl Keen, Kevn Kinney, David Michael Kennedy, Julius Lester, Vini Lopez, Tom McCrae, Michael McDermott, David Means, Jim Musselman, Willie Nile, David Pesci, Chuck Prophet, Mark Radcliffe, Tom Russell, Jim Sampas, Jim Sclavunos, Jeremy Searle, Southside Johnny, Brett Sparks, David Spelman, Mark Spence, Michael Timmins, Willy Vlautin, Sean Wilentz, Dar Williams and Steve Wynn.

David Burke is a native of Mullingar in Ireland, now living in the UK. His first book, *Crisis In The Community: The African Caribbean Experience Of Mental Health*, was published by Chipmunka in 2008. He works as a television subtitler and writes for *R2* magazine (formerly *Rock 'n 'Reel*).

Also available from Cherry Red Books:

Johnny Thunders - In Cold Blood
Nina Antonia

The Secret Life Of A Teenage Punk Rocker: The Andy Blade Chronicles
Andy Blade

Hells Bent On Rockin': A History Of Psychobilly
Craig Brackenbridge

Tom Waits: In The Studio
Jake Brown

Best Seat In The House – A Cock Sparrer Story
Steve Bruce

Heart Of Darkness – Bruce Springsteen's 'Nebraska'
David Burke

All The Young Dudes: Mott The Hoople & Ian Hunter
Campbell Devine

Bittersweet: The Clifford T Ward Story
David Cartwright

Kiss Me Neck – A Lee 'Scratch' Perry Discography
Jeremy Collingwood

Celebration Day – A Led Zeppelin Encyclopedia
Malcolm Dome and Jerry Ewing

Our Music Is Red - With Purple Flashes: The Story Of The Creation
Sean Egan

The Doc's Devils: Manchester United 1972-77
Sean Egan

The Rolling Stones: Complete Recording Sessions 1962-2002
Martin Elliott

The Day The Country Died: A History Of Anarcho Punk 1980 To 1984
Ian Glasper

Burning Britain - A History Of UK Punk 1980 To 1984
Ian Glasper

Trapped In A Scene - UK Hardcore 1985-89
Ian Glasper

Those Were The Days - The Beatles' Apple Organization
Stefan Grenados

PWL: From The Factory Floor
Phil Harding

Irish Folk, Trad And Blues: A Secret History
Colin Harper and Trevor Hodgett

A Plugged In State Of Mind: The History of Electronic Music
Dave Henderson

Embryo - A Pink Floyd Chronology 1966-1971
Nick Hodges And Ian Priston

Goodnight Jim Bob - On The Road With Carter USM
Jim Bob

Indie Hits 1980 – 1989
Barry Lazell

Fucked By Rock (Revised and Expanded)
Mark Manning (aka Zodiac Mindwarp)

Music To Die For – The International Guide To Goth, Goth Metal, Horror Punk, Psychobilly Etc
Mick Mercer

Independence Days - The Story Of UK Independent Record Labels
Alex Ogg

No More Heroes: A Complete History Of UK Punk 1976 To 1980
Alex Ogg

Random Precision - Recording The Music Of Syd Barrett 1965-1974
David Parker

Prophets and Sages: The 101 Greatest Progressive Rock Albums
Mark Powell

Good Times Bad Times - The Rolling Stones 1960-69
Terry Rawlings and Keith Badman

Quite Naturally - The Small Faces
Terry Rawlings and Keith Badman

The Legendary Joe Meek - The Telstar Man
John Repsch

Death To Trad Rock – The Post-Punk fanzine scene 1982-87
John Robb

Rockdetector: A To Zs of 80s Rock / Black Metal / Death Metal / Doom, Gothic & Stoner Metal / Power Metal and Thrash Metal
Garry Sharpe-Young

Rockdetector: Black Sabbath - Never Say Die
Garry Sharpe-Young

Rockdetector: Ozzy Osbourne
Garry Sharpe-Young

Please visit
www.cherryredbooks.co.uk
for further info and mail order

We're always interested to hear from readers, authors and fans - for contact, manuscript submissions and further information, please email books@cherryred.co.uk

www.cherryredbooks.co.uk